I0841208

The Fractured Equinox

The Definitive Edition

A.M. Pozon

Paragon Publishing

To my wife, Felice—thank you for standing beside every crazy idea, for grounding me when I needed it, and for believing in this story before it ever found a page. To my son, Jericho—you are the reason I began writing again, the reason I wanted to build a world worth handing down. I hope one day, these stories will be yours to tell in your own voice. And to my parents, Alvin and Elsie—everything begins with you. Your love, your sacrifices, and your unwavering presence made this possible. Without you, none of this would exist.

Preface

This second edition of The Fractured Equinox marks a new beginning for the story that started it all. Originally, this book was meant to stand alone. A single story in a single world. But after its first release, the characters wouldn't let me go. New ideas came, deeper arcs took shape, and what began as a standalone novel quietly unfolded into a trilogy. With that shift came the need to return, revise, and rebuild the foundation. This version tells the same core story, but with higher stakes, sharper clarity, and a closer look at the trio who carry it: Kaelen, Elara, and Dorian. My hope is that they feel more real this time around; more flawed, more human, and ultimately, more worth rooting for. To everyone who read the first version, thank you. And to those discovering Elyndor for the first time, welcome. I hope you enjoy what's ahead. Thank you for being here.

Act I: The Fractured World

Chapter 1: Shadows of Forgehelm

A dead automaton twitched beneath Kaelen's boot, its rusted limbs spasming one last time. A hiss of steam escaped its shattered core, curling into the smog-choked air like a dying breath. Overhead, rusted gears screeched in their housings, half-swallowed by Forgehelm's endless haze. The city was alive, but only in the way a great machine devoured everything to keep its gears turning.

Kaelen pulled his collar up against the sting of burning coal in the air. The lower-tier streets teemed, bodies flowing between makeshift stalls hawking rusted tools, salvaged parts, and food as dubious as the hands passing it. He moved through it like smoke—silent, quick, unnoticed. Forgehelm had two kinds of people: the ones who kept moving and the ones who got stepped on.

He clutched the satchel at his side, fingers brushing over the blueprint hidden within. It was one of Orlan's old designs, a stolen fragment of Orlan's last work. A design he wasn't supposed to have. A reminder that his uncle had seen the dangers of unchecked ambition long before anyone else.

Kaelen knew better than to linger. Enforcers marched past, boots hammering rhythm into the cobblestone. They weren't looking for him specifically—not yet—but they always had a reason to pry. He kept his head down, ducking past a group of grimy workers unloading crates from a transport rail, his movements quick but controlled. He couldn't afford to draw attention.

Above him, the upper tiers of Forgehelm stretched toward the sky, a world of polished stone and intricate automaton constructs. The wealthy resided there, far from the choking smog and the endless toil of the lower districts. He had heard tales of shimmering gardens, of streets paved in white marble, of crystalline lights that mimicked the stars the lower tiers could no longer see. But to someone like Kaelen, those were nothing but stories—illusions painted by those who had never set foot in the reality of Forgehelm's underbelly.

A mechanical bird screeched as it passed overhead, its brass wings clinking in rapid succession. Kaelen paused, watching it disappear between the towering buildings. Someone in the Collegium had probably built it, another project funded by the elite who sat in their sky-bound halls.

The Collegium. His destination.

He adjusted the strap of his satchel, the weight of it grounding him. The blueprint inside burned in his mind—a fragment of something larger. He wasn't just gathering scraps today. He was chasing an idea—one his uncle had started but never had the chance to complete.

He adjusted the strap and wove deeper into the labyrinth of alleys, toward the scrapyard where the remnants of Forgehelm's industry lay discarded. It was time to find what he needed.

Time to build something new.

The scrapyard loomed ahead, a graveyard of twisted metal and forgotten inventions. Kaelen moved swiftly, keeping to the shadows as he approached the rusted perimeter fence. He ran his fingers over a familiar gap between the bars—a narrow opening just wide enough to squeeze through. He had done this before.

The city's waste ended here—half-buried automaton husks, shattered runestones, rust and silence. To the people of the upper tiers, it was a junkyard. To Kaelen, it was an archive of lost potential. He pulled his goggles over his eyes, shielding them from the dust and sparks that occasionally flared from unstable remnants of Mechcraft.

His target was deeper inside. He wasn't scavenging for parts at random this time. Orlan's blueprint had called for something specific—old core casings, preferably from the old era. A near impossibility in Forgehelm, where anything linked to the old era was considered contraband. But Kaelen had a theory: some of the older scrap, the remnants of past wars, might still hold what he needed.

He kept low, moving between stacks of rusted plating and hollowed-out machine limbs. His pulse quickened as he neared the older sections of the yard, where the metal was warped from age and battle. A gloved hand reached into his satchel, pulling out a small device—a makeshift scanner he had cobbled together from salvaged parts. The screen flickered, displaying faint energy signatures beneath the wreckage. Most were dead, their power sources long since depleted. But one reading pulsed faintly, hidden beneath a collapsed automaton frame.

Kaelen smiled. There.

He wedged his shoulder against the rusted plating and shoved, muscles straining as the metal groaned in protest. The automaton's remains shifted just enough to reveal a glimpse of something beneath—curved metal, smooth and untouched by rust. His fingers brushed over the surface, tracing the unfamiliar rune markings carved along its edges. This was it. This was what Orlan had been searching for.

A sound snapped him to attention.

Footsteps.

Kaelen tensed, instinctively pressing himself into the nearest pile of debris. The sound was faint, but deliberate. Someone else was in the scrapyard.

A cloaked figure moved through the wreckage, picking through the scrap. The dim light of a flickering lantern cast jagged shadows across the man's scarred face. His movements were precise, but there was a tension in his posture, like he was searching for something. Or someone.

Kaelen's grip tightened on the core casing. He had what he came for, but now he had a choice—slip away unseen, or stay and see what this stranger was after. His gut told him that this was no ordinary scavenger.

Then, as if sensing the weight of his thoughts, the man stilled.

And turned to face him.

Kaelen's breath caught in his throat. The stranger's gaze locked onto him, sharp and assessing. For a moment, neither moved, the scrapyard's usual symphony of distant hissing vents and shifting metal fading into tense silence.

Then, the man took a step forward.

Instinct kicked in. Kaelen spun on his heel and darted deeper into the wreckage, weaving between rusted automaton frames and heaps of discarded gears. His satchel thumped against his side, the weight of the old-era tech inside a grounding reminder of what was at stake. He wasn't leaving without it.

A quick glance over his shoulder confirmed the worst—the man was following.

Kaelen reached into his belt, fingers brushing against a handful of scrap spheres he had rigged together with rudimentary explosive powder. Not lethal, but enough to cause a distraction. He tossed one over his shoulder without breaking stride.

A sharp crack split the air as metal shards burst outward in a flash of sparks. The stranger halted, shielding his face, giving Kaelen the precious seconds he needed. He rounded a towering heap of broken parts and pressed his back against the cold metal, forcing his breath into slow, measured exhales.

Silence.

The footsteps had stopped.

Had the man given up? Was he waiting?

Kaelen carefully unclipped his scanner from his satchel and reactivated it. The flickering display picked up scattered readings—mostly inactive metal—but one pulsed steadily, faint but undeniable. Just ahead, beneath a collapsed automaton, something was still alive.

He dropped to his knees and clawed at the debris, wrenching away jagged plating piece by piece. His fingers burned from the effort, but he ignored the pain. A few more layers and—

A pulse.

Kaelen froze as a low, steady hum vibrated beneath his fingertips. He swept the last of the scrap aside and found it: a smooth, palm-sized object, partially embedded in the dirt. Unlike the rusted machinery surrounding it, this piece was untouched by time—its surface sleek, its intricate carvings unweathered. Runes shimmered faintly across its metallic shell, their symbols shifting before his very eyes.

A relic of the old era.

A thrill surged through Kaelen, equal parts exhilaration and apprehension. He reached out, fingers hovering over the artifact. He could feel the energy radiating from it, something ancient and powerful. Every logical part of him screamed caution, but his gut told him something else entirely.

It had been waiting.

The moment his fingertips brushed the relic's surface, a jolt shot up his arm—not painful, but overwhelming, like a silent current of static charging through his nerves. His scanner shorted out instantly, its display flickering before going dark.

Kaelen's breath hitched. He had scavenged countless old parts before, but nothing like this. Whatever this relic was, it didn't belong in the scrapyard. It didn't belong anywhere near Forgehelm.

A noise behind him yanked him from his daze.

The stranger had found him.

Kaelen scrambled to his feet, his instincts screaming at him to run. But as he took his first step, the man's voice cut through the haze.

"Put it back, boy. You have no idea what you're holding."

Kaelen's grip tightened around the relic. His pulse thundered in his ears as he turned to face the stranger fully. The man stood a few paces away, his tattered cloak barely concealing a wiry frame. His face, now visible under the flickering scrapyard lanterns, bore the scars of time and hardship. His sharp, piercing eyes locked onto Kaelen with an intensity that sent a chill down his spine.

"Put it back," the man repeated, his voice lower, almost pleading. "You don't know what you've just unearthed."

Kaelen hesitated, his fingers flexing over the relic's smooth surface. He had risked too much to leave empty-handed. "If you know what this is," he said, keeping his tone even, "then tell me."

The stranger took a slow step forward, his gaze flicking to Kaelen's satchel. "That's not something you can just take and tinker with, boy. That relic belongs buried. It was never meant to be found."

"Buried by who?" Kaelen shot back. "The enforcers? The Collegium? Or people like you who think knowledge should be lost forever?"

A flicker of something passed across the man's face—anger, regret, or something deeper Kaelen couldn't place. "I watched them kill a man over one of those," he said, his voice dropping to a whisper.

"You think you're clever, boy? You think you found something special? You found a death sentence."

Kaelen's heartbeat stuttered.

A shrill whistle split the scrapyard air. Then came the clank of armored boots. Enforcers.

"You've already been seen," the stranger muttered. "They're coming for you now."

Kaelen's breath caught. He hadn't been careful enough. His mind raced—if the enforcers found him with the relic, there'd be no talking his way out of it.

The man took a step back, melting into the shadows. "Listen to me, boy. If you want to survive, leave it here. Walk away."

Kaelen tightened his grip on the relic. He had a thousand questions, but no time for answers. His path was set the moment he touched it.

The clang of metal echoed closer.

The stranger didn't wait for agreement. "Then run."

Kaelen didn't need to be told twice. He bolted, shoving the relic deep into his satchel as he disappeared into the scrapyard's maze of wreckage. Behind him, the enforcers' voices rang out in the dark.

The hunt had begun.

Kaelen's boots pounded against the uneven ground, his breath sharp and ragged as he tore through the scrapyard's maze of metal. The relic burned in his satchel, a weight heavier than it should have been. Behind him, shouts rang out, the enforcers closing in fast.

The scrapyard was a maze of rust and ruin—but Kaelen knew its spine. He vaulted over rusted plating, ducked beneath collapsed scaffolding, and slid through gaps too narrow for the armored enforcers to follow easily. The air was thick with the scent of oil and rust, the night alive with the mechanical groans of shifting scrap.

A harsh beam of light swept past him—one of the enforcers had activated a search lantern. Kaelen skidded to a halt, pressing himself into the shadow of a gutted automaton husk. His pulse hammered as the light hovered inches away.

"There! By the south stacks!"

Kaelen cursed under his breath. No more hiding. He had to move.

He bolted, weaving between towering heaps of scrap. The enforcers' heavy boots clanged against the walkways above, some taking higher ground to cut him off. He needed a way out—fast. His eyes darted to the transport rail overhead, an old mechanism used to ferry scrap to the furnaces. The tracks led straight out of the scrapyard and toward the lower districts.

A plan formed. It was reckless, but reckless was better than captured.

Kaelen sprinted for the nearest support beam and scrambled up, fingers slipping against the greasy metal. The enforcers saw his intent too late.

"Stop him!"

Shots rang out—burst rounds from a rifle. Sparks erupted as bullets ricocheted off metal. Kaelen gritted his teeth, pushing himself higher. His arms burned, his grip threatened to give, but he lunged, fingers catching the edge of the transport rail's platform. He pulled himself up just as the machinery groaned to life, a cargo transport whirring toward the exit.

Kaelen didn't think. He ran.

With one final, desperate leap, he landed atop the moving rail cart, his body jolting from the impact. The enforcers shouted below, but he was already slipping out of reach. He braced himself against the railing, pulse crashing in his ears as the scrapyard disappeared.

But he knew this wasn't over.

He had the relic.

And now, the entire city would be looking for him.

The rail cart rattled as it carried Kaelen away from the scrapyard, the night air thick with the scent of burnt oil and smog. He remained low, his fingers gripping the metal edge as Forgehelm's industrial skyline passed in a blur of flickering lights and towering smoke stacks. His heart still pounded, but the chase was behind him. For now.

The moment the cart slowed near the lower tiers, Kaelen rolled off, landing in a crouch. He stuck to the shadows, navigating familiar alleyways until he reached the worn metal door of his workshop. He pressed his palm to the scanner beside it—a simple mechanism he'd built himself. The lock clicked, and he slipped inside, bolting it behind him.

The air in the workshop was thick with the scent of metal shavings and oil, a cluttered but familiar chaos of half-built machines, scattered blueprints, and discarded tools. A small forge glowed in the corner, casting flickering light over the mess. This was the only place in Forgehelm where Kaelen felt truly at home.

His satchel hit the worktable with a dull thud. With shaking fingers, he unfastened it, pulling out the relic. Even under the dim workshop light, its runes still shimmered, shifting as if aware of his gaze. But he set it aside—for now, there was something even more important.

He reached into his satchel again, this time retrieving the blueprint Orlan had given him. Its edges were worn, the ink smudged from years of careful study. It was the last thing his uncle had entrusted to him: a design unlike anything else in Forgehelm. A small, lizard-like automaton, crafted with precision and imbued with a level of intricacy that surpassed even the Collegium's best constructs.

Wiz.

Kaelen ran a hand over the blueprint, his pulse steadying. This was why he had braved the scrapyard, why he had risked everything—to bring Orlan's creation to life. He spread out the salvaged parts across the worktable, assessing each piece. The core casing, lightweight and undamaged. The servos, slightly worn but still functional. And the intricate gears that would form the automaton's inner workings.

With a deep breath, he set to work. Sparks flared as he welded the frame, each movement measured, each angle precise. He shaped the limbs, ensuring each joint was flexible yet sturdy. The delicate circuits and fine-tuned mechanisms required absolute focus, but Kaelen welcomed the challenge. This was more than just a machine. It was proof of his skills. Proof that Orlan's trust in him had not been misplaced.

Hours passed, unnoticed. The workshop remained silent save for the steady hum of his tools and the crackling fire of the forge. Finally, he installed the final piece—a small power core, one of the oldest components he had scavenged, its origin unknown, but its energy stable. He connected it to the frame, holding his breath as he activated the first sequence.

A whir.

Then movement.

The automaton's eyes flickered to life, a soft blue glow illuminating its delicate frame. Its tail twitched, joints adjusting for the first time. Then, with a curious chirp, it lifted its head, staring directly at him.

Kaelen laughed, breathless. "Welcome to the world, Wiz."

Wiz stretched, then scrambled up Kaelen's arm to perch on his shoulder. Its metal claws gripped his vest, but not hard enough to hurt. Kaelen smiled, a rare warmth spreading through his chest.

For the first time in what felt like forever, something had gone right.

But as his gaze flicked back to the relic sitting on his worktable, its shifting runes still glowing faintly, he knew that his night was far from over.

Wiz was just the beginning.

Kaelen places the relic on his workbench, turning it over in his hands. The runes shift subtly under the dim light, unreadable yet strangely familiar.

He freezes.

"Where have I seen this before?"

He grabs an old, dust-covered blueprint from the back of his workshop—one of Orlan's unfinished designs. His fingers trace the faded ink, his breath catching.

There, etched along the edges of the schematic—the same runes.

Kaelen's hand started trembling as he dropped the blueprint on the floor.

"No. That's impossible."

Orlan never finished this project. He was executed before he could. Forgehelm erased all records of his final works.

So why is a piece of his research buried in a scrapyard, inside forbidden Mechcraft tech?

Wiz, his automaton, attempts to scan the relic, but the device immediately malfunctions, sparks flying. Kaelen jerks back, shaking out his hand. The scanner's fried.

His pulse quickens.

This wasn't just a discarded relic. It was something Forgehelm wanted buried. And now, somehow, it's in his hands.

His fingers tightened around the blueprint, his breath shallow. He should tell someone. He should—

Dorian.

The name surfaced before he could stop it. Dorian, with his damnable sense of duty. If Kaelen showed him this relic, would he see the truth, or would he see a crime?

Dorian was his closest friend, but he was also a Titanbreaker. A soldier first. A loyal enforcer of Forgehelm's will.

He shoved the blueprint aside, cutting the thought short. No. Not yet.

He wasn't ready for that conversation.

A sharp knock on the door shattered the hum of the workshop.

Kaelen tensed, his pulse spiking. No one came here unannounced—not unless they had a reason. His first instinct was to shove the relic into a drawer, but Wiz, perched on his shoulder, chirped in alarm.

Another knock. Louder this time.

His fingers twitched. He moved toward the door. He pressed his eye to the small viewing slit before unlocking it. The moment he saw who it was, his grip on the handle tightened.

Dorian.

Kaelen hesitated before pulling the door open just enough to let him inside. Dorian entered, the ever-present Forgehelm mist clinging to his shoulders. The Titanbreaker's imposing frame filled the small space, his heavy boots clanking against the metal floor. He smelled of iron and oil, a constant reminder of his place within the enforcers.

"You're hard to find," Dorian said, voice calm but edged with something else.

"I wasn't hiding," Kaelen muttered, shutting the door behind him.

Dorian's gaze swept the room, taking in the scattered tools, the still-lit forge, and finally, the blueprints on the worktable. His eyes lingered on Wiz, who studied him with mechanical curiosity. The automaton tilted its head, chirping softly.

Dorian raised an eyebrow. "That's new."

Kaelen swallowed. "Finished him tonight."

Dorian reached out, and Wiz hesitated before cautiously stepping onto his gauntleted arm. The Titanbreaker studied the small automaton. Something passed behind his eyes—recognition, maybe regret—but his voice stayed even. "Orlan's design?"

Kaelen nodded.

Dorian set Wiz back on the table with surprising gentleness. Then his voice sharpened. "Kael, enforcers are searching for someone who fits your description. They've locked down the lower tiers."

Kaelen forced himself to stay composed. "And you came here to warn me?"

"I came here because I need to hear the truth," Dorian said, no longer hiding the weight behind it.

Something in his tone sent a wave of unease through Kaelen. He crossed his arms, choosing his words carefully. "I don't know what you're talking about."

Dorian pressed his lips together before speaking. "Don't do that. We both know I'd cover for you, but I can't do that if you don't tell me what's going on. What did you take?"

Kaelen hesitated, then reached into his satchel and slowly pulled out the relic. The runes pulsed faintly, shifting like liquid metal. He set it on the table between them.

Dorian took a step back. "Kael… where did you get this?"

Kaelen clenched his fists. "Scrapyard. I didn't steal it. I found it."

Dorian's gaze flicked between the relic and Kaelen, and for the first time that night, Kaelen saw something close to fear in his friend's eyes.

"You don't understand," Dorian murmured. "People disappear over things like this."

Kaelen straightened. "Then help me figure out why."

Dorian's conflicted expression was answer enough. Whatever this relic was, it was bigger than both of them. And now, there was no turning back.

Sleep did not come easily.

Kaelen sat at his workbench long after Dorian had left, his fingers tracing the shifting runes on the relic's surface. Wiz rested on the table beside him, mechanical tail flicking occasionally, its systems idly scanning the object that had turned Kaelen's world upside down.

His thoughts were tangled—memories of Orlan, the chase through the scrapyard, the fear in Dorian's voice. Everything led back to this relic. And still, no answers.

A sigh escaped him. Maybe he was overthinking it. Maybe it was just another forgotten artifact of the old era, left to rust with the rest of Forgehelm's discarded progress. Maybe—

The runes shifted.

Kaelen blinked. He hadn't moved, hadn't done anything—but the symbols rearranged themselves, realigning in fluid patterns across the relic's metallic shell. A faint hum resonated in the air, barely perceptible but deep enough to settle in his bones.

Then, everything went black.

The workshop disappeared.

Kaelen stood in the middle of a battlefield. He had no memory of getting there—one moment he was at his desk, the next he was surrounded by twisted metal and scorched ground. The air crackled with energy, thick with the scent of burning oil and something older, something raw.

In the distance, two figures clashed. Their movements blurred between past and present, shifting between solid form and something spectral. One was wreathed in flame, his massive hammer carving arcs of fire through the air. Above him, a great phoenix with red and black feathers circled, embers trailing from its wings.

His opponent stood firm, golden energy radiating from the staff in his grasp. Each movement was precise, deliberate, as though channeling something far greater than himself. A giant eagle, feathers shimmering like molten gold, hovered above him, watching with piercing eyes.

The ground trembled beneath their battle, the very sky fracturing above them.

Then, a voice—ancient, hollow, and heavy with something deeper than time itself.

"The Equinox comes."

Kaelen gasped, stumbling back—

And slammed into his chair, the vision snapping away like a flame extinguished.

His breath was ragged, his hands gripping the edges of the workbench to keep himself grounded. The relic sat before him, untouched yet changed. Its glow had faded, but its presence was undeniable.

Wiz chirped in alarm, nudging Kaelen's arm as if checking for damage. He barely registered it. His heart still pounded, his skin cold with sweat.

The Equinox.

He had no idea what it meant.

But he knew one thing—

This relic wasn't just a machine.

It was a warning.

The knock came just as Kaelen finished securing the relic in a hidden compartment beneath his workbench.

Three slow, deliberate raps against the metal door. Not Dorian.

Wiz tensed beside him, tiny servos clicking as the automaton registered the sudden change in atmosphere. Kaelen swallowed hard and wiped his hands on his vest, trying to steady himself. Whoever was on the other side of that door wasn't here for pleasantries.

He forced himself to move, adjusting the scattered tools on his work table as though nothing was amiss. Then, with a deep breath, he approached the door and cracked it open just enough to see who had come calling.

A Forgehelm enforcer captain stood on the threshold, flanked by two armored soldiers. The captain's uniform was pristine, his mechanical gauntlet polished to a mirror sheen. Their helmets hid their faces. Their posture said the rest.

"Can I help you?" he said, like he hadn't just hidden a relic under the floor.

The captain's gaze swept the workshop, sharp and calculating. "We're conducting an investigation. Unregistered individuals were spotted trespassing in the scrapyard earlier tonight."

Kaelen feigned a frown. "Happens all the time. That place is crawling with scavengers."

The captain tilted his head slightly, as if assessing Kaelen's every twitch. "And yet, the description we received was rather specific."

Kaelen shrugged, forcing a casual tone. "You think every grizzled mechanic in Forgehelm looks the same?"

The captain didn't smile. "Mind if we come in?"

Kaelen's stomach twisted, but he stepped aside, keeping his movements slow and measured. The enforcers entered, their boots clanking against the metal floor. One of them swept a scanning device across the room, its light pulsing as it cataloged every piece of equipment.

Stay calm. Don't give them a reason to search deeper.

The captain approached his workbench, running a gloved hand over a set of blueprints. "You're quite the inventor," he remarked. "Self-taught?"

Kaelen nodded. "Mostly."

"Impressive." The captain lifted a small automaton arm Kaelen had been working on earlier. "Would be a shame if talent like yours were wasted."

Kaelen forced himself to remain still. "I keep my head down and my work clean. That's all Forgehelm asks, isn't it?"

The captain's lips curved into something that wasn't quite a smile. "Indeed."

The scan finished, beeping twice before the enforcer holding the device turned toward the captain. "No anomalies detected."

Kaelen let out a slow breath through his nose.

The captain gave one last lingering glance around the workshop before turning back to Kaelen. "If you hear anything… suspicious, you'll report it immediately."

Kaelen nodded. "Of course."

The captain studied him for a moment longer before finally stepping back toward the door. Without another word, the enforcers exited, their footsteps fading into the night.

Kaelen waited until he was sure they were gone before exhaling fully. He turned to Wiz, who had remained motionless throughout the entire exchange. The automaton blinked once, tilting its head.

That was too close.

He reached beneath the floor, fingers brushing over the relic's cool surface. They hadn't found it this time.

But Forgehelm was watching.

And it was only a matter of time before they knocked again.

Kaelen didn't sleep.

He sat at his workbench long after the enforcers had gone, the weight of the relic pressing on his thoughts. He turned it over in his hands, watching as the runes flickered, shifting in patterns he still couldn't decipher. The encounter had shaken him more than he wanted to admit. The enforcers weren't just suspicious—they were waiting for him to slip up.

He couldn't afford to.

Wiz chirped softly from the table, watching him with bright mechanical eyes. Kaelen reached out and ran a finger along its metallic head. "We can't stay here," he muttered.

He needed a plan. Fast.

His gaze flicked to the holomap on the far wall, its surface flickering as he powered it on. The city's layout spread before him in lines of glowing blue, every tier and pathway marked with routes he had memorized over years of navigating Forgehelm's underbelly. There were ways out—dangerous, unpredictable, but possible.

He zoomed in on the lower tiers, tracing potential escape paths when his workbench terminal let out a sudden beep.

A message.

Kaelen frowned and turned to the screen. His hands hovered over the keys as he opened it. No sender. No traceable origin.

Just a single line of text:
"You're not the first to find it. You won't be the last. Run."

A cold weight settled in Kaelen's chest.

Wiz let out a warning chirp as Kaelen shot to his feet, eyes darting around the workshop. The walls felt smaller. The air is heavier. Someone out there knew exactly what he had.

And if they could send this message, they could find him.

He powered down the holomap, grabbed the relic, and shoved it deep into his satchel. His hands shook.

He turned to his workbench. Blueprints still covered the surface, unfinished, their edges curled from years of handling. His gaze drifted to a half-built automaton arm on the shelf, the joints still stiff, the wiring exposed.

Three more days, and I could have finished it.

I could still hide the relic.

I could destroy it.

Maybe it's not too late—

A sudden clang from outside. Heavy boots.

Kaelen closed his satchel shut.

No. It was already too late.

He secured his tools, tightened his vest, and adjusted Wiz on his shoulder. Then, with one last glance at the place that had been his home, he flipped off the workshop lights and slipped into the shadows.

Forgehelm had never been safe.

But now, it was hunting him.

Chapter 2: Echoes of the Past

Kaelen moved like a shadow through Forgehelm's underbelly, his breath tight in his chest. The moment the enforcers had left his workshop, he knew his time in the city was over. Now, with the bounty declared and his face undoubtedly plastered across every notice board, staying in Forgehelm was a death sentence.

Chaos simmered in the lower tiers. Word traveled fast underground, and Kaelen didn't need to hear the declarations to know the weight of the accusations against him. High treason. Theft of forbidden technology. A price on his head that would make even allies reconsider their loyalty. Worse still, Aldric was leading the hunt personally.

Kaelen slipped into a dead forge, its once-glowing embers long extinguished. He pressed his back against the cool stone wall, forcing himself to steady his breath. Through the warped slats of a broken window, he watched as enforcers swept through the streets, torches slashing through the smog. The rhythmic clank of their heavy boots echoed through the alleyways, a grim reminder that Forgehelm had no room for fugitives.

A bounty meant one thing—Kaelen wasn't just an inconvenience to the council. He was a threat.

He needed to disappear. Now.

His mind raced through possible escape routes. The underground tunnels beneath the old foundries? No, the enforcers would already be blocking those exits. The trade routes out of the city? Impossible without forged documents, and those took time he didn't have. That left the smuggler routes—dangerous, unpredictable, but his best option.

Before he could move, a voice rang out from the street.

"Search everything. No one leaves this district until we have him."

Aldric.

Kaelen dared to peer through a crack in the wall. The man stood in the center of the street, his polished enforcer armor catching the torchlight, making him stand out even in the gloom. His presence sent a clear message—this wasn't just another fugitive hunt. This was personal.

Kaelen knew Aldric by reputation, though they had only crossed paths a handful of times. The man had grown up in the upper tiers, a son of Forgehelm's ruling elite. To him, Kaelen—just another poor, lower-tier scrapforger—was a stain on the city's legacy. Worse still, he was Orlan's kin, a reminder of the man the Forgemasters had executed for treason.

That, more than anything, made Kaelen a target.

Aldric had always despised the lower tiers, believing that the weak had no place in Forgehelm's future. But Kaelen wasn't just another nameless vagrant—he was connected to a man who had defied the city's rulers, who had dared to challenge the Forgemasters. Aldric wouldn't allow such defiance to resurface.

Kaelen tightened his grip on his satchel. If Aldric found him, there would be no trial, no chance to plead his case. The council wanted him erased.

A group of enforcers turned down his alleyway. Kaelen swore and bolted, slipping through a side passage that led toward the industrial ruins. His mind whirled with a single thought—he needed to get out before Forgehelm swallowed him whole.

And he was running out of time.

Dorian knelt before the towering statue of Vardun, the Forgeborne god of destruction, fire, and innovation, his hands clasped tightly in front of him. The grand chamber of the Forgehelm temple flickered with the glow of molten metal, its walls lined with intricate engravings depicting the city's history—war, conquest, progress. The heat radiated from the forge pits at the center of the chamber, filling the air with the scent of burning coal and smoldering iron.

But tonight, the fire brought him no clarity.

He had come seeking guidance, but the weight in his chest only grew heavier. The council had spoken. Kaelen was to be hunted, branded a traitor to Forgehelm. If Dorian was the man he was supposed to be—the enforcer, the Titanbreaker—there would be no hesitation. The city demanded order. The council's will was law.

So why did he hesitate?

The sound of footsteps echoed against the stone floor. He straightened, already knowing who it was before he turned.

Aldric.

"You look troubled," Aldric said, his tone smooth, calculated. He stepped closer, his enforcer's cloak barely shifting despite the heat of the chamber. "Praying for the strength to do what needs to be done?"

Dorian stood slowly, turning to face him. "I'm seeking clarity."

Aldric scoffed. "Clarity? There is nothing unclear about this. Kaelen Virel is a fugitive. He has stolen from the council and is a direct threat to the order of Forgehelm." He stepped forward, his piercing gaze locking onto Dorian's. "And I need to know where your loyalty stands."

Dorian clenched his teeth. He had known Aldric for years, trained alongside him, and fought beside him. But there was always something lurking beneath the man's polished demeanor—a coldness, a cruelty that made him a perfect enforcer, but a dangerous leader.

"The law is clear," Dorian said carefully. "But the council has been wrong before."

Aldric's eyes narrowed and for the first time, true hostility flared in his eyes. "Watch your words, Titanbreaker." He stepped even closer, lowering his voice. "You and I both know that the council doesn't make mistakes. But traitors? They are mistakes that need correcting."

Dorian held his ground, refusing to look away. His fists tightened at his sides.

Aldric shook his head, tone full of mock disappointment. "I hope I'm wrong about you, Dorian." He turned to leave but hesitated, glancing over his shoulder. "Because if I find out you've helped him, I'll see you kneeling before the council in chains."

The words lingered in the air long after Aldric was gone. Dorian looked back at the towering statue, searching for some kind of sign.

But the flames gave him nothing.

Kaelen's lungs burned as he weaved through the ruins of the industrial district, the sound of enforcer boots pounding against metal grates behind him. His escape routes were narrowing—every major path blocked, every alley patrolled. Caution hadn't been enough. Aldric's enforcers were too efficient, too relentless.

He had minutes, maybe less.

Sliding into a narrow gap between two collapsed structures, Kaelen pressed his back against the cold metal, chest heaving. His fingers brushed against the satchel at his side, where the relic was still hidden. He couldn't lose it. He couldn't afford to be captured. The city would swallow him whole.

A flicker of movement ahead made him tense. A figure emerged from the shadows, his stance unhurried, his steps eerily quiet against the rusted ground.

The man from the scrapyard.

Kaelen's pulse spiked as he recognized the cloaked stranger who had warned him before. But this time, the man wasn't disappearing into the darkness. He was waiting.

"Not the best night for a stroll, boy," the stranger muttered, his voice carrying a dry amusement. His sharp eyes flicked to Kaelen's satchel. "Still carrying that weight, I see."

Kaelen barely had time to react before the echo of enforcer voices cut through the streets. Too close.

"I don't have time for this," Kaelen snapped, pushing off the wall.

The man's hand shot out, gripping his arm. "No, you don't. Which is why you're coming with me."

Kaelen started to pull away, but something in the stranger's gaze stopped him. There was no hesitation, no uncertainty. Just grim certainty.

"I told you before—you don't know what you're holding," the man continued, his voice low. "But I do."

Kaelen hesitated for only a second before a searchlight swept dangerously close. The enforcers were closing in. He had no choice.

"Fine," he muttered. "But if this is a trick—"

The stranger didn't wait for him to finish. With a swift motion, he pulled Kaelen deeper into the ruins, navigating through hidden pathways Kaelen had never noticed before. The man moved with certainty—each turn deliberate, every step exact. This wasn't someone running blindly—this was someone who knew the city better than even the enforcers hunting them.

After several tense minutes, they reached a concealed hatch in the ground. The man knelt, pressed his palm to a barely visible panel, and the metal door creaked open.

"Inside," he ordered.

Kaelen hesitated, but the sound of enforcers shouting nearby made his decision for him. He dropped into the passageway below, landing on a grated floor. The man followed, sealing the hatch above them just as the patrol passed overhead.

For the first time since his escape began, Kaelen took a full breath.

The stranger straightened, dusting off his cloak. "You remind me of your uncle. Stubborn, reckless… but not without promise."

Kaelen's stomach twisted. "You knew Orlan?"

He watched Kaelen for a moment. "I did." He reached up, pulling back his hood to reveal sharp, weathered features. "My name is Rindun Veladra."

Kaelen's mind reeled. The name meant nothing to him, but the way Rindun looked at him—like he had already decided something—sent a fresh wave of unease through him.

The warmth left Rindun's tone. "And if you want to survive what's coming next…"

Aldric stood before the council for the second time in a week—no ceremony, no escort. Just silence thick enough to smother.

The chamber felt colder tonight, though the molten channels still pulsed beneath the floor. Every seat was filled. No whispers this time. No pretense.

Magnus Rooke didn't look at him right away.

"It seems your proof has turned to ash," Councilor Veren said, not bothering to mask her contempt. "Kaelen is gone. Again."

"And your enforcers," muttered Luthan, "are becoming the city's newest joke."

Aldric remained still. "He hasn't left Forgehelm. Not yet."

"You said that last time," Magnus said flatly. "And the time before."

Aldric didn't flinch. "I still believe it."

Veren leaned forward. "Belief isn't worth the heat it wastes. You were told to prove yourself. You failed."

"I didn't fail," Aldric said, voice low. "I underestimated him. That won't happen again."

"Spare us the conviction," Luthan spat. "You're asking for full control after three failures. Give us one reason why we shouldn't strip you of command entirely."

Aldric looked at Magnus. "Because no one else is closer. Because I know how he thinks. And because if I'm right, and he's carrying what we all suspect—then the only worse outcome than my failure is giving this task to someone who doesn't understand the cost of it."

Magnus steepled his fingers. "And if you fail again?"

The room quieted.

Aldric didn't hesitate. "Then let the cost be public. Strip me of my name. My title. My command. Let all of Forgehelm know that Aldric Rooke—son of Forgemaster Magnus Rooke—could not catch a scrapforger."

He let the words sink in.

Magnus finally met his gaze. "So be it."

The declaration landed like a verdict.

"You have full authority," Magnus continued. "Command of the enforcers, unrestricted access to every district, and no barriers from this council."

"But you fail again…" Veren added, "and we don't exile failures. We erase them."

Aldric bowed once—not out of humility, but ritual.

"I understand."

As the council adjourned, Aldric turned toward the exit, the weight of expectation crushing, clarifying. He would not be humiliated. He would not fall.

Kaelen Virel would be caught—because Aldric Rooke had nothing left to lose.

Kaelen followed Rindun through the dimly lit tunnels beneath Forgehelm, the scent of sewage and refuse thick in the air. The path twisted and turned, winding deeper into the forgotten veins of the city. Here, the sounds of enforcers, of the ever-churning forges, faded into silence, swallowed by the weight of stone and secrecy.

"Where are we going?" Kaelen asked, his voice hushed but sharp.

"To the only place left in this city where the truth hasn't been burned away," Rindun muttered. His steps were steady, confident, as though he had walked these tunnels a thousand times before.

Kaelen kept pace, his fingers brushing against the satchel at his side. The relic inside had been silent since his escape, but its weight felt heavier now. The words of the council, of Aldric's relentless pursuit, rang in his mind. This wasn't just about survival anymore. This was about understanding why he was being hunted.

After several more minutes of winding through the underground maze, Rindun finally stopped before a reinforced metal door, its surface covered in rusted bolts and faint etchings of old symbols. With a firm push, the door groaned open, revealing a workshop filled with scattered schematics, aged tomes, and relics of machinery long forgotten.

Kaelen's breath caught. This place… it was like his own workshop, but older, untouched by the city's rules. A sanctuary of forbidden knowledge.

Rindun looked at him for a long moment, something solemn in his gaze. "Your uncle once stood where you are now. He was one of the few who saw what Forgehelm was becoming."

Kaelen swallowed hard. "You knew Orlan." It wasn't a question this time.

"I fought beside him," Rindun said. "And I watched as the council erased his name from history." He stepped closer, his voice steady but filled with something deeper—conviction, or perhaps regret. "Orlan wasn't just executed for treason. He discovered something the council feared. Something they buried."

Kaelen's grip tightened on the strap of his satchel.

"The Celestine Convergence," Rindun said, almost as a whisper.

Kaelen held the relic tighter. "Why does it react to me?"

Rindun's face hardened. "Because you remind it of someone. Someone who held it before you."

His heart pounded. "Who?"

A shadow crossed Rindun's face. "Your uncle. Orlan Virel."

Kaelen's throat tightened. "He was a mechcrafter—he built machines. Not—whatever this is."

"He was more than that." Rindun leaned closer. "The Forgemasters killed him because of what he was—what he could become. And if they find out about you, they'll finish what they started."

Kaelen's mind reeled. Orlan had never spoken of a grand rebellion, only of the dangers of unchecked ambition, of the corruption in Forgehelm's highest ranks. But if this was true—if the Celestine Convergence had played a role in his uncle's death—then this was bigger than Kaelen had ever imagined.

Rindun stepped past him, pulling a dusty tome from a shelf and flipping it open to a series of sketches—diagrams of the relic, symbols he had seen shifting across its surface. "You were never supposed to find it, Kaelen. But now that you have, the council will stop at nothing to erase you the way they erased him."

The weight of it landed. He wasn't just running from Forgehelm.

He was running from the fate that had already claimed his uncle.

Dorian marched through the barracks with measured steps, his mind racing. The Forgeborne temple's walls had felt suffocating, but here, in the cold corridors of the enforcer stronghold, the weight of expectation threatened to crush him. The enforcers he passed gave him wary glances, their trust in him eroding with each rumor that spread through Forgehelm's ranks. He knew why he had been summoned. Aldric wasn't the type to let disloyalty fester.

He reached the command hall's doors and pushed them open. The room was dimly lit, the glow of rune-laced sconces casting flickering shadows across the polished steel walls. A single figure stood near the center, back turned to Dorian, hands clasped behind him. Aldric.

"You took your time," Aldric said without turning. His voice was as smooth as ever, but there was an edge to it, a sharpness honed by ambition and suspicion.

"I came as soon as I was summoned," Dorian replied evenly.

Aldric finally turned, his piercing gaze locking onto Dorian's. He held up a parchment—an official order stamped with the council's seal. "This came down an hour ago. You've been reassigned."

Dorian frowned. "Reassigned?"

"Effective immediately, you are relieved of your command. You are to be taken into custody for aiding and abetting a fugitive."

The words hit harder than any blow. Dorian's fists clenched, but he forced himself to remain still. "You know that's not true."

Aldric took a slow step forward, his smirk barely concealed. "What I know is that you've been… hesitant. You were seen at the temple, speaking to the priests. Speaking about justice." He spat the word like it was poison. "The council doesn't need soldiers who hesitate, Dorian. They need enforcers. Loyal ones."

Dorian didn't look away. "Loyalty and blind obedience aren't the same thing."

Aldric's voice stayed level. "You always thought you were better than me. Thought your faith made you righteous. But faith isn't what keeps Forgehelm standing. Strength is. And I am stronger than you."

A tense silence stretched between them. Then, Aldric tossed the parchment onto the table between them. "You still have a choice. Give me Kaelen. Tell me where he's hiding, and I will see to it that you walk away from this unscathed."

Dorian stared at the parchment but didn't move. His mind raced. If he betrayed Kaelen, he would betray everything he believed in—everything Orlan had stood for. But if he refused, Aldric would see him shackled and dragged before the council like a common traitor.

He took a deep breath and met Aldric's gaze. "I won't do it."

Aldric's smirk vanished. "Then you've made your choice."

The doors burst open behind Dorian. Enforcers moved in, their armored boots clanking against the stone floor. The cold grip of steel gauntlets seized his arms, rune-bound shackles locking around his wrists. He didn't resist. There was no point.

Aldric leaned in close, his voice a whisper only Dorian could hear. "You should have chosen differently."

As Dorian was led away, he didn't look back. His path was set, and there was no turning back now.

Kaelen crouched in the shadows of the abandoned tunnels beneath Forgehelm, his breath steady despite the tension thrumming in his veins. Rindun Veladra stood beside him, his posture relaxed but his eyes sharp, scanning the dimly lit passage ahead. The air was thick with the scent of damp metal and old oil, the remnants of an age when these tunnels had been used for smuggling and illicit dealings. Now, they were the only thing keeping Kaelen from the enforcers hunting him above.

"They're getting closer," Rindun murmured. His voice barely carried over the distant clanking of boots against steel.

Kaelen nodded. He could hear them too—enforcers combing the city, methodical in their search. If Aldric had put the full force of the council behind this manhunt, then they had little time left.

"We need to move," Kaelen said, gripping the strap of his satchel. "There's an old access point that leads out past the district walls—Orlan showed me once."

Rindun smirked. "Your uncle always did have an exit strategy."

A metallic echo rang through the tunnels, closer this time. Kaelen and Rindun pressed themselves against the cold stone, listening as armored figures passed above. Their muffled voices carried down, distorted but clear enough.

"Spread out. The moment you see him, signal."

Kaelen didn't move. Didn't blink. The moment they were spotted, it was over.

Rindun drew a rune-etched device from his belt. With a flick of his wrist, it emitted a soft hum, and the tunnel walls around them shimmered briefly before dulling back to their normal state.

"Concealment device," Rindun explained. "It won't last long, but it should mess with their tracking tools. Let's go."

They moved swiftly through the tunnels, Kaelen leading while Rindun covered their rear. The passage grew narrower, forcing them to duck under rusted beams and step over collapsed supports. Every so often, Kaelen glanced at the relic secured in his satchel, its presence a constant weight. He still didn't understand its full purpose, but he knew one thing—it was worth killing for.

A sudden noise from behind—Rindun spun, his weapon half-drawn. A burst of torchlight illuminated a figure at the tunnel's mouth.

An enforcer.

"Run!" Rindun barked. "I'll hold him back."

Kaelen bolted, the tunnel walls blurring past him. He heard the clash of steel, a sharp grunt of pain, but he didn't look back. Rindun had made his choice, and Kaelen knew better than to waste the opportunity. He sprinted toward the access hatch Orlan had once shown him, his mind racing.

He reached it just as another shout echoed from behind. The enforcers were coming. Kaelen threw his weight against the rusted hatch, the metal screeching as it gave way. He scrambled through, emerging into the cold night air beyond Forgehelm's outer ring.

For the first time since the chase began, Kaelen felt the sheer vastness of the world beyond the city. And he had no choice but to run into it.

Rindun's last words echoed in his mind.

"Find the others before it's too late."

Aldric stood before the Forgeborne Council, his posture rigid, his face was a mask of discipline. The chamber, carved from dark stone and reinforced with intricate golden inlays, pulsed with the weight of authority. The gathered council members, cloaked in ceremonial robes, sat in a semicircle around him, their gazes unreadable. At the head of the assembly sat Magnus Rooke, Aldric's father, his face impassive as he tapped his fingers against the armrest of his throne-like chair.

"The boy has escaped," one of the elder councilors said, voice thick with disapproval. "Again."

"Not for long," Aldric replied, as if it were fact—not a promise.

Magnus Rooke leaned forward, his piercing gaze settling on his son. "Your enforcers have failed at every turn. First, the Collegium. Then the scrapyards. And now, the tunnels." His voice was calm, but every word cut deep. "Tell me why I should trust you with this task when you've already failed me three times."

Aldric forced himself to meet his father's eyes, unwilling to show weakness. "Because I understand him better than anyone." He took a slow breath. "Kaelen is not just running. He's searching. He will not leave Forgehelm until he finds what Orlan left behind. That makes him predictable."

One of the councilors scoffed. "And yet, you let him slip through your grasp."

"I was cautious," Aldric admitted. "I will not make that mistake again."

Magnus studied him for a long moment, then turned his gaze to the rest of the council. "What say you?"

Murmurs filled the chamber, some voices favoring caution, others demanding swift action. Finally, one of the elder councilors, a woman with iron-gray hair and piercing blue eyes, spoke. "The boy cannot be allowed to roam free. If he uncovers what Orlan knew—" She stopped herself, glancing at Magnus. "We cannot afford another rebellion."

Aldric seized the moment. "Then let me deal with it as I see fit. Give me full authority, and I will ensure Kaelen never becomes a problem again."

A silence followed. Then, Magnus nodded once. "Very well."

Aldric felt the weight of victory settle on his shoulders as Magnus continued. "The enforcers are yours to command. If you fail again, do not return."

Aldric bowed his head. "I will not fail."

The council rose, the meeting adjourned, but Magnus remained seated as the others left. Aldric turned to go, but his father's voice halted him.

"Aldric."

He turned back, his pulse steady despite the sudden shift in tone. Magnus regarded him with something dangerously close to disappointment. "You seek to be more than a soldier. You want power."

Aldric didn't deny it. "I want what is best for Forgehelm."

Magnus's lips curled slightly, though there was no humor in it. "Then prove it."

Aldric inclined his head once more before leaving the chamber, the weight of his new authority pressing down on him. He had wanted this for years. Now, he would show them all what he was capable of.

And Kaelen Virel would be the first to learn just how relentless he could be.

Dorian sat in the dimly lit chamber of his quarters, his wrists bound in rune-etched shackles. The cold metal bit into his skin, but it was nothing compared to the weight pressing against his chest. He had always known that choosing faith over obedience came at a cost, but he hadn't expected the price to be this steep—his rank, his freedom, and soon, perhaps, his life.

The heavy door creaked open, and Aldric stepped inside, his polished enforcer's armor gleaming in the flickering lamplight. He moved with the slow, deliberate confidence of a man who had already won. Two armed guards flanked him, but Aldric raised a hand, dismissing them. The door shut behind him, leaving them alone.

"You had your chance," Aldric said, pacing the room. "You could have walked away with your honor intact. Instead, you threw it all away for some foolish notion of faith and justice. Tell me, was it worth it?"

Dorian met his gaze, unflinching. "Yes."

Aldric's smirk faltered for the briefest moment before he let out a short, humorless laugh. "That's what I always despised about you. That self-righteousness. That belief that you stand above the rest of us. But tell me, Dorian—where has it gotten you? Chained like a criminal. Stripped of your command. Branded a traitor."

Dorian said nothing. He wouldn't give Aldric the satisfaction of seeing doubt.

Aldric leaned in, voice low. "The council has already made its decision. You'll be transferred to the lower cells at dawn. A public trial will follow, but let's not pretend it will be anything more than a formality. The people need to see that betrayal has consequences."

Dorian met his stare. "If you think fear will make them follow, you're wrong. They may obey, but they will never follow."

A flicker of tension crossed Aldric's face, but it vanished beneath a smirk. "That's the difference between us, Dorian. I don't need them to follow. I need them to submit."

A knock on the door interrupted the tension. Aldric turned as one of his officers stepped in, face grim. "Sir, we have a situation. The prisoner is needed for immediate transfer. Orders from the council."

Aldric frowned but nodded. "Very well."

The officer stepped aside, and another figure entered—a cloaked figure, her features hidden beneath the hood's shadow. She moved with purpose, her stance unfamiliar. Dorian's instincts screamed at him—this was not what he was expecting.

Before Aldric could react, the woman struck. With a flick of her wrist, a small explosive rune ignited on the floor, sending a concussive blast that knocked Aldric backward. The guards outside shouted, but the cloaked figure was already at Dorian's side, slicing through his restraints with a concealed blade.

"Time to go," the stranger said. Her voice was steady, calm.

Dorian didn't hesitate. He surged to his feet, his muscles burning from disuse, but there was no time for weakness. They had mere seconds before the alarms triggered.

Aldric, coughing, pushed himself up from the ground, fury contorting his face. "You think this changes anything? You're only delaying the inevitable!"

Dorian spared him one final glance. "No, Aldric. I'm choosing my own fate."

Then he followed his rescuer into the night, leaving behind the life he once knew.

Kaelen stood at the city's outer edge, his breath ragged, his boots coated in dust from the forgotten roads that led beyond Forgehelm. The city loomed behind him, its towers stretching toward the sky like jagged iron teeth. Patrol lights blinked through the haze, their searchlights sweeping over the ruins and forgotten pathways that marked the city's end. He had made it this far, but the weight in his chest told him this was only the beginning.

He pulled the bounty notice from his satchel, his own face staring back at him beneath the bold proclamation:

WANTED—DEAD OR ALIVE. The ink was still fresh. Aldric hadn't wasted any time.

Wiz, perched on his shoulder, let out a low mechanical chirp, scanning the darkness beyond the city's reach. Kaelen took a slow breath, steadying himself. He had no plan, no allies beyond Dorian—wherever he was now. He knew only one thing: he couldn't stay here.

The road ahead stretched into the unknown, its dangers unseen but inevitable. The Godless Lands loomed far beyond the city's borders, a place of whispers and myths, a place people feared to tread. But right now, fear was a luxury Kaelen couldn't afford.

He adjusted his satchel and took his first step forward. Then another. And another.

The city behind him was already beginning to fade into the night.

A gust of wind kicked up dust along the cracked road, and Kaelen pulled his cloak tighter around his shoulders. Every instinct screamed at him to turn back, to find another way, but there was none. He thought of Rindun's sacrifice, of Dorian's choice, of Orlan's legacy. He wasn't just running—he was carrying something far greater than himself.

Wiz clicked softly and shifted on his shoulder, its sensors still scanning for movement. Kaelen reached up and ran a gloved hand over the automaton's metal frame. "Looks like it's just us for now, Wiz."

The automaton gave a short, warbling chirp, almost reassuring. Kaelen didn't answer. He couldn't match that kind of calm. He wished he shared Wiz's certainty. He had grown up among the smog and steel of Forgehelm, where the hum of machines never truly faded. Out here, in the vast openness beyond the city walls, the silence pressed against him like a weight.

Somewhere in the distance, the call of a night beast echoed across the plains, a stark reminder that the world outside Forgehelm was not barren—it was wild, untamed, and dangerous in ways he had yet to understand. He had studied maps, read stories, but nothing could prepare him for what lay ahead.

He glanced one last time over his shoulder. The spires of Forgehelm stood unwavering, but to him, they were nothing more than a prison he had finally broken free from. He turned away, steeling himself. There was no turning back now.

And so, he walked on, into the unknown, where only fate would decide what awaited him next.

Chapter 3: The Great Canopy's Secret

The grand chamber of Eldoravell's Council Hall, The Wardens of Aeldrin, stood in defiant silence, its emerald-streaked marble reflecting the pale light of the bioluminescent lanterns hanging from the vaulted ceiling. The chamber's central table, a circular construct of intertwined roots and polished stone, was surrounded by the most powerful figures in Verdant society. Elara Thorne sat among them, her back straight, her hands folded in her lap, masking the fire burning in her chest.

The High Warden, an elder draped in ceremonial Verdant green, steepled his fingers. "The rumors from Greenhold grow with each passing season," he intoned, his voice slow and deliberate. "The people whisper of imbalance, of omens in the sky. They speak of war."

Her voice stayed level, but the edge was unmistakable. "And how does this council intend to address such fears? By pretending they do not exist?"

A murmur of disapproval rippled through the chamber. Across from her, Tarian Thorne, her elder brother and a rising figure within Verdant's military order, shot her a warning glance. She ignored it.

The High Warden folded his hands. "It is the duty of the Council to ensure stability. Aeldrin's will has held this land in balance since the first Equinox. Do you truly believe that has changed?"

"I believe the people deserve the truth," Elara countered. "Fractured harvests. Erratic tides. Aggression from the southern front. These aren't coincidences. They are warnings."

Another councilor, an aging noble named Veshar Delorne, scoffed. "Lady Thorne, we are not here to entertain myth and superstition. You speak of omens like a star-chaser lost in children's fables."

Elara's fingers curled into her palm. "It is no fable that every Equinox throughout history has marked a turning point for our world. What if this one is different? What if Verdant is not prepared?"

Tarian leaned forward, his posture still composed. "Elara," he said, his tone meant for her ears alone. "Tread carefully."

She met his gaze, unflinching. He was trying to protect her, she knew, but she would not be silent.

"The people will not accept ignorance for long," she said, addressing the Council once more. "Refusing to act won't stop the storm. And we will be blind to it."

The High Warden studied her for a long moment before speaking. "The prophecy of the Equinox is Verdant's oldest myth. A tale of balance, not of destruction. If you wish to chase shadows, Lady Thorne, you do so at your own peril."

The meeting concluded with no resolution, only thinly veiled dismissal. As the Council members rose and began murmuring amongst themselves, Elara remained seated, frustration coiling in her stomach.

Tarian lingered beside her, lowering his voice. "You push too hard. There are lines, sister, even for you."

Elara stood slowly."Then perhaps it is time those lines were redrawn."

The Wardens called them "warnings," but Elara remembered the fields outside Greenhold.

No crops. No life. Just withered stalks under a sky too heavy with silence.

They could sit in their towers and debate, but Elara knew the truth— something was coming. And if no one stopped it, Verdant would burn.

She turned on her heel and strode toward the exit, the echoes of the Council's indifference ringing in her ears. If they would not seek the truth, then she would.

The corridors of Eldoravell's upper halls stretched before Elara, their walls woven with vines that pulsed faintly with Verdant's natural magic. Councilors and attendants moved through the space in hushed conversation, their gazes flickering toward her with wary disapproval. The meeting had ended, but the weight of her defiance lingered like the echo of a storm yet to break.

"Elara Thorne, the ever-spirited visionary."

The voice was smooth, laced with amusement, and unmistakably condescending. Elara turned to see Lord Calion Varess, heir to one of the oldest Verdant bloodlines, leaning against an ivy-wrapped pillar with the ease of someone who had never known true struggle. His golden cloak draped like punctuation—an exclamation of status.

"If you want fairy tales, perhaps you should visit the old archives—if they'll let you in, that is." Calion mused, a smirk tugging at the corner of his lips.

Elara stiffened, recognizing the barb beneath the feigned politeness. "Perhaps I will. Some of us find value in knowledge rather than complacency."

Calion chuckled, pushing off the pillar with an infuriatingly casual air. "Then by all means, indulge your curiosity. But don't be surprised if you find nothing but dust and forgotten ink. Some things are lost for a reason."

With that, he strolled away, his presence leaving behind an air of smug satisfaction. Elara watched him go, her mind already working through the implications of his words. The Great Canopy—Verdant's central archive—was no secret, but its deeper records were tightly restricted. If the prophecy had been deemed unimportant by the Council, why would its records be hidden at all?

She took a steady breath, glancing toward the distant towers where the archives stood, their canopies stretching high above the rest of Eldoravell. The Wardens of Aeldrin wanted her to let this go. Tarian wanted her to be cautious. But caution would not bring her answers.

Calion meant to mock her. Instead, he gave her something far more dangerous: a direction.

Elara moved swiftly through the winding pathways of Eldoravell, her destination clear—the Great Canopy, Verdant's vast archive of history, knowledge, and prophecy. The towering structure was an intricate fusion of ancient stone and living wood, its upper levels vanishing into the thick, emerald foliage above. It was a testament to Verdant's devotion to preservation—yet, as Elara approached, she couldn't help but wonder how much of that knowledge was hidden rather than shared.

The entrance to the Great Canopy was flanked by two Verdant sentinels, standing like part of the architecture itself—unmoving, unreadable. She expected no resistance here—after all, she had visited the archives many times before. But as she stepped forward, a familiar figure blocked her path.

Overseer Revand Durlain, the custodian of the archives, stood with his hands clasped before him. He was an aging man, his robes marked with the insignia of Verdant's scholarly order. His sharp, hawkish eyes regarded her with scrutiny.

"Princess Elara," he greeted, voice measured. "I assume you have business here?"

"I do," she replied, lifting her chin. "I require access to the historical records regarding the Equinox prophecy."

Revand's lips pressed into a thin line. "I'm afraid those records are restricted."

Elara narrowed her eyes. "Since when? I've accessed archive records on Verdant's histories before."

Revand did not flinch. "Some knowledge is best left to the Council and those deemed worthy of its burden."

Elara crossed her arms. "And who decides what knowledge is a burden? You? The Council?"

A flicker of something unreadable passed through Revand's gaze. "Some questions are better left unasked, Lady Thorne."

Elara's frustration burned. First the Council dismissed her, now she was being barred from the very place meant to hold Verdant's knowledge? She would not let this stand.

She considered her options. She could attempt to argue further, but Revand would not budge. She could appeal to Tarian, but he would urge her to leave this alone. That left her only one choice—she would have to find another way inside.

Offering Revand a polite nod, she turned and walked away without another word. But as soon as she was out of sight, she veered down a side passage, her mind already working through the possibilities. If the Council thought they could keep the truth from her, they were sorely mistaken.

Elara moved through the dimly lit corridors of the Great Canopy's lower halls, her steps careful, her breath steady. The scent of aged parchment and polished wood filled the air, an intoxicating reminder that this place held more than just history—it held secrets. The overseer's refusal still burned in her mind, but she had learned long ago that when the Council closed a door, one had to find a window.

The records she sought were not in the public halls. If the Equinox prophecy was deemed too dangerous for common study, then its true accounts would be buried within the restricted archives. And she knew exactly where to look.

After ensuring the hallway was clear, she pressed her hand against a carved relief along the wall—a twisting depiction of Verdant's founding, its stone grooves worn smooth by time. With ease, she traced a specific sequence of runes hidden within the vines. A soft click echoed in the silence, and a narrow panel in the wall shifted open.

Slipping inside, she found herself in a forgotten alcove of the archives, a space where dust clung to untouched tomes and neglected scrolls. The Council hadn't expected anyone to come looking here.

She moved quickly, fingers skimming across the spines of the oldest records, searching for any mention of the Equinox. Most texts held only the sanctioned version—the one she had heard repeated her entire life:

Aeldrin, the Verdant god of balance, created the Equinox as a symbol of order, ensuring neither faction would ever rise unchecked.

But then, buried beneath a stack of worn ledgers, she found something different—a brittle scroll, its edges charred as if someone had once tried to destroy it. Carefully, she unrolled it, her heart hammering as she read.

The Equinox is not balance—it is an event. A catalyst. The moment when the Great Unity stirs once more.

Her breath caught. The Great Unity. A being said to have existed before the gods themselves. A myth, if the Council was to be believed. And yet, the script before her told a different story.

One line was burned deep into the parchment, its letters dark and etched with undeniable force:

"The Unity never left. He waits."

Elara swallowed hard, the weight of the revelation settling over her. If this was true, then everything Verdant had taught her—everything the Council upheld—was a lie.

Footsteps echoed in the distance.

She stiffened, quickly rolling the scroll and tucking it beneath her cloak. Truth in hand. Escape first.

Elara's fingers trembled as she carefully rolled the brittle scroll, tucking it beneath her cloak. The words still burned in her mind—The Unity never left. He waits. If this were true, then the Council had hidden far more than she ever imagined. But why? And what did it mean for Verdant's future?

She turned back to the shelves, scanning the faded titles, hoping for more. If the Great Unity had been erased from history, there had to be more traces buried beneath the Council's deception. Her gaze landed on a wooden chest pushed against the far wall, its surface covered in a layer of dust untouched by recent hands. The lock was weak, rusted with age.

A sharp glance toward the door confirmed she was still alone. She crouched and pried it open.

Inside, stacks of faded parchments lay nestled against delicate, wax-sealed scrolls. At first, they appeared to be simple lineage records—family trees, noble decrees, the type of documents the Council saw fit to preserve. But then, beneath the top layers, something caught her eye—a crest. Not just any crest. Her family's.

Elara's breath caught. She carefully lifted the parchment, her heart pounding as she took in the intricate design. It was almost identical to House Thorne's sigil—except for one difference. A single symbol had been woven into the vines of the crest, so seamlessly hidden it was easy to miss.

The same symbol from the prophecy.

A rush of realization chilled her blood. House Thorne had always been loyal to Verdant, deeply entwined with its history—but nowhere in her family's records had this mark ever appeared. If it was here, buried in a forgotten archive, it meant only one thing:

Her family had been part of the Equinox—before the Council erased them.

She carefully unfolded the attached document, scanning the faded ink. The script was old, written in a formal tone, its words weighted with meaning:

The duty of House Thorne is eternal. Through the ages, we remain the stewards of the Equinox, the watchers of the turning cycle. As was sworn by our blood, so it must remain, lest balance be lost.

Elara's grip tightened on the parchment. The Council had hidden this. They had erased her family's role.

Why?

A thousand possibilities flooded her mind. Had her ancestors once stood against the Council? Had they tried to reveal the truth? Had they, like her, questioned Verdant's devotion to the gods' will? If they had been cast aside, then what did that mean for her now?

She wasn't just digging into forbidden history. She was reclaiming a duty her family had sworn to uphold.

A sound outside the chamber made her freeze.

Footsteps. Close.

Her heart slammed against her ribs as she shoved the parchment beneath her cloak. She had what she needed—but now, she had to get out before the Council ensured she never asked another question again.

Elara pressed herself against the wooden shelves, her breath held as the footsteps outside the chamber grew louder. The flickering glow of lantern light crept through the cracks of the door. Someone was there. Watching. Searching.

Had she already been discovered?

Her fingers clenched around the parchment beneath her cloak. She had come too far to be caught now. Carefully, she edged toward the opposite side of the room, scanning for another way out. The chamber was small, lined with ancient texts and dust-covered tomes, its scent thick with the passage of time. No doors other than the main entrance. No windows. No escape.

The footsteps stopped.

Elara stiffened, her heartbeat hammering in her ears. Then—a faint rustling. Not from outside. From within the room.

Her eyes darted to the nearest shelf. Some of the oldest scrolls had been disturbed, their stacks uneven, pages missing. Someone else had been searching here before her.

Then she saw it.

A message, carved roughly into the wood of the shelf, as if by a dagger's tip. The edges were splintered, the letters uneven but deliberate.

"The Equinox comes."

A chill ran down her spine. Someone had left this behind—someone who had read these records, someone who had found the truth before her. But had they fled? Or had they been silenced?

She reached out, running her fingers over the grooves of the carved letters. The urgency of the message was clear. This was not a historian's note. It was a warning.

The footsteps outside moved again—closer this time. A shadow passed beneath the door.

Elara swallowed hard. There was no more time to think. She turned back to the shelves, scanning the scattered pages, searching for anything else of value. Some were missing. Burned edges lined the gaps where scrolls had once rested. Whatever knowledge had been here, someone had tried to destroy it.

But why leave the warning behind?

A hand rested against the door outside. The wooden frame groaned softly under the pressure.

Elara's pulse quickened. If she didn't move now, she would have the answer to her question far sooner than she wanted.

Carefully, she stepped away from the carved message, retreating into the shadows. The moment the door cracked open, she would have only seconds to act.

The truth was slipping through her fingers.

And she wasn't the only one looking for it.

Elara barely had time to slip behind a tall shelf before the door creaked open. The dim lantern light cast long shadows over the chamber, flickering across the ancient tomes and dust-laden scrolls. She held her breath, pressing herself against the cold wood, heart hammering as footsteps crossed the threshold.

The overseer.

Elara watched through the gaps in the shelving as Revand moved with slow deliberation, his sharp eyes scanning the room. His gaze flicked to the disordered shelves, lingering on the gaps where missing scrolls should have been. Then his fingers brushed against the carved message on the wood. **The Equinox comes.**

He inhaled sharply.

Elara could see the tension in his shoulders as he traced the letters with a gloved hand. A flicker of something crossed his face—recognition? Fear? Whatever it was, he masked it quickly. His head turned slightly, as if listening for something unseen. Then he spoke, his voice calm but edged with something colder.

"You're not the first to search here," he murmured. "But you might be the last."

Elara's breath caught. Was he talking to himself? Or did he know she was there?

Revand lingered a moment longer, then turned abruptly. He strode toward the entrance, but instead of leaving, he reached for something just outside the door. The sound of metal scraping against wood sent a jolt of panic through Elara.

He was locking the chamber.

She had seconds to act.

As the heavy mechanism slid into place, she grabbed a loose scroll from the nearest shelf and stepped out, forcing her expression into one of feigned surprise. "Master Revand?"

He stilled, his hand still on the latch. Slowly, he turned, eyes narrowing as they landed on her.

"Lady Thorne," he said, his tone unreadable. "Curious place for a noble to wander."

Elara gave a small, polite smile, keeping her grip on the scroll firm. "The Council has tasked me with expanding my research into Verdant's foundational texts. I thought this chamber might hold something of value."

Revand studied her in silence, and she knew he was weighing her words. He didn't miss details. If her logic cracked, he'd see it—and exploit it.

At last, he spoke. "History is delicate, Lady Thorne. It is easily misunderstood by those who seek more than they are meant to know." He gestured to the door, stepping aside. "Perhaps you should return to the texts deemed… appropriate."

Elara didn't argue. She bowed her head slightly, moving past him, forcing herself to walk at a measured pace. She didn't breathe until she was clear of the chamber.

As she stepped into the corridor, Revand's parting words followed her, tranquil but heavy with meaning.

"Be careful where you dig, Lady Thorne. You may not like what you unearth."

Elara moved swiftly through the winding halls of the Great Canopy, her heart still racing from her encounter with Master Revand. She had escaped, but barely. And his words lingered in her mind like an unshaken whisper: You may not like what you unearth.

She needed answers—but she also needed caution. And as she stepped into the moonlit courtyard beyond the archives, she realized she was not alone.

"Tarian."

He'd been waiting. Still, arms crossed, gaze fixed—not with judgment, but something close to fear.

"Elara," he said, voice hush but firm. "Tell me you weren't in the restricted archives."

She hesitated. Lying to Tarian had never come easily, and she could see in his eyes that he already knew the truth.

"I found something," she admitted, lowering her voice. "Something about our family—about House Thorne's past."

Tarian scanned the room before stepping closer. "I was afraid of this." His voice dropped. "Elara, you don't understand how dangerous this is."

She lifted her chin. "Then explain it to me. Why is our name in a prophecy no one speaks of? Why did the Council erase our family's role?"

Tarian ran a hand through his hair, frustration breaking through. "Because history is only as true as the ones who write it." He lowered his voice. "Verdant is built on balance. The moment you question that balance, you break it. And if you break it, Elara, you break us."

She searched his face, reading the conflict there. He wasn't just worried for the Council—he was worried for her.

"You think they'll exile me?" she asked.

Tarian didn't answer immediately, but the weight in his gaze spoke for him. "I think they'll do worse."

A chill ran through her, but she held her ground. "Then I need to be sure the truth is worth the risk."

Tarian let out a slow breath, then placed both hands on her shoulders, steady and strong. "Then I'll be by your side," he said firmly. "But you need to be careful, Elara. If you push too hard, they won't just come for you. They'll come for our entire house."

Elara's resolve did not waver. "Then I'll find a way to keep us safe. But I can't stop now."

Tarian's grip tightened slightly before he let out a weary sigh. "If you're going to do this, at least let me help where I can. Just… don't shut me out."

She nodded, a small sense of relief settling in her chest. She wasn't entirely alone. Not yet.

With a final glance at her, Tarian turned toward the Great Canopy's towering trees. He didn't speak again. Just stood a moment longer, like he wanted to say more—but didn't.

Elara watched him go, determination settling in her bones. Whatever the Council was hiding, she would uncover it. And this time, she wouldn't be the only one fighting for the truth.

Elara paced her chambers, the weight of the night's discoveries pressing heavily on her shoulders. The candlelight flickered against the worn parchment she had unrolled across her desk—the secret history of House Thorne, buried beneath layers of Council-sanctioned lies. Tarian's warning echoed in her mind, but it only strengthened her resolve. The Council had erased the past, but they could not erase the truth she now carried.

Her fingers traced the altered crest, the unfamiliar symbol woven into the vines. The same mark had appeared in the prophecy, in the archives' forbidden texts. There was a connection, but she couldn't yet see it clearly.

She needed more.

A gust of wind rattled the wooden shutters of her balcony doors, drawing her attention to the towering trees of the Great Canopy beyond. The Council claimed that Verdant's history had always been guided by Aeldrin's will—that their order ensured balance. But what if the truth had been buried, just like her family's legacy?

Frustration curled in her chest. She turned back to her desk, reaching for the drawer where she kept her family's old records. As her hand brushed the wooden panel, something shifted beneath her fingertips. A faint groove—a seam she had never noticed before.

Elara stilled.

Slowly, she pressed against the hidden panel. With a soft click, a compartment slid open beneath the drawer.

Inside, nestled in the darkness, was an object of metal and stone. The surface was marked with the same symbol from the prophecy—the sigil of the Great Unity.

Elara's breath caught in her throat. She reached for it hesitantly, her fingers grazing the cold surface.

Elara's fingers traced the smooth edges of the relic—no larger than her palm, cold despite the warmth of the room. Its surface was covered in delicate carvings, almost too faint to see.

Her hand trembled as she gripped the relic tighter. "I'm trying—why won't you tell me what I need?"

The runes flared. For a moment, Elara felt something else—a presence, old and watchful.

She froze.

The air seemed heavier, the candlelight flickering wildly. Then—a whisper, too faint to be real.

"They executed him before he could finish it."

Elara's breath hitched. She turned sharply, but the room was empty. No one was there.

Her pulse pounded against her ribs. Slowly, she looked down at the relic again. And this time, she saw the writing.

Faint, nearly erased. But still there.

"The Equinox was stopped before it began."

"One was betrayed. One was silenced."

"The cycle begins again."

A voice—distant and hollow—echoed through the air.

"They were stopped before the Equinox began. If it fails again, the Veil will be severed."

The last word rang in her ears— the veil. What Veil? And what happens if it severs?

Elara staggered back a step. The relic felt heavier in her hands.

She swallowed hard, gripping the relic more firmly. If the Great Unity had truly vanished, then why did this still exist? Why had her family hidden it?

The Council had spent centuries ensuring Verdant's history remained unquestioned. They had silenced voices, erased records, and buried secrets.

But they had failed to bury this.

Elara held the relic tightly, its weight pressing into her palm. This was proof that the Great Unity was more than a forgotten myth.

And now, she had something the Council never intended for her to find.

Elara turned the relic over in her hands, its weight both solid and unreal. The flickering candlelight caught the edges of the engraved sigil, casting twisting shadows against the walls of her chamber. A thousand questions swirled in her mind, but none had answers—not yet.

A chill ran through her despite the warmth of the room. The Unity never left. He waits. The words from the prophecy resurfaced, pressing against her thoughts like a whispered warning.

Then—

A noise outside.

Elara's pulse spiked. She stiffened, fingers tightening around the relic as she turned toward the balcony doors. The shutters creaked softly, disturbed not by wind but by movement. Someone was there.

Carefully, she extinguished the candle, plunging the room into darkness. She crossed the room without a sound, slipping to the wall and watching through the shutters.

A figure stood just beyond the railing, cloaked in shadow, motionless except for the slow rise and fall of their breath. The faintest glimmer of moonlight caught on something metallic at their hip—a blade.

Elara swallowed, forcing herself to remain still. Whoever they were, they were watching her. Waiting.

Her mind raced. Had the Council already discovered what she had found? Had Master Revand sent someone to follow her? Or was this another seeker of the truth—one who had been searching just as she had?

The figure shifted, tilting their head slightly, as if aware of her gaze.

Then, without a word, they turned and vanished into the canopy of Verdant's towering trees, disappearing as quickly as they had come.

Elara let out a slow breath, her heartbeat still thundering in her chest.

This was no coincidence. Someone knew.

And now, she wasn't just chasing the truth.

She was being hunted for it.

Chapter 4: Iron Pursuit

The Iron Flats stretched endlessly before Kaelen, an ocean of rusted soil and fractured metal plates, remnants of a war fought long before his time. The sun hung mercilessly above, its scorching heat beating down on his back as he ran. Every step sent up clouds of dust and ash, coating his skin in the metallic scent of old blood and forgotten battles. The land beneath his boots was treacherous, riddled with sinkholes where ancient mining tunnels had collapsed, threatening to swallow the careless whole.

And behind him, the Enforcers were closing in.

Distant voices cut through the dry wind. Forgehelm enforcers had picked up his location. Kaelen cursed under his breath, forcing his legs to move faster. Aldric's men had tracked him through Forgehelm, chased him beyond its smog-choked borders, and now pursued him into the wastelands. There was no doubt in his mind—Aldric would not stop until Kaelen was either captured or dead.

The Celestine Convergence pulsed faintly in his satchel, the heat of the relic nearly searing through the fabric. Was this worth it? The thought clawed at his mind as exhaustion crept into his limbs. He had risked everything for this artifact, but at what cost? He was alone, hunted, with nowhere left to run.

But then, the relic shuddered. A faint surge of energy coursed through his fingers as he adjusted his grip on the strap. It was as if it were reminding him—you cannot abandon me.

A burst of steam erupted from the cracked ground ahead, a pressure vent from the unstable caverns beneath the Flats. Kaelen veered to the side, narrowly avoiding the scalding spray.

His lungs burned, his muscles screamed for rest, but he couldn't stop—not now.

The enforcers are getting closer. He could hear the sound of their voices. Aldric's voice rang out from the ridge behind him.

"Virel! You can't run forever!"

Kaelen ignored him, pushing forward. Behind him, the sounds of pursuit grew louder—heavy boots crunching against dry ground, the mechanical whir of enforcer gear.

Kaelen stole a glance over his shoulder. Too close. Aldric's forces had spread out in a wide formation, cutting off every possible escape route. They weren't just chasing him—they were herding him.

Kaelen knew Aldric could track him down in an instant, but he wasn't. He was playing with him—maybe out of arrogance, maybe for some other reason. Either way, it gave Kaelen precious time to make his escape.

Wiz skittered beside him, the small automaton barely keeping up in the oppressive heat. His delicate servos whined, struggling against the magnetic interference in the Flats. Kaelen gritted his teeth. He needed to find cover, a way to break the enforcers' line of sight—

His foot hit something sharp.

A jagged shriek of pain ripped through him as his boot slipped against rusted metal, sending him crashing forward. The impact drove a twisted scrap shard deep into his calf, tearing through fabric and flesh alike.

Kaelen barely swallowed a cry, his fingers digging into the cracked dirt as he fought against the wave of pain. Blood seeped into his boot, hot and slick. He couldn't stop. He had to move.

Wiz let out a sharp, worried chirp, nudging against his side.

Kaelen forced himself up, biting back a groan. His leg screamed in protest, but he pushed forward, half-limping, half-running. No time to bandage it. He didn't stop. Didn't let himself think.

The voices behind him grew sharper.

He had seconds to decide.

Kaelen sucked in a breath, clenched his fists, and leapt.

The world tilted as he plunged into the trench, his boots skidding against loose gravel. He barely managed to keep himself upright, staggering forward into the shadows of the wreckage.

Aldric's voice rang out, sharp and commanding.

"Find him."

Kaelen pressed his back against a warped metal husk, sucking in air through clenched teeth. His pulse hammered in his ears, his leg throbbed, but he stayed silent.

Wiz huddled close, its small frame vibrating in distress. Kaelen reached down, his fingers brushing against its metal plating in reassurance.

The enforcers were close now. Too close.

Kaelen gritted his teeth, forcing himself to stay still. If they found him now, it was over.

The heat of the Iron Flats was relentless. The sun hung like a molten brand in the sky, baking the cracked land and turning every breath into a struggle. Kaelen's boots pounded against the rust-colored ground, his lungs burning as he pushed himself forward. Every step sent sharp jolts of pain through his leg—the wound from the scrap field was slowing him down.

The jagged metal had torn deep, staining his pants with dark streaks of blood. He clenched his teeth, forcing himself onward. There was no time to stop, no time to bandage the wound. Not when Aldric and his enforcers were just behind him.

Wiz scurried at his side, the small automaton struggling against the heat. His usual quick, agile movements were sluggish, his delicate mechanisms clicking unevenly. The Iron Flats were thick with residual magnetic interference—scrap metal from old battles littered the landscape, remnants of war machines long since abandoned. It was throwing off Wiz's internal balance.

"Not now, Wiz," Kaelen muttered, gripping the construct tightly as it let out a series of strained chirps. "I need you to hold on."

A distant howl tore through the air—not an animal's cry, but something cold and mechanical. Aldric had unleashed the tracker hounds. He'd been toying with Kaelen all along, dragging out the chase like a predator savoring the hunt. But now? Now, he was done playing.

Kaelen's heart pounded harder. He had to find cover. Now.

Up ahead, the land sloped downward into a deep trench where shattered remnants of old war constructs had been left to rot. The jagged debris cast long, thin shadows across the rusted wasteland. It wasn't much, but it was his best chance.

Kaelen pushed forward, ignoring the fire in his leg. He reached the edge of the trench and slid down, his boots kicking up loose gravel and dust. Pain exploded up his leg, a sharp cry escaped his throat before he could stop it. He hit the ground hard, barely managing to roll to absorb the impact.

The enforcers' voices grew closer. The mechanical whir of the hounds getting louder.

"Spread out! He's close!" Aldric's voice was unmistakable—calm, controlled, but carrying the weight of a man who had no intention of letting his quarry slip away.

Kaelen pressed himself against a crumbling metal husk, holding his breath. Wiz lay still at his side, his systems dimmed to conserve energy.

A shadow passed over the trench's edge. Boots crunched against the dirt above him.

Kaelen didn't dare move. He could hear the faint whir of a tracking device scanning the area. Any movement, any sound, and he was caught.

Seconds stretched into an eternity. The heat pressed down on him, his wound throbbed in protest, but he remained still.

Then, finally—

A voice called from the other side of the trench. "Nothing here! Keep moving!"

The shadows shifted. Footsteps retreated.

The silence held. A few minutes. Maybe.

He turned to Wiz, pressing a hand against his cooling chassis. "We have to keep moving," he whispered. "But we need another way out."

Wiz clicked weakly, his sensors flickering back to life. Then, after a moment, he let out a soft, distinct chirp—one that Kaelen recognized.

A signal.

Wiz had found something.

Kaelen followed Wiz's gaze toward a collapsed section of the trench wall, where remnants of an old transport tunnel jutted from the rubble. It was a risk, but if it meant avoiding Aldric's enforcers, it was one he had to take.

Kaelen's breath came in sharp, uneven gasps as he pressed his back against the rusted hull of a long-forgotten war machine. His leg throbbed, the wound pulsing with every frantic heartbeat, but he couldn't stop moving. Not yet.

Above the trench, the enforcers swept the area, their voices cutting through the dry, stifling air.

"He's close," one of them muttered. "The hounds are circling back. They are having issues with their tracking systems, it must be the magnetic field of this place."

He forced the panic down. He didn't have much time.

Wiz chirped softly, his optics flickering with low power warnings. The heat and magnetic interference were affecting his systems too. If wiz shuts down now, he'd have to navigate the Iron Flats by himself—another disadvantage he couldn't afford.

A shadow passed overhead. Aldric.

Even without seeing his face, Kaelen could hear the authority in his voice.

"Lock down the perimeter," Aldric ordered. "He's bleeding. That means he's slowing down."

Kaelen sucked in a breath. Damn it. They were reading the terrain, tracking him not just with their hounds but with logic. He had minutes at best.

He forced himself to move, creeping along the base of the trench, staying in the wreckage's shadows. Every step sent sharp stabs of pain up his leg, but he bit back any sound.

Then—movement ahead.

Kaelen barely had time to react before a dark figure dropped down into the trench before him. His instincts screamed fight or run, but he could do neither fast enough. The figure surged forward, grabbing him by the arm.

Kaelen swung, but his weakened stance made the strike easy to deflect. He was shoved back, his boot slipping in the dirt—

Then the figure spoke.

"Kaelen, stop!"

The voice froze him. Impossible.

Dorian.

Kaelen stared in disbelief. He thought Dorian was still in Forgehelm. He had assumed his friend was either locked away in Forgehelm or—

No. Not now.

Dorian looked like a ghost of himself—leaner, rougher, eyes hollowed by more than exhaustion. His armor was stripped of rank insignias, his hammer slung across his back.

"What—how—" Kaelen stammered, his thoughts a tangled mess.

"No time," Dorian said sharply. "We have to move. Now."

Kaelen barely had a second to process before a gunshot rang out.

Dorian shoved him aside, drawing his hammer in one fluid motion. The shot ricocheted off the wreckage beside them, sending a burst of sparks into the air.

The enforcers had spotted them.

Dorian planted his feet, hammer ready. He wasn't running. He was staying to fight.

Kaelen cursed. Of course he was.

"We don't have time for this," Kaelen hissed, tugging at Dorian's arm. "You just saved me—don't waste it by dying here!"

Dorian didn't look at him. His gaze was locked on the trench's edge, where figures were already descending.

Then, finally—

"Go," Dorian muttered, shoving Kaelen toward a path through the wreckage. "I'll cover you."

Kaelen hesitated. He had just gotten Dorian back. He wasn't about to lose him again.

But the look in Dorian's eyes told him everything.

Dorian wasn't here just to save him. He had his own reasons for being here.

Another shot rang out, forcing Kaelen's choice.

He ran.

Dorian's hammer swung upward, meeting the first enforcer mid-strike. Kaelen heard the crunch of impact as he forced himself forward, his leg screaming in protest.

Wiz beeped anxiously, but Kaelen didn't stop. He couldn't.

As he disappeared deeper into the trench, Dorian's voice rang out behind him—

"I'll find you again, Kaelen! Just keep running!"

Kaelen's breath burned in his throat as he stumbled through the wreckage, forcing his wounded leg to keep moving. The Iron Flats were vast, an endless expanse of rusted metal and forgotten machines, but nowhere felt far enough.

Dorian had stayed behind to fight. Again.

A part of Kaelen wanted to turn back. He had barely processed that Dorian was alive—had barely gotten more than a few words out of him before they were separated again.

But he knew the truth.

Dorian was strong. Stronger than him. If anyone could survive, it was him.

The only way Kaelen could help was by making sure Dorian's risk wasn't wasted.

Wiz chirped weakly from his perch on Kaelen's shoulder, his systems barely functioning in the oppressive heat.

"I know, I know," Kaelen muttered. "We need to find shelter."

The terrain ahead sloped downward, leading toward a stretch of jagged rock formations and half-buried tunnels—old war shelters from a battle long forgotten. The perfect place to disappear.

Kaelen adjusted Wiz's weight, gritting his teeth through the pain in his leg. He had no way of knowing if the enforcers were still tracking him, but he had to assume they were.

He staggered forward, moving as fast as his injury allowed.

Then—movement.

Kaelen froze, pressing himself against a rusted metal wall.

A figure in the distance.

At first, he thought it was an enforcer. But no—the shape was wrong. The stance was too deliberate. Whoever they were, they weren't searching in a panic like Aldric's men.

They were watching.

A wave of unease rolled through Kaelen's chest.

The figure was too far to make out any details, but something about them felt off. Like they weren't just another pursuer, but someone who had been here all along.

Kaelen sucked in a slow breath, edging deeper into the shadows. If they were an enemy, he couldn't afford a fight. Not like this.

Then, suddenly—

The distant wail of an enforcer alarm echoed across the Flats.

Kaelen tensed, expecting the figure to react. To move. To hunt him down.

But instead, they walked away.

Not toward him but toward the enforcers.

Just… gone.

Kaelen's gut twisted. Who was that?

No time to think.

With one last glance toward where the stranger had disappeared, Kaelen forced himself onward, slipping into the tunnels ahead.

Somewhere in the distance, the mysterious figure watched.

And for now, she let him go.

Kaelen didn't stop until the tunnel swallowed him whole. The air inside was stale, thick with the scent of rust and damp soil. Darkness wrapped around him, a stark contrast to the sun-scorched Iron Flats above.

His legs trembled, exhaustion setting in, but he forced himself to keep moving. He couldn't afford to collapse now.

A flicker of movement ahead made him freeze.

Kaelen's fingers curled around the closest piece of scrap metal he could grab—a twisted length of steel, rusted but solid. He held his breath, his pulse hammering in his ears.

Then—

"Kaelen."

Relief and irritation crashed through him at once.

Dorian.

Kaelen let out a breath, dropping his makeshift weapon. His friend stood near the entrance of a larger chamber, barely visible in the dim light.

"You made it," Kaelen muttered. "Guess you didn't die after all."

Dorian's stance didn't ease. "Glad to see you're concerned."

Kaelen shoved past him, moving to sit against a cold rock formation. The pain in his leg had become unbearable, but he refused to acknowledge it. "You left me no choice. You didn't give me a second. You just threw yourself into the fight."

Dorian didn't immediately respond. Instead, he crouched down, pulling a cloth from his belt. "Let me see your leg."

"I can handle it."

"You're bleeding everywhere."

Kaelen scowled but didn't fight when Dorian reached for his injured leg. As his friend began wrapping the wound, his touch careful but firm, Kaelen tried to focus on something—anything—other than the sharp sting of torn flesh.

"How did you escape?" he asked, his voice low.

Dorian hesitated. "I had help."

Kaelen's eyes narrowed. "Help?"

Dorian tightened the bandage slightly, making Kaelen hiss. "An old friend of mine, her name is Riven. I don't think you've met her before."

That uneasy feeling in Kaelen's gut returned. He thought back to the figure on the horizon. The one who had simply… left.

Had that been the same person?

He rubbed a hand down his face. "This keeps getting worse."

"Yeah, no kidding." Dorian sat back on his heels, watching Kaelen closely. "So, are you finally going to tell me what is so important about that relic?"

Kaelen tensed. His fingers instinctively moved toward his satchel, where the relic was carefully hidden.

Dorian's voice dropped, flat and steady. "You don't even trust me with this?"

Kaelen hesitated. It wasn't that he didn't trust Dorian. It was that he barely knew what he was holding.

Before he could answer, something strange happened.

A faint pulse of light flickered from his bag.

Kaelen and Dorian both froze.

The glow was subtle, brief—but Kaelen knew Dorian had seen it.

The silence between them stretched.

"…What was that?" Dorian asked.

Kaelen hesitated, then finally spoke.

"I think it's responding to you."

Dorian said nothing. Just watched Kaelen like the rules had changed.

For now.

Kaelen skidded to a halt, dirt and shattered metal crunching beneath his boots. Ahead, the ground dropped into a sheer cliffside, jagged rock formations vanishing into the smog below. The edge was unstable—crumbling beneath the weight of time and erosion—but there was nowhere else to run.

Dorian was beside him, his gauntleted fists clenched as he scanned their surroundings. "Damn it," he muttered. "They herded us here on purpose."

Kaelen's pulse pounded. Aldric's forces fanned out behind them, cutting off every possible escape route. The enforcers' plated armor gleamed beneath the dim glow of their tracking drones, their mechanical hounds pacing at the front line, metal teeth bared. At the center of it all stood Aldric, still as stone. Watching. Waiting. Certain they had nowhere left to run.

"You're out of options, Virel. And it looks like Dorian is with you now too." Aldric called out. His voice carried over the wind, smooth and confident. "Surrender now, and maybe the council will be merciful to you two."

Kaelen's grip tightened on his satchel, feeling the faint pulse of the Celestine Convergence through the fabric. He couldn't let it fall into Aldric's hands. "Not happening," he shot back.

Aldric sighed, shaking his head. "I was hoping you'd say that." He raised his hand. "Take them."

The enforcers advanced. The hounds lunged.

Then—

A sharp crack split the air, followed by the high-pitched whine of malfunctioning machinery. One of the tracking mechs sparked violently, its limbs twitching before collapsing in a heap of broken metal. The sudden disruption sent the enforcers into momentary disarray.

"What was that?!" one of the soldiers barked.

Aldric spun, scanning the ruins. "Find the shooter!"

Kaelen barely had time to process what had happened before Dorian grabbed his arm. "Move!"

They bolted.

As they ran, Kaelen risked a glance over his shoulder. Just for a second, he caught a glimpse of movement—a figure cloaked in shadow, perched on the wreckage above. The dim light of the collapsing mech reflected off the weapon in their hands—a phase-rifle, the weapon shimmered—metal and magic fused. Not a regular soldier's tool. A Quantum Stryker's tool.

Then she was gone.

Kaelen didn't stop running, but his mind raced. Who was she? And why had she helped them?

The question lingered as they vanished into the darkness, Aldric's enraged shouts echoing behind them. The hunt was far from over.

<hr>

Kaelen and Dorian ran, their boots pounding against the fractured terrain, the wind howling in their ears. The Iron Flats stretched endlessly before them, but their path was growing narrower, bordered by jagged ridges and unstable ground. Behind them, the shouts of enforcers and the metallic snarls of hunting mechs echoed, closing in.

Then the ground gave way beneath them.

A sudden, deafening crack split through the air as the weakened ground crumbled. Kaelen barely had time to gasp before the world dropped out from under him. Dust and debris spiraled in every direction as he plunged into darkness, his body tumbling through open air. He reached desperately for something—anything—to slow his fall, but his fingers found only emptiness. The wind tore at his clothes, the weight of his satchel pulling him downward.

The impact came hard. Kaelen hit the ground with a bone-jarring thud, rolling onto his side as loose stone and dust rained down from above. He coughed, forcing air back into his lungs, the taste of iron thick on his tongue. Somewhere nearby, he heard Dorian groan.

"Dorian?" Kaelen rasped, pushing himself up. His limbs ached, but nothing felt broken. He turned his head, his vision adjusting to the dim, eerie glow that pulsed faintly in the cavern around them.

"I'm—" Dorian's voice came from a few feet away, gruff but alive. "Still in one piece."

Kaelen exhaled in relief, but his reprieve was short-lived. As his senses sharpened, the weight of the cavern pressed against him—the air here was different. Charged. Heavy. It thrummed with an unnatural energy, sending an uneasy shiver down his spine.

Wiz, who had managed to remain latched onto Kaelen's vest during the fall, chirped in alarm. The small automaton's mechanical eyes flickered as he scanned the surroundings. A moment later, Wiz let out a sharp beep—anomalous signals detected.

Kaelen glanced at his satchel. The Celestine Convergence was pulsing, almost in response to the cavern itself. "It's reacting to something," he muttered.

Dorian dusted himself off, wincing as he stretched his arm. "I don't like this," he admitted, his voice lower now. "Where are we?"

Kaelen took a slow step forward, the ground beneath him uneven and damp. The walls of the cavern stretched high, vanishing into shadow, ancient runes barely visible along the jagged rock. Some glowed faintly, pulsing in an erratic rhythm—as if they were alive.

A drop of water echoed somewhere in the distance, but the sound felt distorted, stretched too long before fading. The entire cavern felt like it was breathing.

"We might have made our situation worse," Kaelen murmured.

Dorian's hand went instinctively to his weapon. "Yeah," he said grimly, scanning the darkness. "I got the same feeling."

They had escaped Aldric's forces, but in doing so, they had stumbled into something far older. And Kaelen had the sinking realization that whatever had been waiting down here—it had been waiting for them.

Aldric knelt beside the jagged fissure where Kaelen and Dorian had fallen. Aldric scanned the chasm, dust swirling around his boots. The drop didn't bother him. What mattered was what survived it. The dust was still settling, filling the air with the scent of scorched metal and broken ground. His enforcers stood at attention behind him, their hunting mechs prowling restlessly along the cliff's edge, scanning the chasm below.

He reached down, fingers brushing against something half-buried in the dirt. A torn scrap of fabric—Kaelen's. A slow smirk curled at the edges of his lips as he lifted it, turning it over in his palm.

"They're not dead. And if they are, it makes no difference," Aldric muttered. "Bring them back—whether they're breathing or not."

He straightened, rolling the cloth between his fingers before tucking it into his belt. The wind howled over the Flats, kicking up dust, but Aldric remained unmoving, his gaze fixed on the chasm. He had underestimated Virel's resilience, but it didn't matter. The boy was only delaying the inevitable.

"My lord," one of the enforcers hesitated before speaking, his helmet tilting toward the wreckage of a downed tracking mech. Sparks flickered from its exposed wiring, the remains of a clean, precise shot disabling its core. "This wasn't an accident."

Aldric turned sharply, his eyes narrowing at the ruined machine. He approached it, kneeling to inspect the damage. The shot had been calculated, expertly placed to disable but not destroy. Whoever had done this was skilled—too skilled to be a random mercenary.

Someone was interfering.

Aldric rose slowly, but something in him had recalibrated. This wasn't improvisation. This was precision. Intent. First, Kaelen's impossible escapes. Now, an unknown player is disrupting the hunt. This wasn't just about the mechcrafter anymore. Something larger was at play.

He stood, dusting off his gauntlets before addressing his enforcers. "We move at dawn," he ordered. "Sweep every passage, every tunnel leading beneath these ruins." His voice dropped, the weight of command pressing down on every syllable. "I want him found. I don't care what's waiting down there."

The enforcers saluted, their hunting mechs recalibrating for the next pursuit. Aldric cast one final glance toward the dark chasm below.

Kaelen could run. He could hide.

But there was nowhere in Elyndor he wouldn't be hunted.

The cavern stretched endlessly before them, the damp air thick with something unseen—a presence. Kaelen felt it in the way the ground pulsed beneath his boots, in the faint whisper of energy curling through the stone walls. Wiz's small frame shuddered on his shoulder, its sensors clicking wildly.

Dorian moved ahead, his torch casting long, wavering shadows along the jagged rock. "This place doesn't feel right," he muttered.

Kaelen agreed, though he couldn't bring himself to say it aloud. The deeper they had gone, the more the walls changed—from raw, untouched stone to something shaped, forged. Strange markings, neither Verdant nor Forgeborne, lined the tunnel's edges, their faint glow pulsating in an erratic rhythm, like a dying heartbeat.

Then they saw it.

An archway, carved from obsidian and laced with veins of shimmering metal, stood at the cavern's farthest end. Its frame was etched with runes older than any Kaelen had seen before, their inscriptions twisting unnaturally in the dim light. The air around it shimmered, like heat rising from a forge, though the cavern itself was cold.

The Celestine Convergence flared to life.

Kaelen gasped as his satchel vibrated against his side. He yanked it open, and the relic pulsed—its glow matching the rhythm of the runes on the archway. Energy crackled between them, an unseen current linking the two, like the final pieces of an ancient puzzle falling into place.

Dorian took a slow step forward, his fingers tightening around the hilt of his hammer. "What is this?"

Kaelen swallowed, his mind racing. "A gate," he whispered. "A portal to somewhere."

Dorian glanced at him, then at the Celestine Convergence. "And it's waiting for us."

Kaelen hesitated. The relic was reacting—but to him, or to Dorian? The Equinox prophecy had always been vague about its chosen ones, its wording shifting between singular and plural. Was it him? Was it them both?

Dorian didn't wait for an answer. He stepped forward, reaching toward the runes. The moment his fingertips brushed the obsidian, the portal roared to life.

Light surged through the cavern, illuminating the space in waves of blue and gold. The air vibrated with raw energy as the archway's runes ignited, spinning into patterns too complex for Kaelen to follow. The glow of the Celestine Convergence intensified, casting shifting shadows across the walls.

Then, deep within the portal, something stirred.

Kaelen's breath hitched. Whatever lay beyond this gate, it had been waiting.

And now, it had noticed them.

The portal pulsed with raw energy, its swirling light stretching out before them, beckoning—demanding. The air vibrated, thick with power that neither Kaelen nor Dorian could fully comprehend. The Celestine Convergence still thrummed in

Kaelen's grip, its glow syncing with the shifting patterns within the gate, as if guiding them toward something inevitable.

Dorian tightened his grip on his hammer. "We either go through," he said, voice steady despite the storm raging around them, "or we wait for Aldric to find us."

Kaelen hesitated for only a second longer. The weight of everything—the chase, the relic, the prophecy—pressed against his chest. But the moment his gaze met Dorian's, he knew there was no turning back.

Together, they stepped forward.

The moment they crossed the threshold, the world shifted. The cavern, the portal's towering arch, the very air around them—everything bent and twisted as if being unraveled and rewoven at the same time. Kaelen felt himself pulled forward, his body weightless yet impossibly heavy, as if gravity itself had forgotten what to do with him. Sound warped into a deep, echoing hum, and for a fleeting second, he swore he heard whispers—not words, not voices, but something older, something watching.

Then, with a rush of blinding light, they were gone.

The cavern fell silent once more, save for the faint crackling of residual energy still coursing through the stone. From the shadows above, a lone figure remained, watching.

Riven Locke lowered the scope of her rifle, the glow of the portal reflecting in her sharp eyes. A smirk tugged at the corner of her lips, but there was no amusement there—only calculation.

"Good luck, boys," she murmured, voice barely above the whisper of the fading magic. "You'll need it."

Then, as silently as she had arrived, Riven disappeared into the darkness, leaving no trace she had ever been there at all.

Act II: The Prophecy Ignites

Chapter 5: The Broken Path

The transition was not gentle. The moment Kaelen and Dorian stepped through the portal, the world twisted and warped, the space around them folding in on itself. Then, just as suddenly as it had begun, the chaos snapped back into place.

They stumbled forward onto solid ground. The air was thick with an ancient stillness, the kind that clung to forgotten places. Obsidian Reach stretched before them, its sprawling ruins rising from the darkness like jagged bones of a long-dead titan. Towers of blackened metal and stone loomed overhead, some half-collapsed, others still standing defiantly against time. Bridges stretched between the structures, their edges crumbling, hanging precariously over a seemingly endless abyss below. Mist curled through the streets, obscuring whatever lay beyond the immediate path.

Dorian adjusted his stance, shifting the weight of his hammer across his back. "Feels like we're being watched," he muttered, eyes tracking the edges of the dark.

Unease pricked at Kaelen's skin as he stepped forward. The city felt… wrong. Not lifeless, but watching. The moment his boots touched the ancient stone, a faint pulse rippled beneath his feet. The sensation crawled up his spine, like a machine awakening after centuries of slumber.

Wiz, perched on his shoulder, let out a sharp mechanical chirp. The automaton's optics flickered as it scanned the environment, its tail twitching with unease.

Then Kaelen noticed it.

The runes.

Faint glyphs glowed along the pathways, shimmering in response to their presence. Not all of them—only those beneath Dorian's steps. Kaelen frowned, stepping to the side, testing the reaction. Nothing. The runes only flared brighter as Dorian moved.

Dorian saw it too. "What does that mean?"

Kaelen's frown deepened as a cold knot tightened in his gut. "It means this place isn't responding to me."

Dorian turned to face him, confusion laced in his expression. "But the prophecy—"

"Yeah, I know," Kaelen snapped, then sighed, rubbing a hand over his face. "I don't know. Maybe we're both supposed to be here, but… something is different."

The relic inside his satchel remained cold and dormant, no longer humming with the same intensity it had before. The city wasn't rejecting him, but it wasn't welcoming him either.

Dorian, however, the city seemed to be expecting him.

Kaelen shook off the thought. This wasn't the time for self-doubt. They needed to move.

The wind howled through the towering ruins, carrying whispers that weren't entirely from the breeze. Shadows flickered in the mist, shifting in the periphery of Kaelen's vision, but when he turned, there was nothing there.

Dorian rolled his shoulders, his voice low. "Feels like we woke something up."

Kaelen's grip tightened on his satchel. "Yeah." His gaze flicked toward the looming structures ahead, the broken roads leading deeper into the heart of the city. "And I don't think it's happy to see us."

The scent of soil and wildflowers filled the air as Elara stood before her assembled squad in Verdant's outer barracks. Sunlight filtered through the canopy, casting dappled light over the gathered warriors. Each of them had sworn their loyalty to Verdant, to protect its lands and people, yet the mission before them was unlike any they had faced. Greenhold was in danger, and the Council refused to act. So Elara would.

She straightened her shoulders, looking over the faces of those who would accompany her. "We leave at dawn," she announced. "Greenhold needs us, and we can't afford hesitation."

Among the group, Lysandra Merrow, her mentor and one of Verdant's most formidable Thornblades, regarded her with measured approval. The older warrior, clad in leather reinforced with natural woven fibers, had seen more battles than most. Her twin swords rested at her hips, ready as always. "You've taken on a heavy burden, Elara," Lysandra said, her voice calm but firm. "Leadership is not about the fight—it's about making sure everyone lives to see another day."

Elara met her gaze and nodded. "I understand."

To Lysandra's side stood Sylva, a Wildshot archer whose sharp silver eyes held an amused glint. She rolled her shoulders, adjusting the sleek bow slung across her back. "I assume we're not expecting a warm welcome," she quipped. "Just tell me where to aim."

Elara smirked. "I'll count on you for that."

But not all of those she had hoped to bring stood among them. Her brother, Tarian, was absent, tied to pressing Council affairs. He had fought to stand beside her, but duty demanded otherwise. And then there was Arin Merrow, Lysandra's daughter and Elara's closest friend since childhood. A fellow Grovecaller, with her vibrant green eyes and healer's grace, had been forced to remain behind.

Arin placed a gentle hand on Elara's arm. "You'll do fine," she said quietly. "You already know what needs to be done."

A few steps away, Sylva adjusted her bowstring, eyes scanning the treeline as she tested the weight of an arrow in her hand.

Elara forced a small smile, though the absence of both Tarian and Arin weighed on her. This was the first time she would be truly on her own, without their familiar support. But this wasn't about her—it was about the people waiting in Greenhold, the ones who had no voice in the Council's decisions.

She turned back to her squad, determination solidifying in her chest. "We leave at first light. And no one gets left behind."

The warriors gave sharp nods, their faces set with resolve. Whatever awaited them in Greenhold, they would face it together.

Kaelen's fingertips grazed the ancient archway, the carved runes beneath his touch pulsing with an eerie rhythm. The moment stretched long, the energy humming through the stone setting his nerves on edge. There was something here, something waiting.

A shift in the air behind him sent a prickle of unease down his spine.

"You have a habit of meddling with things you don't understand."

Kaelen spun around, heart hammering. A figure emerged from the shadows of the ruined city, moving with the kind of confidence that spoke of deep familiarity with this place. His cloak, worn and dusted with time, swayed with each step. Silver-streaked hair framed sharp, calculating eyes that studied Kaelen and Dorian in turn.

Recognition struck Kaelen like a thunderclap.

"The scrapyard," he breathed. "You were there." His mind whirled, fitting the pieces together. "And in the tunnels… You helped me escape Forgehelm."

Rindun inclined his head, just enough to acknowledge the truth. "So you do remember." His gaze flicked to the archway, then back to them. "I suppose I shouldn't be surprised you made it this far. But Obsidian Reach does not open its doors so easily."

Dorian took a step forward, his hammer shifting slightly in his grip. "Who are you?"

Rindun paused, weighing the moment. "A watcher. A guide. Perhaps a warning, depending on your choices."

Kaelen frowned. "You knew about this place. You knew we would come here."

Rindun didn't confirm or deny it. Instead, he turned his attention fully to the archway. "Obsidian Reach only reveals its truths to those who can survive its trials." His voice was calm, but there was an unmistakable weight to his words. "And two must always come."

Kaelen exchanged a glance with Dorian. "Why?"

Rindun studied them for a long moment before answering. "Because this city does not choose one. It chooses unity." He let his gaze settle on Dorian, watching him intensely. "Or at least… that is how it was meant to be."

Kaelen's stomach twisted. It wasn't choosing him.

Dorian scowled, shifting under Rindun's scrutiny. "I never asked for this."

"That doesn't matter," Rindun said simply. "The city does not ask. It only decides."

The words hung there. Kaelen said nothing, the weight of it crawling up his spine. He had come here searching for purpose—for answers. But the city wasn't looking at him. It was looking past him. Choosing Dorian instead.

The runes along the archway pulsed again, brighter this time. The city was awake. Watching. Waiting.

Rindun's tone cooled, the edge of finality unmistakable. "If you truly intend to walk this path, be warned." His voice, still yet unwavering, carried an edge of finality. "Obsidian Reach does not tolerate the unworthy."

The banners of Verdant fluttered in the early morning breeze as Elara and her convoy rode through Eldoravell's grand eastern gate. The towering trees cast shifting shadows across the worn stone path ahead, their gnarled roots winding through the city's foundation like the veins of something ancient and unyielding. The weight of what lay ahead pressed against her chest, but she kept her posture firm, her gaze steady.

At her side, Tarian rode in silence, his back straight, his knuckles pale on the reins. The tension between them had only grown since the Council meeting. Though he hadn't openly opposed her, his warnings had been clear.

"You're making enemies, Elara," he said finally, breaking the silence. His green eyes, so like their mother's, flickered with concern. "Lord Corvyn won't let this go unanswered."

Elara kept her gaze forward. "If Corvyn wants to stop me, he'll have to do more than whisper threats from the shadows."

Tarian shook his head. "This isn't a game. There are whispers of extremists—people who believe the prophecy is a lie meant to weaken Verdant. If they think you're endangering our people with this pursuit, they won't hesitate."

Elara's fingers tightened on her reins. She had seen the reports, the coded messages warning of growing unrest. Someone in Verdant's leadership was quietly working against her, but she couldn't yet prove who.

Behind them, the convoy rode in disciplined formation. Lysandra Merrow led a vanguard of Thornblades, their hands resting near their hilts, their eyes sharp. Sylva, ever the contrast to the rigid discipline around her, twirled an arrow between her fingers as she rode, her silver braid catching the light. She caught Elara's glance and smirked. "Starting to feel real now, isn't it?"

Elara allowed herself the faintest smile. "It's been real since the moment the Council ignored Greenhold's call for help."

Tarian remained stiff beside her. "I should be riding with you," he muttered. "Not—" He broke off, shaking his head. "Not stuck dealing with the Council's politics."

Elara looked at him, then, some of her frustration softened. "Verdant needs you here. If someone is working against me, I need you to root them out."

His lips pressed into a thin line, but after a moment, he nodded. "Just… be careful. You're heading straight into danger."

Elara turned her gaze forward again, her resolve solidifying. "I know."

As the convoy disappeared into the emerald expanse of Verdant's outer reaches, the wind carried with it an unease she couldn't shake. The road to Greenhold had only just begun, and already, the shadows of opposition were closing in.

And if Tarian was right, this would not be a simple journey. It would be a war before the first battle was even fought.

The chamber pulsed with an oppressive energy, thick and unrelenting. At its center stood the Vein of Judgment—a jagged column of obsidian, its surface webbed with pulsing veins of light. The runes carved into its stone flickered weakly, like dying embers, their meaning lost to time. The air itself vibrated with an unseen force, pressing down on Kaelen and Dorian like a silent challenge.

Rindun Veladra stood at the chamber's edge, watching them with expectation. He was still, unbothered by the weight in the air—as if he already knew how this would end.

Kaelen stepped forward first. Because, of course, he did.

He had spent his entire life chasing Orlan's shadow, trying to prove he was more than the boy everyone assumed he would be. This was his chance. If he could pass this trial, if he could prove himself here, then the city would have to acknowledge him.

The doubt clawed at him—but he moved anyway. His hand met the Vein.

The world shattered.

The chamber was gone. Kaelen stood in the heart of Forgehelm, but it was wrong—the forges burned too hot, and the sky churned with a sickly red glow. His limbs felt heavy, as though weighed down by something unseen. Then he saw it—Orlan, bound and on his knees, the execution platform looming above.

Kaelen's breath caught. This moment had already happened. He had stood in the crowd, watching, helpless, as Orlan's sentence was carried out.

But this time, it wasn't Magnus Rooke who stood over him.

It was Kaelen.

His fingers curled around the handle of a hammer, slick with sweat and ash. He tried to move, to stop himself, but his body refused to obey. Orlan lifted his head, his expression calm but broken.

"Will you make the same choice?"

Kaelen's chest tightened. He wanted to drop the hammer, to back away, to reject this nightmare—

The world fractured.

Through the cracks, he saw two figures standing beneath a burning sky. One was Dorian. The other—a woman he didn't recognize. She stood with her head held high, her silhouette framed by the inferno.

Kaelen barely had time to process the vision before he was thrown backward. He hit the ground hard, and the breath ripped from his lungs. His heart pounded as he looked up at the Vein of Judgment. It no longer reacted to him.

And then, Dorian stepped forward.

Unlike Kaelen, he hesitated. He didn't want to do this. The city wanted him, but he never asked for it. But as his fingers hovered over the Vein, something in him urged him forward. His hand trembled as he pressed it against the stone.

The reaction was immediate.

The runes flared violently, the chamber vibrating with power, as if the city had been waiting for him all along.

Dorian's vision swallowed him whole. He was back in Forgehelm, but it was a ruin. The walls had collapsed, the streets burned, and in the heart of the devastation, the Titans walked again. A throne of flame stood at the city's center—empty.

A realization settled deep in his gut. If he did not take that throne, the world would burn.

Then he saw Kaelen—at the throne's foot. Bloodied. Alone. Too late.

Dorian ripped his hand away, as if burned. His face twisted in fury. "It's choosing me—but I didn't ask for this."

Kaelen, breathless, pushed himself up, bitterness curling in his chest. "Maybe it's because you don't care that it wants you."

The words hung between them, raw and ugly.

Rindun's tone carried a flicker of amusement—but something older stirred beneath it. "This city does not choose lightly," he said, his voice softer now, almost reverent. "Two must walk this path—but only one will hold the weight of fire. Together, you might succeed where the last Chosen failed." His gaze flickered, distant. "Alone… well, you've already seen how that ends."

Kaelen's fists clenched. "What else aren't you telling me about Orlan?"

Rindun's gaze met his. He didn't say much but just murmured, "I knew his heart."

Before Kaelen could demand more, the Vein of Judgment trembled, and the air cracked with distant thunder.

Something was changing.

And whatever it was, they were now part of it.

The mist was thicker than it had any right to be.

It pressed low against the forest floor, soft as breath, curling around hooves and ankles as Elara's convoy wound its way through the eastern trail of the Mistwood. The trees loomed high overhead, gnarled and knotted, their canopies blotting out most of the light. Fog clung to every surface, muffling hoofbeats and conversation alike.

Elara rode near the front, staff resting across her lap, fingers brushing the polished wood as if expecting it to whisper some warning. It didn't. But the relic nestled in her bag pulsed again. A slow, rhythmic throb against her skin.

Her eyes drifted toward the forest's edge. No birds. No insect drone. Just the hush of breath and hoof and bristling silence.

Beside her, Lysandra shifted in the saddle. "It's too quiet."

Elara nodded. "Even the forest is holding its breath."

A scout emerged from the fog, his horse lathered and wide-eyed. "Found a wreck just ahead. Looks like a merchant caravan. No bodies, but signs of a struggle. Cargo's half-burnt."

Lysandra's hand was already on her sword. "This reeks of bait."

Elara glanced at the soldiers flanking them—ten riders, two grovecallers, and a few lightly armored scouts. Most looked alert. One—Talin, barely older than seventeen—was fidgeting with his bowstring.

"We can't ignore it," Elara said. "If someone survived—Verdant or not—we don't leave them."

Lysandra didn't argue further. She gestured to her second. "Fan out. Keep it tight. If you see movement, don't chase."

The column slowed. Fog thickened. Elara dismounted, boots sinking slightly into moss. The air here felt colder, as if something was drawing the warmth out of it.

The wreck was upturned like a broken beast. One wheel shattered, the other torn off. Burn marks scarred the canvas and frame, but not from wildfire—these were patterned, intentional.

The Verdant crest had been burned off in a circular motion, like an erasure.

Her relic pulsed again. Harder. Urgent.

Elara frowned and turned. "Lysandra—"

That's when the first arrow hit.

It punched through Talin's neck. He fell without a sound. Then a second—another scout. Then five more.

The forest erupted.

Verdant attackers poured from the treeline—painted faces, vine-stitched cloaks, masks carved from ashwood. They moved like phantoms through the fog, coordinated, silent. For the first three seconds, they didn't speak.

Then came the cries.

Not war shouts. Chants.

"Restore the balance!"

"By root and ash!"

Lysandra bellowed, "Form up!"

Elara raised her staff. The runes flared to life. She slammed it into the ground, summoning a thicket of vines in a sweeping arc. A wall coiled up to protect the wounded behind her. Roots twisted out and lashed at the enemy, but they were met by opposing grovecallers—Verdant magic wielded by traitors.

Elara cast again. Vines burst upward beneath three enemies, tangling legs and arms. One broke free, only to be impaled by a wooden spike hurled from a nearby rider.

Then the ground shook.

A flare of heat. A blast of spores. Something exploded just behind the caravan, sending three guards flying. Elara felt the impact in her ribs.

"Pull back to the wreck!" Lysandra shouted.

She didn't make it far.

An arrow slammed into her lower side. She stumbled, coughing, blade dropping from her hand. A grovecaller tried to cover her with a wall of bramble, but it burned away in a flash of red light.

Elara screamed her name and ran.

Vines whipped out to clear her path—not enough. She took a glancing hit to the shoulder, but kept going. She reached Lysandra, grabbed under her arms, and dragged her toward the overturned cart.

The staff shook in her hand as she cast a shield of bark to cover their retreat. It held long enough for them to crawl under the wreckage.

Inside: darkness, blood, splintered wood. A tight crawl space, rank with the smell of burned cloth and old rot. Elara laid Lysandra down and pressed her hands to the wound. Magic surged through her palms.

Light gathered. Slow. Too slow.

"I'm not leaving you," Elara said, breath shaking.

"Wasn't going to ask," Lysandra muttered.

Outside: silence.

Then footsteps.

Slow. Methodical. One set, then another.

"They're not looting," Lysandra whispered. "They're hunting."

Elara's spell pulsed. The bleeding slowed, but not enough. She reached for more power, but the forest around her felt distant now. Like it was watching.

A shadow passed over the wreck. A murmur. A prayer in old Verdant.

They know who she is.

The figure paused. Then moved on.

Time passed—she wasn't sure how long. The silence stretched, heavy and unbroken.

The fog was thicker than before. The air was still.

Most of her squad were killed or missing.

Bodies were everywhere. Talin. The other grovecaller. A captain from her personal guard slumped against a tree with bark growing from his mouth.

The attack hadn't been an ambush. It had been a message.

Her relic is still pulsing.

She couldn't cry. Not yet.

Then she saw them.

Cloaked figures.

Five. Maybe six. Emerging from the fog like statues waking from sleep. Their robes were clean. Hands gloved. Faces hidden. No weapons drawn. No threat voiced.

But they didn't belong here. Not to Corvyn. Not to the forest.

Elara raised her staff. Vines twitched at her heels, sluggish and thin.

"If you've come to finish it," she said, "do it."

No reply.

The Vein of Judgment was silent now.

The chamber had dimmed. Whatever current had been running through the runes—whatever unseen force had been listening—was gone. Only the stone remained, black and cold, its flickering light now a memory. The walls no longer hummed. The pressure in the air had lifted, but the weight in Kaelen's chest hadn't.

He sat slouched against the far wall, arms on his knees, eyes fixed on the cracked floor. Not speaking. Not looking at Dorian.

Dorian stood across from him, hand still curled into a fist, as if the Vein might flare again if he reached for it. It hadn't. It wouldn't. Whatever choice it made, it had already passed judgment.

Rindun Veladra leaned against a pillar on the edge of the chamber. Watching. Always watching. He hadn't spoken since the visions ended. He hadn't needed to.

Kaelen broke the silence first.

"You saw something too."

It wasn't a question.

Dorian nodded once, slowly.

Kaelen didn't look up. "Was I dead in yours, or just broken?"

Dorian hesitated.

"Does it matter?"

Kaelen's laugh was short. Flat. "Guess not."

The silence threatened to settle again, but Dorian didn't let it.

"I didn't ask for any of this."

"No. You just got it anyway."

Kaelen stood, slow and stiff. He didn't close the distance. Didn't need to. His voice did the work.

"You walk in here, you touch the stone for five seconds, and it lights up like it's been waiting for you. You don't even want it, and it still picks you."

Dorian didn't flinch, but his stance shifted—subtly, reflexively. "You think that makes it easier?"

Kaelen's eyes finally met his. "I think it makes you dangerous."

For a moment, neither moved. They weren't shouting. That would have been easier. There was nothing theatrical about this. Just two people who knew too much about each other, standing in a place that had judged them both.

"You think I wanted to see you like that?" Dorian asked. "On the ground, broken, at the foot of that throne?"

"Then maybe don't sit on it."

Dorian stepped forward. "You don't know what it showed me."

Kaelen didn't flinch. "I know enough."

Rindun shifted. Not a warning. Just movement. Like a man bracing against a wind that hadn't started blowing yet.

"The Vein doesn't offer answers," he said. "It offers exposure."

Both men turned to look at him.

"What you saw was not the truth. It was pressure. The weight you carry, laid bare."

Kaelen spoke without looking away. "And what happens when the weight picks favorites?"

Rindun tilted his head. "It doesn't. It reflects them."

He stepped forward slowly, not imposing, but deliberate.

"The Vein showed you the shape of your fear. And him the cost of his doubt. One feared being nothing. The other feared doing nothing."

Dorian watched him. Warily.

"Then what does that make you?"

Rindun smiled, almost gently. "A man who has seen this dance before."

Kaelen's brow furrowed. "How did Orlan fail?"

Rindun didn't confirm. But he didn't deny it either.

"I knew the burden he tried to carry alone."

He let the words settle. Not heavy, but precise.

"You think he failed because he wasn't strong enough. But that wasn't the failure. The failure was that when the weight began to crush him, no one stood beside him to carry it."

Dorian looked away.

Kaelen didn't. "And now it picks you. The official Chosen."

Rindun's voice was quieter now. "He is. And you are not."

Kaelen stiffened.

Rindun went on, calmly. "The Convergence was designed to find two. One to preserve. One to burn. But you're neither. And both."

Kaelen's fists clenched. "So what am I, then? A mistake?"

"No," Rindun said. "You're what the prophecy never accounted for."

Kaelen stared at him.

"You think that brings me comfort? Being the anomaly in someone else's broken myth?"

"It shouldn't," Rindun said. "It should bring you caution. You are the question the world is now forced to answer."

Kaelen turned back to Dorian. "And what does that make you? The answer?"

Dorian shook his head. "I don't even know the question."

Kaelen looked away, bitterness flickering across his face.

"Then you'll do exactly what they did to Orlan. You'll follow the prophecy. You'll let it use you. And you'll let it erase anyone who doesn't fit."

He turned to go.

"I won't be erased."

Kaelen walked to the chamber's edge, past the Vein, past Rindun, toward the stairwell that led out. He paused only once, not looking back.

"I won't stand in your shadow anymore. And I won't burn in your future."

Then he was gone.

Dorian stayed where he was. Eyes on the stone. Still not glowing. Still silent.

Rindun watched him.

"He doesn't hate you," he said.

Dorian didn't respond.

Rindun stepped beside him.

"But he might. If you stay silent."

Dorian finally looked at him.

"And if I speak, what then?"

Rindun's voice was quiet.

"Then perhaps, this time, the Chosen will not be alone."

Dorian didn't move as the chamber fell silent again.

Rindun remained a moment longer, watching the place where Kaelen had stood. Then he turned his gaze to the Vein, now dark and cold.

Softly, as if to the stone itself:

"It always begins in dust and ash. Never flame. The fire comes later."

"You must bring the Celestine Convergence to Nocturne's Edge, that is where you must complete the ritual before the Equinox."

Then he, too, left the chamber in silence.

The mist swirled tighter.

Then something shifted.

An arrow sliced through the air, followed by three more. Elara barely registered the sound before a wall of stone and root erupted in front of her, shielding the wrecked cart with a thunderous crack. The arrows embedded in the makeshift barrier with a hiss.

The cloaked figures moved fast, coordinated. One vaulted over the stone wall, landing in a crouch between Elara and the attackers. His arms were wrapped in gauntlets etched with faint blue runes, and as he raised his hand, the ground buckled again, twisting upward into jagged spikes that shattered the terrain.

Elara blinked. Elemental magic? But it wasn't natural—it moved too sharply, too precisely. Not Sylvanar. Not exactly. There was tech grafted into the movements—thin copper lines running along his forearms, pulsing in rhythm with each cast.

Another figure flanked him, using a short, compact staff with an emitter tip. A burst of kinetic force disrupted a grovecaller's vines mid-cast, snapping them like brittle twine. The cloaked stranger spun through two assassins, moving with Forgeborne efficiency and Verdant control. Each strike ended quickly.

Elara crouched beside the wreck, shielding Lysandra with her body. Arrows whistled again, but none reached them. The barrier held. The figures—whoever they were—fought with a strange unity, like they'd trained against these tactics for years.

A third one landed beside her. Elara tensed—until she saw the soft glow of green magic pooling at his fingertips.

"I won't hurt you," he said—voice calm, even accented. "Let me see her."

She hesitated, then shifted aside.

The man pressed a hand to Lysandra's wound. He drew out a vial from a belt pouch, poured it over her side—it fizzed where it touched flesh. Then he placed two fingers at Lysandra's temple. Vines bloomed from the ground, but they were laced with something else—threads of silver coiled in the stems. The vines wrapped gently around Lysandra's waist, tightening like a brace.

Elara watched, stunned. "That's not Verdant healing."

He gave a brief nod. "Not entirely."

"Who are you people?"

Footsteps crunched behind them.

The one who'd led the charge approached, lowering his hood.

He was tall, medium build, with features marked by sharp clarity. His skin was olive-toned, his hair dark and cut short, and his eyes a deep, steady brown. The kind of face that didn't invite easy trust—but didn't need to.

His armor was matte black and grey, reinforced with materials Elara didn't recognize. He moved like someone who didn't waste effort.

"My name is Sariel," he said. "You're safe now."

Elara didn't lower her staff. "Says who?"

"Says us." Sariel didn't flinch. "We've been watching for a long time."

Elara scanned the others. The attackers—the extremists—were all down. Some unconscious. Some not. It had taken less than a minute.

The cloaked warriors were already fanning out, checking bodies, securing the perimeter.

Elara narrowed her eyes. "You're not Verdant. And you're not Forgeborne."

"No," Sariel said. "We're called the Forgotten by others. But we call ourselves Equinox."

Elara's grip on her staff tightened.

Sariel didn't approach further. He gestured to the one healing Lysandra.

"She'll live. Thanks to Orren."

Orren—still focused—glanced up briefly, then returned to adjusting the vines. Lysandra stirred faintly beneath his hands.

Elara stared at the tech-laced healing. The barrier. The strange synergy of magic and machinery.

"What do you want from me?"

Sariel's expression didn't change. "Right now? Nothing but for you to rest."

Elara frowned. "And later?"

Sariel stepped back into the mist. "Later, we'll talk about the future."

Moments later, one of Sariel's men came back carrying a woman. Sylva. "We found her unconscious, we managed to heal her but the rest didn't make it."

Around them, the forest remained still. But the balance had shifted.

Not just in Elara's survival.

In what had come to save her.

The sky above Hollowgrove was pale and cloudless, a false calm over a place built on ruin. Stone arches leaned crookedly over moss-covered buildings, remnants of an older civilization reshaped into something livable. Elara moved through it slowly, staff in hand, cloak wrapped tightly against the wind that never seemed to stop whispering.

She stopped at the edge of a shallow rise, where a row of graves marked the outskirts of the settlement. The markers were simple: carved wood, some etched with names, others only symbols. Lysandra's squad. Her people.

Elara knelt. The soil was freshly turned. She placed her hand on the nearest grave.

"I should've seen it coming," she whispered. "I should've done more."

Her relic didn't pulse. It had gone silent since the forest. Or maybe she had.

A breeze stirred the tall grass around her. No words came. She didn't need them. Guilt had its own gravity.

Footsteps approached.

Sariel.

He stopped a respectful distance behind her. Said nothing until she stood.

"What is this place?" she asked.

"A settlement," Sariel said. "Hidden. Old. We call it Hollowgrove."

She glanced back toward the leaning towers, the strange blend of architecture and overgrowth. "You built all this?"

"We salvaged it," he said. "Adapted it. Like everything else."

"And your people—the Equinox?"

Sariel gave a small nod. "The world calls us the Forgotten. But we're not. We remember too much."

Elara's grip tightened around her staff. "You said you were here to protect me. Why?"

Sariel didn't answer immediately. Instead, he gestured toward the relic beneath her cloak. "Because of that," he said quietly. "It's not just reacting to you. It's recognizing you."

Elara frowned. "Recognizing me?"

"The Celestine Convergence is more than a relic. It's a call. A warning. It responds to those who embody its ideals—and it awakens in moments of danger."

She looked down. The relic pulsed faintly now, a soft echo of the surge it gave during the ambush.

"You're saying I'm—"

"The Verdant Chosen," Sariel said. "Yes."

She stepped back. "No. That's not possible. I'm not—"

"You are. The relic doesn't care about titles. Or blood. It awakened because you acted. Because you refused to let them take everything from you."

Elara said nothing. Her eyes lingered on the grave at her feet.

"The prophecy was never meant to be fulfilled by one side," Sariel continued. "You are one half of what the world needs. And the other half is already moving towards Nocturne's Edge."

A beat.

Elara swallowed. "How long do we have?"

Sariel looked up toward the sky, where the pale sun hovered low.

"The sky is starting to turn. The first omen is gathering, not yet here—but close."

He turned to her.

Elara didn't speak. She didn't move. Her eyes stayed on Sariel, narrowed slightly. "And I'm just supposed to believe you? That this relic makes me some prophesied savior?"

Sariel's tone didn't change. "You don't have to believe me. Just watch what the world does next. The relic will keep responding. And the more you fight it, the louder it'll get."

Elara said nothing, but her grip on the staff didn't ease. Sariel gave her a moment, then added, "We'll help you. But the path ahead isn't ours to walk. It's yours."

It began with silence.

Not peace. Not calm.

The kind of silence that waits at the edge of something vast.

In Hollowgrove, Elara felt it first—a pressure in her chest, not from fear but from recognition. The air tasted metallic. Her staff buzzed faintly in her grip.

Above her, the clouds began to turn.

They moved too slowly to be natural. A spiral coiling inward. No wind. No sound. Just shape—divine and deliberate.

And then the sky split open.

A jagged arc of crimson lightning carved a line across the heavens—unnatural, blood-bright, and terrifying in its silence. It didn't flash and vanish. It lingered. Burned. Observed.

Beneath her cloak, Elara's relic exploded with light.

She dropped to one knee, breath caught, fingers clenched around the Verdant half of the Celestine Convergence—a relic that had only pulsed before. Now it surged. Alive. Aware.

Sariel stood beside her, face unreadable.

"It has begun," he said. "The first omen."

Kaelen stepped into the light just beyond the city's edge—a basalt overlook cut into the side of the mountain, where you could see both sky and ash plains. He hadn't gone far. Just far enough to breathe.

The wind died. The stone stilled. And the sky above twisted into a whirl of smoke and storm.

Then it struck.

Lightning—red as fresh blood—spanned the sky from ridge to ridge. It moved sideways, not down. It didn't flash. It declared.

Kaelen froze. He felt no pain, but his skin prickled, his lungs caught mid-breath.

And behind him—closer now—Dorian came running up the path.

"Kaelen—what—"

Then he saw it too.

The sky.

The light.

And the Forgeborne half of the Celestine Convergence—Dorian holding the relic in his hand—erupted with light.

White fire poured from the seams, painting the stone in stark contrast. The hum was so loud it felt like pressure in the skull.

Kaelen staggered back.

"It's reacting."

Dorian didn't answer. He was staring at the relic. Then in the sky. Then at Kaelen.

"No," he said. "It's not reacting to you. It's reacting to your counterpart."

Elara forced herself to her feet. The clouds still churned overhead—massive and symmetrical. No storm moved like that. No storm waited to be seen.

Her relic pulsed again, rhythmic and deep, like a war drum in her ribs. She looked at Sariel.

"You said I was the Chosen. Verdant half."

He nodded.

"And the other?"

"With him. The Forgeborne. It's been passed to the right hands."

One stood among iron and stone.
One stood beneath roots and mist.
One stood between.

And across every sky they could see—the same lightning.

There were only two halves of the Celestine Convergence.

But now, the bridge had awoken.

And time—true time—was running out.

Forty days.

The Equinox had begun.

Chapter 6: The Convergence

The wind in Obsidian Reach had a way of carrying silence like it meant something.

Kaelen stood on the crumbling edge of the platform, gazing out over the valley. The horizon stretched before him, painted in muted shades of grey. The sky was clearing now—if crimson lightning could ever be called clarity. The storm had passed, but something heavier remained in the air. Not static. Expectation.

Behind him, Dorian approached with cautious steps.

"Are you planning on staying here until the next omen hits?"

Kaelen didn't turn. "Depends. That one was just clouds and lightning. Might be fire next time."

Dorian stopped a few paces behind him, arms crossed. "I spoke with Rindun. He said we don't have time to wait for the next sign."

Kaelen snorted. "Did he say where to go? Or did he just spout more riddles and disappear into a dramatic pause?"

Dorian hesitated. "He gave me something. Told me to go to Nocturne's Edge before the Equinox."

Kaelen finally looked back. "Yeah? Don't we need to find the Verdant chosen one first?"

"There's a Verdant settlement not far from here. Small. Quiet. Neutral ground. If we head there, we might get information. Maybe even intercept whoever's holding the other half of the Convergence."

Kaelen gave a tired nod. "Safe bet."

"It is," Dorian said evenly. "And we need safe bets."

Kaelen stepped past him, moving toward the stone stairway that led down the ridge. "Except safe bets are the ones the prophecy expects. And if the last one failed, maybe the ones it expects aren't enough."

Dorian frowned. "What are you saying?"

Kaelen stopped halfway down the stairs, resting his hand on the cold stone rail. "Rindun said something else. Not directly, but he meant it."

Dorian waited.

Kaelen turned back. "He said, 'Where ash never settled.'"

Dorian raised an eyebrow. "That could mean anything."

"No. It means Cinderhollow."

Dorian folded his arms. "That place is a myth."

"It was." Kaelen stepped down to the next landing. "Now I think it's something more. The lightning didn't just split the sky over us—it touched Hollowgrove too. If someone is carrying the other half of the Convergence, they're not hiding in safe villages."

Dorian's gaze narrowed. "You think she's there."

"I think if she's anything like us," Kaelen said, "she'll go where the world tells her not to."

They stood in silence for a beat. Somewhere deep within the Reach, the stone vibrated faintly—residual energy from the relic, or something else.

Dorian spoke first. "So that's it? We chase ghosts and riddles instead of solid leads?"

"No," Kaelen said. "We chase the ones who aren't afraid to answer them."

Dorian gave a short nod. "If this is the path… then we walk it together."

Kaelen gave a thin smile. "That's a start."

The two moved through the fractured corridors of Obsidian Reach, the stone walls echoing every footfall.

Somewhere deeper in the settlement, children's voices rose—not loud, not joyful. Just steady. Rhythmic.

Kaelen slowed. "You hear that?"

Dorian nodded. "Sounds like a song."

They turned a corner and paused—half-hidden behind broken beams, a small group of children sat in a loose circle near a flickering crystal torch, voices weaving in and out like a round:

"One shall rise, the other fall,
And sacrifice will answer all…"

"In shadows deep, the whispers call,
The moment's near, the dawn will fall…"

The last line fell into silence. One of the children looked up at the men briefly—then looked away.

Dorian's voice dropped. "The Forgotten Song."

Kaelen raised an eyebrow. "You think that's what it was?"

"Close enough."

"Didn't sound like a prophecy. Sounded like something meant to be buried."

Dorian didn't answer at first. Then:
  "They say no two people remember it the same way. Even the verses shift depending on who's telling it."

Kaelen muttered, "Maybe that's the problem."

Dorian gave a dry smile. "Or maybe it was never supposed to be understood—just survived."

The wind picked up again, curling around the stone towers of Obsidian Reach like a whisper repeating itself.

The mist hadn't lifted from the edge of Hollowgrove. Morning light struggled through it, casting long streaks across the half-ruined paths that led out of the settlement's eastern ridge.

Elara stood at the overlook, one hand resting on her staff, the other curled around the strap of her pack. She hadn't spoken in some time.

Behind her, Sariel broke the silence.

"If we head west, we can avoid open roads. Keep low. Quiet. It's the safer route."

Elara didn't turn. "Safer for who?"

Sariel stepped beside her. "You're still healing. Lysandra's not out of danger. You have no guard, no transport. And whatever storm just cracked the sky—if that was the first omen, then we don't have time to walk into traps."

Elara's grip on her staff tightened. "Cinderhollow wasn't a trap. It was a memory."

Sariel frowned. "A graveyard."

"That too."

He waited, but she didn't elaborate. Instead, she turned toward the old northern path—barely more than a weathered trail now, lined with thorned underbrush and broken trees.

"Do you know what Cinderhollow was before it became ash?" she asked quietly.

Sariel didn't answer.

"It was where the last of the original order of Wildlancers stood. Before they fractured under the council decree. Before the prophecy broke." She looked at him. "It's where balance failed."

Sariel gave no hint of emotion. Only the truth. "You walk into a place the Wardens of Aeldrin tried to erase."

Elara gave a small, dry breath. "Then maybe that's exactly where truth still lives."

She turned away and walked back toward the infirmary, where Sylva was carefully packing salves into a linen pouch, her movements precise but slow. The girl looked up, eyes red-rimmed but steady.

"You're leaving."

Elara nodded. "I have to."

Sylva stood. "Lysandra's not strong enough to travel."

"I know."

The pause stretched.

"Will you come back?"

Elara knelt, resting a hand on Sylva's shoulder. "I will. When I can. But you both need to stay hidden. If anyone comes looking for me…"

Sylva nodded. "We say we haven't seen you. We don't know where you went."

A small smile touched Elara's lips. "You're getting good at this."

She stood and stepped into the dim room where Lysandra lay propped up against a bundle of cloth, half-awake, pale but alive.

"I heard you arguing," Lysandra rasped. "You're still as stubborn as I remember."

Elara bent close. "And you're still as reckless. Next time, dodge."

Lysandra's eyes fluttered. "Next time, don't let me get shot."

They both smiled—just a little. Then Elara took her hand.

"I'll come back. I swear it."

Lysandra nodded. "Don't die."

Elara left the room without another word.

Outside, Sariel was already waiting. He didn't ask again.

She passed him in silence, staff in hand, cloak pulled tight, boots finding the north path like she'd known it all her life.

This wasn't an escape.
 It was a return.

And somewhere beyond the horizon, the other half of the storm was walking toward her.

The chamber beneath Cindralis was dark, cold, and silent—until Aldric spoke.

"Say it again."

The enforcer bowed low, armored fists pressed to the floor in the old tradition. His voice was steady, but thin. "Two confirmed sightings, Lord Commander. One of Kaelen Virel, the other Dorian Asher. Northwest of the city limits. Both passed through an old copper vein checkpoint two nights ago."

Aldric stood with his back to the room, facing a steel-forged map inset into the far wall. Cindralis blazed at its center. The northwest quadrant glowed faintly now, two marks etched in red.

"And their direction?"

"They were seen heading southwest, into the lower Wildglen region."

Aldric nodded slowly. "So they're not running. They're converging."

He tapped one finger against the map, metal clinking against metal. "Where does that line lead?"

The enforcer hesitated. "Southwest would take them toward the edge of Verdant territory. Possibly—Cinderhollow."

A sharp breath from Aldric. "Cinderhollow doesn't exist."

The enforcer didn't reply.

"Or maybe that's what they're counting on."

He turned. "Prepare four squads. One rides southwest—intercept. The others spread north, west, and south. Fan the net. I want eyes on every pass, every crossing, every ruin."

The enforcer bowed. "And if we find them?"

Aldric's voice was low, final.

"You don't find Kaelen and Dorian. You **remove** them."

He paused. "But if possible… bring them to me alive. I want to see which one breaks first."

As the enforcer rose and turned to leave, Aldric stepped back toward the wall-map. His gloved hand hovered over the southwest path—the old, faded trail that led to a place no map marked anymore.

Cinderhollow.

He traced the line with his fingertip, a faint groove left in the dusted metal.

"Let's see if the prophecy bends to steel."

They reached the edge of Cinderhollow just past midday.

The forest gave way to ruin slowly—trees thinning, brush fading into brittle ash. The wind shifted. Even the birds had gone quiet. No real path marked the boundary, just a slow decay of green into gray.

Kaelen's pace slowed. A faint hum drifted up from beneath his coat. He pulled the relic from its pouch. It wasn't pulsing. Just… resonating. Low and constant, like it knew something was coming but didn't want to startle it.

He glanced at Dorian.

"You're the Chosen One. Remind me why I'm the one holding this thing?"

Dorian didn't miss a beat.

"Because the last time I carried it, it nearly blew a hole through the tower floor."

Kaelen smirked. "Right. Wouldn't want to damage any perfectly good ancient architecture."

Dorian nodded. "Or you know, yourself."

Kaelen tucked the relic back under his cloak. "Fair."

Kaelen stepped into the clearing first, hand resting near his belt but not on his weapon. His eyes swept the terrain like a smith checking for warps in cooling steel.

A single tree stood at the center. Blackened. Twisted. Scarred down one side with a jagged line like it had been struck by lightning and left to remember it. The ground around its roots was bare.

"That it?" Dorian asked quietly.

Kaelen nodded. "Yeah."

Dorian circled wide, scanning the rise and drop of the land. Shallow cover at the treeline. Some old stonework near the eastern slope. No high ground, but at least three angles to retreat if things went wrong.

"If we get flanked, we pull north. That ridge has enough bend to break the line of sight."

Kaelen pointed south. "There's a run-off channel there. If we have to split—"

"We don't split," Dorian said flatly.

Kaelen didn't argue. Just kept moving.

He looked at Dorian.

Kaelen's mouth thinned. "I think it's trying to talk to the other half."

Dorian didn't respond right away. He stood at the edge of the clearing, watching the scarred tree.

"If this is the meeting," he said, "we go in ready. Not righteous."

Kaelen gave a short nod.

They didn't move any closer. Just stood there—two halves of a broken world, waiting for someone they didn't know but already felt.

A shift in the wind.

Kaelen turned sharply toward the far end of the clearing.

Two figures stepped from the forest edge—one tall and cloaked, the other slimmer, shoulders square, staff in hand. The mist coiled around them as if unwilling to touch them. They moved with purpose.

Then the relic flared.

Half of the Celestine Convergence nestled beneath Kaelen's coat ignited with sudden, heatless light. A pulse, deep and unmistakable.

Dorian reacted first.

He stepped forward, placing himself between Kaelen and the advancing figures, one hand near his belt. "That's not nothing."

Kaelen drew the relic into view just enough to glance down at it.

"It's not reacting to them," he said. "It's reacting to something else."

Across the clearing, Elara stopped near the scorched tree. Her own relic—hidden beneath her cloak—began to glow in rhythm. A sharp, tightening awareness crawled up her spine. The sensation wasn't unfamiliar. But this time, it was… amplified.

She locked eyes with the figure in the coat. The one holding the glowing relic.

Her first thought wasn't awe.

It was recognition. "He's the Forgeborne Chosen One."

Sariel's stance shifted behind her.

Kaelen saw it too—just a step, subtle, but enough to signal the weight in the moment.

Dorian's voice stayed low. "We don't know who they are."

Kaelen's relic pulsed again, stronger now—synchronizing with something. Not another device. Another half.

Only two exist. Only two are meant to respond.

Dorian didn't flinch. But something in his grip tightened—enough for Kaelen to notice.

Kaelen looked at the girl—no, the woman—with the staff. The one staring straight at him like she already knew what he was.

"She thinks I'm the Chosen."

He didn't say it aloud.

Dorian didn't speak, but the weight in his stare said enough. He knew what Kaelen had just realized.

Elara held her ground. Her fingers curled tighter around her staff.

Her relic was pulsing in time with his.

It has to be him.

The clearing held its breath.

Three figures. Two relics. One misunderstanding.

Kaelen's voice was quiet. Dry.

"You ever get the feeling we're being misread?"

Dorian didn't answer. He didn't need to.

No one moved.

The relics—one in Kaelen's hand, one pressed to Elara's chest—beat like a shared drum, syncing faster now. Not violent. Not calm. Just imminent.

A choice waited here.

And none of them knew who would make it first.

The pause held like drawn breath.

Dorian stepped forward, his cloak shifting behind him, one palm raised just enough to signal restraint. His voice was level, controlled.

"We don't want a fight. Not unless you make one."

Sariel's hand drifted near the blade at his side.

"Then don't cross the tree."

His tone was quiet, even—but the warning was clear. The burned tree between them had become a border.

"Step closer, and the roots won't ask questions," Elara added, holding her staff ready to cast her grovecaller magic.

Kaelen looked at Elara. "Funny. I thought nature was supposed to heal, not ambush unsuspecting people."

"Your kind burns forests, then asks if the smoke was necessary." She retorted.

Dorian snapped, clearly fed up with the banter. "Enough. We came to talk—not trade graves."

Meanwhile, Sariel looked disgusted at the words they said. "Children of Druvalandrine. Still thinking like soldiers."

Elara stepped beside Sariel, eyes fixed on Kaelen.

She sees the relic in his hand. Sees Dorian hesitate. Sees Kaelen step forward. Of course it's him. How could it not be?

"Is it you?"

Kaelen didn't respond.

"He's not—" Dorian said, too quickly, like he needed her to believe it before he could.

Kaelen raised a hand.

"Does it matter?"

Elara blinked.

Kaelen's voice was calm but flat.

"If you already believe what you want to believe, what's the point in me saying anything?"

That landed harder than it should have. Not just for Elara. Even Sariel's posture stiffened.

The relics were humming again. Not chaotic—but louder. Nearing a pitch that could tip either way.

Elara took one step forward.

Dorian shifted with her. Not aggressively. But ready.

Sariel's fingers flexed once. He hadn't drawn, but he wasn't far.

Kaelen stood still. His coat brushed against the hilt of the tool at his side. He didn't reach for it.

The clearing shrank.

Every breath felt sharper. The sky above hadn't changed since the omen, but the light around them felt filtered—like whatever force had split the sky was now watching to see who blinked first.

"You think you're the Chosen," Elara said quietly. "Then say it."

Kaelen tilted his head.

"I think I'm holding something that wants a fight less than we do. That's enough for now."

Sariel's tone sharpened.

"So you hide behind mystery."

Kaelen looked at him, then Elara.

"No. I hide behind uncertainty. Big difference."

Dorian took a breath.

"We didn't come here to posture. We came to see if this meant something. And it does. Clearly."

"So talk," Elara said. "Tell me why your relic flared the second I arrived."

Dorian looked at Kaelen.

"Go on."

Kaelen met Elara's gaze.

"Because it recognizes you."

It wasn't an accusation. It wasn't reverent.

It was a statement of fact.

Elara's grip on her staff didn't ease. But she didn't take another step.

The relics thrummed together—steady, matched. Not urgent. Not yet.

"This isn't the part where we kill each other," Kaelen said. "That comes later if we screw this up."

Sariel didn't smile. But he didn't draw either.

The tension held.

And for the first time, all three stood not as strangers, but as answers to the same question:

What are you willing to risk when the world is watching?

They hadn't made peace.

They had made space.

They moved at the same time.

Elara's staff dipped forward, more instinct than intention. Kaelen shifted his weight. Dorian stepped into his stance. Sariel's squad started to fan wide, hands near weapons, breaths shortening.

One breath away from ignition.

Then the sky split.

A bolt of crimson lightning dropped from the clouds in a perfect vertical line. It slammed into the scarred tree between them with impossible speed.

No sound.

Just force.

A shockwave burst outward from the point of impact. The ground lurched. Air collapsed inward. Kaelen was thrown backward, boots skidding. Dorian dropped into a half-crouch but still stumbled, catching Kaelen by the elbow before they both hit the dirt. Elara collided with Sariel's shoulder, her staff dragging a mark into the ground as she steadied herself.

The dust settled in seconds. But the silence that followed didn't feel like stillness.

It felt like judgment.

The tree didn't burn.

It changed.

Cracks in the bark glowed from within—red at first, then gold. Veins of color spread slowly, like roots blooming in reverse. Old runes surfaced across the trunk, not carved, but revealed, pulsing with ancient rhythm. The blackened shell began to peel back, fractured, shedding.

And from that ruin, life returned.

One leaf, then another. Branches groaned quietly as they lifted, no longer sagging under the weight of ash. Green pushed out from the bark. Not fast. Not magical. Just certain.

The tree was not healed.

It was becoming.

Dorian trying to get up from the dirt, shaken. "That was aimed. It didn't just land—it chose."

Kaelen stayed on one knee, breathing hard. "It's watching us. The relic... It's not just reacting—it's remembering."

The Forgeborne half of the Convergence was still clutched in one hand, its glow now fading.

Elara's relic had also gone still, the pulse gone silent against her ribs. "I've called Aeldrin my whole life. He never answered—until now."

Behind Elara, one of Sariel's squad fell to a knee and muttered something reverent in the Verdant tongue. Another bowed their head. One looked terrified. The others just stared at the tree like they had seen the edge of something not meant for human eyes.

"It's an omen," someone whispered.

"No," Kaelen said, still catching his breath. "That was a message."

Dorian remained quiet, eyes flicking from the tree to Elara, then to Kaelen.

The relics no longer pulsed.

Whatever force had spoken, it didn't care who was holding what.

Sariel stepped forward, just one pace, then stopped. His eyes stayed on the tree.

No one crossed the clearing now.

The branches kept reaching skyward, leaves catching a light that hadn't been there before.

Kaelen rose slowly and dusted off his coat.

"So," he said, glancing between Elara and Sariel, "are we still doing this?"

No one answered.

Because whatever fight had been building between them—

It had already been interrupted by something far larger.

The light faded, but the silence didn't.

The tree stood tall now, green with new leaves, gold lines still pulsing faintly along its trunk. It was impossible. Sacred. Unanswerable.

Sariel dropped to one knee.

"It's him," he said, voice barely above breath. "Druvalandrine lives."

Elara didn't look at him. She was still watching the tree, face unreadable, shoulders locked. But she didn't speak to correct him either.

Dorian's brow furrowed. His eyes went from the tree to Kaelen, then to the relic in his hand.

"They didn't warn us," he said slowly. "The relics. They didn't react to a threat. They brought us here."

Kaelen didn't respond.

Elara did.

Elara didn't look at him. Her eyes never left the tree. Whatever she felt, it was buried deep—but her stance held.

"You were ready to fight."

Kaelen blinked. "So were you."

Her voice didn't rise. That almost made it worse.

"That's what this power does to people."

Dorian didn't speak. But whatever warmth had been there—wasn't anymore.

"Or maybe," he said, "it's what people do to power."

No one answered that.

The tree continued to sway gently, as if untouched by the words being traded beneath it. The leaves didn't glow. The relics didn't pulse.

Kaelen closed his hand around the Forgeborne half, dull now in the light.

"I didn't ask for it," he said, almost to himself.

Dorian heard it, but didn't comment.

Elara turned back toward the tree. Her grip loosened around her staff. She didn't step forward. She didn't kneel.

She just watched.

The moment had been divine. But the aftermath was entirely human.

None of them agreed on what they'd seen.

And that was how prophecy always started to break.

Kaelen shifted first. He glanced at Dorian, then toward Elara and Sariel's group.

"We're doing this, aren't we?"

Dorian gave a short nod. "Might as well know what kind of mess we're in."

They stepped forward, cautiously, the way you might approach something that had stopped trying to kill you—but hadn't promised it was done.

Elara matched their movement. Not with full confidence. Not with threat. Her posture had changed—not yielding, but measured.

She stopped a few paces short, staff grounded again.

"I'm Princess Elara Thorne. Of Eldoravell."

Dorian offered a slight bow of his head. "Dorian Asher, ex-enforcer of Forgehelm."

Kaelen hesitated a beat longer, then said, "Kaelen Virel, also from Forgehelm."

He didn't offer more.

Sariel stood slowly, brushing dust from his cloak. Whatever reverence he'd felt had passed—his eyes now moved like a man weighing outcomes.

"Keep your eyes sharp," he said to his squad. "The sky may have calmed, but the world hasn't."

The Equinox soldiers nodded and moved quickly. One circled wide, scanning the edges of the trees. Another unslung a strange-looking device from their back—half metal, half vine-wrapped wood—and planted it near the ridge.

"This tree," one muttered to Sariel, "it might become a beacon. Unwanted eyes will see it."

"They already do," Sariel replied. "We're just the first to understand what it means."

He kept his eyes on the three in the clearing.

He was waiting to see what they'd do next.

And so was the world.

The stillness didn't last.

Another pulse struck the air—sharper than the rest. Not like the first awakening. Not like the convergence. This one carried weight behind it. Direction.

The relic in Kaelen's hand flared white-hot. "You feel that? Something's wrong."

Dorian turned instantly. "Wait. Where's the sound?"

They realize the clearing has gone eerily quiet.

"That wasn't from the tree."

Kaelen's grip closed around the relic.

"That one I recognize."

The wind shifted.

Far off, somewhere beyond the northern ridge, a horn blew—low and deep, with the warped echo of something forged, not carved. Then another, closer. Sharper. A signal call, carried on steel and structure.

Elara stiffened. "It's the relic again. But it's not… afraid. It feels angry."

Sariel turned quickly toward his squad.

"Positions. Now."

The Equinox soldiers moved at once. No shouts. No scramble. Just reflexes shaped by routine. One vanished into the forest edge. Two others crouched behind the edge of the ridge, eyes fixed west. The fourth drew a compact crossbow from under his cloak and readied it without a word.

Another horn blast sounded—closer now. Ground-level.

Then a voice cut the clearing clean in half.

"The gods may be watching, but I brought something louder."

They turned.

A man stepped from the trees beyond the far slope, flanked by two armored enforcers. His cloak dragged against the dirt, black and sleeved with trim that shimmered faintly like burned metal. His hair was silver at the roots, cropped close. His voice was smooth and unhurried.

"Look at you. All three," he said. "How convenient."

Kaelen's blood ran cold.

Dorian didn't move.

Elara took one slow step back, staff sliding toward a ready angle.

Aldric smiled without warmth.

"I was told prophecy had a pattern. That it staggered. One at a time. A Verdant. A Forgeborne. A disaster." His eyes passed over each of them. "And here you are. Standing in the same clearing. Right on schedule."

Sariel stepped forward, placing himself half in front of Elara.

"You shouldn't be here."

Aldric didn't even glance at him.

"I'm exactly where I need to be."

Another horn blast sounded behind him. More enforcers emerged—first in pairs, then in disciplined clusters. Three more squads took shape along the perimeter. Some bore heavy shields. Others carried long-range rifles rigged with arcane enhancements.

One of Sariel's scouts dropped down beside him.

"We're surrounded. At least sixteen, maybe more. He brought an entire patrol column."

Sariel tapped his scout's shoulder twice—an old signal. "Hold formation. Watch the flanks."

"Keep the perimeter tight. If they breach, fall back to the north ridge. Don't break formation unless I call it."

Kaelen's fingers flexed around the relic.

Dorian's eyes swept the northern ridge. He was already calculating options.

Elara watched Aldric's line expand, slow and methodical.

They had been brought here by prophecy.

But they had also been followed.

The convergence hadn't just opened the path forward—it had lit a beacon.

And now the wolves had come to feed.

The first shot cracked across the clearing.

A bolt from one of Aldric's riflemen ripped through the air and splintered the stone beside Sariel. The response was instant—his squad unleashed a volley of return fire, bolts and arcane projectiles arcing toward the treeline.

Kaelen ducked low, the Forgeborne relic still gripped tight. Dorian took a step forward, drawing the hammer from his back, eyes locked on the closest incoming squad.

Sariel turned just enough to shout, "Hold the line! Break the flanks before they close the gap!"

Equinox soldiers moved in rhythm—fast, trained, but outnumbered.

Kaelen crouched behind a jut of broken stone. "We can hold them! Just long enough—"

Dorian cut him off. "Or we fight through. Straight line. I take the front, you cover—"

"No!"

Elara's voice snapped like a crack of thunder.

She stepped between them, staff raised, eyes blazing.

"No one dies here today. We run."

Neither moved.

She didn't wait.

Her hand grabbed Kaelen's coat, the other hooking Dorian's arm, yanking both men back with force that surprised even her.

"We don't run!" Kaelen protested.

"You're not dying for a tree." Dorian grabs Kaelen as he ducks to avoid the bullets.

Another blast tore through the clearing. A tree behind them shattered.

Elara commands both. "Move! You want to argue prophecy, do it after we're alive!"

Sariel glanced over his shoulder just long enough to see them retreat.

"North path! Get them out!" he barked. "The rest of you, buy them time!"

His squad broke formation just enough to collapse the center, funneling Aldric's forward push into a bottleneck of stone and tangled roots. Two Equinox fighters stayed behind, blades drawn, intercepting the first enforcers to break through.

Elara charged toward the overgrown trail, half-hidden behind thorned brush and broken ground. She didn't look back.

Dorian stumbled once as a bolt clipped the ground beside him. Kaelen kept pace, ducking low, the relic glowing faintly under his coat.

They vanished into the trees just as another horn sounded—closer this time.

Their first act as a unit was not to stand and fight.

It was to live.

And that was Elara's choice.

The forest swallowed them.

Roots tangled their feet. Thorns grabbed at their cloaks. None of them spoke. There wasn't time. The sounds of battle behind them grew quieter, but not distant enough. Not safe.

Kaelen moved fast, ducking branches, half-guided by instinct and half by whatever force seemed to drag him forward. The relic's glow had dulled, but its weight hadn't. It still throbbed faintly in his coat—like a warning that hadn't expired.

Elara spoke in a ragged voice, barely catching her breath. "Those are your people, why are they hunting you... And me?"

Dorian kept close behind. His hammer was still drawn, even as they ran. No hesitation. No wasted motion. Just movement. Measured and sharp.

"To stop the prophecy, I assume you have someone chasing after you, too?"

Elara led. Not because she knew the way, but because she refused to stop.

"Yes, and I barely made it out alive if it weren't for the Equinox people. Sariel, my guide, saved me and two others from my group; everyone else was killed."

The overgrown path bent sharply and spilled into a narrow ravine, half-hidden beneath an old canopy. She spotted the shadow before the entrance—barely a sliver between boulders—and veered hard toward it.

"In here," she hissed.

The cave opened just enough for them to slip inside, one by one, pressed between stone and darkness. Dorian took the rear, holding his hammer, eyes scanning the tree line until the last moment. Then he ducked through.

Inside, the air was cold and damp. Not deep—just far enough to mask them.

Elara collapsed to one knee. Not from injury. From release.

Kaelen paced once, twice, then leaned against the cave wall. His breath came fast, sharp. He didn't realize his hands were shaking until he saw them in the dim light.

Dorian stayed near the mouth of the cave, listening.

Minutes passed.

When the silence finally settled, it was Kaelen who broke it.

"She thought it was me."

Elara looked up.

Dorian didn't turn. "I thought it wasn't."

She stood slowly. "And I think we just passed a point of no return."

They were quiet again.

"You saw what happened," Elara added. "What the relics did. What the tree became."

Kaelen ran a hand through his hair. "Yeah. Hard to forget a divine lightning bolt breaking up a fight."

Elara stepped closer to the mouth of the cave, her staff now braced lightly against the stone. "This isn't about prophecy anymore. It's already moving. We're just trying not to get crushed beneath it."

Dorian finally put away his weapon. "It chose you. And it chose me."

He glanced over his shoulder at Kaelen.

"But you're still holding mine."

Kaelen met his gaze. "And it still reacts to me. Not sure what that says about your prophecy."

Elara broke the silence. "It says we don't know enough. About the relics. About each other. About what happens next."

Dorian nodded once. "We should've died back there."

"We will," Kaelen said. "If we keep acting like three people who just happen to be in the same cave."

That hung in the air longer than it should have.

Outside, the wind stirred the leaves. No horns. No pursuit.

For now.

Elara set her staff down beside her and sat. She didn't fully relax. None of them did. But for the first time, she didn't feel completely alone.

"We stay the night," she said. "Take turns keeping watch. Then we move."

Kaelen gave a short nod.

Dorian sat opposite her, one hand resting on the floor. His eyes didn't leave the entrance.

They weren't allies yet. Not really.

But the divine had seen them.

The enemy had chased them.

And now, whether they trusted each other or not, they were on the same side.

Together.

For better or worse.

They didn't speak. The relics had gone quiet. But none of them believed the silence would last.

Chapter 7: The Long Way Around

Kaelen stopped, one foot perched on a mossy rise. The trees parted just enough to offer a glimpse of the distant ridgeline—and with it, the truth.

"We're headed west," he muttered. He unrolled the old map again, squinting at the faded ink. "Damn it."

Dorian stepped up behind him, arms folded tight across his chest. "You're just figuring that out now?"

Kaelen didn't answer right away. He scanned the landmarks again, lips tight. "These trails don't match the cartography. Half the markers are gone. This map predates the last border shifts."

"Or you just led us the wrong way."

Elara leaned against a nearby tree, arms crossed, silent.

"We followed the river bend," Kaelen said. "The same one listed here. It veered south before looping west. Nothing on the map suggests—"

"Because your plan was to outpace the Verdant patrols and take the lesser-known route. Right?" Dorian stepped closer. "Shortcut your way to glory. Now we're gods know how many leagues off-course."

Kaelen didn't answer the accusation—just stared back. "We're not lost."

"No? Then point to Floralis." Dorian stabbed a finger toward the map. "Right now."

Silence.

From behind them, Elara finally spoke. "So this is the 'united front' we're supposed to be."

Both men turned. She didn't raise her voice, didn't look at either of them. Her fingers traced the bark of the tree beside her, gaze fixed on the wilderness beyond.

No one replied.

As the trio continued on their journey they passed an old Verdant shrine—charred, half-buried, desecrated.

"This shouldn't be here. This far west? It was a place of healing." Elara was astonished.

"Looks like someone disagreed," Kaelen responded.

Dorian inspecting the shrine. "Or made sure no one else got the chance."

The forest around them had grown denser, the canopy blotting out the sun in wide patches. Vines crept across the trunks in unfamiliar patterns, thicker than before, pulsing faintly with Verdant energy. These weren't borderlands. This was old growth, untouched for decades.

Even the air had changed—damp, charged, carrying the scent of moss and distant bloom. No birdsong, only the rustle of underbrush and the slow creak of trees shifting in the windless quiet.

"Floralis is east of Irondale," Kaelen said, voice low. "We've veered west. But... we're not far. If we shift course, we can still—"

"We've been walking in the wrong direction for over a day," Dorian snapped. "How far is 'not far' now?"

Kaelen didn't answer.

Elara stepped forward. "Arguing isn't helping. If we're truly near Floralis, we'll need to be cautious. We're deep in Verdant territory now, whether we meant to be or not."

Dorian huffed. "We're lucky not to have been seen."

"Or maybe we were," Kaelen muttered. "And they're just waiting."

A silence settled between them, heavier than before.

The path ahead curved through a break in the trees, revealing distant light—the kind that suggested a clearing, perhaps even the outer ridges of Floralis. Kaelen saw it and stepped forward, slower now.

"We keep moving," Elara said. "And we do it together. No more grand plans. No more blame. We move east. That's all that matters."

Neither man replied, but both fell in behind her.

They didn't speak for the rest of the day.

The trail had emerged by mistake. But their own path—whatever it was supposed to be—remained tangled.

And the wild didn't care how or why they'd come.

The rain started soft—just a faint patter on the leaves above—but it thickened fast. The kind of downpour that turned trails to trenches, soil to soup. By the time they found cover, they were already soaked.

A shallow overhang beneath a moss-slicked rock face was the best they could manage. It was barely wide enough for the three of them and the gear. Not much room to stretch, no room for a proper fire, and no chance of staying dry.

Dorian worked to clear a small space with his boot. "We should've pushed further," he muttered.

"We couldn't see ten feet ahead," Kaelen said. "You want to fall off a ravine?"

"I'd take that over sleeping in a puddle."

"Then keep walking."

Elara said nothing. She laid her pack against the inner wall and sat beside it, water dripping from her hood. Her staff rested across her lap.

Wiz slogged in behind them, his limbs caked with mud, ears drooping. He tried to sit, slipped, and tried again. Kaelen crouched down and wiped the worst of the muck off the creature's legs, steadying him against the stone.

"He's grown," Dorian said quietly.

Kaelen glanced back. "Wiz? Yeah. Little buddy keeps absorbing power every time the relic pulses."

Wiz leaned into Kaelen's side, grateful for the touch. His breathing was steady now, tail twitching slowly as the worst of the chill passed.

Elara watched from where she sat, eyes tracing the creature's outline. She didn't speak at first.

"He reminds me of…" Her voice trailed off.

Kaelen looked up.

Elara shook her head slightly. "Thalvoryn. He reminds me of Thalvoryn."

Dorian raised an eyebrow. "That a name or a place?"

"The legendary dragon. Lived alongside Druvalandrine. Eyes like wildfire. Always knew more than it let on." She catches herself—realizes she's getting too personal

Kaelen responded with skepticism. "Sounds like a myth."

"Or history. Depends who you ask." She says in a defensive tone.

The storm wasn't hard, but it didn't stop. Water dripped steadily from the edge of the rock, soaking their boots, their tempers. The fire Kaelen managed to coax out was small and bitter, more smoke than warmth.

Nobody moved to speak again. They sat close, but it didn't feel close. Not yet.

But the silence wasn't hostile. Just unfinished.

The rain refused to quit. It had become a thin sheet, steady and indifferent, soaking through cloaks and dripping down into boots. Even under the rock overhang, water found its way in.

They didn't speak as they worked.

Dorian moved through the underbrush, boots squelching with every step. He returned with a handful of foraged tubers, a few sprigs of something that looked edible, and a glare that dared anyone to question the haul.

Kaelen took the supplies without comment. He wiped the roots down with the corner of his cloak and set them in the battered tin pot with a few inches of rainwater collected from a runoff stone. The pot hissed as it met the meager flame.

Elara stayed where she was, her back to the rock wall, arms folded. She hadn't moved much since they'd set camp. Her eyes stayed half-lidded, watching the fire without actually watching it.

The roots boiled slowly. Dorian leaned against the outer curve of the shelter, arms crossed, fingers tapping against his sleeve. Kaelen kept stirring the pot with a flat twig, occasionally glancing into the flickering orange light as if hoping it might cook faster just by staring.

The food, when it was finally passed around, was bland and watery. Kaelen took the first bite, made a face, and passed it to Dorian, who ate in silence. Elara accepted the pot last, she ate without a comment—just a faint twitch in her brow giving her away.

No one complimented the meal.

Kaelen poked the fire with a stick.

"Fine cuisine. Might open a tavern when this is over."

Elara didn't look up. "Then learn how to season something."

"I'm working with what nature gave me."

"Then maybe ask nature to try harder."

Dorian cleared his throat. "At least it's warm."

Kaelen smirked. "Just barely. Like our charming conversation."

"You're one sarcastic remark away from eating alone tomorrow," Elara said.

Dorian tried again. "We're all tired. Maybe we give each other some space tonight."

"We're already sharing five square feet," Kaelen muttered. "How much more space can we give?"

"Emotional space," Dorian said flatly.

Elara snorted. "Right. Because that's easy in the middle of nowhere while being hunted."

The fire crackled, the only sound brave enough to stay.

Wiz curled beside Kaelen's pack, belly rising and falling slowly, the only one truly at ease. His warmth bled into Kaelen's leg, but the comfort didn't reach far.

Dorian shifted against the wall and rested his head back, staring up at the rock ceiling as if trying to see stars that weren't there.

Kaelen leaned back and shut his eyes.

Elara stayed where she was, back straight, eyes open, watching the fire shrink.

They could sit around the same flame. They could pass the same pot.

But each of them burned alone.

And the silence, this time, wasn't just tired—it was resigned.

The fire had settled into a low, steady flicker, more ember than flame. Rain still tapped at the rocks above, but the worst of it had passed.

They hadn't moved in a while.

Kaelen sat with one knee up, poking absently at the coals. Elara leaned forward slightly, her fingers steepled just above her knees. Dorian remained behind, his shoulder pressed against the stone, eyes half-closed but still watching.

The silence deepened again, not comfortable but settled.

Kaelen finally spoke, his tone dry.

"So. Anyone else feeling like a divine scavenger hunt with no map and rigged clues?"

Elara glanced at him. "You Forgeborne always this poetic?"

He grinned faintly. "Only when we're lost in the rain and out of decent food."

Dorian stirred. "We've been reacting to signs. That's not the same as understanding them."

Elara's eyes narrowed. "We were taught the prophecy pointed to a Verdant Chosen. One paired with a Forgeborne. But we never expected yours to survive the trials."

Kaelen looked up. "Because you thought the Verdant half would carry the weight alone?"

"No," she said. "Because none of the histories said the Forgeborne half made it this far before."

Kaelen's smile vanished. "That's rich. Even our own people barely believe in the prophecy. The only ones who pushed it were the Council—and they used it to execute Uncle Orlan."

Elara flinched slightly but said nothing.

Dorian's voice cut in, quiet. "Then none of us knows the truth. And maybe someone wanted it that way."

That line hung between them longer than the silence that followed.

Kaelen leaned back. "So the Verdant lied to you. The Forgeborne lied to us. And the relics—"

"—say nothing," Elara finished. "They just pulse when they want, glow when convenient, and leave us guessing the rest."

"No," Dorian said. "They brought us together."

The fire popped. A spark jumped, curled, and died in the dirt.

No one spoke after that. But the silence had changed.

This time, they weren't just alone together.

They were betrayed together.

The fire had burned down to a circle of coals, warm but dim. Outside, the rain had slowed to a mist, whispering across leaves and stone.

Elara's voice broke the silence. "Why do your people build things that burn and explode?"

Kaelen looked up from the fire. "That's specific."

She didn't smile. "Your machines. The weapons. The furnaces. Even your transport rigs—we saw what they did to the riverbank outside Hollowgrove."

Kaelen shrugged. "Because they work."

"That's not an answer."

Dorian shifted. "She's not wrong. You deflect every time this comes up. Tell her what you told me in training."

Kaelen hesitated. Then he picked up a shard of wood from the edge of the fire and turned it in his hand.

"We don't build things to last forever," he said. "We build things to hold long enough to keep going."

He tossed the wood into the coals. It hissed, caught, and blackened.

Elara frowned. "That's… pragmatic."

"It's survival," Kaelen said. "In the forges, time costs lives. You hold the line or you lose it. Permanence is a luxury."

Dorian gave a small nod. "And if it breaks, we build the next one better."

Elara traced a small knot in the wood beside her. "We don't do that. Verdant shaping doesn't force things into form. We persuade it. We borrow structure from the world around us."

Kaelen raised an eyebrow. "You're saying you ask the forest's permission to build a house?"

"In a way."

"That's incredibly inefficient."

"It's sustainable."

Kaelen didn't argue. Not right away.

Elara looked back at him. "Your cities grow upward like towers racing the sun. Ours grow outward. Into the land. With it."

"And when the land says no?"

"Then we listen."

The fire cracked again. More sparks curled and faded.

For the first time, they weren't just speaking across a divide. They were looking into it.

And trying to measure how wide it really was.

The fire had faded to little more than warm coals. Morning hadn't arrived yet, but the edge of night was beginning to fray. The rain had thinned to a whisper, barely touching the forest floor.

Kaelen stood just outside the shelter, swinging a heavy wrench in wide, deliberate arcs. Not with the grace of a trained fighter—but with the kind of repetition that said he'd done this more than once. His footing was solid. His swings were efficient. Practical.

Dorian watched from the rock ledge, arms crossed.

"Why don't you craft a sword?" he said. "Or something sharp, at least."

Kaelen stopped mid-swing and lowered the wrench. "Swords aren't really my thing."

Dorian tilted his head. "And a wrench is?"

Kaelen shrugged. "It works. But…" He paused, thinking. "I saw this mechcrafter once. Back at the Collegium. Built a mechanical gauntlet—had a powered grip, integrated impact coils, even a retractable spike for close quarters. It was… pretty damn cool."

Dorian raised an eyebrow. "You could build that?"

"If I had the blueprint." Kaelen smiled faintly. "Which I don't. But I remember enough of the design to sketch something close. Maybe. If we had a forge. And parts. And time."

Dorian smirked. "We might have two of those things eventually. Maybe all three."

Kaelen looked at the wrench in his hand. "Still, this hasn't let me down yet."

Elara, sitting nearby with her staff across her knees, looked up. "It suits you. Ugly. Heavy. Functional."

Kaelen pointed the wrench at her like a scepter. "And you carry a stick."

"It listens better than you do."

Dorian chuckled. "You two are going to get along horribly."

Kaelen turned the wrench once more in his hand, slower now, thoughtful.

The idea lingered. Not a sword. But something better.

And maybe, finally, something his own.

All three were quiet. Then all of a sudden, the relics—each one stored differently—start to emit a faint hum at the same time.

It lasted for five seconds—no heat, no blinding light. Just a synchronized reaction.

Then it stops.

Kaelen scratching his head. "That's not comforting."

"It's never done that before." Elara looking shocked.

"Maybe they're listening," Dorian said, trying to ease the group's unease.

Kaelen added. "Maybe they are waiting."

The forest had gone still again. Whatever threat might've followed them had given up—or waited. The rain had stopped, replaced by a thick silence that pressed into the night.

They took turns keeping watch.

Kaelen's shift overlapped with Elara's first. The fire was low. Most of the coals had turned to ash.

She sat with her back against the rock wall, eyes on the forest edge. Kaelen stood a few paces away, wrench resting across his knees.

"You didn't correct me," Elara said suddenly.

Kaelen glanced over. "When?"

"When I called you Chosen."

He shifted his weight. "Because I didn't know what I was either."

Elara didn't respond right away. "And now?"

Kaelen shrugged. "Still figuring it out."

She nodded once, and the silence returned.

Later, Dorian relieved her. Kaelen stayed a little longer than needed, poking at the fire as Dorian sat down beside him.

"She listens to you," Dorian said.

Kaelen didn't look up. "That surprises you?"

"A little."

Kaelen set the stick down. "Maybe because I don't lie."

Dorian scoffed. "That's a low bar."

"It's also rare. Especially in cities built on lies."

Neither smiled. But neither looked away.

"Back in the clearing—when she said you were the Chosen. You let her believe it."

Kaelen looking surprised about what Dorian asked him. "Would it have changed anything if I corrected her?"

"It might have."

"Then maybe that's the problem," Kaelen replied abruptly, cutting off the conversation.

Dorian's shift continued in silence. Eventually, Elara returned, brushing the damp from her cloak as she approached.

They didn't speak at first. Then Dorian said, "You trust him?"

"I trust what I see," Elara said. "Most days."

"And what do you see?"

Elara tilted her head. "Someone trying. Same as you."

Dorian glanced up at the trees. "Think the gods are testing us?"

Elara's voice was quiet. "Some days, I think they're laughing."

There was an awkward silence between the two, but then Elara spoke again.

"You move like a soldier."

Dorian shifted awkwardly. "I was trained that way."

"Trained… or broken?" Elara pushed.

Dorian quickly replied. "Does it matter?"

Elara trying to break the awkwardness between them. "It should. But no one ever seems to think so."

The fire cracked once, a spark dancing into the dark.

They didn't smile.

But neither looked away.

The night passed, heavy with the weight of too many truths.

They weren't allies.

Not yet.

But they weren't just tolerating each other anymore.

Dawn broke slowly, filtered through the mist that clung to the canopy. The forest was quiet—too quiet—but not in a way that felt threatening. Just watchful.

Elara crouched near a patch of flattened moss, her map unrolled across her knees. Not one made of parchment, but traced in memory—lines of star paths and sacred markers etched into stone and bark. She turned her gaze upward.

Above, the clouds had finally parted enough to reveal a fractured sky. Constellations blinked through the thinning fog, faded but visible. Her eyes followed them like old friends.

"There," she said, pointing at a cluster above the eastern ridge. "If we're beneath the Crown of Leaves, then the path curves south toward the Wyrmbark grove. That should bring us within two days of Floralis."

Kaelen walked over, peering up at the same stretch of stars. "That's not on any map I've ever seen."

"Because your maps weren't written by the forest," Elara replied.

Kaelen knelt beside her. "Still. That's the first useful navigation we've had in days."

"I'll try not to be offended."

He offered the faintest grin. "Try harder."

The wind shifts all at once. The trees stop swaying mid-gust. Everything stills. The air feels too heavy for a few moments—like they're being watched. Then a distant rumble—no storm, no lightning. Just the sound.

Dorian looking confused. "Storm?"

Elara answers back. "There are no clouds."

"Doesn't need clouds if it's not weather," Kaelen said.

Dorian joined them, rubbing sleep from his eyes. "So we really are heading toward Floralis?"

Elara nodded. "Apparently the gods want us to argue with nobility."

Kaelen muttered, "Or burn them out of their council chambers."

Elara didn't laugh, but she didn't scold him either.

Dorian knelt, eyes following Elara's markings in the dirt. "So this is Verdant cartography. Memory and stars."

"Memory and listening," she said. "The world leaves markers. If you pay attention."

Kaelen leaned back on his hands. "Maybe the Forgeborne should've tried that before redrawing every border by force."

"No maybe about it," Elara said.

They sat for another minute, gazing at the sky, the forest, the unseen path ahead.

They still didn't walk in step.

But at least now, they were headed the same direction.

It was foggy in the morning.

Not the thick, suffocating kind from days earlier—but light, rolling mist that hovered just above the ground. The trees looked cleaner in it. The path clearer, even if it still wound through unknown terrain.

No one argued. No one needed to.

Kaelen crouched beside Wiz, adjusting a loose panel on the creature's casing. The latch had started sticking again, and the last thing they needed was another cracked component. He worked quietly, his hands steady.

The relic in Elara's coat started humming, then pulsed with static.

Wiz briefly shorts out, twitching like he's picking up interference.

Elara's vines retract on instinct. The Forgeborne relic flares in defense.

Then silence. Everything returns to normal.

Kaelen, clearly surprised by what happened. "Okay. That's new."

Elara responds. "They're reacting to something."

Dorian stood nearby, watching. He didn't offer to help, arms folded across his chest. "Or to each other."

Kaelen silently resumed fixing Wiz's loose panel.

Kaelen muttering. "Stupid gods. Stupid wrench. Stupid prophecy."

"You could ask for help." Elara notices Kaelen's growing frustration.

Kaelen brushed off her comment. "Don't start."

Elara sat with her back to a tree, running a whetstone along the ironwood edge of her staff. The motion was slow, rhythmic. Not urgent. Just necessary.

There were no jokes. No jabs. But the silence between them had changed.

When Kaelen stood, he reached into his pack and pulled out a second tool—slightly shorter than his main wrench, curved and battered, but balanced.

He held it out toward Dorian. "Spare."

Dorian took it with a nod. "Thanks."

Elara looked over, but didn't flinch. Didn't question. Just watched.

They packed up without needing instruction. Each moved in rhythm—not perfectly, but without hesitation.

The trail ahead stretched east, dappled in faint morning light.

They didn't speak when they started walking.

They didn't need to.

It wasn't peace. Not yet.

But it was momentum.

And that was enough to keep going.

Act III: Fractures in Flight

Chapter 8: The City That Does Not Forget

The forest changed before they saw it.

The air shifted—cooler, sharper, thick with energy that hummed just beneath the surface. The scent changed too, from wet soil and pine to something more fragrant—like crushed flowers and old bark. The trees here were older than any Kaelen had seen, their trunks wide enough to house entire rooms, bark dark with age, canopies stretched into a cathedral of green and gold. Light filtered through in slanted beams, catching dust that glimmered like spores drifting between the leaves.

Then the city revealed itself.

Floralis wasn't built. It had grown. Towers spiraled up from massive tree trunks, their bark wrapped in bioluminescent veins that pulsed gently like living circuits. Bridges arched between limbs like woven thread, walkways stitched from root and vine. Some were narrow, fit for a single person, others wide enough to carry a procession. Birds circled high overhead, their feathers streaked with green and silver. Somewhere deeper in the city, music—or something close to it—carried faintly on the wind, rising and falling like wind through reeds.

Kaelen let out a slow breath. "Well, subtle it isn't."

Dorian didn't respond. Dorian intently watched the blooming tower. "It's not what I expected."

Elara stepped forward, reaching into her pack and pulling out two cloaks dyed in deep green. The fabric shimmered faintly, threads of silver and violet catching the light. Sigils stitched into the hems glowed only when turned toward the city.

"Put these on," she said.

Kaelen examined the stitching, studying how the threads responded to light. "Clever design."

Dorian didn't move.

"I'm not hiding," Dorian said.

Elara turned, voice sharper than before. "It's not hiding. It's surviving."

"We've come this far. We're not sneaking in like criminals."

"You're Forgeborne." Her tone dropped lower. "Walk in there wearing your pride and see how long you last. The guards won't ask questions. The people won't care what side of the prophecy you're on."

Dorian's fists tightened at his sides. "Forgeborne don't hide."

"Then be proud in chains," Elara snapped. "Or be smart in the shadows."

Kaelen, already draping the cloak over his shoulders, spoke without looking up. "Call it tactical camo. Or fashion. Either way, I'm not getting stabbed because someone doesn't like my hometown."

Dorian looked at him, then back at Elara. Tension pulled tight between them like a drawn bowstring. Finally, Dorian took the cloak and threw it over his shoulders—not tying it, not adjusting it. Just there. Begrudgingly.

They walked the rest of the path in silence.

As they drew closer, the outer wards of Floralis came into view. Small shrines grown from twisting vines lined the trail, each shaped with care, their forms different but all familiar to Elara.

Some resembled animals, others abstract patterns grown into domes or spires. Each pulsed faintly with protective enchantments, the light shifting like breath.

Elara slowed as she passed them, her eyes moved swiftly to each one with familiarity. She paused at one shaped like an open palm and touched the vine-woven edge. The enchantment responded with a soft pulse, as though recognizing her.

Kaelen watched her fingers drift to the relic beneath her coat. It hadn't reacted since the lightning, but something in her expression made him wonder if she was waiting for it to.

Dorian kept scanning the perimeter—every shadow between the roots, every movement in the canopy above. Even now, his instincts stayed ahead of his thoughts.

They crested a final rise, and the trees parted just enough to reveal the path into the city proper. It was quieter than Kaelen expected. No border guards. No fanfare. Just a smooth arch grown from two trees that had bent together over decades.

Elara stopped and looked over her shoulder.

"From this point on, let me talk first. We're not on neutral ground anymore."

Kaelen gave a single nod. Dorian followed a beat later.

They weren't allies here.

They were intruders with a purpose. Strangers under a sacred canopy.

And the city ahead had not forgotten the wars that had shaped them all.

Whatever happened next, they were walking into it together—but not yet side by side.

The city's edge held no walls, no gates—only the intention of a place that had never needed either. Floralis opened gradually, its paths winding into layered terraces and spiraling halls grown from the forest itself. The trees became buildings. The roots became roads.

Guards flanked the main artery into the city. They stood beneath canopies of flowering vines, still as carved wood, armor masked in layers of moss-colored cloth. Their eyes followed the trio as they passed—polite, but fixed for too long.

Kaelen felt it first.

The air shifted again, heavier this time. Not the kind of weight you could see. The kind that settled into your spine when you were being watched. He tugged the edge of the cloak tighter across his chest, not to hide, but to mute whatever it was they thought they saw in him.

"They're staring," he muttered.

"They're trained to," Elara replied, not breaking stride. "Verdant guards memorize every stranger's face the moment they step through."

"Feels more like measuring."

"Probably both."

A child pointed at Wiz peeking from Kaelen's pack. The parent grabbed the child's hand too quickly. No words. Just retreat.

As they passed under an arched gateway, the sound of water filled the space—a silent stream running through the walkway itself, its current traced with glowing petals. Dorian looked down but didn't stop. Kaelen glanced at the guard nearest the bend, who nodded once and said nothing.

A vine twitched above Kaelen's head. He stopped. It didn't move again.

Elara didn't speak, but her grip on the staff tightened.

Elara spoke quietly as they walked. "If you see a Sylvanar, don't provoke them."

Dorian frowned. "Who are they?"

"Elementalists. Fire, wind, water, ground. They're not guards—they're the elite. The last line of defense Floralis never speaks of."

Kaelen raised an eyebrow. "Sounds like a lovely welcome party."

"It's not a welcome," Elara said. "It's a warning."

They crossed into the heart of the city. Terraced platforms rose ahead, each one lined with gardens that seemed untouched by human hand. Vines swayed gently in a wind no one could feel. People passed them in pairs and small groups, their clothes draped in forest tones, their eyes cautious, always glancing twice.

Eyes followed them, but mouths stayed shut. Floralis didn't speak its suspicions—it just observed until they became facts.

No one spoke to them. But no one looked away, either.

A mother tugged her child behind her cloak as the group passed, whispering something sharp and hurried in Verdant.

Every wall, every path, every living structure was designed to feel open—and yet, Kaelen had never felt more enclosed.

Floralis was beautiful.

But it did not forget.

And it did not trust.

The square opened like a clearing between the towers—an amphitheater of woven stone and living wood, canopied by flowering branches that swayed with the breeze. Lanterns shaped like luminous blossoms drifted in slow orbits overhead, suspended by subtle enchantments.

Subtle, that is, until one of them jolted sideways and crashed into another.

Conversation quieted wherever they walked—like their presence drew a thin fog no one wanted to breathe.

A fruit vendor saw Dorian's hammer that was wrapped with cloth and subtly turned his stall's sign from open to closed without saying a word.

A sharp gust tore through the space, scattering petals and tipping over a display of ceremonial herbs. One lantern struck a second mid-spin—too hard. The impact ignited a pocket of dry pollen with a sharp whump, sending flame curling along the edges of silk.

"Nonononono—"

A young woman sprinted in from the edge of the square, her cloak half-fastened, hair frizzing outward like she'd fought with both wind and static.

She raised her arms and bellowed, "Water!"

A surge burst from the nearby basin—too much. It blasted the burning lantern into the air before drenching the entire nearby platform. The fire died with a hiss... and so did the lantern's frame, which crumpled under the flood.

The woman's momentum carried her two steps too far. She slipped, skidded, and landed with a splash in a decorative planter.

She emerged soaked, one sandal missing, a flower stuck defiantly to her cheek.

The entire square froze.

A dozen nearby onlookers stared in silence. Someone coughed politely. No one clapped.

Elara stiffened at the edge of the walkway.

Dorian blinked. "That's a Sylvanar?"

Elara winced. "Supposedly."

Kaelen gave a low whistle. "And I thought Forgeborne had chaotic energy."

The woman stumbled upright, water streaming from her sleeves.

She grinned at the crowd with theatrical flair and shouted, "Liora Greenwood. Don't forget the name!"

Then the woman's eyes landed on them—and she froze, her grin faded, replaced by something quieter. Like she had found what she didn't realize she'd been looking for.

She stared. Squinted. Took a tentative step forward.

Kaelen straightened. "She sees us."

Elara was already turning away. "Keep walking."

Dorian didn't argue.

They left the square at a steady pace, not hurried, not casual—just wrong enough to catch eyes. Behind them, the woman stood motionless, still dripping, watching them go.

Floralis remained polite. But its eyes lingered long after they passed.

And it would remember this.

The inn stood near the eastern edge of the city, tucked beneath a canopy of low-sweeping trees that formed a natural roof over its upper floors. Its walls were carved from living bark, shaped into a structure that flexed gently with the wind. Lanterns by the door pulsed with a soft green glow—rooms available.

Elara stepped in first, her cloak still damp from the earlier rainfall. Inside, the air was thick with the scent of herbs and varnished wood—pleasant, but heavy. A vine-draped counter curved along one wall, behind which stood the innkeeper: polite face, motionless posture, gaze too sharp.

"Two rooms," Elara said, laying a few polished Verdant tokens on the counter.

"East-facing alcoves," the innkeeper replied smoothly. "Quiet and private."

His voice was all hospitality. His eyes betrayed the rest—flicking from Elara, to Kaelen, then lingering a beat too long on Dorian.

The innkeeper's smile never moved. But his fingers tapped twice on the counter—soft, rhythmic, deliberate.

Not a nervous habit. A signal.

Kaelen caught it. Said nothing.

He didn't speak. Just adjusted his weight—like someone preparing for something.

Dorian stayed near the door, back straight, gaze scanning. One hand hovered close to where a weapon would've been.

They took the stairs in silence. Narrow halls. Moss-lined floors. Everything too soft, too deliberately soothing. The kind of comfort meant to lower defenses, not provide it.

Inside, the rooms were simple. Clean. A little too undisturbed. Kaelen ran his fingers along the windowsill—fresh grooves in the curtain rod. Recently moved.

Downstairs, the common area murmured with half-conversations and peaceful music from a hanging reed instrument. Kaelen paused on the stairwell. His eyes found her instantly.

Liora.

Dried off. Cloak re-fastened. Sitting at the bar with a fig in one hand, posture casual, mouth running. The barkeep wore the look of someone who'd surrendered to the conversation a while ago.

Elara moved past Kaelen, stopping beside the bar but not sitting.

"If you're trying to follow us," she said quietly, "don't."

Liora blinked. Still smiling, but not as wide. "Just here for the figs. You're the ones dragging mystery and tension into my inn."

"Not your inn," Kaelen muttered.

"Fair," she said, chewing.

Elara's voice was low. "We're just passing through. That's all you need to know."

Liora nodded, unfazed. "Sure. Passing through. With two Forgeborne, one of them armed with nothing but posture and judgment."
 She glanced toward Kaelen's cloak. "And something buzzing in your pack. Cute, by the way."

Kaelen stepped closer. "You've been watching us."

"You're not exactly subtle."

Elara met her eyes one last time. "Don't follow us."

She turned and walked away. Kaelen and Dorian followed. None of them looked back.

But Kaelen felt it anyway—the weight behind them, the conversation that shifted as they left. The pause in the music. The subtle pull of attention, like gravity bending toward a falling object.

At the end of the hallway, the innkeeper stood motionless, hands folded, gaze fixed not on the ledger—but on them. No smile. No blink. Just silence.

He turned away as they passed—but too late to pretend he hadn't been listening.

Floralis welcomed visitors the way a forest welcomed fire.

And every tree had ears.

Night settled over Floralis in layers. The soft pulse of the lanterns outside the inn dimmed to a low green glow, mimicking the rhythm of resting flora. The city itself never truly slept—its structures breathed, its pathways hummed faintly—but the activity dulled, as if the forest encouraged rest. In the upper rooms of the inn, even the walls felt quieter, as though they'd absorbed the noise of the day.

In their shared room, Dorian sat near the window, the forge-tempered head of his hammer resting across his lap. He rotated it slowly, inspecting every notch, every scar left behind by time and violence. His fingers moved over the carved runes along the haft, reading them in silence. They weren't just decorative—each mark recorded a lesson, a moment, a cost.

Across the room, Kaelen was sprawled on the floor, sleeves rolled up, smudges of charcoal on his knuckles and cheek. A thick pad of parchment lay open in front of him, filled with sketches—some clean and precise, others scratched out in frustration. He had already drawn three variations of segmented shoulder plating, none of which pleased him. Off to the side, a rough outline of a gauntlet sat unfinished, surrounded by annotations and aborted designs.

"No point wearing iron if you can't move in it," Kaelen muttered, erasing a contour and redrawing it.

Dorian didn't respond at first. He traced the worn edge of the hammer again, eyes narrowing at a hairline crack near the joint. "We'll need better tools than this inn has."

"Anviltown," Kaelen said without looking up. "It's southeast of here. Has parts we need. Might even have an old gearhouse if it hasn't been dismantled."

Dorian nodded slowly. "You sure it'll have what we need?"

"Depends on what we need."

Kaelen flipped back a few pages, revealing diagrams of a compact harness design—something rigged for maneuverability and flexible joint protection. His writing in the margins was tight, almost surgical. Weight ratios. Heat dispersion.

Dorian leaned closer, eyeing a half-drawn weapon sketched near the center. "That?" he asked, pointing. "What's that supposed to be?"

Kaelen paused, then tapped the page with the charcoal. "It was supposed to be a short-blade hybrid. Something light. Something fast. Just enough reach to keep someone away."

"But you didn't finish it."

Kaelen shrugged. "I build. I break. I don't kill." He set the charcoal down, hands resting in his lap. "Not if I can help it."

Dorian studied him for a long moment. "But you still carry a weapon."

Kaelen didn't look away. "Because not everyone gives you the choice."

The fire in the hearth had died down to faint coals. The room was dim but not cold. Outside, the leaves rustled lightly against the wooden frame, like whispers just out of earshot.

Kaelen turned the page and began sketching a new gauntlet design. This one looked heavier—reinforced knuckles, interlocking plates over the wrist. But its structure wasn't made for offense. It was defensive. Something that could absorb impact. Shield, not strike.

It wasn't a compromise.

It was intended.

Dorian returned his gaze to the window, watching the flickering lights of the city below. "We'll hit Anviltown if we keep east, then from there we go south to Smeltport and finally take a ship down the river towards Irondale," he said.

Kaelen nodded, still drawing. "We get the parts. We build smart."

Dorian tapped the hammerhead once against his knee. "And maybe then we'll be ready for what's coming."

Kaelen didn't answer right away. He added one final stroke to the gauntlet sketch and leaned back.

Some things you didn't say out loud.

You just built toward them.

And hoped it was enough.

The room held its silence like a held breath. The hearth crackled low, casting long shadows against moss-lined walls. The beds were clean, the blankets dry, the lanternlight soft—but none of it reached beneath their skin. Not yet.

Kaelen sat on the floor near the fire, sleeves rolled up, working a worn tool between whetstone and cloth. Sparks of metal dust clung to his boots. Dorian leaned against the wall near the door, arms folded, not quite resting. Elara sat with her staff across her lap, gaze fixed on the flames.

They hadn't spoken much since arriving.

The city had welcomed them, yes. With tranquil eyes and hushed words. The kind that watched, measured, waited.

"We weren't supposed to be here," Kaelen said finally. His voice wasn't bitter—just tired.

Dorian didn't move. "Cinderhollow. Mountain pass. North to Nocturne's Edge. That was the path."

"And then it wasn't." Elara didn't sound surprised. Just resigned.

Kaelen chuckled once. "Takes talent to be this lost with a map."

"You weren't the only one making calls," Elara said.

Dorian opened his eyes. "We all knew what we were risking."

Kaelen nodded. "Doesn't make it any less frustrating."

Silence returned. This time, it settled between them instead of over them.

"So what's next?" Elara asked softly. "What do we think is waiting beyond Floralis?"

Kaelen didn't look up. "Questions. The kind no one wants to ask out loud."

Dorian: "Answers. If we're lucky."

Elara: "And danger. The kind you don't walk away from unless you know who's walking beside you."

They sat with that.

Not in agreement. Not in defiance. Just in the space between.

Kaelen leaned back against the wall, tossing the cloth onto the bedframe beside him.

"Well," he muttered. "At least nothing's exploded yet."

Dorian arched an eyebrow. "You're counting that as progress?"

Kaelen smirked. "In a week like this? Absolutely."

Elara didn't laugh. But she didn't argue either.

The fire burned steady. The silence didn't press as hard.

It wasn't comfort.

But it was enough.

The creak of the inn's main door was too quiet to draw attention at first. But Kaelen's ears caught it anyway.

Footsteps followed—measured, padded, intentional. More than one set.

He rose from his seat slowly, gaze locking with Dorian's. The other man was already standing, posture shifting from still to ready. His hands hovered just close enough to look casual—just close enough to act.

Downstairs, voices murmured. Then one broke through the calm.

"They're Forgeborne," the innkeeper said. "Armed. I feared for my safety."

Not surprise. Confirmation. The bastard had sold them out.

Elara stood, staff in hand. Her silence said exactly how this would go.

Then came the footsteps on the stairs.

Three guards appeared in the hallway, cloaks trimmed in the floral sigils of Floralis lawkeepers. Their armor was dyed in forest tones, shaped to echo the natural elegance of the city around them. They didn't draw weapons—but their hands lingered just above their hilts. Calm. Controlled. Waiting.

The lead was tall, her face composed, almost serene—save for her eyes, which were just a little too sharp.

"You're asked to come with us for questioning," she said. "Quietly."

Dorian didn't move. He just exhaled—tired, almost disappointed.

"They're not enemies," he said, glancing at Kaelen and Elara. "Just misled."

Kaelen's hand shifted toward his belt. No blade there, but his fingers curled anyway.

Elara stepped between the guards and her companions.

"We've done nothing wrong. This isn't justice. It's performance."

The lead guard didn't blink.

"Perception becomes truth. And truth invites scrutiny."

Downstairs, someone moved. A footstep. Then silence.

Outside, beneath the inn's arched window, Liora crouched behind a stack of wood bins, half-shadowed by overgrowth. She hadn't meant to follow them back. She told herself she was just curious. Just walking.

But then she heard the innkeeper's voice—too smooth, too rehearsed. Like someone reading a part they'd practiced for weeks.

Then the guards arrived.

Now she knelt motionless, breath tight in her chest.

"If I help them," she thought, "I'll be branded a traitor. I'll lose everything. Training. Sponsorship. Home."

"I'll be the Sylvanar who betrayed her own."

But if she didn't—

A voice drifted through the open window. Dorian's. Low. Controlled.

"They're not enemies. Just misled."

And that's what hit her.

They still believed in mercy.

Even now.

Liora closed her eyes. Bit the inside of her cheek until the sting cleared her vision.

"If I walk away, I'm exactly what this city made me to be: quiet, obedient, forgettable."

She stood.

"But if I act... maybe I get to be something else."

She wiped her palms on her cloak. Flexed her fingers. The magic trembled there, raw and unbalanced.

"Don't screw this up," she whispered to herself.

Then she moved.

Upstairs, the air pressed in.

Kaelen stepped forward—not aggressive, but defiant.

"If you're going to arrest us," he said, "do it plain. Don't wrap it in civility. Don't pretend this is anything but fear."

The guard met his gaze. "We are here to maintain order."

"Then say it." His voice sharpened. "You think we're a threat. Say it."

She opened her mouth—

—and the fire in the hearth surged.

A gust of heat swept across the room. The lanterns trembled. Elara's relic pulsed against her ribs like a drumbeat.

This wasn't going to stay civil.

She moved beside the others, her staff angled low.

"No one wants this," she said.
 Dorian's voice followed, steady. "But it's already begun."

The guards drew their weapons—measured, controlled. Not as intimidation. As protocol.

Outside, shadows passed between the trees. Kaelen counted six. Possibly more.

The hallway tightened. The light dimmed. Everything shrank.

And then—

A burst of wind slammed through the hallway.

It came from the stairwell—uncontrolled, uneven, too much at once. Papers scattered. Dust sprayed. One guard staggered, her cloak twisting into her face.

Liora vaulted up the last two steps, both hands glowing faintly.

"Bad timing," she muttered. "Sorry in advance."

She didn't wait for approval.

Her hand swept out. The floor trembled—not much, just enough to shift a guard's stance. Her second spell summoned water from the air itself—more splash than force, but it hit like a thrown pail.

Dorian didn't need more than a second. He surged forward, knocking one guard into the wall with a shoulder-check. Kaelen grabbed Elara's arm and shoved her toward the window-side stairs.

"Move!"

A blade swung—too slow.

They barreled down the hallway as Liora shouted, "Go left! There's a back exit by the kitchens!"

One guard stumbled after them. Another cursed behind.

They barreled down the stairs two at a time. The inn groaned under the weight of chaos—shouts behind them, the scrape of boots, the distant crack of something magical going wrong.

In the scramble, Kaelen's pouch snagged on a twisted stair rail. Papers burst loose, fluttering down the steps like wounded birds.

One blueprint skidded across the landing and slid beneath the rail.

Kaelen cursed, twisted back.

"Wait—!"
His hand shot out toward the paper.

Dorian grabbed his shoulder. "We don't have time."

"I can get it," Kaelen said, already moving.

Elara blocked his path, staff low. "It's gone. We're not."

He froze—torn, teeth gritted.

The shouting upstairs grew louder. Steel hit wood.

Every muscle screamed to retrieve the blueprint. Kaelen walked anyway.

Elara flung open a service door and led them into a narrow passage lined with drying herbs. Kaelen kicked over a storage rack behind them as they passed. Bottles shattered.

The back door opened onto a narrow garden path—overgrown, dimly lit, framed by twisting roots and hanging moss. No guards. No shouts. Not yet.

They didn't speak.

They ran.

Elara led them through the corridor of trees and stone, ducking beneath woven arches and skirting behind tall hedges. Kaelen's boots slammed against packed earth. Dorian moved like a shadow—controlled, quick, watching every corner.

Only once they ducked beneath a crumbling trellis, half-hidden by ivy and dripping lantern moss, did they stop to breathe.

Still inside Floralis.

Still being hunted.

A wall to their right rippled—just for a second. Bark flexed, like it was breathing.

Dorian slowed. The light embedded in the root above them pulsed red, then faded.

"We're not just being followed," he muttered. "We're being tracked."

Kaelen turned, breath sharp, heart still racing—and saw Liora, doubled over, hands on her knees. Her sleeves were scorched at the cuffs. A patch of mud streaked her cheek. One of her boots squelched every time she moved.

Still catching his breath, Kaelen turned to her. "I thought you were the one who turned us in."

Liora didn't flinch. She looked up, eyes tired. "Yeah. So did I."

Kaelen didn't blink. "Then why help us?"

She straightened, slowly, like every muscle ached.

"Because I saw what they were about to do."

Her voice wasn't angry—just quiet. Steady.

"And I got tired of pretending this city knows what justice looks like."

The silence that followed wasn't trust.

But it wasn't rejection either.

They didn't thank her.

But they didn't leave her behind.

The alleys of Floralis weren't made for flight.

They twisted, split, rejoined. Arches of woven bark dipped too low, roots erupted from walkways like barricades, and living walls pulsed with Verdant enchantments that tracked heat and movement. Every corner felt like it might bend behind them, like the city itself was trying to remember their shapes.

Dorian led. Elara flanked. Kaelen kept pace beside Liora, who was struggling not to limp.

"That way!" Dorian pointed, veering beneath an arch formed by two grown-together trees. The tunnel ahead was narrow and dim, lit only by pale glowcaps sprouting from the walls.

"Is this a path or a drainage vine?" Kaelen muttered.

"Don't ask questions with 'drainage' in them," Liora panted. "Just keep running."

Behind them, boots struck wood. A voice shouted—closer than before.

Elara twisted, staff raised, and sent a burst of magic across the entrance behind them. Vines grew in a rapid snarl, tangling the passage just long enough to stall their pursuers.

Kaelen glanced at her. "That trick only works once."

"Then we'd better make it count," Elara snapped.

They emerged into a wider corridor—part marketplace, part overgrown plaza. Empty at this hour, but not silent. Lights swayed. Windows opened. Someone was watching from above.

A horn sounded—sharp and distant.

"They've signaled the outer patrols," Liora said.

"Which means?" Dorian asked.

"Every living vine in this quarter is about to become our enemy."

A root jerked up under Kaelen's foot. He nearly went down but caught himself with a grunt.

"Not helping your city's tourism pitch," he growled.

Liora grabbed his sleeve and yanked him left, down a split in the path. "Come on, I know a shortcut—sort of. Maybe. Hopefully."

They ducked through a curtain of hanging moss and into a chamber-like pocket between grown buildings. The air was damp and close. The floor flexed underfoot, like they were running across a giant leaf.

Elara hesitated. "This can't be right—"

"It's temporary," Liora said, dragging a palm across one of the walls. "This part of the city regenerates. The path closes behind us every hour. If we make it to the other side before it seals, we vanish. If not..."

A vine slammed down behind them, closing off the entrance.

"Too late to turn around," Kaelen muttered.

The walls shimmered with Verdant script—some kind of old guidance system. Elara read it in pieces, calling turns in a tight voice.

"Right. Left. Sharp curve—watch the ridge!"

A guard's voice echoed faintly behind the wall—trapped, confused. They hadn't followed into the growth channel.

The path pulsed underfoot, reacting to their heat, their motion, their intent.

"This place is alive," Dorian muttered. "I don't like it."

"You're not supposed to," Liora replied. "You're Forgeborne. The city doesn't trust you."

"Neither do the people," Kaelen added.

"Yeah," Liora said. "But I'm starting to."

They rounded one final curve and emerged into a tranquil grove wrapped in lightroots. The tunnel behind them sealed with a low hum.

Silence.

Just for a moment.

Everyone breathed.

The group pushed forward, slipping through root-bridges and narrow outer trails that wound away from the heart of Floralis. The ground here was uneven—part stone, part living wood—and the trees grew closer together, their branches twisted like fingers clutching secrets. Ferns grew wild in the crevices, glowing faintly with the bioluminescent tint common in deeper Verdant paths. The deeper they went, the more the forest closed around them, familiar to Elara and foreign to the others.

Their footsteps were uneven, breaths ragged. The adrenaline from their escape had started to fade, replaced by the gnawing awareness that they were still being hunted. Not with torches and swords—but with silence, with shadows, and with spells they didn't fully understand.

They crossed a narrow bridge of gnarled limbs, the space between it and the forest floor dizzyingly wide. The roots shifted under their feet, creaking like old bones. Dorian took point, scanning every tree line and bend in the path. Kaelen followed close, occasionally glancing at the pouch under his arm as if the sketches inside might offer some way out of this mess.

Kaelen paused at the center of the bridge, panting. "We need to stop. Just long enough to—"

A flare lit the sky.

Bright green, laced with gold, it burst above the canopy like a signal fire. A Verdant flare spell—meant to mark movement. And territory. The pulse it released vibrated faintly through the canopy, setting birds into flight and making even the leaves tremble.

Kaelen cursed under his breath. "That's close."

Dorian didn't break stride. "We don't have time to fall apart."

Elara, a few steps behind, snapped, "They don't even know why they're chasing us."

"They don't care," Dorian replied. "We're not citizens. We're symbols."

Liora, stumbling slightly as she caught up, gave a dry, breathless laugh. "Welcome to Floralis. We're real big on justice, just not the fair kind."

The silence that followed was jagged. Tension returned to their limbs, heavier than before.

They cut through another trail, low-hanging vines brushing their faces, damp leaves clinging to clothes and skin. Every turn felt the same, every shadow deeper than the last. Somewhere in the distance, a distant echo—hoofbeats? No, drums. A low rhythm carried on the forest's breath, too faint to place, too steady to ignore.

Kaelen finally slowed, chest heaving. "They're not going to stop, are they?"

Elara's silence said more than agreement. She clutched the staff like it was the only thing holding her together.

"They think we're a threat," she said at last. "And threats don't get questioned."

"They just get chased," Kaelen muttered.

"We didn't start this," Dorian said. "But we'll finish it. When we're ready."

"Or when they give us the chance," Liora added, wiping a streak of dirt from her cheek. "Which they won't."

The group paused at a fork in the trail—one path sloped upward toward a thicker canopy, the other dipped into the roots of a hollowed-out tree formation.

Elara pointed toward the hollow. "That way. We can circle wide, hit the old glade near the western ridge."

Kaelen gave a dry laugh. "You sound like you've done this before."

"I've run from things before." Her voice was quiet. "But not like this."

They ducked under a low archway of roots, emerging into a moss-laden clearing. For a moment, the trees held their breath.

A moment of stillness. A brief reprieve.

But no one relaxed.

They had escaped the inn.

But not the city.

And not each other.

Floralis didn't forget.

And neither did the roots beneath their feet.

The moss-laden clearing gave way to a thinning tree line. Beyond it, the forest sloped downward into wild grass and silver-thorned bramble—open land that marked the edge of Floralis's reach. The sky overhead remained streaked with the remnants of the Verdant flare, now beginning to fade into twilight. The fading light bled through the treetops, turning the moss and bark shades of amber and blue.

They stopped near a half-fallen tree whose roots curled like claws into the soil. Everyone was breathing hard, faces damp with sweat or rain—no one could tell anymore. Their silence said more than words: they had gotten away. But they hadn't escaped.

Elara leaned her back against a tree trunk, eyes scanning the distance. Dorian crouched low to check for signs of pursuit. Kaelen adjusted the straps on his pouch, glancing back the way they came. They all moved like people not used to running, but learning fast.

Liora stood near the edge of the treeline, arms crossed, back to them. Her breath was still uneven, shoulders rising and falling like she hadn't quite shaken the sprint—or the choice she just made.

She didn't speak at first. When she did, her voice barely reached them.

"I just threw away my home for three people I barely know."

The words hung in the air like smoke.

Kaelen glanced at her. Elara turned fully. Dorian said nothing.

Liora shifted, arms dropping to her sides.

"I know what happens now," she said. "They'll mark me. Maybe not officially. But I won't be trusted again. No mentor will take me. No squad will train with me. Floralis forgets quickly—unless you screw up. Then it remembers forever."

She turned to face them. Her smile was crooked, but real this time—tired around the edges.

"So no, I didn't help you because some prophecy told me to."

"Then why did you?" Elara asked.

"Because it was the first time I had a chance to do something that felt... worth it. And I couldn't walk away from that just to stay safe."

She glanced away, biting her lip, then added, more quietly:

"And because I'm tired of being a joke in a city that trained me to fail."

That stopped the conversation.

She didn't flinch. She didn't pretend it didn't matter. She just let it hang there—truth, bare and without decoration.

Then, finally: "A man once told me I'd meet three people who'd change my life."

Elara frowned. "What?"

"He said they'd drag me into something impossible. Said I'd become the Sylvanar Elyndor remembers."

She gave a one-shoulder shrug. "I thought he was being dramatic."

Kaelen arched an eyebrow. "Let me guess—old guy, smelled like moss and metal?"

"Yeah. Bit hunched. Cane made of roots and brass. Talked like he was reading the world backwards."

"Rindun Veladra," Dorian said quietly.

Liora snapped her fingers. "Hmm not quite. I think it was Alden Varidnur. He told me to just call him Alden. Anyway…"

Elara stepped forward. "He told you this would happen?"

"No," Liora said. "I think he made it happen."

Her voice steadied. "He didn't act like someone waiting for fate. He acted like someone was nudging it."

A heavier silence settled across them. The kind that made everything feel closer. Realer.

Liora looked at each of them in turn. "I'm not a good Sylvanar. I know that. My magic flails more than it flows. I've failed every practical exam. I set a rain cloud loose in a library once. It still smells like mildew."

"Sounds like you're exactly what we need," Kaelen muttered.

"Why?" she asked. "Why me?"

Elara stepped beside her.

"Because you made the choice anyway. And that's more than most ever do."

Dorian gave a slow nod. "Prophecy didn't name you. But it noticed."

Liora let the words settle. Then she squared her shoulders.

"I'm in," she said. "Not because I'm brave. Because I'm screwed. So I might as well screw something back."

"And maybe... maybe I'll finally matter for something."

Kaelen cracked a tired smile. "You just ran from your city. Not many exits left."

"Then I'll go where you go." She looked at each of them again. "And make myself useful along the way. Or die trying."

"Let's hope it doesn't come to that," Elara said.

"Let's hope it does," Liora replied, grinning. "That's when I'm at my best."

And just like that—without oaths or orders—she became part of the story.

Not because she was destined.

But because she chose to matter.

And that made all the difference.

The grove was still. No horns. No footsteps. No watching eyes.

For the first time in what felt like hours, they could breathe.

Kaelen sat on the edge of a raised root, elbows on his knees, head down. He hadn't said much since they stopped. Just adjusted his gear. Checked his pouches.

Now he sat still, staring at the dirt.

Elara glanced over. "You okay?"

Kaelen didn't answer at first. Then he nodded—once. "Just thinking."

"About what?"

He hesitated.

"I dropped a blueprint."

That caught Dorian's attention. "Something important?"

Kaelen shrugged, but it wasn't casual.

"Could've been. I don't even know which one."

Kaelen paused.

"Didn't label them. Just... kept refining ideas until one stuck."

Elara stepped closer.

"You still have your tools. Your mind. It's just paper."

Kaelen's eyes didn't move.

"Yeah. But it was mine. And now it's in a place I can't go back to."

No one said anything.

Liora sat a few paces away, wringing the water from her sleeves. She opened her mouth, then closed it again.

Finally, Dorian spoke. "We'll find you more paper."

Kaelen huffed a laugh. It wasn't cheerful. "It's not about the paper."

They let the silence settle.

This was what it meant to run—not just from people, but from parts of yourself that couldn't keep up.

A sharp pulse rippled through the air—both relics glowing where they hung at Elara's and Kaelen's sides.

They froze.

Kaelen's hand went to the Forgeborne half. "You feel that?"

Elara nodded. "It's danger. But why now? We're clear of the guards."

The sky above them darkened, not with a storm but with something mechanical. A flicker of motion overhead—a drone, its frame small and angular, drifted into view. Red lights blinked on its undercarriage.

It hovered. Beeped once. Twice. Scanned.

Then it shot off, low and fast, vanishing behind the tree line.

Dorian rose slowly. "That wasn't Verdant."

"No," Kaelen said. "That was something else."

Then a voice broke the silence—low, firm, coming from somewhere just beyond the clearing.

"Come out. I know you're hiding there."

They turned as one.

The forest had gone still again.

But someone had found them.

Chapter 9: Pursued By Shadows

The forest clearing fell into a strained silence, broken only by the rhythmic ticking of Kaelen's mechanical companion and the distant rustle of leaves. The drone hovered overhead, a Forgeborne scout model—sleek, precise, inescapably menacing. Its single red sensor eye blinked twice, as if confirming what it already knew.

Kaelen didn't move. His eyes tracked the drone's arc, his breath shallow. "It's real," he murmured. "That's a V-9 Observer. Military grade. Range-finders, heat scanners, vocal imprint targeting. Fully autonomous if needed, but usually enslaved to a handler nearby."

Dorian kept his gaze on the drone. "So they know we're here."

"Worse," Kaelen said. "They know who we are."

The drone let out one final chirp, then banked left and vanished behind the treetops. Leaves fluttered in its wake, and for a second, it almost felt like nothing had changed.

For a moment, no one breathed.

Then came the voice.

Calm. Measured. Male.

"Kaelen Virel. Dorian Asher. Elara Thorne of the Verdant line. Step forward."

The three froze. Kaelen's shoulders went rigid. That voice. It shouldn't be here. Not this far from Forgeborne borders. Not in the middle of nowhere.

From the shadowed edge of the clearing, figures emerged—two enforcers in full Forgeborne combat gear, flanking a tall man with smooth, calculated movements. His armor wasn't as bulky as Aldric's—it was refined, precise, etched with utility runes and ports Kaelen recognized all too well. Modular chassis. Adaptive joints. It wasn't for intimidation. It was for efficiency.

"Clyne," Kaelen said under his breath. The name tasted like iron.

Elara whispered, "Who is he?"

Kaelen didn't answer right away. His gaze stayed locked on the Mechcrafter in the center. His old instructor. His worst influence. His best mistake.

Clyne stepped into full view. Behind him, two mechanical hounds moved in sync—sleek, predatory constructs with gleaming fangs and pulse-coils humming faintly at their sides. They made no sound, but their eyes—those same red optics—never stopped moving.

"You've improved," Clyne said, voice almost casual. "Didn't think you'd get this far. But here we are."

Kaelen took a single step forward. "Why are you here?"

"Retrieval." Clyne gestured lazily to the enforcers. "The orders are simple. I bring back the relic. Or what's left of it."

Dorian moved beside Kaelen, his posture defensive. "You're not taking anything."

"No," Clyne said evenly. "I'm giving you a choice."

He lifted a small device from his hip—a transmission key, glowing faintly.

"You come with us. No restraints. No conflict. Just cooperation. Or…"

The mechanical hounds took one synchronized step forward, their paws making no sound on the forest floor. Their mouths opened just enough to show a shimmer of internal wiring and heat vents.

"…we shift to containment protocols."

Elara's fingers tightened on her staff. "How did you find us?"

"The relic pulses. We track it. Simple. You lit up half the valley with that tree trick. And Kaelen? You're still transmitting faint biometric tags. You always were messy with calibrations."

Kaelen didn't hide the bitterness in his voice. "You taught me those calibrations."

"And now I've surpassed them," Clyne said, almost with a shrug. "I warned you years ago—no invention is ever neutral. It either serves, or it gets scrapped."

Liora's voice broke the tension. "Uh. So… this isn't part of the prophecy, right?"

No one answered.

Clyne looked at her briefly, then dismissed her entirely. His gaze returned to the trio. "You're outnumbered. Outgunned. And frankly, out of time. But I'm offering a courtesy. One chance. Surrender. Walk back on your own legs."

Kaelen stepped back beside Dorian and Elara. He didn't need to speak. The answer was already written in their stances—the slight shift of Dorian's weight to his dominant side, the way Elara adjusted her grip on her staff without realizing it, the stillness Kaelen had learned to carry when he knew a fight was inevitable.

The clearing shifted from silence to tension in a heartbeat. The fight hadn't started yet—but it had already begun.

The hounds didn't lunge. The enforcers didn't raise their weapons. That was what made it worse.

Clyne didn't need to posture. He had already won, and he knew it.

He stood at the center of the clearing with the composure of someone who had rehearsed this moment a dozen times and was now watching it unfold exactly as expected. His eyes moved past Elara and Liora without pause, as if they were terrain, not people.

"Elara Thorne," he said flatly. "You're not my concern. Nor is your companion." His gaze flicked once to Liora, then away. "Verdant matters don't intersect with my directive."

Liora's shoulders tightened. Elara shifted her stance but didn't speak. The message was clear—they weren't targets. Just irrelevant.

Clyne's full attention returned to Kaelen and Dorian. "This isn't a pursuit. This is an opportunity. Repatriation. You return. Under observation, of course. No prison. No collar. But boundaries. Terms. Structure."

Kaelen gave a bitter half-smile. "You think that's appealing?"

"I think it's inevitable." Clyne gestured slightly, and the hounds relaxed by a fraction—just enough to emphasize that they didn't need to be tense in the first place.

"You walk back now," he continued, "and your names are cleared. No charges. No exile. You'll even get your workbench back, Kaelen. Clean slate."

Dorian crossed his arms. "And what do we give up?"

"Autonomy," Clyne said without hesitation. "But you'll be alive. That's not a luxury for those who defy orders in wartime."

"You still think loyalty's about chains. I serve Forgehelm too—but I won't follow it off a cliff." Dorian responded.

Kaelen didn't respond. Not yet. His hand drifted instinctively toward his satchel, tightening around the strap like it might offer balance.

Clyne saw the gesture and smiled—thin, knowing. "About that."

He tapped a command into the transmitter at his hip. A projection flickered into life beside him—schematics, line work and arc measurements rendered in Forgeborne orange. A gauntlet. Half-complete, but unmistakably Kaelen's design.

Kaelen's breath hitched.

"Scanned during the drone flyby," Clyne said. "Low-res, but our systems filled in the gaps. Your shorthand is still sloppy, by the way. You always rushed your margin annotations."

"You didn't finish it. You guessed."

Clyne responded. "We completed it. You just didn't like the ending."

Kaelen stared at the floating design. It wasn't just a copy. It was a reassembly. Polished. Filed. Stripped of his intent and slotted into a database like it had never belonged to him.

"Already reconstructed," Clyne added. "Neatly indexed under your name. You'll find it in the Central Archive, if you ever return."

Kaelen said nothing.

He didn't have to. His silence was louder than anything he could've shouted. He wasn't just angry. He was undone.

"They were mine," he said at last. His voice was low, but it cracked.

"They were," Clyne replied, almost gently. "Now they're ours."

The hounds stood ready.

The offer still hung in the air.

But Kaelen wasn't hearing it anymore.

Clyne didn't step closer. He didn't need to. Words were his scalpel, and Kaelen was already open—exposed in a way only someone who knew him intimately could orchestrate.

"You were always the sharpest of the lot," Clyne said. "Not the strongest. Certainly not the most obedient. But clever. Efficient. Ideas bigger than your station."

Kaelen stood motionless, but his fists clenched tighter at his sides. The words weren't praise—they were a diagnosis.

"You could've redefined our systems," Clyne continued, tone almost wistful. "A new age of modular weaponry. Seamless resonance transfer. You saw those things before anyone else did."

"You sketched blueprints that the Forgeborne will be using for the next decade. But you walked out like a fool expecting the system to pause and ask permission."

"You could've been the future of Forgehelm. Instead, you became a symbol for its undoing."

Kaelen's lips twitched, but he didn't speak right away. The weight of memory hung behind his eyes.

"Maybe I figured out the system wasn't worth finishing," he said at last.

Clyne ignored it. His eyes dropped briefly to Kaelen's satchel, then back up. "Still carrying that thing around?"

Kaelen shifted slightly, too fast. A tell. "He's not a thing."

"Right. He's a reflection. That's what makes him so easy to break."

Clyne smiled. "The automaton. Wiz, was it? Emotional crutch cobbled together from scrap and sentiment. The kind of distraction we train out of proper engineers."

"You don't know anything about him," Kaelen snapped.

"Oh, I know exactly what he is," Clyne said. "A patchwork mascot. Symbol of your rebellion. Proof that you still can't let go of things you outgrew. You built a pet to clap when no one else would. Programmed applause. That's not innovation—it's loneliness with gears."

The words hit harder than a blow. Kaelen's face hardened, but his stance faltered.

Clyne made a casual hand signal.

The mechanical hounds reacted instantly—moving not toward Kaelen, but around him. Flanking. Searching. The clearing narrowed with their presence, silent but full of intent.

Kaelen turned sharply, too late.

One hound dipped low near his pack, the red sensors flashing as it locked onto a heat signature. It tilted its head, whirred, and let out a short ping.

"No—stay back—Wiz, don't—"

Wiz bolted.

The tiny automaton launched from the flap of Kaelen's satchel like a kicked gear. Sparks trailed behind him as he darted past Kaelen's legs and into the underbrush, small limbs pumping in perfect sync.

"Wiz!" Kaelen shouted, lunging a step forward.

The underbrush rustled violently as the automaton vanished into the shadows.

Clyne's smile deepened, but he didn't give chase. He didn't need to.

"You see?" he said. "Still running from everything you can't control."

Kaelen's hand hung in the air, arm extended toward where Wiz had disappeared. But he didn't move. Couldn't. The entire group watched him, but he was alone in that moment—unanchored.

Dorian shifted beside him but said nothing.

Elara's staff was lowered, but her stance wasn't passive. She was waiting—for a signal, for a target, for an excuse.

Liora took half a step forward, then stopped.

The moment stretched. Kaelen's chest rose and fell, shallow and rapid. But he didn't chase after Wiz. He didn't call again.

That was the pressure point.

Clyne had found it.

And he was pressing.

The silence shattered.

From the shadows beyond the clearing, a shrill whir of overclocked servos burst forth—thin, high-pitched, and defiant. Wiz shot back into view, his tiny frame propelled not by logic but by fury. Arms outstretched, his body vibrating with unstable power, the automaton launched himself at the nearest mechanical hound with a warble that was half-shriek, half-spark.

"No!" Kaelen shouted, too late.

Wiz struck with everything he had—five pounds of desperation against two hundred of killing design. The lead hound snapped its head up, sensors blinking as it adjusted to the new movement.

It caught him mid-air.

One metal paw clamped down around Wiz's chassis, and with a single twist, the hound spun and slammed him into a nearby tree. The impact rang through the clearing like a dropped forging hammer. Sparks exploded from Wiz's body. His limbs jerked once, twice, and then went still. Smoke curled from his back panel. A small gear rolled away into the grass, clicking faintly as it spun to a stop.

Kaelen froze.

Dorian stepped forward, hand halfway to his weapon. Elara took a breath, eyes locked on the fallen automaton. Her staff dipped slightly, as if she too had lost air from her lungs.

Liora gasped, barely stifling it with both hands. "He was just trying to help," she murmured, but the words fell flat under the weight of what had just happened.

Clyne didn't laugh. He didn't need to. The sound of metal tearing was insulting enough.

"End of your legacy," he said.

He wasn't mocking anymore. He was delivering a eulogy. Cold. Final.

Kaelen stared at the broken shape on the forest floor. Wiz, who had followed him through Forgehelm. Wiz, who had carried spare tools in his side compartment and squeaked when anxious. Wiz, who had powered through the Iron Flats. Who had walked beside him when no one else would.

Who had tried—always tried—even when the odds were stacked against him.

Kaelen's knees bent slightly. Not out of weakness, but tension. Contained fury.

He didn't speak. Didn't breathe. His mind tunneled into every moment that had led to this—the late nights soldering Wiz's circuits by dim lamplight, the experimental power cells they tested together, the jokes he made when no one else was around to laugh. Every screw and wire had meant something. And now it is gone.

Something inside Kaelen snapped—not like glass, but like a lever pulled past its resistance point.

The hesitation was gone. It burned away, fast and clean.

He didn't look at Clyne. Didn't look at the others. He stepped forward once, eyes blazing.

"I'm going to rebuild him," he said quietly, every word grounded in steel.

And then—

"And I'm going to start with you."

The threat wasn't shouted. It didn't need to be. It hung in the clearing like ozone after a lightning strike—charged, real, and about to ignite.

Dorian moved first.

He didn't shout or warn—he simply launched forward, hammer in hand, and collided with the nearest enforcer like a battering ram. The sound of metal slamming against armor reverberated through the clearing. The enforcer went flying, crashing into a tree with a bone-jarring thud.

"You two are Forgeborne. That doesn't mean you have to carry all the weight."

Elara raised her staff and thrust it toward the treeline. Vines erupted from the ground like grasping fingers, wrapping around trunks and branches to form a thick curtain of greenery. Sightlines vanished. The clearing became a fortress of roots and foliage. "They can't shoot what they can't see," she muttered.

Liora's hands flared with unstable light. "Okay, Liora. Don't screw this up. Just do anything helpful." she told herself, already panicking. She stomped the ground and flung her arms outward. A burst of wind roared from her palms, knocking over one of the mechanical hounds. It landed hard, legs flailing, its movements awkward. Not disabled, but delayed.

Kaelen didn't hesitate. He bolted for Wiz's body, skidding to a stop beside the limp automaton. One look confirmed it—sparks still hissed from exposed wiring, the core was dim. Kaelen gritted his teeth and scooped Wiz up with one arm, clutching him protectively against his chest.

From the inside of his coat, Kaelen pulled a small circular disc and slapped it against his bracer. With a mechanical chirp and a flare of blue energy, a magnetic pulse field sprang to life around him. It hummed—a shimmering dome of improvised shield tech. "Don't fail me now," he muttered.

The shield absorbed a scattershot burst from an enforcer's rifle. Kaelen flinched but held the line.

"Flank right!" Dorian called out, swinging again. His hammer connected with a second enforcer's gauntlet, cracking the armor and sending the weapon flying. The enforcer staggered back.

"Already flanked!" Kaelen shouted, ducking under a second blast and adjusting the field output. Wiz's body twitched once in his arms, and he winced. "Hang on, buddy."

Elara backed toward him, staff still glowing. "We need to split them—cut the lines-of-sight, separate the tech from the handlers."

"Done," Liora cried, another wave of air pushing foliage across the open ground. Her spell was sloppy, unstable—but it worked. Visibility dropped. The mechanical hounds hesitated, their programming faltering without clear targets.

Clyne didn't move.

He stood still in the haze of magic and mayhem, arms folded behind his back. Clyne didn't move. He watched—calm, composed, already seeing five steps ahead.

He was waiting for something.

Kaelen noticed—and that made him furious.

"Dorian!" he yelled, gesturing toward the left side of the clearing. "We move! Now!"

Dorian nodded, parried another swing, and started toward the flank. Elara fell in behind them, guiding Liora with a hand at her back.

The fight wasn't over.

But the initiative had shifted.

They weren't just reacting anymore. They were moving with purpose.

And Clyne, though unmoved, now had something new in his gaze.

Curiosity.

He wanted to see what they'd do next.

And they would show him.

With every step, every strike, every refusal to fall—they would show him.

The fracture wasn't just in their enemy's line.

It was in the hold he thought he had over them.

And it was widening.

Kaelen ducked under a blast and rolled across the damp soil, one arm still cradling Wiz's broken body. The forest floor scraped at his skin, but he didn't stop. When he came up, he reached behind his belt and yanked out his old standby—a thick-forged wrench, scarred from years of field repairs and sleepless nights. The weight felt familiar in his grip. Grounding. Like an old voice in his palm saying, "You've survived worse."

He charged.

An enforcer met him halfway. Kaelen swung low, the wrench colliding with the armored shin, knocking the soldier off balance. Sparks flared from the impact. He pivoted for a follow-up strike, twisting his body into the momentum—but the soldier recovered faster than expected. The butt of a rifle slammed into Kaelen's ribs, stealing the breath from his lungs. Pain rippled outward.

The wrench flew from his hand.

Kaelen hit the ground hard, coughing, vision flickering at the edges. He rolled onto his back, barely able to shield himself.

Across the field, Clyne stepped forward for the first time.

He didn't run. He didn't shout. He simply raised his arm.

The gauntlet on his right hand flickered to life—sleek metal segments locking into place with a hiss of pneumatics. No blade. No weapon casing. Just seamless form. Pure, refined utility. Arcs of static pulsed along its surface, dancing from his knuckles to his wrist, coiling like restrained serpents.

Then he moved.

Not fast. Not showy. Just deliberate. Efficient.

Kaelen scrambled to his feet, still clutching Wiz protectively. His chest burned, ribs protesting every breath. He swung anyway—bare knuckles, full of heat and instinct.

Clyne caught the punch mid-air, barely needing to shift. With a smooth twist, he turned Kaelen's arm and sent him stumbling. The gauntlet flared again—an elegant flick of the wrist discharging a shallow arc of current. It nicked Kaelen's shoulder, sending a jolt through his spine. He staggered, teeth clenched against the shock.

But something else sparked.

Kaelen's eyes locked on the gauntlet. Not the glow. Not the force. The design.

The way it moved.

It wasn't a weapon—it was a philosophy.

No bulk. No handle. No distance between thought and execution.

Not a tool. Not a copied schematic. Not a borrowed design from a half-read textbook.

An extension.

His breath caught—not from pain, but revelation.

It wasn't repurposed tech. It wasn't a patchwork idea from someone else's discarded notes. It didn't beg for approval.

It belonged to Clyne. Completely. That was the part that cut deepest.

And Kaelen realized, for the first time, that he had never built something entirely his. Not really.

Not yet.

He could do better.

He would do better.

Not to mimic. Not to impress. But to break away from everything that told him what invention should be.

He ducked another strike, turned low, and swept his leg at Clyne's knees. The motion wasn't elegant—it was raw, born of street fights and workshop brawls. But it worked. Clyne stumbled, just enough.

Kaelen didn't press the advantage with another gadget. He stepped forward, fists raised.

His stance was uneven. Guard too high. Shoulders too tight.

But it was his.

He lunged again—fist-first.

Sloppy.

But bold.

And it landed.

Clyne staggered half a step. Not from force. From surprise.

Not just at the hit.

But at the shift.

The fight had changed.

And Kaelen wasn't fighting like a student anymore.

He was fighting like someone who had nothing left to prove—except to himself.

Liora stood near the edge of the clearing, heart pounding, hands trembling at her sides. The battle unfolded in staccato bursts—Kaelen staggering from Clyne's gauntlet, Dorian locked in a brutal exchange with a second enforcer, Elara holding back a flanking charge with rapidly thinning vines. The forest around them seemed to contract, drawn tight by tension and smoke.

She wasn't strong enough to stop any of it. But she couldn't stand still.

Liora's breaths came shallow and fast. Her pulse thudded against her ears. She took a shaky step forward, eyes wide as chaos played out in front of her. She saw Kaelen bleeding from the shoulder, trying to hold his ground with bare fists. She saw the mechanical hounds circling back into formation, relentless. She saw Elara biting back exhaustion as her spells faltered.

Liora closed her eyes for half a second and stretched her arms wide.

"Elements, listen," she whispered. "Please, just this once."

She called them all.

Wind came first—immediate, too eager. It surged around her, lifting her off her heels and throwing leaves and ash into the fray. It knocked Elara's staff off course and sent Kaelen's coat whipping sideways. One of the mechanical hounds miscalculated its step, sliding in the churned-up mud. Unhelpful, but not entirely useless.

Then water. It answered slow, pooling in the soil beneath her feet. It trembled, then burst upward in a geyser where no one stood. A tree branch groaned, soaked from the sudden pressure, and snapped under its own weight with a dull crack. Steam hissed into the air.

Earth followed.

That was the one that answered properly.

With a thunderous crack, the ground beneath the second mechanical hound gave way. A jagged rock, swollen and twisted by Verdant energy, surged upward with the force of a battering ram. It slammed into the underside of the hound, lifting the entire construct off its feet and hurling it into a nearby tree.

The impact shattered bark. The hound crumpled, limbs spasming from internal damage. The core inside its chest flickered and died.

Liora fell to one knee, gasping. Her hands were smoking faintly, tinged with soil and sap. She looked up through blurred vision.

It wasn't clean. It wasn't graceful.

But it worked.

The sudden shock in the enemy's formation rippled outward. Dorian turned and dropped his current opponent with a crack of his hammer, while Elara stepped forward and launched a precise volley of thorny vines at the last enforcer, forcing them into a defensive crouch. The vines wrapped fast and tight, pinning one arm to the enforcer's side.

Kaelen saw the shift, too.

He didn't wait for orders.

He charged forward, a fresh roar building in his chest, and forced Clyne to take a step back for the first time since entering the clearing.

"Fall back," Clyne ordered flatly. "Now."

The remaining enforcers moved quickly, grabbing what they could and retreating into the underbrush. One of them limped, dragging a twisted ankle. Another kept a rifle raised in case the retreat turned into a rout.

Clyne lingered for one heartbeat longer. His eyes swept across all three of them—Kaelen, Elara, Dorian. Then to Liora.

Then he met Kaelen's eyes.

"This isn't over."

"No," Kaelen said. "It's finally started."

And just like that, Clyne vanished into the trees, melting into the undergrowth like smoke slipping through fingers.

Liora, still panting, looked around the clearing. Her arms were trembling now, and her legs barely held her upright. "Did I—was that...?"

"You tipped it," Elara said, stepping through the wreckage and offering her a hand.

Liora blinked. "On purpose?"

Elara didn't answer. Just helped her up.

Dorian walked past them both, quiet, glancing down at the crumpled hound. Then at Liora.

"Whatever it was," he said, "it was enough."

But for the first time, Liora didn't feel like a mistake.

She felt like part of something.

And this time, no one tried to take it away from her.

They didn't run so much as stumble.

The clearing behind them faded into fog and ruin. The trees that had once seemed distant and reverent now loomed in silence, like sentinels bearing witness to a fight that wasn't finished. No one said a word. No one dared to. Dorian led the group deeper into the grove, one hand pressed tight against the gash in his side. Each breath sounded ragged, shallow, forced. Blood soaked the edge of his tunic, leaving a dark trail on the moss-lined path with every dragging step.

Elara moved behind him, summoning glowroots with a wave of her staff. Thin tendrils of bioluminescent vines rose from the soil, curling up like small spirits. They pulsed with a pale green light, illuminating the twisted roots and uneven ground just enough to keep them from tripping. It wasn't enough to feel safe. Just enough to see where their feet landed—and to see each other's weariness reflected back.

Kaelen lagged slightly behind, clutching Wiz's frame close to his chest. The automaton still sparked faintly, the shell dented and scorched beyond anything Wiz had endured before. One of his arms hung at a crooked angle, the light in Wiz's sensor eye dim but flickering now and then, as if he were dreaming in code. Kaelen didn't speak. His grip never loosened, and his eyes never left the trail. Like if he looked away—even once—Wiz might vanish from his arms.

Liora trailed the rear. Her cloak dragged through wet undergrowth, heavy with muck and wet soil. Her hands were still smudged with dirt and residue from her last, chaotic spell. She kept glancing at the others—Kaelen's hunched shoulders, Dorian's bleeding side, Elara's silent focus—as if waiting for someone to yell, to snap at her, to confirm the guilt she already carried. Her lips were pressed into a hard line, and every snapped twig underfoot made her flinch.

They passed under twisted boughs, the branches low and heavy with age. The canopy thickened, muting the light and muffling the world. The deeper they went, the quieter the forest became—as though even the birds had decided not to intrude.

When they finally stopped, it wasn't because they found safety.

It was because they couldn't walk any further.

Dorian slumped against the base of an old tree, his breathing uneven. Blood soaked through the bandage Elara had tried to apply mid-walk. She dropped to her knees beside him again, hands glowing faintly with healing light, and pressed them gently against his wound. He winced but didn't move away. Neither of them spoke.

Kaelen knelt beside a fallen log and gently set Wiz down atop it. He removed his coat and laid it beneath the automaton's frame, shielding it from the cold ground. He didn't try to repair him. Not yet. He just stared, as though memorizing every scorch mark, every misaligned hinge, every little detail that made Wiz more than just a machine.

Liora stood apart, arms wrapped tightly around herself. She looked between them all, eyes wide, guilt written in every line of her face. Then she looked down at the ground. She opened her mouth once, then shut it. When she finally spoke, it was barely louder than the wind.

"I almost killed us. Again."

No one answered. Not because she was wrong—but because it wasn't the time for blame. Or forgiveness. The silence that followed wasn't harsh. Just hollow.

Elara sat back on her heels, wiping blood from her fingers. "We're still here," she said softly.

Kaelen didn't look up. "For now."

Dorian leaned back against the tree. "That was a message. Not just a retrieval."

"A warning," Elara added. "We're not out of reach anymore."

Liora slowly sat on a moss-covered rock, still hugging her arms. "I don't think I can do this. I'm not like you."

Kaelen finally looked up. His voice was tired but firm. "None of us were ready for this. Doesn't mean we stop."

They had survived.

But it wasn't a victory.

It was a fracture, raw and spreading.

But it had motion.

And sometimes, motion was the only thing that kept you from breaking entirely.

The others slept, or tried to. Dorian leaned back against the tree trunk, his breathing steady but shallow, a strip of bloodied cloth pressed to his side. Elara sat cross-legged nearby, her staff resting across her lap, eyes half-lidded in meditation between shifts of healing pulses. Liora had curled into her cloak, knees to chest, unmoving except for the occasional twitch of a dream she likely wouldn't remember.

Kaelen didn't sleep.

His mind refused the stillness. The memory of Wiz's impact, Clyne's voice, and the sight of the gauntlet danced behind his eyes like static.

He waited until Elara's last spell flickered out and the forest stilled—until even the hum of danger seemed to ebb. He didn't think Clyne had stayed. That kind of man didn't retreat to hide. He retreated to report.

So, without a word, he rose and slipped away, moving through the trees in silence. The forest floor was soft underfoot, scattered with fallen leaves and broken branches, damp with the lingering scent of smoke.

He followed the same path they'd taken in retreat, but now in reverse. The world felt different in his absence—emptier, stripped of the urgency that had driven them. The clearing came into view, ghostly in the moonlight, with its wreckage frozen in the stillness of the aftermath.

The clearing looked undisturbed—no fresh footprints, no humming drones overhead. Whatever command Clyne followed, he hadn't circled back.

A faint shimmer pulsed across the field—Elara's doing. A subtle warning ward, left in case the enforcers returned. It hadn't gone off.

That meant he was alone. Probably.

Scorched bark marked where lightning had hit. Pieces of fractured tech lay strewn across the clearing like discarded bones. One of the mechanical hounds still lay half-buried where Liora's magic had thrown it, the core exposed and flickering faintly. The remnants of the fight were not just evidence—they were opportunities.

Kaelen stepped into the mess like it was a workbench.

He moved silently, methodically. Not hunting. Not mourning. Just collecting. His hands moved with precision, plucking parts from ruin with the same care he used to take in assembling delicate charge valves. His mind wasn't replaying what was lost—it was sorting, designing, adapting.

He knew it was reckless. He also knew no one else would understand what these pieces meant—not the way he did.

He knelt beside the shattered gauntlet Clyne had used. Its surface still hummed with residual energy. He touched it carefully, then pried loose two intact servo coils from the casing. He rolled them in his palm, feeling the tension wound into the metal, the potential still locked inside. Compact. Reliable. Useful.

Next, he moved to the mechanical hound. The plating was warped but salvageable in parts. He ran his fingers across the torn metal, tapping lightly until he heard the hollow ping of an unruptured segment. Beneath a layer of dust, a fractured joint node caught the moonlight. Kaelen extracted it, cleaned it with the edge of his sleeve, and tucked it into his satchel.

He paused then, crouched among wreckage and ruin.

Each piece went in without ceremony. No sketches. No blueprints. No measuring or marking. He wasn't mapping something.

He was building toward it.

Kaelen stood and looked around the clearing once more, his eyes sweeping over the battlefield not as a graveyard—but as a blueprint. Every broken circuit, every scorched fragment, was a line in something new.

Armor. Not decoration.

Not rank.

Just function.

He reached to his belt, pulled out the old wrench—the same one he'd fought with, trained with, nearly died gripping. The symbol of everything he had clung to when nothing else made sense.

He turned it over in his hand, thumb brushing the worn grip.

Then, without fanfare, he set it down at the base of a tree. Not buried. Not broken. Just placed. A tool, retired with respect.

The past didn't need to be destroyed.

It just didn't belong to this version of him anymore.

"I saw enough to remember the structure," Kaelen said quietly. "But it's not his blueprint I want—it's the flaw."

He turned and walked back through the trees, his steps heavier but his heart steadier. The servo coils clinked faintly in his pocket. Behind his eyes, the first sketch of something new began to take shape—not drawn on parchment, but engraved in purpose.

"The next time I build something," he said, wiping ash from his cheek, "Not until I know it won't be taken again."

His evolution had begun.

Quietly.

But with purpose.

The forest clearing was silent again.

Not peaceful—just emptied. The air hung thick with the residue of smoke and ozone, a haunting stillness settling over the remnants of conflict. The trees bore fresh scars—burned bark, fractured limbs, blackened roots that crackled beneath the lightest step. The underbrush was trampled, the moss turned to mud beneath the scuffle of boots and claws. Shattered plating from fallen hounds glinted dully in the moonlight.

Clyne sat alone on a moss-dusted stone near the center of the clearing. His posture was casual, but there was a weight to his stillness. One leg crossed over the other, hands folded calmly in his lap. His gauntlet, dark and dormant now, rested across his knee like a relic cooling after use. Its energy coils had faded to a soft blue-gray. Silent. But not forgotten.

Above him, the drone hovered in a slow, deliberate arc. It moved without urgency, sweeping from side to side like a pendulum. Its sensors blinked in rhythm—red, green, red again—scanning the battlefield, recording data, silently parsing movement signatures left in the soil and air.

Clyne tilted his head slightly, speaking aloud with the same surgical calm he brought to engineering labs and interrogation rooms. The words weren't for the drone—they were for the log.

"Subject escaped. Combat protocol not authorized. Tracking beacon deployed. Awaiting next position."

The drone emitted a soft two-tone beep in acknowledgment. A confirmation pulse blinked across its lower console.

Clyne reached inside his coat and pulled free a slim projection disc. With a flick of his thumb, he activated it. A soft hum preceded the light, and a schematic display shimmered to life in midair. The image rotated slowly: Kaelen's satchel, rendered in cold, precise lines. Zoomed in, a single point of red pulsed at the edge of the rear strap.

A tag.

Placed with surgical timing. Quiet. Undetectable during the chaos.

Clyne studied the projection in silence for several seconds, watching the red dot blink like a heartbeat. There was no malice in his eyes—just purpose. The slow machinery of a larger plan grinding into motion.

He reached forward and tapped the display once. Coordinates populated beneath the schematic.

No smile. No reaction. Just the next step unfolding.

Just inevitability.

"Forgehelm is watching," he said, almost to himself.

He flicked the disc again. The projection folded into itself and vanished with a faint hiss.

The drone rose a meter higher, pivoted toward the tree line, then began to drift westward—silent and invisible in the night canopy.

Somewhere, deep in the woods where Kaelen now walked—unaware, exhausted, and half-focused on salvaged coils and fractured tech—a faint red light blinked beneath the stitching of his satchel.

They hadn't shaken the Forgeborne.

They'd invited them.

And now, they were being watched.

Every step.

Every word.

Marked not just by a beacon.

But by a question hanging in the dark:

Will Forgehelm's prodigal sons be able to escape its shadow?

Chapter 10: Marked

The trail had no end—just more rock, more dust, more angles wrong for walking. Kaelen stepped over a sun-cracked root, half-sure it shifted behind him. He didn't check. No one was talking.

Elara paused mid-step.

The relic at her side gave a faint pulse—nothing strong, just enough to tug at her awareness.

She glanced over her shoulder, frowning.

Kaelen asked. "What is it?"

"I don't know. Just… static. Like danger, but distant."

"Residual tension. We've been running for days." Dorian added.

Elara didn't argue. But her fingers stayed near the relic for the next mile.

A rustle to the east snapped them alert. Kaelen crouched, one hand on his wrench. But it was only a juvenile mossboar—thin, scarred, and more frightened than them.

Dorian's hand pressed low on his side. The bandage beneath his coat had gone from white to rust hours ago. He walked like it didn't matter, but his limp said otherwise.

Elara glanced his way. Once. Then again. Still, she said nothing.

Liora broke the silence. "Do you think we're almost there, or do you think Nocturne's Edge is just a myth invented to keep wanderers busy?"

No one answered. Kaelen checked Wiz instead. It gave a weak series of chirps—three long, one short—then went silent again.

"Still working on a sense of humor," Kaelen muttered.

Elara slowed her steps, then stopped. "Dorian."

He paused mid-stride, but didn't turn.

"Let me see it."

He hesitated, then relented, pulling back the edge of his coat. Blood had seeped through the cloth again, darker now, thicker. Elara knelt beside him, already unrolling fresh bandages.

"Sit."

Dorian obeyed with a grimace.

The others gave them space.

Her fingers moved efficiently, but not indifferently. Her fingers worked quickly—too quickly. But not carelessly. When she wrapped the bandage around his side, her hand brushed his.

She didn't pull back.

Neither did he.

When she tied the final knot, she lingered. Just a second too long.

Dorian watched her, but said nothing. When she stood, he did too.

No one mentioned it. The group kept walking.

The trail didn't get easier. But none of them asked to stop.

"That slope over there," she said, "if we hug the edge and cut east, we might shave half a day."

Dorian followed her gaze, unimpressed. "That's a cliff."

"It's cliff-adjacent," Liora said. "Totally passable. I think. Probably."

Elara didn't even look. "We'll stick to the forest."

Kaelen grunted. "One miracle at a time."

Liora threw up her hands. "Fine. But when we're running from death tomorrow, I'm saying 'I told you so' on the way down."

The sun hadn't risen yet, but the sky had begun to shift—blue and pale around the edges, like something hesitant to return. The forest quieted. Even the birds seemed to hold their breath. The trail ahead was still shrouded in mist, damp from dew and the scent of moss thick in the air. The only sound was the soft crunch of boots on damp leaves and the occasional chirp of a tired machine.

Kaelen hissed, flinging a component into the underbrush.

"That one was burning. Residual current, maybe. Or worse."

Dorian looked at Kaelen. "You sure it wasn't tagged?"

Kaelen shaking his head. "Didn't get a ping. Nothing active. If it was, the relic would've screamed."

"Can we just not take souvenirs from people trying to kill us next time?" Liora added.

Kaelen didn't respond. But later, when no one was looking, he checked the lining of his satchel again.

Kaelen felt the heat first.

It pulsed through the strap of his satchel, subtle at first, then sharp enough to sting. He stopped in his tracks and swung the bag around, unbuckling the flap. Inside, buried beneath coiled wires, notes, and scavenged plating, a faint orange glow pulsed from the base of a fractured servo unit—one of the pieces he'd recovered from Clyne's gauntlet.

"Wait," he said sharply.

The others halted. Dorian's hand went to his hammer, instinct taking over. Elara shifted her weight, staff angled low and ready. Liora blinked, already tensing for another incoming threat.

"It's not the relic," Kaelen added quickly, seeing the alarm in Elara's eyes. "I'd know if it was."

He reached in and pulled the component free. Half-melted and still warm, the metal thrummed with a rhythmic pulse—not unlike a heartbeat. It was too steady, too structured to be ambient energy. Something was wrong.

Elara stepped closer and opened the pouch at her side. Her half of the relic sat still in its cradle—no hum, no pulse, no reaction. She frowned. "Then what is it?"

Kaelen turned the piece over in his hands, brow furrowing. The pulsing didn't waver. He looked at the array of circuits, and a creeping realization settled in.

"It's not a beacon," he muttered. "Not exactly."

Liora leaned in, eyes narrowed. "Then what is it?"

The words tasted bitter as he said them. "A data node. Live… Clyne must've wired it for remote sync—probably to monitor field performance in real time. Which means…"

Dorian's face darkened. "They've been watching us."

Kaelen nodded grimly. "Since the fight. Maybe longer if the sync was running before I even picked it up."

He dropped to one knee and pulled out a slim tool from his belt. Sparks lit as he pried at the casing. A small cluster of micro-tethers twitched like nerves. One twist—nothing. The second twist made the glow sputter. The third cracked the housing entirely, and the pulse died with a soft electrical whine.

Smoke rose in a thin line, curling into the canopy like the last breath of a dying signal.

For a long moment, the group stood still. No one spoke.

Then Elara said what none of them wanted to admit.

"They know exactly where we are."

Kaelen stood slowly, brushing dust off his hands. "Not anymore. But they'll know where we were and in which direction. Maybe how many of us. Maybe more."

Dorian scanned the treetops like he expected drones to descend. "So what now?"

"We move," Kaelen said. "Fast. Silent if we can, but fast either way."

Liora swallowed, tightening her pack. Her face had gone pale. "So… there's a chance more are already inbound?"

Kaelen didn't answer. He didn't have to.

The trail behind them wasn't just a memory now.

It was a record.

Kaelen tossed another hot coil into the dirt with a hiss, shaking out his fingers.

"I don't like this," he muttered.

Dorian glanced over. "That makes all of us."

Then—snap.

A sharp crack echoed through the trees. Too loud. Too clean. Not the wind.

Everyone froze.

Kaelen dropped into a crouch. Elara pressed a hand to her relic. It pulsed once—then went still.

Liora had already ducked behind a root, her voice barely audible. "That was close. Real close."

Dorian shifted his weight, eyes narrowed toward the sound. "North ridge. Ten meters out."

Kaelen whispered, "Is it them?"

No one answered.

For a moment, they stayed like that—half-breaths, twitching fingers, nerves coiled tight. Then a shadow moved behind the underbrush—

—and bolted.

Not a patrol.

Just a lean forest deer, white-striped, startled and gone before anyone could breathe.

Liora winced. "Okay. New rule. No dramatic twig snapping unless you're about to die."

Kaelen stood slowly. "Could've been worse."

Elara didn't relax. "That's the problem. It still could be."

The signal had been quieted, but not before it sang its location to whoever was listening.

Elara glanced at her relic again.

Still nothing.

"Maybe it was just nerves," she muttered.

In the trees behind them, high on a distant ridge, a drone flickered past.

They hadn't been followed.

They'd been tracked.

And now they had to outrun what came next.

They moved faster now, but not together. The silence between them had changed—no longer cautious, but brittle. The forest had narrowed into denser undergrowth, forcing them into a single file. Kaelen walked ahead, his shoulders rigid, Wiz tucked protectively against his side. His steps were deliberate, but the tightness in his grip betrayed the storm inside him.

Dorian followed, boots landing hard enough to announce every step. The wound at his side had reopened slightly, the blood seeping through the fresh wrap Elara had tied that morning. Still, he said nothing. He didn't need to. The tension between them was a living thing now—dense, like the air before a lightning strike.

It was Dorian who broke first.

"You should've left that piece behind," he said, voice low but cutting. "Your habit of collecting junk nearly got us killed."

Kaelen didn't turn. "It wasn't junk. It was data. Insight. Things we'll need if we want a shot at staying ahead of them."

"You gave them a shot at us instead."

Kaelen stopped walking and rounded on him, boots skidding slightly on the damp forest floor. "We can't all fight with hammers and good intentions. Some of us have to build solutions from the scraps we're given."

Dorian stepped forward, eyes narrowed. "Some of us know when to stop tinkering and pay attention to the threat breathing down our necks."

Kaelen's fists clenched at his sides, shoulders tight as cable wire.

Elara stepped between them, arms slightly raised—not defensive, just a barrier. "That's enough," she said, voice firm but quiet. "We don't have time for this."

Dorian didn't say anything—but backed off. Kaelen turned sharply and resumed walking, muttering under his breath.

The silence that followed wasn't peace. It was distance. Liora trailed behind them, hands jammed into her sleeves, eyes on the ground. She glanced up once, hoping someone would break the silence. No one did.

"I liked it better when the trees were trying to kill us," she muttered. It wasn't loud, but loud enough.

No one laughed. But the tension shifted, softened. Kaelen's pace eased slightly. Dorian adjusted his grip on the hammer across his back. Elara offered the faintest smile—nothing more, but it was enough.

They kept moving.

A gust of wind passed overhead. Elara froze, her grip on her staff tightening as she scanned the trees.

"That wasn't natural," she said under her breath.

"I'll check ahead," Liora offered suddenly. Her voice was too casual, but her eyes were alert.

Dorian looked at her sideways. "You?"

"I can sneak," she insisted. "Or at least... not stomp. And if I die, I promise to scream helpfully."

Elara's eyes tracked Liora for a second. "Don't go far. Just eyes, Liora. No heroics."

Liora gave a crooked salute with the wrong hand, then ducked beneath a low branch and disappeared into the underbrush.

The path bent again, climbing into a thicker stretch of moss-covered roots and leaning trees. When the terrain leveled and the heat of the argument had cooled to a dull memory, Elara stepped closer to Dorian. She didn't speak. Just reached out and placed a hand on his shoulder as they walked.

It lingered a second too long to be just reassurance.

He didn't flinch. His posture straightened slightly. When she moved ahead again, his eyes followed her for a while.

Kaelen glanced over his shoulder once. He didn't say anything either. Just kept walking, his eyes fixed forward, but something about his stride had changed—less rigid, more focused.

Liora came back breathless, leaves in her hair and twigs caught in her sleeve. She grinned as she dropped into a crouch.

"Good news—nothing waiting to murder us. Bad news—I face planted into a fern. We are now emotionally bonded."

The group moved on. Together.

The sky darkened slightly as clouds drifted in, blotting out what little warmth the morning had offered. The canopy above thickened, knitted branches forming an uneven ceiling that left only fractured shafts of light to fall below. Damp air clung to their skin. The forest felt closer now—tighter, more aware.

It started as a faint hum. Just a tremor in the silence. Then it grew—a rising note of artificial tension, sharp and mechanical. It vibrated through the trees like something searching.

Kaelen froze. "Drone," he hissed.

All of them dropped low.

They scrambled beneath a tangle of roots that had grown from the hillside, arching overhead like a ribcage. Elara pressed herself into the dirt beside Dorian, her staff tucked close. Kaelen ducked in last, clutching Wiz to his chest, the automaton's frame making a soft whir of distress. Liora scrambled in behind him, her sleeve catching on a root. The moss snagged against her tunic as she squeezed in, face pale.

The drone passed overhead, its undercarriage blinking red. The buzz intensified, rising to a high whine as it hovered. Its movement wasn't random. It swept in deliberate arcs—left, pause, right, pause—as if listening for something more than sound. The shadows above twisted as it scanned, red light flickering like a warning brand.

Liora's breathing quickened. She clenched her fists. The air around her shimmered, disturbed by the surge of unstable magic coiling beneath her skin.

"Don't," Elara whispered sharply, grabbing Liora's wrist.

"I can't hold it," Liora whispered, voice cracking.

"Yes, you can." Elara's tone hardened. "Focus. You're not alone."

Liora squeezed her eyes shut. Slowly, the shimmer faded. Her hands steadied. The glow bled out into stillness.

The drone paused above them, its red light pulsing in place.

Kaelen reached into his belt pouch. His fingers fumbled through scraps and salvaged remnants until they found the slim sink coil—a hacked-together frequency jammer from a piece of old Forgeborne wreckage. One use left. Maybe. He didn't hesitate.

He twisted the dial and pressed the core. The coil vibrated, emitting a faint pulse of feedback—barely audible, but just enough. The red light on the drone blinked once. It twitched mid-air, let out a static chirp, and veered away west.

The sound faded. The silence returned.

Kaelen dropped the burnt-out coil into the mud beside him. It hissed on contact.

"That was our last clean jammer," he muttered, voice flat.

"Are you sure it worked?" Dorian asked, his grip still on his hammer.

Kaelen nodded once. "If it hadn't, we wouldn't be having this conversation."

They waited another minute. Another two. Then crawled out from under the roots, one by one, muscles aching from the tension.

Liora wiped her palms on her cloak. "I don't like hiding."

"Then next time, stay quiet," Dorian said, a little sharper than he meant.

Liora didn't argue. She just nodded, still shaken.

Elara looked to Kaelen. "We'll need another plan. Something longer-term. That drone wasn't random."

"No," Kaelen agreed. "That was a sweep. Coordinated. They're not just looking anymore. They're closing in."

He looked down at his belt—his tools lighter, his pouch emptier.

The forest had always felt alive. But now, it felt like a trap.

They kept moving, feet crunching the damp leaves, every glance cast upward.

The grove no longer offered shelter.

And Kaelen had one less tool to protect them.

They'd bought time. But the cost was catching up.

They made camp in silence. Not because they wanted to—but because there was nothing left to say.

The clearing they chose was half-sheltered by a broken canopy and ringed by thick roots that curved in like bent fingers. No fire. No warmth. Just the muted glow of Elara's staff, planted upright in the soil and pulsing faintly like a heartbeat too slow. The light was enough to see each other's silhouettes, nothing more.

Kaelen sat with his back to a moss-covered stone, tools scattered in a semicircle around him. Wiz lay across his lap, core flickering like an injured eye. He didn't speak as he worked. Every movement was careful—tightening a bracket here, realigning a limb there. He didn't hum, didn't sigh, didn't curse. The silence was full of focus and fatigue.

Liora sat nearby, legs tucked beneath her. She hummed, soft and aimless—an old Verdant melody, maybe, or something she made up to fill the space. It didn't mask the weight in the air, but it softened the edges of it. Her hands stayed clasped in her lap, knuckles white from the strain she wasn't showing on her face.

Kaelen stood and sat nearby, adjusting a wire in Wiz's frame. He glanced over. "You're quiet."

"Trying something new," she muttered. "Don't ruin it."

He didn't. Not right away.

After a while, she said, "Do you ever feel like you missed the moment when you were supposed to matter?"

Kaelen didn't look up from his work. "Constantly."

Liora nodded once, then smiled without teeth. "Cool. Just checking."

Dorian sat against a twisted tree trunk, eyes half-lidded but not asleep. He hadn't spoken since the drone. His breathing had evened out, but the tension in his shoulders never left. Blood had dried along the edge of his tunic. Elara approached slowly, her cloak brushing the ground behind her.

"Let me look again," she said.

He didn't argue. He just shifted, pulling back the fabric.

The wound had closed but not cleanly. The edges were angry, the skin around it swollen and tender. Elara crouched beside him, her fingers cool as she inspected it.

"You're going to scar," she said softly.

Dorian gave a faint smirk. "Means I get to remember it right."

She didn't answer. But she didn't move away, either.

She dipped her fingers into a small vial at her hip—some mixture of sap and Verdant herbs—and pressed it gently to the wound. Dorian didn't flinch.

"My magic," she murmured, "grovecaller healing—it doesn't work well with Forgeborne wounds. Your body pushes back against the energy. Too much iron in the blood. Too much heat."

"Doesn't surprise me," Dorian said. "We were built to resist interference."

"Or connection," Elara said quietly.

Their eyes met. Neither looked away.

After a long pause, she bandaged the wound again, hands steady, then rose to her feet without another word. But she lingered there a moment longer than necessary.

Kaelen watched from the edge of his work but said nothing. He returned to his repairs, eyes narrowing as he adjusted Wiz's damaged leg.

The fireless camp held its breath. The tension hadn't vanished. But it had shifted—no longer a threat, but something quieter. Something waiting.

They didn't rest easy.

But they rested.

The trail picked up again at dawn, the forest around them painted in bleached grey and hues of muted green. The clouds above hung low and heavy, stealing the color from the sky. Fog clung to the underbrush like old breath, curling around their legs as they pushed forward through uneven ground and damp soil. Every step sank just slightly into the ground, their boots leaving behind tracks that the moss would erase within hours.

No one spoke. Not from tension this time—but from exhaustion.

It was Elara who stopped first.

Her eyes caught something out of place—just beyond a knot of bramble, tangled and wet with dew. She raised a hand for the others to pause, then moved forward slowly, carefully. The others watched in silence as she crouched by the thorns.

Among the twisting branches, a scrap of cloth fluttered faintly. It was small, stained, partially hidden in the green. Elara reached forward, threading her fingers through the thorns with grace. She avoided each barb like she'd done it a hundred times before. When the fabric came loose with a soft tear, she held it up.

It was a bloodied bandage, unraveling at the edges. At first, it looked like a simple piece of discarded cloth—another leftover from one of the many skirmishes that had bled into the forest. But then Elara turned it over, her brows drawing together.

There—woven into the inner lining—was a greenish-gold thread. Subtle. But unmistakable.

She brought the fabric closer to her face, inhaling slightly. A faint scent rose from it. Herbal. Sharp. Precise.

"Kingsward," she murmured.

Kaelen stepped forward, careful not to step on any of the thorns. "What is that?"

"A healing herb," Elara replied. "It grows in the deepest sanctums of Verdant groves—only there. It's almost impossible to cultivate outside that environment. And even harder to preserve." She ran her thumb over the stain. "But this isn't just Kingsward. It's processed. Royal-apothecary level."

She looked up, eyes shadowed beneath her hood. "Only one group uses this."

Dorian's brow lifted. "Is that going to be a problem?"

Liora had been watching quietly but now stepped closer, her voice hushed and reverent. "The Verdant Royalty."

The words lingered in the space between them, heavy as stone.

Kaelen glanced between them, then to Elara. "Your people?"

She shook her head. "Not quite. My superiors. My protectors—once. But not allies. I don't know anymore."

"So either they're close," Dorian said, "or they passed through recently."

"They don't pass through anywhere randomly," Elara added. "If they're here, they're tracking someone."

Liora stepped back from the thorn patch. "Kingsward breaks down quickly. That smell? It fades fast. If we can still sense it, they can't be far."

Kaelen took the bandage from Elara's hand and turned it over, inspecting the frayed threads. "It was torn. Rushed. Someone left it behind in a hurry. Not deliberate."

Elara nodded. "Whoever used this wasn't trying to leave a trail."

"Which means they're either being hunted," Dorian said, "or doing the hunting."

The group stood still, each processing what that could mean.

Elara folded the bandage with a care that bordered on reverence and tucked it into one of her pouches. Her fingers lingered over the flap for a second before securing it.

"If the Royals are this close," she said quietly, "they'll see everything. Hear everything. Even if they're not looking for us now, we're in their path."

"And they don't ask questions when they find someone," Liora added. "They assume answers."

"Then we keep moving," Kaelen said. "Quiet. No trails. No mistakes."

Dorian shifted his grip on his hammer. "We're running out of forest to disappear into."

They set off again with more urgency, but the air had changed. Not from fear alone—but from possibility.

Hope stirred in the thought that they weren't alone. That someone might be ahead. Someone who could help.

But behind that flicker of hope, something colder took root:

If the Verdant Royalty were near, danger wasn't just close.

It was inevitable.

They had walked in silence for another hour. The terrain had begun to slope upward, and the fog slowly thinned, but the forest around them remained dense—old trees with bark like folded leather and moss so thick it muted their steps.

Then it came—a sound that didn't belong to the wind or bird or branch.

A bird call.

But not just any call. Three chirps, a pause, then one short trill. It echoed once through the canopy, then faded.

Elara stopped like she'd been struck.

The others turned to her.

Her eyes scanned the trees, every muscle in her body suddenly alert. But not afraid. Focused.

Elara's brow furrowed. "That call… it could be him."

The second bird call came—three chirps, pause, one trill.

She straightened, eyes wide. "No. That is him."

Kaelen furrowed his brow. "Who?"

She stepped forward slowly, eyes still fixed on the canopy. "When we were little… we used to run off into the groves. The palace was—too much sometimes. Tarian and I would sneak out, and that call—it was how we'd find each other again. One of us would hide. The other would follow the sound."

Another call echoed. Same pattern. Same rhythm.

Elara turned toward it, the bandage with Kingsward all but forgotten in her pouch.

"It's him."

Dorian glanced at Liora, then back at Elara. "Is that good news?"

Elara nodded, her voice firmer than it had been in days. "If he's near, we're not alone. And we're not being hunted. Not by him."

Kaelen checked the horizon through the trees. "Then let's not lose the signal."

They moved again—but faster now, with direction. For the first time in days, Elara's steps led with certainty.

Whatever came next, they were no longer chasing shadows.

Someone was out there.

And he remembered her.

Liora stayed near the back, still clutching the edge of her cloak.

"So," she whispered to Kaelen and Dorian, "either someone's coming to rescue us, or that bird call was Verdant code for 'run faster.'"

Dorian gave her a sidelong look. "Always helpful."

"I am helpful," she said, a little too defensively. "Statistically. Sometimes."

Kaelen smirked. "You're improving."

Liora grinned. "And that's the scariest part."

<hr>

The bird call echoed again—three chirps, pause, one trill—guiding them like a thread through the trees.

The terrain shifted beneath their feet as they moved. What had once been a gentle decline became a steady slope, the kind that demanded attention with each step. The underbrush thinned, replaced by tufts of grass and pockets of bare stone. Roots that had once clawed across the surface disappeared into soil, giving way to a descending forest path lined with trees so tall and old their branches wove a roof overhead.

Kaelen stopped first, his hand shooting up as a signal. The others stilled. He dropped into a crouch behind a half-toppled trunk wrapped in dry moss. The others followed without question, muscle memory and tension guiding them into place.

He scanned the slope below, eyes narrowing.

Movement.

There—between the trees. Not animal, not random. Shapes moved in rhythm, in silent formation. A dozen figures swept the perimeter of a basin. Their armor gleamed in patches beneath forest-green cloaks edged with gold. Each step was deliberate. These weren't scouts. They were soldiers.

"Figures ahead," Kaelen said under his breath. "Uniformed. Moving clean."

Dorian shifted beside him, adjusting the weight of his hammer. "Ambush?"

Kaelen shook his head. "Not a scramble. Too precise."

Elara leaned closer. Her eyes locked onto one of the soldiers as the figure turned—just enough for the sigil on the pauldron to catch the light.

A stylized branch curled around a single thread of golden light, shaped like a coiled serpent.

She inhaled sharply. "That's my brother's unit."

Liora let herself breathe—just a little. "So we're safe?"

Elara's answer didn't come quickly. Her gaze remained pinned on the basin below.

"They don't know we're here yet," she said finally. "And just because it's Tarian's unit doesn't mean they'll see us as allies."

Dorian glanced at her sidelong. "Your brother wouldn't protect you?"

"It's not about him." She shook her head. "It's about what I've done. What I've chosen. The moment they see me with Forgeborne, it'll raise questions."

Liora knelt beside them, her voice low. "What kind of questions?"

"The kind that get you detained before they're answered."

Kaelen tapped his finger against the wood of the fallen trunk. "Then we stay hidden until we're sure."

Elara frowned. "That's not how Tarian operates. He moves fast. He'll see our tracks eventually—he's trained to."

Dorian's eyes swept the tree line again. "Then we use this moment to decide. Step out, or stay in the shadows?"

Another bird call rang out. This one was fainter. Further.

Liora looked at Elara. "Was that still him?"

Elara nodded. "He's signaling the edge of his sweep. We're just ahead of it."

A long silence passed between them.

Then Elara stood.

"If we wait too long, they'll find us anyway—and that'll look worse."

Kaelen stood with her. "So we go down?"

She nodded. "Together."

The four of them started moving again—slowly, quietly—toward the basin. Toward the place where certainty and danger waited, standing shoulder to shoulder in green and gold.

Whatever came next, there would be no hiding from it.

At the edge of the slope, just before the trees opened into the basin, the group came to a halt. The air had gone still, unnaturally so, as if the forest itself was waiting. Even the wind had quieted, leaving only the faint rustle of shifting gear and the soft, rhythmic hum of distant movement below.

The basin was open, but not empty. Distant figures moved with coordination—Verdant guards in full gear, their cloaks patterned like the forest around them, the shimmer of polished armor beneath green and gold. They hadn't seen the group yet. Not clearly. But it was only a matter of time.

Elara turned to face the others. Her staff hung at her side, its carved vines catching the last glint of filtered light through the trees. Her eyes were calm, but her stance was anything but passive. Every inch of her body held intent.

"This is it," she said, her voice low but unwavering. "Let me go first."

Kaelen didn't move, just tracked the guards below. He didn't like it. But he trusted her. His gaze swept over the figures in the basin, calculating odds. He knew better than to challenge her at this moment.

Dorian looked like he wanted to protest. His brow furrowed, and his fingers flexed once near the strap of his hammer. But then he caught the look in Elara's eyes—a look of certainty—and relented. He gave a slow nod.

As she moved past him, his hand reached out, brushing hers. Just for a moment. A simple contact. But it carried weight. A gesture that said: I'm here, be careful and everything he couldn't speak out loud.

She didn't look back.

Kaelen returned her a small, steady nod. No questions. No flair. Just acknowledgement. Liora stood beside him, her usually animated features subdued. Her eyes flicked between Elara and the guards below, uncertainty curling around her like smoke. But she didn't speak.

Elara adjusted her grip on the staff and stepped out from the safety of the tree line.

The forest receded behind her, replaced by the sloping descent of the basin. With each step, the ground leveled. The air felt cooler here, thinner somehow, touched by tension.

The unit below began to stir. A few turned. A signal passed from one to the next. Subtle, efficient. They hadn't raised weapons—but they had noticed her.

She didn't waver.

Behind her, the others followed. Not in a line, not in formation, but in unity. Careful. Deliberate. Dorian walked just behind her, his presence grounded and heavy. Kaelen kept to the right, one hand still resting near Wiz's shell. Liora lingered slightly behind, her boots light on the leaves, her gaze darting.

No one drew a weapon.

No one said a word.

Whatever came next—whether reunion or confrontation, embrace or arrest—it would begin here, in this clearing, beneath this sky.

Not with violence.

But with truth.

Not just a shift in direction.

A shift in trust.

Chapter 11: Bonds of Blood and Truth

The basin welcomed them with measured silence. Elara led the way, eyes sweeping between movement and shadow. The silence said enough. The weight of home, of memory, pressed heavy on her shoulders.

Behind her, the others moved in lockstep—though the unity was recent, uneasy. Dorian's gaze never left the tree lines. His hammer remained strapped but within reach. Every breath he took felt like restraint. Kaelen scanned the trail with a technician's eye, noting the unnatural spacing in the forest floor, the carefully packed earth that had been cleared and maintained. "They've got perimeter patrols," he muttered. "Regular ones. This whole area's been grid-mapped."

Wiz gave a soft, mechanical whimper from Kaelen's pack.

Kaelen's shoulders twitched slightly at the sound. "Easy, buddy," he said under his breath.

Wiz didn't respond. He simply curled deeper into the canvas folds, trembling faintly as the glint of armored guards became clearer.

Liora, unusually quiet, reached out and laid a hand over the pouch. "Me too, buddy," she whispered. The words came without humor. Just solidarity.

The camp revealed itself in pieces—tents built into the natural curvature of the basin, camouflaged walkways braided with vine-stitched rope, signal towers masked in branches. Guards watched them from elevated posts. No one moved, but the tension rippled like wind against taut cloth.

Then came the sound of heavier boots.

A squad of four approached from the south path—flanked by another two pairs at their flanks. At their head, taller than the rest, was a man in deep green armor etched with leaf-script.

Tarian.

Tarian didn't break stride. But when he saw the unfamiliar faces behind Elara, his hand went to his sword—without hesitation.

"Elara!" he barked. "Step aside!"

Kaelen's hand shifted toward his belt.

Dorian tensed.

But Elara moved first. She stepped between her companions and the soldiers, staff raised—not threatening, but firm.

"They're with me," she said. Clear. Commanding.

Tarian halted. The soldiers behind him didn't lower their guard, but they didn't advance.

"I said they're with me," Elara repeated. "All of them."

The pause that followed was long. Measured.

Tarian's gaze flicked to each of them—Dorian, armored and rigid. Kaelen, tense but alert. Liora, wide-eyed but standing her ground.

He didn't argue. Just nodded. "Then they'll be watched."

"We expected nothing less," Elara said.

The soldiers stepped aside, allowing the group to pass through the outer edge of the camp. They were not welcomed, not truly—but they weren't stopped.

And sometimes, that was enough.

The moment the group crossed into the main encampment, the air shifted. More eyes turned toward them—some curious, some wary, all alert. Every movement was measured, each guard calculating distance and posture. Tension clung to the clearing like dew, silent and heavy. Yet even through the scrutiny, one figure on the far side of the camp didn't hesitate.

Arin.

She broke from the line of Verdant soldiers like a snapped arrow, her cloak billowing behind her in a green streak. There was no hesitation in her feet, no glance toward her commander for permission. The guards nearest her flinched in surprise but didn't move to stop her. No orders barked. No warnings issued. Whatever protocols existed crumbled in the wake of the raw emotion propelling her forward.

She sprinted across the clearing, closing the distance with reckless speed, and Elara barely had time to register it before Arin collided with her. Her arms wrapped around Elara's shoulders and back, pulling her in like she was anchoring herself to the last thing in the world that still mattered.

It wasn't neat. It wasn't ceremonial. It was desperate and all-consuming, the kind of embrace that carried months of silence and miles of guilt.

"You idiot," Arin whispered fiercely, her voice thick with something unspoken. "You're late."

Elara laughed into her friend's hair, her hands locked tight around Arin's back. "I know."

She closed her eyes for a second longer than necessary, letting herself feel the weight of another heartbeat against her own.

For a moment, everything else vanished—soldiers, weapons, loyalties. There was just this: breath shared between friends, no—sisters, who hadn't seen each other in far too long.

Tarian approached slower, his steps heavy with relief wrapped in discipline. His armor was ceremonial and functional all at once, but his eyes betrayed everything else. The moment he reached them, his stance eased.

He didn't smile, not quite, but his voice was lighter. "You heard the signal?"

Elara pulled back from Arin just enough to look at him. "We heard it."

"We tried it near the northern edge," Tarian said. "Didn't think anyone would actually be listening. But we picked up signs—scattered trails, old campsite marks. Thought maybe it was you. Tried the call on instinct."

"Well," Elara said, glancing back at the group trailing behind her, "it worked."

Arin turned then, she looked them over with the calm scrutiny of someone used to triage: catalog first, trust later.

"I got Sylva's message, we knew you survived the ambush." she said to Elara. "It looks like they are safe with the Equinox people. She didn't say where they are, though."

"Too risky," Elara replied. "Wardens might have intercepted it."

"She figured that," Arin said. "We knew to look close, but it's been days of guessing. And hoping."

"Welcome to the club," Kaelen muttered, just loud enough for Elara to hear.

She ignored the remark, eyes still on Tarian. "Thank you—for listening. For trusting it might be me."

Tarian finally extended a hand, placing it briefly on her shoulder. "You're not easy to track. But you always leave a thread."

It wasn't a promise. But it was something.

For the first time since the ambush, Elara's shoulders relaxed. Just a little.

They weren't safe—not fully. But they weren't alone anymore either.

And for now, that made all the difference.

As the emotional high of the reunion faded, reality began to settle in. The rest of the camp hadn't moved. Verdant soldiers still lined the edges of the clearing, watching the Forgeborne with thinly veiled suspicion. Their weapons remained holstered—but only just.

Dorian kept his distance. His stance was loose, but his eyes were sharp, moving from soldier to soldier, scanning for patterns, exits, weaknesses. Every glance was a calculation. He didn't trust this place, not even with Elara's word vouching for them. And he didn't hide it. His posture read as restraint—barely.

Kaelen lingered near the rear, a hand resting protectively on his satchel, shielding Wiz from view as best he could. His eyes weren't on the people, but the gear they wore. The armor wasn't forged—it was cultivated. Bark-like plating interwoven with glowing fibers that pulsed with some inner current. Lifelight, maybe. Or something stranger.

He muttered under his breath, "This armor wasn't built. It was grown."

Wiz let out another mechanical whimper from the pack, a faint stuttering chirp. Kaelen reached back and gave the bag a gentle tap, wordless reassurance.

One of the nearby soldiers—a tall Verdant woman with sun-worn skin and a hawk's posture—locked eyes with Kaelen. Her gaze held no warmth. It was judgment, sharpened by fear and years of conflict. Kaelen didn't flinch. He met her stare with a raised chin, his fingers curling slightly.

Another Verdant soldier muttered. "My cousin was murdered by one of them in a skirmish. Ruthless animals."

The woman next to him added. "...and now Lady Thorne is working with them. I don't want to be branded as a traitor too."

Tension rippled outward like a dropped stone in water. Before it could escalate, Tarian stepped slightly forward and gave the soldier a barely perceptible shake of the head. She blinked, broke eye contact, and turned away without a word.

Elara, sensing the moment teetering toward danger, stepped forward. Her voice was calm but carried weight.

"These are my allies," she said, clear and steady. "Dorian Asher. Kaelen Virel."

Tarian hesitated—just for a breath—then stepped forward and offered his hand.

Dorian's grip was solid. He didn't mask his wariness. "I know how this looks," he said, tone flat.

"It looks like a risk," Tarian replied. "But Elara says it's worth taking. That's enough—for now."

Then came Kaelen. His handshake with Tarian was shorter, stiffer. Tarian didn't squeeze hard, but there was force in his grip—a message: I'm watching.

Kaelen didn't try to read too far into it. He simply nodded.

"They're polite," Kaelen murmured, nodding toward the guards. "In that 'you-don't-belong-here' way."

Liora stood to the side, arms crossed, her brow lifted as she took in the tension surrounding them. Her usual humor simmered just beneath the surface.

"So..." she said under her breath to Elara, "are we guests or prisoners with better lighting?"

Elara didn't answer right away. Her eyes scanned the guards still circling, the guarded posture of the camp, the way no one fully turned their back on them.

"Ask me tomorrow," she said.

They were inside the camp.

They were alive.

But they weren't welcome.

Not yet.

Later that evening, after the soldiers had settled back into their routines and the fire pits flickered low across the basin, Tarian asked Elara to walk with him.

They moved through a quieter part of the encampment, beyond the main cluster of tents, where the light of the fires no longer reached and shadows ruled the paths. The forest loomed around them, its silence broken only by the occasional hiss of wind threading through the canopy. Insects buzzed in the distance, and the thick scent of moss and woodsmoke filled the air. Here, away from the others, the burden of titles fell slightly away. But only slightly.

Their boots crunched softly over fallen leaves. Tarian kept his eyes ahead, while Elara's gaze drifted up toward the star-streaked canopy. For a few long strides, they didn't speak.

Then Tarian's voice broke the stillness.

"Are you chasing peace or prophecy?"

Elara slowed her pace. The question wasn't meant to corner her—it was genuine. A brother trying to understand. And yet the weight of it landed hard.

She didn't answer immediately. Her fingers tightened around her staff, grounding herself in the feel of the carved wood, and she stared through the trees at the stars barely visible between branches. The silence stretched until it nearly became an answer itself.

"Both," she said at last. "But not because someone told me to. Not because of a vision, or a council decree, or a family name. Because I've seen what happens if we don't. I've seen the ruins. I've seen war brewing under every treaty."

She turned to face him fully.

"I carry a relic. One half of something ancient. The Verdant half. The other... it responded to Dorian. And Kaelen—he's not one of the Chosen. Not officially. But the relic reacts to him too. He bridges something in the prophecy that none of us fully understand."

Tarian watched her. There was no disbelief in his eyes—only calculation. His mind turned over every word, every implication.

"You trust them?" he asked.

"With my life," she said. "And maybe more than that."

Tarian folded his arms. "You know the Council won't understand this. Most won't even try. You bring Forgeborne into a Verdant stronghold and speak of relics, of ancient pacts—it sounds like blasphemy to them."

"I know," Elara said. "But we don't have time to wait for them to catch up."

He studied her face. Then gave a slow nod.

"Then I'll stand by you," he said. "For now. But don't mistake that for approval from the rest. You've already drawn a line, Elara. And not everyone will stay behind it with you."

"I wouldn't ask them to," she said.

As the tension in the tent eased, Tarian gestured for Arin to join them.

"There's more," he said, glancing between them. "The council didn't sanction our search. I wasn't supposed to come."

Elara blinked. "What?"

Arin sighed, folding her arms. "It was strange. Even for them. The council wouldn't even allow a small scouting party. No resources. No permission. Just silence."

"So I invoked royal privilege," Tarian said, calm but firm. "It was reckless. Could cost me my seat. But I didn't care."

He met Elara's eyes. "You're my sister. And no title means more than that."

Arin nodded. "We knew the risks. But we had to know you were alive. We had to see you."

The silence that followed wasn't heavy—it was grounding.

They stood there a moment longer, surrounded by the rustling trees and soft torchlight. Two siblings. One mission.

And a dozen consequences they hadn't yet begun to count.

Kaelen moved along the outer rim of the camp as night fell deeper. The glow from the central fire pits didn't reach here, leaving only pale moonlight threading through the high canopy. It painted the ground in fractured silver, broken by long, waving shadows. Each step he took was deliberate—soft but purposeful, boots brushing quietly over the undergrowth.

A passing soldier gave Kaelen's satchel a lingering stare—eyes narrowing at the faint pulse of residual Forgeborne energy.

Kaelen didn't meet it. Just adjusted the strap and kept walking.

Wiz peeked out from the top flap of his pack, optical lenses dim and flickering. A faint scan beam pulsed from the small automaton as he locked onto a supply crate nearby—grown from woven root and lined with crystal compartments. Wiz chirped, a quick series of beeps and warbles.

Kaelen reached back and tapped the side of the pack. "Shh. Not now."

The chirps cut off instantly, but Wiz trembled slightly and withdrew again into the pack.

The gear stacked nearby didn't resemble anything Kaelen had ever studied—sleek bows grown from living vinewood, blades that shimmered with inner light rather than sharpened edges. There were no screws. No weld points. Just seamless, grown design. Natural and precise. It unnerved him.

He crouched next to one of the crates, running a finger along a curved edge. It flexed slightly, like a warm bone.

"Feels weird, doesn't it?"

Kaelen looked up to see Dorian approaching from the shadows, hands tucked into his belt. He moved without sound, but the weight of him pressed into the air like gravity.

Kaelen straightened. "Feels temporary," he said.

Dorian looked out toward the trees beyond the camp, where the stars blinked in gaps between the leaves. "We're not resting. Just pausing."

"Exactly."

They stood side by side in the stillness, just outside the ring of light. The sounds of the camp continued in the background—quiet voices, the occasional clang of armor or staff—but out here, the silence was thicker.

Neither man said anything for a while. They didn't have to.

They both stayed at the edge—half-in, half-out.

It wasn't distrust. Not entirely.

It was a survival instinct. And neither of them had unlearned it yet.

Later, as the moon crept higher and the camp's torches began to dim, Arin found Elara seated near a small moss-covered stone, her staff resting across her knees.

Without speaking, Arin sat beside her and pulled something from inside her cloak—a sealed letter, edges crinkled, and a silver pendant shaped like a leaf caught in frost.

Elara stared at the pendant, breath halting.

"Lysandra sent this with one of the Equinox messenger doves," Arin said. "It found us a couple of nights after we learned what happened with the convoy. We weren't sure we'd get the chance to deliver it."

Elara took it slowly, her fingers brushing over the seal—Verdant wax, faded but intact. She opened the letter.

It was short. Barely four lines.

Trust what you carry. Even if you don't understand it yet. That's enough. That must be enough.

Elara read it twice. Then again. No instructions. No coordinates. No warnings. Just words that sat heavy in her hands.

She looked down at the pendant and turned it over in her palm. It was Lysandra's. The one she wore beneath her collar, always hidden. Always close.

"What does it mean?" Arin asked gently.

Elara shook her head. "I'm not sure. But it sounds like goodbye."

Dorian, nearby, glanced at her. "You think she meant the relic?"

Elara shook her head. "No. I think she meant me."

She folded the letter, tucked it carefully into her satchel, and said nothing more. Her throat tightened, but no tears came. Only a deeper silence.

The burden was still hers. But now, so was the reminder—of who had helped carry it before.

Lysandra's voice returned to the story. And Elara could no longer pretend it was just hers alone to finish.

The camp was quiet, but tension lived in its corners. Elara walked along one of the outer paths, letting her staff rest against her shoulder as she passed torch-lit sentry posts and low-lying vine structures. The forest beyond was dark, but the camp itself buzzed with restrained energy. Conversations dropped to whispers when she passed.

Near a moss-hung watchpoint, she heard the sharp edge of a hushed argument.

"She brought them here," a scout muttered. "Forgeborne, into our camp. She'll break us from the inside."

"She's Verdant," came the reply. "She's one of us."

"Not anymore. Not if she sides with them."

Elara stopped briefly in the shadows, unseen. The voices didn't rise again, but they didn't stop either. It was enough.

Later that night, Tarian joined her near the edge of the encampment, his face half-lit by the flickering light of a small fire. He crouched by the fire without a word. The camp might be split—but he wasn't.

"I heard the same thing you did," he said quietly. "I can keep them in line. But not forever."

Elara didn't pretend to be surprised. She nodded slowly. "We won't stay longer than we have to."

Tarian looked toward the fire, then back at her. "You don't have to break a wall," he said. "Just find the hairline crack."

His meaning lingered in the silence between them. This camp, this alliance—it wasn't built for what she was trying to do. It might support her for a while. But not forever.

The fracture had already started. Now it was only a matter of time.

They walked back toward the center together, but both knew the stability under their feet had started to shift.

The sun filtered through the upper canopy in gentle beams as the camp stirred with slow, steady movement. The morning air was cool, laced with dew and the hum of insects in the trees. In a quieter part of the camp, away from the patrol lines and guarded tension, Liora sat near a moss-covered bench, fiddling absently with a tangle of vine string she'd pulled from her sleeve. She hadn't meant to be here, exactly—but wandering had a way of making her less anxious.

Arin joined her with a small nod, a folded satchel of dried herbs tucked beneath one arm. Liora stiffened slightly, caught off guard by the serene but confident presence.

"Oh," she said. "Hi. I'm just, you know... loitering."

Arin raised a brow. "You're in a camp. I think that's called resting."

"Is it?" Liora pulled at the vine string, then gave up and dropped it. "Doesn't feel like it."

"Liora, right?" Arin asked. "You look like the kind of girl who forgets she left the tea steeping for three hours."

Liora grinned. "Only twice. That I know of."

A silence stretched, not quite awkward—just waiting for a shape. Then Arin settled on the bench beside her.

"You're a Sylvanar," she said.

Liora winced. "That obvious, huh?"

"Mostly the scorch marks on your sleeves."

Liora looked down, sighed, and gave a lopsided shrug. "I've got a full set of elemental attunements and none of them work right. My wind is twitchy, fire's scared of me, earth gives me bruises, and water... well, water mostly just splashes me in the face."

Arin smiled. "I'm a grovecaller."

Liora blinked. "Oh. So you're the competent kind."

Arin laughed. "And you're the brave kind. You stuck around, didn't you?"

Liora glanced away, smiling despite herself. "I guess."

They sat together for a while, letting the birdsong fill in the spaces where words didn't need to be.

Later that day, Elara found Arin near the supply tent and waved her over.

"Can you look at Dorian's wound?" she asked, lowering her voice. "It's been sealed, but it hasn't healed right."

Arin nodded without hesitation. "Of course."

Dorian sat near the perimeter, one hand braced against the tree behind him. He didn't protest when Arin knelt beside him. Elara stood back, watching as Arin unwrapped the bandage with deft fingers, murmuring soft words under her breath.

Liora watched from a few feet away, fascinated.

A faint green glow pulsed through Arin's hands, flowing into the angry red tear along Dorian's ribs. The skin smoothed. Muscle knitted. The pain dulled and drifted away.

A wry smile cracked through. "That's... better than Elara's salves."

Elara crossed her arms, but there was no heat in her glare. "I never said I was the best healer."

Arin looked up at her friend. "You have other strengths."

Elara nodded once, but didn't answer. There was pride in her gaze—but something else too. Awareness. Of what she could do. And what she couldn't.

And sometimes, that mattered more.

Liora leaned toward Arin as they walked away. "Next time I nearly set myself on fire, I'm coming straight to you."

"You wouldn't be the first," Arin replied.

They laughed together—quiet and genuine. And for the first time in a long while, the tension in the camp didn't feel like the only thing holding it together.

The night was clear—clearer than it had any right to be. The clouds that had lingered earlier had scattered, leaving the sky sharp with stars. A breeze drifted through the trees, cool but not cold, rustling the leaves in soft waves.

Elara stood near the edge of the camp, just outside the circle of woven root lanterns that gave off a low amber light. She didn't know if she was waiting for something or avoiding everything.

Her staff was planted in the ground beside her, forgotten for the moment.

She heard him before she saw him.

Dorian stepped into view, silent but present, his posture more relaxed than usual—but only slightly. He looked up first, scanning the stars as if trying to name constellations that no longer matched anything in Forgehelm charts. Then his gaze dropped to her.

"You're still standing," he said. "After all this."

Elara smiled without turning. "You think I never flinch?"

"I've seen you bleed," he said. "But I haven't seen you hesitate."

She didn't answer right away. "I've done both. Just not where people could see it."

A beat passed. Then two.

Their hands brushed.

Not by accident. Not fully.

This time, neither of them pulled away. They let the contact sit between them—skin against skin, neither grasping nor retreating. Just connected.

Dorian's voice dropped. "I don't know what will happen next."

"Neither do I," she said. "But that's not new."

His thumb shifted slightly along her knuckles. A slow movement. Intentional.

Elara looked at him then. Really looked. The firelight didn't reach this far, but the starlight was enough. Enough to see the tired lines around his eyes. The small scar that hadn't been there before. The way he stood like he expected to be needed again at any second.

He was too tall. Too Forgeborne. Too wrong for everything she'd been told.

And yet.

She didn't step back.

He didn't step forward.

There was no kiss. No whispered promise. Just breath between them. A shared silence. And maybe something more inside it.

"Tomorrow's going to be more difficult," she said quietly.

"Probably," he agreed.

Still, they didn't move.

And for one fragile moment beneath the stars, the world didn't ask them to.

Romance didn't bloom. It grew—slow, quiet, and real.

It was well past midnight when Tarian found Elara again. Most of the camp had quieted—only the perimeter guards remained active, moving like shadows beneath the darkened trees. The air had cooled further, and mist crept low across the forest floor, swirling around Elara's boots as she paced slowly near her tent.

Tarian didn't speak at first. He simply joined her walk, matching her stride in silence.

"You heard something," Elara said eventually.

He nodded. "Floralis sent a formal decree to the Council. Word spread fast—faster than I expected."

She stopped. "And?"

Tarian took a breath, glancing around to ensure no ears were too close. "You're not just a rogue Verdant now. You're being named as a destabilizing agent. A threat to inter-faction cohesion."

The news didn't shake her. If anything, it clarified her next step.

"They've labeled you a liability. And they won't wait long to clean up what they don't control."

"Meaning?"

"Meaning someone will be sent. Officially or not."

Elara folded her arms. "That was always the risk."

Tarian looked at her, serious now. "You think I don't know that? I stood up for you, Elara. I put my name on this. But now the Council has a reason to act. And if they do, it won't be with warnings next time."

"I never expected warnings," she said quietly. "I expected war."

He hesitated, then added more softly, "There's talk of Nullification Orders."

She stiffened.

"That's reserved for traitors."

"Or visionaries who move too fast."

The forest around them felt suddenly colder. Not with weather—but with clarity.

Elara turned her gaze back toward the center of camp, where Kaelen, Dorian, and Liora still rested near a low-burning fire.

Peace was fragile.

Peace had an expiration date.

And it was closing fast.

Act IV: Beneath the Burning Sea

Chapter 12: Borderlines

The plateau east of the camp offered a final overlook of the road ahead—dense forest to the north, rolling hills to the east, and silence pressing from every side. It was here Tarian chose to give his orders.

Three squads—thirty-six soldiers in total—formed ranks as he paced before them, the breeze catching the edges of his green cloak. His voice, when it came, was clear but measured.

"We split paths here," he said. "Eldoravell needs to believe we've doubled back. Leave signs, tracks, anything that leads them away from the Verdant border. Our movements must leave false trails."

He pointed east. "You'll return by the southern pass, circle through the Vale, and re-enter from the west. Travel light. No banners."

The soldiers gave a crisp salute, trained to obey without question—but the unspoken tension lingered. No one asked why the captain wasn't returning with them.

Tarian turned to Arin, already standing at attention beside the command tent. His hesitation lasted only a second.

"You should go with them," he said quietly, meant for her ears alone. "It's safer. You'll be an asset to the city—"

"No," she cut in. No sharpness in her voice, only resolve. "I'd rather face danger beside you than be safe in a palace that lies."

Their eyes locked. He didn't argue. Just gave a slow nod. She stayed.

With no further ceremony, the squads dispersed, disappearing into the morning mist. The field emptied, leaving behind only six: Elara, Kaelen, Dorian, Liora, Arin, and Tarian.

Kaelen watched the last figures vanish beyond the ridgeline. "We'll draw attention, traveling like this," he said.

"Less than a full platoon would," Tarian replied. "With luck, they'll think we've splintered entirely."

"Luck's never liked us much," Dorian muttered.

None noticed the scout who lingered behind a half-fallen tree, one of the younger soldiers—name forgotten, face unremarkable. He waited until the others were gone, then slipped westward, breaking formation. In his pouch, a hidden cipher marked for a rogue loyalist faction. He didn't know where the captain was headed—only that someone needed to.

They set out that afternoon, cloaked in the gray hush that followed a farewell. Anviltown lay ahead, unseen beyond the trees, and none among them expected a warm welcome. The road would grow narrower, the threats harder to name. But for now, they moved as one.

Six shadows cast long over the trail.

The mission had changed—but not its purpose.

They left the ridge behind in silence, descending into terrain that didn't welcome them. The trees grew denser here, bent by years of wind and neglect, their branches tangled like grasping hands. Moss coated everything—stone, bark, even the broken trail markers that once offered direction. Half the path had collapsed in places, washed out by old landslides or overtaken by root and rot.

Elara led cautiously, her staff brushing low-hanging vines aside. Behind her, Dorian's steps were heavier, slowed by the uneven footing and his still-healing side. Arin kept close without hovering, her gaze shifting between him and the trail ahead. Kaelen and Liora brought up the rear, flanking Wiz, who strolled low and quiet. The little construct's usual chirps were subdued, its lights dimmed in scan mode.

Wiz pinged faintly. Once. Twice.

Kaelen frowned and tapped the side of his lens. A thin projection shimmered just above his palm—a detection map, low-res and stuttering, but unmistakable.

"Forgeborne residue," he muttered. "Old. Could be machinery. Could be armor."

Elara paused, glancing back. "How old?"

"Hard to say. It's decaying, but the signature's solid. Could be five years, could be twenty."

Tarian, who had remained mostly silent since they'd left the ridge, finally spoke as he stepped over a shattered stone ledge. "These zones were last patrolled a generation ago. Some of the Council elders claim the cost wasn't worth the oversight."

"Meaning?" Dorian asked.

"Meaning they let this land go." Tarian gestured at the overgrowth. "No maintenance. No scouting. The maps stopped being updated. The Council's resources are thinning, and this was the easiest piece to abandon."

Kaelen crouched by a vine-choked marker stone, running a gloved hand across the eroded symbol barely visible beneath the moss. "That's comforting," he muttered. "We're walking blind."

"Not blind," Elara said. "Just uninvited."

The descent steepened, and the path narrowed. Vines looped between trees like tripwires. Each footstep required care, each breath drawn with tension. Birds no longer sang here. Even the wind felt reluctant to pass through.

Liora stepped wrong and slid half a meter before catching herself. Kaelen grabbed her arm before she hit the rocks below.

"Thanks," she breathed. "I hate it here."

"You and me both."

Kaelen had noticed it back in Floralis—the way Liora's hands never stilled. She flinched at sparks. Bit her lip before casting.

He recognized the rhythm. It was the same kind he saw in apprentice mechcrafters right before they blew a charge valve—too much power, not enough control. Not a lack of talent. Just bad wiring.

He didn't pity her. He understood her. That was worse.

They moved slower after that.

Every step was an argument with the terrain. Every scan from Wiz is a reminder that they weren't the first to pass through—and might not be the last.

By midday, they had covered barely a few kilometers. The forest floor dipped into a basin where light barely reached, and the air grew damp and still.

Dorian stopped, scanning the trees above. "I don't like this," he said.

"No one does," Tarian replied.

But they kept going.

Because there was no turning back.

The mist thickened without warning, rolling in from the east like breath from a sleeping giant. It coiled low around their boots and stretched high into the canopy, turning the trees into vague silhouettes and the path ahead into a suggestion more than a direction.

Kaelen adjusted Wiz's sensors to full range, scanning with tight, silent pulses. The automaton hovered in near silence, his lights barely visible in the haze. The only sound was the soft rustle of damp leaves underfoot.

Then came movement.

Behind them. Subtle at first—too regular to be animals, too coordinated to be coincidence.

Dorian slowed his pace. "We're not alone."

Elara turned sharply, eyes narrowing. Shapes drifted between the trunks, vague figures cloaked in pale gray. No banners. No sounds of pursuit. Just forms. Moving with purpose. In formation.

She didn't hesitate.

"Verdants," she said. "Posture's too rigid. Their spacing, their gear—it's Aeldrin loyalists."

"How sure are you?" Tarian asked.

Elara met his eyes. "Sure enough to keep walking."

Kaelen looked back again. "If they're not running, they're watching. That's worse."

Liora pulled her cloak tighter, eyes wide but steady. "Do we run?"

"No," Dorian said. "But we don't slow either."

The group picked up pace, careful not to break into a panic. The path curved along a ravine wall, moss-slick and treacherous. Every glance over their shoulders revealed more shapes in the fog. Never close. Never far.

Just enough to be known.

Just enough to unsettle.

They didn't speak again for an hour. The silence felt thinner than the mist, like one misstep might shatter it entirely.

They were being watched. Tracked.

And whoever followed them wasn't interested in being known—yet.

The hunt had begun.

And the hunted knew it.

Roots snagged at their boots, and the mud thickened as the terrain dipped again, funneling them into a narrow valley veined with crumbling stone. The fog had begun to lift, but it left behind a heavy dampness that clung to their clothes and dragged on every breath.

Liora stumbled again. Her foot slipped on a slick patch of lichen, and she fell hard to one knee.

Arin was beside her in a heartbeat. She said nothing, just reached down and helped her up with a firm grip and a small nod. Liora said nothing, her gaze at Arin a mix of gratitude and mounting fatigue.

Dorian moved ahead of the group, scouting bends in the trail and scanning for high points. He didn't call out, didn't report back. He simply moved with relentless momentum.

Kaelen kept to the middle, checking every side trail like he expected an ambush at each bend.

Elara remained at the rear, her staff in hand, eyes flicking behind them every few steps. The shadows back there hadn't thinned. She could feel them—persistent, patient.

Tarian fell in beside her for a stretch, voice low.

"If we reach Anviltown, we disappear."

Kaelen overheard. "Assuming they let us in."

Elara didn't glance back. "Assuming we make it."

They didn't stop. The forest pressed tighter around them, and the ravine grew narrower, forcing them into single file. Branches clawed at sleeves and cloaks. Stones shifted underfoot.

The sound of pursuit returned—closer than expected. Hooves? No—boots. Fast. Coordinated.

"Split wide," Dorian hissed. "Now."

The group veered off the trail, ducking behind a crumbling stone outcrop. Moss muffled their breath. Elara pressed her back to bark and tried not to twitch.

A patrol passed within yards. Six soldiers, moving in pairs. Not reckless—trained.

One paused. Looked their way.

Kaelen held still, even Wiz going silent inside his pack.

A moment stretched.

Then the patrol moved on, their boots crunching into the trees.

She let her head thump lightly against the stone. "That's the second time I've almost swallowed my own heartbeat today."

Liora breathed hard, but kept going.

Arin stayed close.

Dorian didn't slow.

Kaelen didn't speak.

Elara didn't waver.

But the space between them—between words, between thoughts—grew heavier.

They were still a group. Still moving.

But the seams were starting to pull.

And they all knew it.

The only thing louder than the pounding of their feet was the silence of what followed behind.

Waiting for them to break.

They emerged into a clearing where the forest seemed to thin, not from nature's design but from long-forgotten intentions. Moss grew in thick patches, and shattered stones hinted at where a barrier or marker might once have stood. The ground beneath their boots turned from loam to the cracked suggestion of an old road.

At the center of it all stood a signpost—weather-worn, half-charred, and leaning.

The lettering had been scorched off. Only the faintest remnants of Forgeborne script clung to one edge, blackened and peeling. Elara stepped closer, tracing a finger along a jagged scorch mark. The sign was no accident. Someone had wanted it gone.

Kaelen stood beside her, silent.

Then, a subtle vibration—barely there.

Elara's hand twitched.

Kaelen shifted.

Both reached for their relics in unspoken tandem, each feeling a pulse—not loud, not urgent. A murmur. A change.

"It's not danger," Elara said softly.

Kaelen nodded. "It's something else."

Transition.

Dorian stepped past them, eyes forward. He pointed down the broken trail ahead.

"This is it."

Wiz chirped—a low, tonal beep, like an engine idling beneath awareness. Kaelen's hand hovered near his satchel, watching the automaton's readout. No red lines. No sharp pings. Still, the warning hum persisted.

"What is it?" Liora asked.

"Nothing immediate," Kaelen said, uncertain. "But it doesn't like this place."

No one moved for a heartbeat.

Then Dorian crossed the line.

No alarms. No resistance. Just the soft shift of air, the hush of leaves parting as they entered what had once been—and technically still was—Forgeborne territory.

Elara followed. Then Kaelen.

Arin took Liora's hand and stepped across with her. Tarian came last, his eyes never leaving the forest behind them until the trees fully closed off the view.

No welcome greeted them. No sigils, no patrols.

Only silence.

And the road ahead, empty but waiting.

They didn't stop immediately.

Even after crossing the border, the group pushed on for another half hour through brittle underbrush and abandoned trail remnants. Only when the path widened again—its edges lined by cracked stone and rusted rails from some long-forgotten cart system—did Elara signal for them to pause.

Everyone slowed to a halt.

The silence was heavier here, but not hostile. It had a kind of staleness to it, like a room sealed too long. The wind had stopped entirely. The trees didn't move. Even the birds seemed absent.

Kaelen adjusted Wiz, whose sensors continued their slow sweep, steady but cautious. Dorian leaned against a slanted boulder, one hand pressed to his ribs.

Then Liora turned.

When they finally emerged from cover and crested the ridge, the line of Verdant soldiers stood still—just beyond the threshold of Forgeborne territory.

They didn't shout. Didn't follow.

Just watched.

"They're just standing there," Arin said quietly.

Liora's voice dropped to a whisper. "Why aren't they coming?"

Kaelen, crouched beside Wiz, glanced back. "Because they don't want a war."

Elara: "Then we'd better stay ahead of one."

Dorian didn't speak right away. He kept walking. Then, without looking back he said. "Or maybe they're just smart enough to let someone else fire the first shot."

"Borders don't stop hatred. They just hide it better." He added.

The words landed like weight.

No one answered. Because no one could.

They didn't shout. Didn't aim. Just watched. Like wolves too full to chase—but still hungry enough to remember.

Just silence. The silhouettes didn't move. Didn't raise weapons. Didn't speak.

And then, one by one, they faded—slipping back into the trees like they'd never been there at all.

Elara watched until the last shape vanished. Her grip tightened slightly on her staff, then relaxed.

Tarian stepped up beside her. "They were there to see if we'd cross. Not to stop us."

"They'll report back," Elara said.

"They were always going to."

As the others shifted packs and sorted gear, Liora sat a little apart, eyes darting every time a leaf stirred.

Arin approached with a waterskin beside her. "You've got the same look Elara used to have after night drills," she said softly. "Like every tree's about to whisper a secret you don't want to hear."

Liora gave a half-smile, more a flinch than anything. "I'm used to my enemies having names. And directions. This is... fog."

Arin nodded. "That fog clears. Eventually."

Liora looked down. "You sure?"

"No," Arin said. "But I still walk through it."

Liora didn't reply. But her shoulders eased—just slightly.

No one moved for a while. The fog on the ridge began to thin. The moment passed.

They were free.

But it didn't feel like safety.

It felt like a warning unanswered.

Or a debt postponed.

The trail curved down through rust-bitten switchbacks, curling into a basin that smelled faintly of iron and rust. Then the trees broke—and Anviltown came into view.

Not abandoned. Not hostile. Just hushed.

The gates stood intact but weathered—metal reinforced with grown stone, grimy and silent. No banners flew, but smoke drifted from thin chimneys. Machinery clanked somewhere deeper in. The town breathed—quiet, functional, guarded.

Kaelen scanned the walls. "Still holding."

Dorian stepped forward, eyes sweeping the ridgeline. "I'm staying out here. We don't know how this place will take a mixed group like ours. If something goes sideways, someone has to be outside to pull you out."

Tarian looked toward the gate, then at Dorian. "Then I'll stay too. You cover the retreat—I'll cover the angle."

Dorian gave a short nod. No further debate.

Kaelen turned to the group. "I'll need blueprint parts and components if I'm going to make anything work. Liora, come with me—I could use your eyes."

Liora blinked. "Oh. Sure. Always dreamed of a glamorous career as a parts runner."

He smirked. "Let's not get ambitious."

Elara adjusted her staff and stepped forward. "We can move faster if we split. Arin, come with me—we'll handle food and medicine."

Arin hesitated only a second, then nodded. "We'll be quick."

The group broke naturally—no one following, no one left behind.

Kaelen led Liora under the gate. Dorian and Tarian fanned out to watch from the brush. Elara and Arin peeled off down a side path toward the central market lane.

Anviltown wasn't bustling. But it breathed.

Steam curled from forge vents. Gearsmiths argued over calibration specs behind a shuttered shop. A pair of vendors polished copper rings and memory cores on a portable table—priced, organized, marked with care.

Wiz chirped softly inside Kaelen's satchel, his sensors lighting up.

"He knows this place," Liora said, watching the flicker.

"Of course he does," Kaelen said. "Power signatures here run on dual-phase load. Familiar ground."

They passed a storefront stacked with alloy coils and stabilizers. Kaelen paused, eyes narrowing on a casing etched with the same panel structure Clyne's gauntlet used.

"Start here," he said.

"I'll stay over here and not touch anything that might explode," Liora muttered.

"Perfect. You're learning."

The deeper reaches of Anviltown weren't dead, but they were retreating. Workshops blinked behind shuttered panels. Chimneys spewing weak steam. The air smelled like rust, oil, and old fires no one dared to stoke too high.

Kaelen led Liora down a side lane tucked between two repair yards. One shop still buzzed, its counter scattered with stripped memory coils and outdated servo joints. The others were closed, their signage faded, their doors barricaded with welded scrap.

As they passed a cracked window, a young boy peeked out—then vanished, yanked back by a hand unseen. The curtain snapped shut.

Liora flinched. "They're scared of us."

Kaelen didn't look away. "They're scared of being noticed."

Wiz chirped twice, hopping off Kaelen's shoulder. His sensors pinged low and tight, sweeping the path in a fan-shaped arc.

Then he stopped cold.

A sharp chime rang out—high, clipped, electronic.

"The signal's not local," Kaelen muttered, fingers twitching near his satchel before Wiz even chirped. "We're being tracked."

He dropped to one knee beside Wiz, activating his interface. "Low-res trace. Embedded, not triggered." He toggled through scan filters until a dim red shimmer bled into view—threaded along the corner seam of a wall. Barely visible. Faint. But pulsing.

"Tagging residue," he muttered. "Shit."

Liora leaned closer, brow furrowed. "What kind of tag?"

"Clyne's kind." He stood slowly, brushing metal grit from his fingers. "We must've picked it up from the last encounter—embedded in our gear. Not transmitting. Yet."

He glanced back the way they came. No sign of Elara or Arin. No sign of patrols. Just empty streets and far-off steam vents.

"Wiz found it before it lit up," Kaelen said. "If this thing activates, it sends location data right to Aldric."

Liora stepped back. "Then we need to get out. Now."

Kaelen nodded. "We regroup. Tell the others. Then we run."

Wiz gave a low, uneasy whirr and dimmed his lights.

The red shimmer pulsed once more—soft, like a warning not meant for ears. It wasn't a signal. Not yet. But it was waiting to become one.

Not a beacon.

Not a flare.

Just a whisper buried in the walls.

And for now, it was whispering to the wrong people.

Meanwhile, Elara and Arin are gathering necessary supplies in Anviltown's marketplace.

"They didn't seem angry," Arin said quietly as they walked. "But they didn't smile, either."

Elara glanced back at the last shop they passed. "We're not the threat they're expecting. Doesn't mean they'll trust us."

The wind shifted near dusk.

Dorian adjusted his stance beneath a half-felled column, one hand resting on his hammer's pommel, the other tracing old battle-scars in the stone. Tarian stood a few paces off, arms folded, eyes fixed on the road twisting back toward Anviltown.

They hadn't spoken in a while. They didn't need to.

"They're taking too long," Tarian said eventually, voice low but edged.

Dorian didn't answer right away. He scanned the ridge lines again—no movement, but that meant nothing.

"This place—it's not abandoned," he said. "But it doesn't feel alive either."

Tarian nodded once. "Like a blade that's been sharpened too many times. Still cuts. But you don't trust the hilt anymore."

Dorian huffed, half a laugh. "You sound like one of us."

"I spent years fighting who we were told to hate. Turns out that teaches you something."

A pause.

Tarian glanced sideways. "If it turns south, I'll cover the eastern rise. You cover the gate."

Dorian gave a short nod. "And if it doesn't?"

"Then maybe we let ourselves believe this city doesn't bite. Just once."

Neither looked entirely convinced.

But they kept their watch.

The outskirts of Anviltown were still, the low wind shifting dust across fractured stone paths and metal seams dulled by age. Near the remnants of a collapsed barracks, the group had made camp.

The structure still stood, mostly—walls intact but pockmarked, roof half-patched with sheet metal that clicked with every gust. Glowroot lanterns swung from bent wall brackets, casting green-blue shadows. A cart sat nearby, covered in canvas, its contents cold but organized—tools unused but not forgotten.

Dorian crouched near the outer fence, watching the trail through a slitted visor. Tarian stood further down, half-shadowed, eyes on the ridgeline like he expected pursuit to crest it.

They both turned as Kaelen and Liora approached.

"You were longer than expected," Dorian said.

Kaelen didn't waste time. "We found it. Tracer residue. Same type Clyne used—low signal, but it's on us."

Liora shook her head, still rattled. "It wasn't obvious. It was embedded, passive. Would've gone unnoticed until too late."

"Can he track it yet?" Tarian asked.

"Not real-time. But if we stay put, he'll catch up."

Before the silence thickened, Elara and Arin emerged from the opposite trail, sacks of supplies hanging from their shoulders. Elara's cloak fluttered in the breeze; Arin carried the food and a bundle of medicinal vials, her grip steady.

"No problems?" Dorian asked.

"Not exactly warm," Elara said. "But no one tried to stop us."

"They looked, though," Arin added. "Carefully."

"Cautious. Not hostile," Elara confirmed. "But the longer we stayed, the colder it got."

Kaelen didn't ask for details. "Then we're done here."

But they weren't—not quite.

As night settled over the broken stone and cool mist, the group shifted into quieter tasks. Arin sorted rations. Tarian cleaned the edge of his sword. Dorian sat against a rusted pipe stack, polishing his hammer in even strokes.

Liora crouched near the ash pit, coaxing flame with rhythmic motions. The gesture was practiced—rehearsed even—but her spark flickered, misfired, and finally sputtered out in a sharp breeze.

Kaelen sat nearby, surrounded by scrap and parts—rigging, filament, warped couplers. He watched Liora work. Not judging. Just reading the pattern.

"You're pacing the draw right," he said, after a beat. "But your tether's short. You're correcting too soon."

Liora didn't turn. "Thanks for the poetry."

"I could build something," Kaelen offered. "A channel mod. Focus your casting. Tame the edges."

"We shape stone with chants, not wires," Liora said flatly. "Magic isn't... wired."

He shrugged, twisting a length of copper through an anchor. "Maybe the chant just needs a better echo," Kaelen replied.

Liora stepped away, frustration twitching at her mouth. Smoke and mist drifted from town like old breath. Hammering still echoed—distant and rhythmic.

"You think a coil fixes what I can't?" she asked.

Kaelen didn't look up. "No. I think the best tools don't fix. They meet you halfway."

Liora gave a tired smirk. "Spoken like a true Forgeborne." But her voice had softened.

She glanced back at the firewood—still scattered. Still unlit. Elara and Arin's soft conversation flickered in the background, half-swallowed by distance. The others were steady. Balanced.

She wasn't.

"I've trained for years," she muttered. "Still the worst Sylvanar in the room."

Kaelen smiled faintly. "Maybe the problem's the room."

She hesitated. Then, without a word, sat beside the cold fire again. This time, she didn't try. She just watched.

Kaelen didn't say anything else.

And in the space between them—quiet and unfinished—something began to settle.

Beneath the charred stonework of Anviltown—below collapsed corridors and rust-choked conduits—a sensor flickered to life.

It had been dormant for years. Buried during the siege. Forgotten by most. But not all.

Its activation was silent. No alarm, no siren. Just a ping—sharp, distinct, and unmistakable—broadcast along a narrow encrypted frequency, meant for one receiver only.

Miles away, deep beneath a mountain bunker laced with steel veins and humming relay cores, a console blinked red.

A mechcrafter leaned forward, confusion etched across her brow. "Ping received. Level Four sensor. Latency negligible."

Then the speaker clicked.

A voice answered—cold, flat, and without hesitation.

"Target reacquired. Orders remain unchanged."

The mechcrafter looked up.

On the wall above the console, framed in scorched alloy, a single command slate pulsed with residual heat.

A seal glowed faintly on its surface—the sigil of Aldric, etched in copper and scorched black by command fire.

No alarms blared.

No soldiers moved.

But a series of lights came on across a dormant grid, one after the other, like a machine waking from a long sleep.

In Anviltown, the campfire flickered.

The group didn't know it yet.

But their pursuers had found them again.

Chapter 13: Crossing Lines

Wind carved lines through the fog as the group crested the final ridge overlooking Smeltport. The road curved downward into the coastal city, revealing rusted rooftops and chimneys coughing steam into the mist-heavy air. Smeltport's shoreline wasn't built to impress—just to endure. Rusty, worn metal stuck out from the docks like jagged teeth, and the sea hissed as the tide lapped against the dark, slick stone.

The further they moved from Anviltown, the lighter the air felt—but none of them dared call it safety.

They entered through the east gate, boots scraping across weather-worn plates that had once been clean and proud. Now they groaned under weight and time. Chains clanked from pulley cranes overhead, and every pipe that hissed carried the weight of some unseen pressure.

Kaelen led the way, eyes flicking to every creak and flicker of motion. His gauntlet clicked once, adjusting to the humidity, its sensor node cycling through a quick diagnostic.

Dorian walked beside him, gaze sweeping the city's low skyline. "This place reeks of iron and grudges."

"You're not wrong," Tarian muttered, scanning the crowd. Locals moved with deliberate caution. No one ran. No one greeted. Their glances weren't overtly hostile—but none of them looked past the strangers' boots.

Especially not past the wrapped Verdant staff at Elara's back.

Kaelen muttered, "Let's keep moving. Eyes front."

Behind them, Elara kept her hood low and her step even. She said nothing, but her posture was still too regal, too precise. She didn't blend here. And she knew it.

A cloaked figure stood along the edge of the crowd—still, but not idle. Their hood was low, face obscured, posture relaxed. They leaned against a support beam near a line of crates and watched the group without being obvious. Not following the group directly, not intervening. Just present.

Liora wandered farther off with Arin. The southern plaza opened into a market—open stalls sagging beneath rusted rivets, merchants calling low prices with flatter tones. The fish smelled old. The bread smelled burnt.

Dorian tapped a wind-up crab until it snapped at his fingers; Kaelen lifted a brass token to the light, inspecting the etched tide symbols.

Liora grinned. "You two will bankrupt us before sundown."

Arin, scanning the rooftops, offered a soft smile. "Feels more like a bluff than a welcome."

"Bluffs can collapse," Liora replied. "Still beats a grave."

In the distance, a rust-bitten clocktower wheezed into motion. Noon. The bell didn't chime so much as stutter—metal grating against itself in tired rhythm.

Kaelen stopped in the middle of the road. Dorian slowed beside him. Workers nearby froze for half a second before continuing like nothing had happened.

"Did you see that?" Dorian asked.

Kaelen nodded. "Yeah. They were waiting for that sound."

Tarian's hand rested loosely on his belt. "They're watching for a signal. Let's not give them one."

Smeltport wasn't a city that welcomed travelers. It merely endured them. And it was already measuring the weight of this group's presence.

Liora broke from the others not far from the edge of the market. Her attention snagged on two figures—children, barely twelve years old—carrying a rusted crate between them toward the loading dock near an old warehouse. The boy had a slight limp, the girl a streak of oil across her cheek. Their clothes were too thin for the wind and too worn for this kind of labor.

She approached cautiously. "Need a hand?"

The boy glanced up, half-suspicious, half-amused. "Unless you can grow extra arms, I think we've got it."

"You'd be surprised," Liora said.

The girl snorted, then set the crate down with a grunt. "You talk funny."

"I get that a lot." Liora crouched near them, taking in the details. Calloused hands. Threadbare packs. Forced humor masking fatigue.

"I'm Liora. You two have names, or should I start guessing?"

"Sylas," the boy said. "She's Nyra."

They didn't volunteer more, but the glance they shared said plenty. Liora didn't push.

"Where are you two from?"

"A village," Sylas said. "Doesn't matter now. Left for adventure."

Nyra added, "Now we're broke and mostly just lifting boxes."

Liora offered a dry smile. "Classic start to a legend."

They laughed, but it didn't reach their eyes.

Not far off, Arin stood watching. She didn't interrupt, but her gaze lingered. Something in the way the twins moved triggered a distant familiarity—an echo she couldn't place.

In the corner of the yard, a cluster of rough-looking men leaned against a stack of barrels. Pirates, by the look of them. They didn't speak. Didn't approach. Just watched.

Liora turned just slightly, instinct prickling. But when she looked again, the pirates had turned their backs, muttering low among themselves.

She turned back to the twins. "Are you hungry?"

Sylas perked up. "Is that a trick question?"

"Come on. Let's find a place that overcharges and underwhelms. Perfect for first impressions."

They followed.

And just like that, the group took one more step into a situation already moving beneath them.

Kaelen crouched beside a bench of scrap crates, tightening the final stabilizing loop on his gauntlet. The new frame wrapped over his forearm like a second skin—coated steel plates hugging internal pistons and magnetic disc arrays. He tapped a small switch. With a soft thrum, the gauntlet snapped outward, releasing a compact kinetic pulse that cracked a nearby pebble across the cobblestone.

"Non-lethal," Kaelen muttered. "But persuasive."

Liora stood nearby, arms crossed, watching with furrowed eyebrows. "Looks like it could crack a rib or two."

"Only if they're standing too close."

She didn't respond. But she didn't look away either.

Wiz padded around them, his chassis now almost level with Kaelen's hip. He sniffed at a crate marked with faded glyphs—an odd symbol tucked into the grain like a brand. As soon as his sensors locked on, he chirped. Loudly.

A merchant nearby looked up, scowling. "Hey! Keep that junk dog off my cargo!"

Kaelen yanked Wiz back. "Sorry. He's... curious."

The merchant muttered something under his breath and turned away. Wiz growled softly, a sequence of static huffs that Kaelen recognized as reluctant compliance.

"Crate's marked for outer-isle shipping," Kaelen said under his breath. "Which is odd, considering there are no ships from the isles in port this week."

Liora leaned down. "Smugglers?"

"Or pirates trying not to be pirates. Either way, the wrong kind of silence."

On the far end of the dock, Dorian and Tarian scanned the crowd. Dorian's hand rested loosely on the handle of his hammer, eyes locked on the ship tethered to the end of the pier. A rust-hulled freighter, modest size, but well-kept. Too well-kept for a town like Smeltport.

"See that?" Dorian muttered.

Tarian nodded. "Crew's too alert. No one's relaxing. And they're watching the crowd more than the lines."

"Elara said the route east of the mountains is blocked. If we're taking a water passage, this is it."

Dorian frowned. "Or a trap."

Kaelen joined them, brushing metal dust from his fingers. "Too organized. Either they're military... or something worse pretending to be."

Tarian gave a slight nod. "We stay quiet. No assumptions."

Down the pier, the ship's loading ramp creaked as another crate was pulled aboard. Two men—both in cloaks too heavy for the coastal heat—paused mid-lift to glance toward them. One nudged the other, said nothing, and resumed the task.

The breeze shifted, carrying the tang of salt and smoke.

Liora joined them, Sylas and Nyra trailing behind. The twins were laughing softly, trying to appear unaware, but their eyes kept flicking to the dock.

"There's something wrong with that crew," Liora said.

"You feel it too?" Kaelen asked.

"They look like dockhands. But they move like they're waiting for orders."

No one said it aloud, but the conclusion hung between them.

Whatever was waiting on that ship—it wasn't just cargo.

And if they were going to step aboard, they needed to be ready for whatever followed them up the ramp.

The group gathered near the loading ramp, the last rays of daylight catching the edges of the rusted hull. Crewmen paced the upper deck, pretending disinterest—but the way they paused near the boarding ropes or tracked movement below said otherwise.

Tarian adjusted the strap of his satchel and leaned toward Elara. "Once we're on board, we stick together. No wandering. No chances."

"Agreed," Elara said.

Just as Kaelen stepped forward to speak with the crew, Liora's voice broke in.

"Wait."

The group turned. Liora stood a few paces away, Sylas and Nyra behind her. The twins carried their meager belongings in worn canvas sacks. They looked out of place against the steel and shadow of the ship—too young, too exposed.

"They need to come with us," Liora said.

Dorian was the first to speak. "Absolutely not. We're hunted. This isn't a mission where we adopt children."

Tarian backed him up immediately. "They don't belong in this."

"They don't belong here either," Liora shot back. "They're alone. Stranded. Being watched."

Kaelen's voice cut in, even and quiet. "None of us belong here. That's the whole point."

Dorian turned to him, incredulous. "You want to put them on a ship with armed strangers? What happens when we're attacked again? You think they'll be safer next to us?"

"I think they'll be safer not sleeping in alleyways while pirates circle," Kaelen said.

Elara looked between them. She hadn't said a word yet, but her gaze lingered on the twins—on their tired postures, the way they clutched their satchels like lifelines.

"Bring them."

Tarian stared at her. "You're serious?"

"I am."

Tarian shook his head once. "Fine. But their safety is on you."

Liora beamed and turned, waving the twins forward. Sylas looked stunned. Nyra blinked like she wasn't sure she'd heard right. But they stepped forward, cautious but willing.

Wiz let out a soft chirp as they passed. Kaelen offered a nod, and Liora gave Nyra's shoulder a squeeze.

As Kaelen reached the top of the ramp, he paused. His hand brushed the doorframe leading into the central corridor. Carved faintly into the dark wood—nearly worn smooth by time and salt—was a series of lines:

"For change to come, a life must part,
To mend the world, to heal the heart.
In shadows deep, the whispers call,
The moment's near, the dawn will fall."

Elara stepped up beside him, eyes narrowing at the faded script.

"The Forgotten Song," she murmured.

Dorian joined them, reading over her shoulder. "Just the last verse."

"Maybe that's the only part they thought mattered," Kaelen said quietly.

No one spoke after that. But they all boarded with a little more weight behind their steps.

The air carried the scent of metal and misdirection.

But now, they weren't just six fugitives chasing a broken prophecy.

Now, they were eight.

And with every new step onto the creaking deck, the stakes crept higher.

The ship eased from the dock with a groan of rusted metal and a hiss of steam pressure. Ropes were uncoiled, anchors drawn, and the mooring lines released efficienctly. The deck vibrated underfoot as the vessel pulled into open water, carving through the waves with slow, stubborn determination.

The sky had shifted to that strange color only seen between storms—too gray to be calm, too still to trust. Kaelen stood near the aft railing of the ship, eyes tracing the rolling horizon. His pack rested at his feet. No tools. No distractions. Just sea.

"You've got the look of someone expecting the ocean to answer back," came a voice.

Kaelen turned. A man—older, clean-cut but plainly dressed—stood just a few paces away. He wore no captain's insignia, but something about his posture said he didn't ask permission to be where he stood.

"Just needed air," Kaelen said.

The man nodded. "Ships are good for that. They don't ask what you're running from. They just carry you forward."

Kaelen glanced back toward the horizon. "As long as they don't break apart first."

"The ones that carry too much always creak. Doesn't mean they fail."

A pause. Then, quieter: "Some things just need to be carried by the right hands."

Kaelen turned toward him again—but the man had already started walking off toward the bridge ladder.

He didn't ask for a name. And the man didn't offer one.

Sylas and Nyra were the first to explore, running their fingers along the warped rails, eyes wide as the shoreline pulled away behind them. They ducked between crates, climbed stairs with the reckless energy of children released from confinement. Wiz, not to be outdone, scrambled up the rigging with a clatter of limbs. The line sagged noticeably under his new weight, and a crew member cursed under his breath before stomping off to rebalance the tension.

Kaelen leaned against one of the forward bulkheads, his gauntlet resting idle at his side. He watched the crew as they moved about the deck—coiling lines, adjusting sails, barking short orders. Everything was in order, almost too much so. The crew knew what they were doing—efficient, focused—but it was their silence that struck him. No jokes, no shouting over the wind, no chatter that usually filled the deck of a vessel leaving port.

"Too quiet," Kaelen muttered. Dorian, nearby, gave a slight nod. "Professional. But not merchant work."

"They're men of the sea," Tarian said from behind them. "But that doesn't mean they're the right kind."

Below deck, Liora leaned against a stacked crate, chatting quietly with the twins. Sylas leaned in, voice hushed.

"We saw them earlier. At the dock."

"Who?" Liora asked.

"Pirates," Nyra said. "From before. They didn't look surprised to see us."

Liora frowned. "Why didn't you say anything?"

"They didn't move. Didn't follow. Just… watched."

Above, the ship's prow dipped and rose with the waves, the sea beneath them shifting into deeper blue. Gulls wheeled far behind them, chasing the scent of the mainland. The last sight of Smeltport faded into mist.

Unnoticed by the group, a cloaked figure stood along the starboard edge, halfway between two ventilation stacks. He kept his face low, eyes tracking the crew—not the passengers. He hadn't spoken to anyone. Hadn't drawn attention.

He had boarded just before departure, indistinct from the last few late hands. No one questioned him. No one looked close. But he watched everything. Listened to everything.

The mysterious man kept his hood low and his movements minimal, a silent observer lost in the background.

The ship creaked. The sun dipped. Water churned.

And somewhere in the rhythm of waves and metal and wind, the trap around them began to close.

They were at sea now. And there was no turning back.

Hours passed beneath an ashen sky, the ship carved its way up the broad river in perfect rhythm. By late afternoon, a narrow bend revealed a cluster of wood-planked buildings hugging the muddy banks—more waystation than settlement, nestled where trade routes briefly kissed the water. The current slackened as the ship slowed, anchor dropping with a shuddering clank.

A ramp extended. Three of the ship's crew descended without fanfare, carrying short documents and empty crates. They moved with too much purpose for ordinary deckhands. Dorian, standing near the railing, watched them disappear between the low wooden structures.

"They're not Forgeborne," he said quietly. "Not by dress. Not by movement."

Elara joined him, arms folded. Her eyes narrowed toward one of the men who lagged slightly behind the others. Something clung to him—an aura, faint but distinct.

"There's magic on that one," she murmured. "Verdant. And not natural."

"Subtle enough to pass unnoticed?"

"Barely. Someone masked it—but the residue's still there."

Kaelen stood at the bow, watching the shoreline like it might rise up and speak. Wiz padded up beside him, sensors flickering behind his eyes as he scanned the docks in silence. Kaelen crouched briefly and tapped a port behind Wiz's shoulder joint. A light blinked once across Kaelen's gauntlet interface in response.

"Keep your scan lines running," Kaelen said under his breath. "Low pulse, no alert tones. Just feed me what you see."

Liora approached with the twins in tow, both of whom seemed oblivious to the growing unease. Nyra clutched a small roll of dried fruit someone had given her earlier, while Sylas trailed behind, distracted by the swaying lanterns strung between poles on the docks.

"Why are we stopping here?" Liora asked.

"To pick something up," Kaelen replied, eyes still on the men returning from the riverbank.

More crates came aboard—sealed tightly, stacked too cleanly. No one said what was in them.

Tarian exchanged a brief glance with Dorian. "This stop wasn't on any schedule. That crew knew exactly where to go."

The sky began to darken—not from dusk, but from pressure. The air had shifted. Heavier. Sharper.

Elara's fingers hovered near her staff, and Kaelen shifted his stance just enough to mask a pull on one of his gauntlet's locks.

Something was coiling around them. Not yet sprung, but felt. Known.

As the last crate was loaded and the ship pulled free from the riverside dock, none of the crew spoke. They returned to their stations with mechanical efficiency. Eyes forward. Mouths closed.

Kaelen watched them retreat, each step a confirmation.

"They're not here to sail," he said. "They're here to watch us."

Dorian gave a grim nod.

And still, the ship moved forward—cutting along the wide river, its wake dragging behind them like a tether.

Toward something none of them had agreed to.

The storm was no longer coming.

It was circling.

The river carried them forward under a sky the color of steel, the wind picking up just enough to rattle the rigging. Mist clung low to the water's surface, casting everything in a gray sheen that made distance hard to judge. The ship's rhythm had settled into an uneasy calm, the groan of boards and hiss of steam weaving with the hush of the current. But the crew—those who had barely spoken since the last stop—now moved with a purpose too sharp to ignore.

Kaelen was the first to notice. The crates. They were gone from the deck. Moved below. Too quickly. He opened his mouth to speak—

—and that's when the ship exploded into motion.

Steel flashed. Ropes were cut. Hidden weapons drawn.

The crew were no crew at all.

They moved like predators sprung from hiding—three at the stern, two more from the shadowed hold, another emerging from behind the navigation hub. Faces once blank with maritime routine now twisted with intent, knives and short spears confidently drawn. Predatory. In seconds, the ship was no longer theirs.

The twins screamed. Sylas shoved Nyra toward the mast as a cloaked pirate lunged. Liora leapt forward, instinct overtaking hesitation. Wind burst around her, knocking the pirate sideways, but the man recovered with brutal speed, crashing into her shoulder-first. She grunted, staggering but staying upright.

Kaelen's gauntlet roared to life with a crackle. He surged forward and met an attacker with a kinetic blast, hurling the man into the railing so hard it splintered. Another charged, but Kaelen spun, dropping low and driving his elbow into the pirate's gut. He didn't check if they stayed down—too many, too fast.

"Wiz, flank left!" Kaelen barked.

Wiz zipped from the shadows with a whir of limbs, skirting around barrels and crates. He locked onto a target—and then vanished under a weighted net dropped from the rigging. His cry of static anguish tore through Kaelen's focus.

Dorian had already drawn his hammer, pivoting into the fight with controlled violence. He drove the head into a pirate's shoulder, knocking the man out of formation. Tarian flanked him, blade flashing in clean arcs, his footwork fluid as he parried and countered two blades at once.

But it wasn't enough.

They were outnumbered. Outmaneuvered. Surrounded.

Elara lifted her staff, a burst of green light swirling in her palm—but a silver flash arced toward her. Arin lunged from the side, conjuring vines that caught the blade mid-air. The spell fizzled, redirected too late. A second pirate emerged, striking Arin hard across the back. She cried out and crumpled.

"Elara!" Dorian shouted.

"I'm fine!" she lied through gritted teeth, blood trailing from her temple.

Tarian was driven to a knee, held down by sheer force of numbers. Kaelen tried to reach him but was clipped across the jaw by a hilt. He dropped back, dazed.

Then came the smoke.

A thick hiss from below deck—a chemical bomb, probably from one of the sealed crates. The deck filled with choking mist. Vision blurred. Footing lost. Screams rang out through shadow.

Bindings. Shackles. Screams.

When the chaos cleared, the deck was littered with bruised bodies and broken wood. Ropes coiled around limbs. Blood painted the rails. Elara slumped against the railing, one eye nearly swollen shut. Her staff was gone. Kaelen's gauntlet sparked erratically. He coughed, wiping ash from his mouth.

Dorian and Tarian had been dragged to the mast, wrists bound and weapons stripped. Liora knelt over the twins, trembling, her body angled defensively, her eyes refusing to leave the nearest threat.

Arin lay on her side, struggling to breathe, one arm curled protectively across her ribs.

The attackers did not cheer.

They didn't need to.

The ship was silent except for the faint creak of the hull and the lap of the river against the sides.

They had failed.

Not finally. But undeniably.

And someone else now held the river's reins.

At the bow, a lone figure adjusted their cloak, face still hidden. The shadows clung to him like armor. As the chaos erupted, he slipped back behind a stack of crates, moving without sound.

He hadn't drawn a weapon. Hadn't even moved to help. He simply watched from the dark edges of the hold, eyes scanning, calculating. No one noticed him vanish when the real fighting began.

He hadn't come to join the ambush.

He'd come to see what they would do.

Because this ambush wasn't just about seizing the ship.

It was about what happened next—who rose, who broke, and who was worth following.

And as the smoke thinned and the groans of the injured faded into silence, the hidden observer stayed still.

Waiting.

Because he hadn't decided yet.

Not about them.

And definitely not about himself.

The ship rocked gently, its hull groaning under the weight of silence. Below deck, the light was thin and amber, filtered through slats in the boards overhead. Dust danced in the stillness.

The captives had been split. Elara, Liora, Arin, and Nyra were locked in a small storage cabin—little more than a converted hold with warped walls and crates reeking of fish and iron. The men—Kaelen, Dorian, Tarian, and Sylas—were held somewhere deeper, their voices distant but audible.

Elara knelt near the wall, pressing her palm to the boards. She whispered a grovecaller's incantation, coaxing the roots, searching for moisture, but there was nothing. The wood was too old, too dry. It did not answer.

She closed her eyes in frustration.

Nearby, Liora crouched and placed her arm around Nyra. Liora whispered stories—bad ones, disjointed and half-made-up—but the rhythm was steady, her voice calm. It worked. For now.

Arin sat slumped against a barrel, her breathing shallow but controlled. She hadn't spoken since they were thrown into the hold. Her hand glowed faintly over her side, guiding what healing magic she could.

Meanwhile, in the darker bowels of the ship, Kaelen and Dorian sat back-to-back in a rust-streaked cell lit by a single swinging lamp. Tarian knelt a few feet away, his wrists bound behind him, his eyes as he ran calculation.

"They're going to regroup," Kaelen muttered.

"No," Dorian said. "They already have."

Kaelen flexed his wrists against the rope, glancing toward the shadows. "If I could reach my satchel, I could fry this lock."

"Except they took your satchel. And your gauntlet."

Kaelen scowled. "They're amateurs with lucky timing."

Dorian didn't answer. He looked toward the locked grate, where a faint red flicker pulsed once—then vanished.

Before either of them could speak again, something shifted. A faint creak. A rustle of cloth.

Then the lock clicked.

A hooded figure appeared, framed in the lamplight. He wore no insignia. No armor. Just a long, travel-worn cloak and gloved hands. His face remained hidden, shadows clinging to every angle.

He said nothing. Simply nodded at Kaelen.

The gauntlet—stripped and cast aside in the corner—flickered once, then roared to life. Not violently, but steady. Functional.

Beside it, Wiz stirred with a shuddering whir. His chassis twitched. Lights behind his eyes blinked erratically, then steadied with a soft hum, like a machine rousing from a long sleep. Panels flexed, gears clicked into alignment, and he rose unsteadily to his feet.

Kaelen's eyes widened. He scrambled across the cell and gripped the gauntlet, the familiar weight anchoring him. Behind him, Wiz gave a sharp chirp and scanned the room with renewed alertness.

"Who—?" he began.

The figure raised a hand. Not to threaten. Just to halt the question.

Then he stepped aside.

The door swung open.

Kaelen didn't hesitate. Dorian grabbed Tarian and followed. As they rushed past the stranger, Kaelen stole one more glance back.

The man's posture was still. Measured. And as the trio vanished into the corridor, the figure turned and moved—not toward freedom, but deeper into the ship.

Elara's cell opened next. The same motion. The same silence.

She blinked against the sudden light and saw him—just a silhouette now.

"Who are you?" she asked.

But he was already gone.

Liora stood up, helping Arin to her feet. "I don't care who he is," she muttered. "That's twice we've been rescued by someone we didn't invite."

Nyra looked up, voice thin. "Was he one of the pirates?"

"No," Elara said softly. "I don't think he's with them. I think he was watching."

"And now?" Liora asked.

Elara looked toward the stairs.

"Now he's acting."

The ship had become a battlefield before they reached the top deck. Smoke hung low, mingling with the salty air and the bitter scent of scorched rope. Somewhere, a bell rang—a dull, uneven sound that might have once meant shift change, now a call to chaos.

The cloaked man moved first. He positioned himself just outside the stairwell's frame, guiding the group without commanding them. He wasn't barking orders. He didn't need to. Every motion was precise, efficient, a signal. Kaelen caught on quickly.

"Use the upper corridor," the cloaked figure said quietly, pointing two fingers toward a line of crates.

Kaelen nodded, knelt by Wiz, and tapped the small disc embedded behind the automaton's shoulder plate. A blue line pulsed forward, arcing through the fog like a beacon only the team could see.

"Wiz can track heat signatures. You'll know who's waiting before they know we're coming."

"Three ahead," Kaelen confirmed. "Stacked formation. Waiting for a signal."

The cloaked figure gave one nod.

Liora, crouched near a ventilation pipe, drew the hybrid device Kaelen had cobbled together for her—a sleek metallic bracelet, very subtle and barely Forgeborne in appearance. She whispered something to herself, and slammed her palm down on the side valve.

A hissing roar burst from the pipe. Two pirates, caught mid-sprint, reeled back in a wave of scalding steam. One dropped his blade. The other screamed and stumbled into a stack of barrels, crashing through like splintered driftwood.

From the other side of the deck, Dorian emerged. His hammer returned to him with satisfying weight—he spun once and brought it down across the shoulders of the pirate captain, who barely managed to turn before crumpling.

Tarian flanked two more, his strikes clean and brutal, dropping them before they could rally.

Elara, shielding Arin with one arm, swept her staff low. Vines burst from a nearby railing, entangling the legs of another pirate just as he lunged. He hit the deck hard and didn't rise.

Arin knelt beside a wounded sailor, hands glowing, her magic flowing steady this time. There was no hesitation. No faltering. Just purpose.

Kaelen vaulted over a broken crate, driving his gauntlet into a pirate's gut. The shock discharge sent the man flying into the mast, where he crumpled and slid down unconscious. Wiz, dormant through the early assault, suddenly flared to life with a mechanical whir and a cascade of rebooting tones. His sensors blinked, eyes flaring blue. He zipped around behind Kaelen, projecting bursts of static that disrupted magic and kept the rest of the crew in disarray.

The pirate captain staggered to his feet, bruised but not broken, wiping blood from his lip with the back of a gauntleted hand. "You should've stayed out of this," he spat, voice gravelly. "This isn't about you. It's about them."

He jabbed a finger toward Sylas and Nyra, who froze. The captain's eyes gleamed with something colder than greed—obligation.

Sylas took a hesitant step forward, disbelief painted across his face. "I know you... You serve our father."

The words landed like a blade point-first. Nyra's face paled.

The captain grunted. "Retrieval mission. That's all this is. You come quietly, your new friends stay breathing."

Kaelen's gauntlet sparked. Elara's grip on her staff tightened. Dorian didn't move—but the tension in his frame warned what was coming.

"They're not going anywhere with you," Liora said, stepping forward, eyes locked.

The pirate captain rolled his shoulders, disappointed but not surprised. "Fine. If you want to die for them, so be it. We'll sell your corpses as a bonus."

Then the cloaked figure surged forward, moving through the chaos. A sudden flash of steel deflected a pirate's blade just before it reached Elara's side. The figure pivoted, drove the attacker back, then turned.

He reached up and pulled back his hood.

Elara froze. "Sariel?"

Kaelen blinked. "You've got to be kidding me."

Dorian lowered his hammer, wary. "Where have you been? The last time we saw you, you stayed behind to fight Aldric's forces"

Sariel met Elara's gaze. "Aldric withdrew his forces the moment he saw you three escape. We tried running after them but in the end we knew you three got away safely. I went back to Hollowgrove then I came to find you. To make sure the prophecy stays alive."

No time for more. A final wave of pirates surged forward.

"Later," Sariel said, and moved to intercept.

The twins stayed low near the helm, watching with wide eyes. Sylas looked ready to spring. Nyra gripped his arm tightly, whispering, "Not yet. Let them finish it."

Nearby, Liora crouched protectively in front of them, eyes darting to every movement. Her bracelet clanged on her wrist. She shielded the twins with her magic, a wall of water and steam as another pirate staggered forward, only to be intercepted by Arin, who used her staff to throw him back into a mast support.

Arin moved to Liora's side, casting a protective spell over the trio while maintaining her position near the fallen sailor she had just healed. Her breathing was shallow.

Tarian held the line ahead of them, blades flashing in controlled arcs. He fought like a wall—calculated and punishing. Any pirate who tried to reach the helm was met with his blade. He didn't speak. He didn't need to. His intent was written in the precision of his strikes and the way he positioned himself between the twins and danger.

As the skirmish thinned, the makeshift unit of Liora, Arin, and Tarian held their ground like they'd trained together. They hadn't. But something between instinct and trust kept them from faltering.

Within moments, the fighting slowed. Then stopped.

The remaining pirates—those not unconscious or incapacitated—hesitated, glancing toward their fallen captain. Bloodied and bruised, he stood again, sneering.

"You'll regret this," he snarled. "You just made enemies of The Black Maw. This ain't over—not by a longshot. We've got long memories—and longer knives."

One of the pirates—tattooed, lean, with Verdant-style markings braided into his hair—raised both hands to the sky. The wind shifted. Waves churned beneath the ship. A skiff, small and low in the water, rose from the far side of the hull, held steady by water and wind manipulated through raw elemental power.

The pirate captain leapt onto the skiff, blood dripping from his chin. He locked eyes with the twins, and his final words carried over the deck like a curse.

"You're marked now. Next time, you'll fetch more than coin."

With a snap of his fingers, the mage beside him surged the skiff away, pushing the river behind them in a swirl of power. Water crested in their wake, and then they were gone, swallowed into the mist that drifted over the surface.

Sylas and Nyra stood in stunned silence. Sylas looked like he might throw up.

"He… he works for our father, some of them as well." he finally said.

Nyra said nothing. Her face was pale, locked in unreadable tension. They didn't explain further—and no one pressed. Not yet.

The remaining pirates—those too injured to escape or unwilling to follow their captain—threw down their weapons. A few dove overboard, refusing to face whatever retribution the ship's defenders might offer.

Elara looked up at the sails, half-torn but still standing. The ship listed slightly, but it held.

The ship was theirs again.

Barely.

And no one dared to believe it would stay that way for long.

The storm had passed, but the silence it left behind felt heavier than the fight.

Smoke curled in the broken spaces above deck. Blood streaked across the railings and the floorboards. The sails, though tattered, still caught the river wind. The group stood in a loose circle—battered, breathing, bruised—but standing. The weight of what had just transpired settled on them like a second skin.

Sariel pulled his hood back up, but the weight of his reappearance lingered. Elara hadn't looked away since he'd stepped in. She moved toward him now—not fast, not slow. Just certain.

"You waited this whole time?" she asked, her voice low.

Sariel gave a tired nod. "I had to know. I needed to see if the three of you were what the prophecy truly meant—if you were just echoes or the thing itself. Now I know."

He turned to glance toward the twins, who huddled near Liora. His tone shifted, more grave. "They're not the only ones being hunted."

Kaelen walked to the bow, leaning against the splintered rail. His gauntlet crackled softly as he deactivated the combat pulse. For a moment, he just stared into the river.

"Then it doesn't stop here," he muttered. "Irondale's next."

Dorian stepped beside him, brushing dirt from his sleeve. "This party is getting bigger and bigger each day we get closer to Nocturne's Edge."

Elara joined him, saying nothing. The current whispered beneath them, a slow but relentless pull forward.

Liora knelt beside Sylas and Nyra, who hadn't said much since the pirate captain vanished into the mist. Their shoulders were hunched, their hands still trembling from adrenaline. She placed a hand gently on Sylas's shoulder.

"So. Pirate royalty, huh?" she said with a half-smile that wasn't entirely forced.

Sylas looked down. His voice was a whisper. "It's not something we wanted to be."

Nyra nodded slowly. "We left for a reason. We weren't supposed to be... part of that."

"Yeah, well," Liora said, rising to her feet, brushing dirt from her leggings, "I once set a noble's laundry on fire and accidentally turned a city fountain into a geyser. So who am I to judge?"

The twins blinked. Then, to their own surprise, they laughed—short, shaky, but real.

"You two might've been a terrible choice to bring aboard," Liora added with a chuckle. "But I guess that makes three of us."

Tarian stood off to the side, checking the edge of his blade, but his hand trembled faintly. Arin approached, placing a hand on his arm.

"You held the line," she said gently.

He didn't meet her eyes at first. "You held the twins. That mattered more."

Arin leaned into him slightly. "You're hurt."

"So are you."

She touched the edge of his jaw, where a bruise was already darkening.

"You bruise easier than I thought."

"Only when someone's watching."

They didn't move further. But the air between them shifted—closer, quieter. Something unsaid passed between them, and for once, neither needed to speak it aloud.

At the center of the ship, the wind stilled. The sails fluttered, then hung loose in a hush that settled over the deck.

The stars blinked above them. A sky cleared of clouds, as if even the heavens were catching their breath.

Then, just before the last torch was lowered, a ripple disturbed the water beside the ship.

Barely noticeable.

But moving.

A soft clang echoed from below deck—metal against metal, too deliberate to be wind.

Kaelen turned, just slightly. Dorian tensed. Elara's hand dropped to the haft of her staff.

Then a faint sound—clicks, like something mechanical crawling up the outer hull. Wiz's sensors flickered red.

The water stilled again.

Too still.

Chapter 14: Salt and Sparks

The ship carved through the fog like a wound reopening. Brine clung to every rail and rope, stinging eyes and rusting metal as it creaked toward the jagged coastline. Salt crusted the edges of the deck where waves had slapped high during the night, and the air reeked of seaweed, smoke, and something older—like scorched iron buried beneath sand.

Ahead, the Godless Lands rose from the water like the bones of a broken continent. Cracked bluffs, bramble-choked gullies, and scorched ridges made up the shoreline. Long-forgotten siege engines sagged in ruin near the cliffs, half-swallowed by time. Towering above it all stood a crumbling coastal watchtower—its flagpole bare, its peak blackened by past fire.

Elara stood at the bow, cloak snapping in the wind. She made no move to wave, no attempt to posture or plead. The people of this place had seen too many banners, too many claims of rescue. This wasn't her land, and she wouldn't pretend otherwise.

Behind her, the rest of the group began their preparations. Dorian adjusted the strap on his hammer, scanning the coastline with a soldier's discipline. Kaelen double-checked the magnetic stabilizers in his gauntlet—focused, precise. Liora huddled near the twins, shielding them from the wind with her cloak, while Arin gave Sylas medicine for another bout of seasickness.

Tarian stood near the ship's wheel, hands braced, eyes locked on the dock ahead. "No signal yet," he muttered. "But we're being watched."

No one argued. Figures were beginning to appear through the fog—shapes at first, then silhouettes, then people. Men and women stood along the weather-beaten dock, weapons at their sides. Not a uniform among them. Just layers of salvaged gear and the kind of posture that said they'd survived worse than strangers with a ship.

Many bore visible damage—scars, burns, missing limbs, sun-hardened skin. Some wore armor cobbled from scrap and animal hide. Others had nothing but tools turned into weapons.

The dock itself was barely holding together. Planks warped from salt and time. Nails rusted through. It jutted from the rock like it had no right to still be standing.

Elara said nothing. None of them did. The ship drifted closer, sails already furled, forward motion surrendered to the tide.

Tarian gave a nod. "Ready up."

The group gathered at the edge of the deck. Bags slung. Weapons secured. No one reached for them—not yet.

They hadn't been welcomed. But they hadn't been fired on either.

And in the Godless Lands, that was as good a start as any.

As the crew prepared to descend the gangplank, Liora took one last look around the ship's deck. The wind caught her hair, sending half of it into her eyes, but she didn't care.

She stepped onto a coil of rope like a makeshift podium and cleared her throat with dramatic weight.

"Before we abandon this fine vessel to the salt and the sea" she declared, one arm raised like she was addressing a grand court, "I, Liora Greenwood, do hereby claim her in the name of absolutely no royal house. From this moment forward, she shall be known as the Dawnseeker—fearsome, barely afloat, and mine."

Kaelen looked up from checking Wiz's leg joints. "Is this… official?"

"It is now," Liora said, chin held high. She turned to the twins. "Sylas, Nyra—you're promoted. First Mate and Second Mate. Congratulations."

Nyra immediately pointed at her brother. "Why is he First Mate?"

"Because I'm older," Sylas shot back.

"By two minutes and twenty seconds!"

"Still counts."

Liora crossed her arms. "Settle it on deck or settle it in the brig—oh wait, we don't have one."

Wiz chirped as if in agreement.

Arin smirked from the railing. "You do realize we're not staying on the ship?"

Liora waved her hand. "Technicalities. The Dawnseeker will await our return. Possibly sink in the meantime. Still mine."

Elara shook her head but said nothing. Even now, with storm clouds building in every direction, the moment carved out a small breath of normalcy. And it held—just long enough to remind them all what it felt like to smile without flinching.

Tarian stood near the ship's wheel, eyes fixed on the shoreline.

"They're watching," he said quietly, arms crossed over his chest. "Can't see 'em all yet, but they're there."

Dorian stepped up beside him. "You think we'll get into a fight?"

"Not immediately," Tarian replied. "But I've seen ambushes that looked like welcomes before." He pointed toward the dock's edge, where shadows shifted behind crates and stacked salvage. "We'd be stupid to go in blind."

Dorian nodded once, grim. "Same setup as Anviltown."

"Exactly what I was thinking," Tarian said. "We should post someone on the ship. Two, if we had the numbers. One to scout the dock, one to watch the waterline."

Before Dorian could respond, Elara approached. Arin followed just behind her.

"You're planning for a fight before we've even said a word," Elara said.

"We're planning in case we don't get to say much at all," Tarian replied. "These people aren't Verdant or Forgeborne. If things go sideways, we can't rely on shared codes."

"Which is why we'll need you both with us," Arin said. Her tone wasn't forceful, but it cut cleanly. "If they're hurt or suspicious, they'll need someone to de-escalate. And not just with swords."

"Great," Tarian muttered. "So no one's watching the ship."

"I will," Sariel said.

He was already at the railing, hands clasped behind his back, gaze flicking from the docks to the cliffs beyond. "If it's recon you need, I'm the best chance you have. No one will see me unless I want them to. You'll have my eyes—quiet and steady."

Tarian looked at Dorian. Dorian gave the smallest nod. "He's right. We go. He stays."

Sariel didn't wait for more approval. He stepped back from the group, already fading into the ship's structure like he belonged to it.

"Let's not pretend this is anything but a gamble," Tarian said.

"We've been gambling since Forgehelm," Dorian replied. "Might as well play it through."

He didn't like it. But he moved. "Alright. Let's move."

Then the wind shifted.

And it was time to disembark.

They hadn't made it ten paces off the dock before the welcome committee arrived. Half a dozen militia men and women, leathers patchworked with metal plates and older tech, stepped out from between stacked crates and sand-worn scaffolds. Their leader—an elderly woman, stocky, scar-faced, and squinting against the salty wind—lifted a rusted repeater rifle just enough to make the message clear.

"Names. Purpose. And don't lie. We're short on patience and shorter on water."

Kaelen, Dorian, Elara, and Tarian paused just short of the gathering line of militia. For a breath, no one said anything.

"We need someone to speak," Kaelen murmured.

"I'll go," Tarian said. "Time I did something useful. This might be the one thing I'm good at."

Dorian gave a short nod. "Politics always bored me. You want it, you've got it."

Kaelen glanced at Elara. "Are you good with that?"

Elara hesitated. "I wanted to be the one to speak. But if you're ready for it, Tarian... it's yours."

Behind them, Arin, Liora, and the twins stood close, eyes scanning the militia, ready if the conversation turned.

Tarian moved forward slowly, hands visible and open. "We're not here to take anything. Just passing through. Headed inland."

"Where inland?" the man snapped.

"Northwest, toward Irondale."

The rifle dipped an inch. "You lot don't look like merchants."

"We're not." Tarian kept his tone steady. "But we're not soldiers either. Not anymore."

Dorian remained behind him, arms loose at his sides but his stance unyielding. He didn't speak. Sometimes silence worked better than anything else. Especially here, where words were currency and nobody had much to spare.

Elara stood at Tarian's flank, watching the crowd that had begun to gather near the fringes—dozens of hollowed eyes, hardened hands, and cloaks stitched from mismatched cloth. These were not people waiting for inspiration. They were waiting for a reason not to turn hostile.

"I recognize your voice," one of the militia said to Tarian, narrowing her eyes. "You served in Eldoravell."

"I did," Tarian replied. "I left it, too."

The admission landed with weight.

But the mood shifted when a second militiaman leaned close to the leader and whispered something. She didn't take her eyes off Elara.

"I've seen them before," one of the militia muttered. "Not here, but in a report passed through Mirewatch. A month back. Said a Forgehelm mechcrafter vanished with a relic the council wanted sealed."

Another stepped forward, eyeing Dorian. "And the Titanbreaker who let him go. Turned his hammer on the Forgemasters instead of the Verdant."

The leader didn't move. But her aim shifted—slightly. Not lowered. Just… less certain.

A third voice cut in, quieter but clearer. "The girl's supposed to be dead. Elara of Eldoravell. They sent blades for her. She sent the forest back instead."

For a moment, no one breathed.

"Those stories drift through with the refugees," the leader said flatly. "Half lies."

"Sure," the man replied. "But look at them. You tell me it doesn't fit."

The rifle stayed raised, but the aim softened.

Near a broken post, Arin knelt beside a child hunched against the wall, their arm twisted and bruised. The child flinched when she reached out, but Arin didn't say a word. Her hand hovered over the injury, a faint light pulsing from her fingers—not showy, just deliberate. A breath later, the swelling eased. The child blinked up at her in shock.

Someone noticed. Then another. Not with awe—but with something closer to confusion.

"Why'd she do that?" one man muttered.

"She didn't even ask for a coin."

Liora shifted closer to Elara and whispered, "Do they think we're here to rob them?"

"They think we're here to remind them what they lost," Elara replied.

Kaelen kept his eyes on the surroundings. "We should move before this gets interpreted the wrong way."

But the gruff leader finally lowered her rifle. "You've got two days. You act up, you answer to all of us."

Tarian nodded once. "Fair."

They were granted entry—not with trust, but with tolerance. The first gate cracked open just wide enough to let them through.

Behind them, the wind carried the scent of brine and soil. Ahead, the streets wound through a city that had learned to live in the aftermath—and now had to decide if it would survive a story come to life.

The streets beyond the checkpoint were narrow, sun-bleached, and marked by old fire. Burn lines traced the edges of windows and door frames, a map of past violence etched into every structure. The people here didn't move with discipline or unity—they moved with caution. Not the kind born of fear, but of memory. The kind that came from being left behind.

They weren't Verdant. They weren't Forgeborne. They were the ones forgotten by both. The ones punished not by gods—but by silence.

It didn't take long for a crowd to gather, slow and deliberate. Among them stood an older woman, the village's leader. A thick scar ran from her temple to her jaw, faded but impossible to miss. Her eyes—smoke-gray and unblinking—landed on Elara and didn't look away.

"You," she said. Her voice didn't tremble. "I know your face. Verdant royalty."

Elara stopped mid-step. Dorian moved to her side, ready to intercept, but she raised a hand to halt him.

"You came from towers with gardens that bloom year-round," the woman said. "We came from fields that turned to salt because we didn't pray hard enough. That's what they told us, didn't they? That we were punished. Because we stopped believing."

Elara's voice was steady. "I was taught that, too. I know now it was a lie."

The woman didn't blink. "Knowing that it's a lie will not change what it costs."

Liora stepped in, nervous but trying. "We're not here to claim anything. We're just passing through."

The woman eyed her up and down. "You flinch too easily to be trusted. You've never seen what happens when people like us get told to wait for help. You wait long enough, you learn the help is never coming."

Liora's voice caught. Arin touched her back gently, steadying her without words.

Kaelen stepped forward. "She's not wrong. Not entirely."

That got the woman's attention.

"We weren't sent here by councils or orders. We're not emissaries. We're refugees. Fugitive ones, at that."

"You're Forgeborne," the woman said, tone unreadable.

Kaelen nodded. "And they tried to cut me out the moment I stopped fitting the mold. Dorian too. And Elara? She's standing here because she left her palace behind. Not for power. For something real."

The crowd quieted. No shift in mood, just breath held.

Kaelen continued, not louder—but firmer. "I don't care if you trust us. I wouldn't either. But I know what it's like to be thrown away because someone decided you didn't believe the right thing. That's why we're here. Not to change your mind. Just to survive. Same as you."

The silence didn't break. But it bent—just slightly.

The woman leaned on her cane and stepped back. "Then survive without drawing blood. Do that, and maybe the rest will come."

Someone in the crowd whispered her name: Tessan.

Elara inclined her head. "Understood."

The crowd began to scatter, slow and wary. No acceptance. But no open resistance either. A corridor through grief and suspicion. Just wide enough to pass through.

The elder's words still hung in the air, a bitter truth no one argued. Elara had offered no defense. None would have helped.

Kaelen lingered at the railing, eyes scanning the waterline. The tide slapped against the Dawnseeker's hull, rhythmic and indifferent. Behind him, the crew was quiet. Even the twins stayed back, sensing the shift in mood.

Wiz, crouched at Kaelen's feet, chirped twice—short, abrupt. Not a warning, but not idle chatter either.

Kaelen knelt. "What is it?"

The automaton's sensor array flicked open. A narrow beam of blue light shimmered across the deck and traced down over the side. Kaelen tapped the side of his gauntlet, syncing the feed. What came through wasn't ambient noise. It was a pulse—steady, deliberate.

A Forgeborne signal.

Low frequency. Tracking pattern. Embedded sync markers. Kaelen's pulse quickened. They were being tracked again.

"We're marked," he said.

Dorian stepped in. "Verdant?"

Kaelen shook his head. "Worse. It's Forgeborne. A mechcrafter's tag. They know we're here."

Tarian swore under his breath.

"Can you triangulate it?" Liora asked.

Kaelen nodded. "It's under the hull. Starboard side, just forward of the rudder. Couldn't see it from the dock."

"I can give you a pocket," Liora said. She moved to the edge, hands braced against the rail. The water churned, then pulled back, air rushing into the void like breath filling lungs. Beneath the wooden hull, the tide parted—revealing a hollow chamber just large enough to work in.

Sariel stepped forward. "I'll go with him."

Dorian frowned. "You sure?"

Sariel nodded. "I'm lighter. And quieter."

Tarian and Dorian took up the ropes without question. Kaelen passed Sariel a coil, then dropped down first.

The air pocket was unnaturally still. The hull, worn but intact, glistened in the light filtering through the warped surface of the sea above.

Wiz skittered beside them, claws clicking softly on the wood.

"There," Kaelen said.

Just aft of the stabilizer fin, a spiderlike automaton clung to the hull. It was forged steel, blackened to dull gray, its limbs splayed flat against the surface. The body pulsed faintly—one red eye blinking in rhythm with the signal Kaelen had tracked.

"Not passive," Sariel said. "It's alive."

Kaelen nodded. "Broadcasting a signal every ten seconds. Same frequency I used for short-range comms back in the city. They're not guessing—we're already flagged."

"Can you disable it?"

"Not without tripping it. If it senses tampering, it might trigger a failsafe. Cut the signal or blow the hull. Maybe both."

Kaelen studied the frame—compact, low-profile, but modular. Military issue. This was Forgehelm work. Someone like Clyne, or worse.

Wiz chirped again, scanning the device.

"Alright," Kaelen muttered. "Let's be quick about this."

He tapped a sequence into his gauntlet. A small blade extended from the underside—thin, ceramic-edged, nonconductive. He didn't trust metal near a Forgeborne power coil, especially one humming like this.

The automaton was still. Not dormant, just patient. Its limbs didn't move, but the central eye rotated—not watching them, but constantly scanning, pinging data to a receiver somewhere across the sea.

Sariel crouched low, weight balanced against the hull. "Tell me where to brace."

"Here," Kaelen pointed. "Front left leg. Keep it pinned. If it flexes, the trigger sequence could cycle."

Sariel leaned in, pressed one hand to the automaton's limb, just above the joint. Kaelen could feel the shift—its internal gyros reacting to the added pressure. It was alive enough to notice.

He didn't hesitate.

Kaelen slid the blade behind the eye, cutting under the surface layer. Sparks hissed, but no shock discharge followed. Good. He angled the tip, pried upward, and slid a small copper probe into the gap.

A click. The red glow dimmed, just for a beat. The broadcast paused. Then resumed.

"Failsafe confirmed," Kaelen muttered. "We're not disarming this. We're replacing the output."

Wiz scurried closer and ejected a small pulse coupler from its side panel. Kaelen took it, slid it under the automaton's casing, and clipped it onto the main signal spine.

Sariel shifted slightly. "What's the plan?"

"Ghost loop. It'll bounce the last known coordinates on a closed loop, as if we never moved."

"Will it work?"

Kaelen glanced up. "If Clyne's behind this, it'll buy us half a day. Maybe less."

He adjusted the gain, pulsed a test signal. The red eye blinked, slower now—staggered. The automaton didn't resist. It simply accepted the new command, unaware it had been hijacked.

"Now," Kaelen whispered.

He reached under the device, found the mounting latch, and twisted. The entire spider assembly detached with a soft metallic crack. No alarms. No discharge. Just the subtle hum of a machine losing purpose.

Kaelen caught it in both hands and slid it into a reinforced pouch on his belt. He'd strip it later—see who keyed the beacon signature.

"Let's go," he said.

Sariel gave the rope two quick tugs. Above, the tension shifted. Dorian and Tarian began pulling them up one by one.

But the water stirred before they broke the surface.

Kaelen felt it first—a ripple, then a hard jolt against his boot.

"Something's wrong," he snapped.

A moment later, the hull vibrated. Then came the clicking—dozens of small impacts, tapping against wood, then scraping metal.

Sariel gritted his teeth. "Kaelen. Look down."

A swarm of dark shapes churned through the water—sharp-limbed, carapaced, and fast. The first Brineclaw clamped onto Kaelen's thigh. Another latched to Sariel's side.

Claws like broken glass tore through fabric and scratched at armor joints. The rope strained as both men kicked and struggled, trying to ascend without being pulled under.

"Hold them!" Dorian shouted above.

Tarian dug in his heels. "They're too heavy—something's on them!"

"Brineclaws," Arin said, already at the railing. "They're nesting under the dock."

From the dock, the water near the Dawnseeker had turned black with motion—hundreds of crustacean limbs clawing upward.

Liora froze. Wind howled in her ears. Her heart slammed against her ribs. Tessan's voice rang in her skull.

You flinch too easily to be trusted.

She took a step back.

Then another voice came—Arin's, not shouting, just steady.

"Liora."

Liora inhaled once. Deep. Sharp. Her hands extended—left toward the hull, right toward the sea.

The air pocket beneath the ship held—barely. But her wind surged out like a wall, ripping across the water. It didn't just scatter the Brineclaws—it lifted them, spinning, hurling them into the rocks along the dock where they shattered on impact.

The water cleared in seconds.

Sariel was the first to reach the deck, soaked and bloodied but breathing. Kaelen followed, one leg dragging. Wiz scrambled after him, hissing steam.

Liora dropped to one knee, sweat streaking her temple.

Tessan watched from the edge of the dock, leaning heavier than usual on her cane. Her eyes—gray and sharp as ever—narrowed as she looked at the girl who had hesitated only once.

"I was wrong about you," she said.

Liora didn't answer right away. She was too busy trying to get her breath back. Liora met Tessan's gaze, chest still heaving—but her eyes didn't waver this time.

"You were right," Liora said, standing again. "I was waiting. I just didn't know it."

No one clapped. No one spoke.

But they'd seen.

The tide around them rumbled as the air pocket collapsed beneath the hull.

By the time their boots hit the deck again, the light below had vanished.

Kaelen looked at Elara, then Dorian. "We're not safe here. We weren't the moment we docked."

Elara nodded. "We leave at first light."

Kaelen didn't argue. He turned and headed below deck, the captured device tucked against his side, still warm from the broadcast it no longer controlled.

Below deck, Kaelen sat cross-legged on the floor, the tracking automaton resting between his tools. It was inert now—red light gone, limbs curled inward like a dead insect. But he didn't trust it. Not yet.

He was considering dismantling the core when a voice broke the silence.

"What's that?" Sylas asked, leaning in from the doorway. Nyra trailed close behind.

Kaelen didn't look up. "Tracker. Forgeborne make. Someone tagged the Dawnseeker. We got it off, but the longer I hold on to it, the more likely it resets… and pings our new coordinates."

Sylas crouched beside him. "Why don't we just throw it away?"

"Not good enough," Kaelen muttered. "If it lands nearby, they'll still find us."

The twins exchanged a look. Nyra stepped forward. "What if it doesn't stay nearby?"

Sylas grinned. "Yeah—just tie it to a piece of driftwood. Let the current handle the rest."

Kaelen blinked, then looked up.

Liora, passing by with a crate of supplies, caught the tail end. "I could nudge it along. Bit of wind, some moving water—it'd be halfway to the horizon before they noticed."

The twins laughed, expecting her to be joking.

But Kaelen stood. "No. That's actually… smart."

They found a flat plank, tied the automaton down, and walked it to the shore. Liora stepped into the shallows, murmured something under her breath, and the sea responded—gentle current stretching like a hand. The makeshift raft drifted off, picking up speed, vanishing into the gray chop beyond the cove.

Back at the ship, Sariel met them at the gangplank. "I'll stay behind," he said. "If someone comes looking, I'll see them before they get close."

No one argued. Sariel had a talent for going unnoticed when it mattered most.

The rest of the group turned toward the village.

There was work to finish.

The wind coming off the water was sharp with salt, grit, and something older—like scorched metal buried beneath the dunes. Most of the group had gone quiet, careful not to impose, but Kaelen had drifted toward the edges of the settlement, where utility pipes rattled beneath makeshift stonework and rust-clung scaffolds framed the remnants of a half-collapsed well.

Nobody asked him to go. Nobody welcomed him either.

He crouched beside a rusted valve, eyes narrowing at the way mineral buildup crusted the seams. It was a simple design—old Forgeborne infrastructure, repurposed into something barely functional. He ran his fingers along the ridged piping and tapped it twice with a flat screwdriver. The echo came back too hollow. Clogged.

Behind him, Wiz padded closer on soft servos, his frame sand-dusted and sun-glared. He chirped quietly and extended a tool from his shoulder port.

Kaelen gave a short nod. "Yeah, let's see what we can do."

He adjusted his gauntlet—but paused. The stabilizer ring jolted slightly, vibrating out of sync. Kaelen frowned and tapped the lens again. The display flickered. Distorted.

"Gauntlet's not reading properly," he muttered. "Too much interference."

Wiz whirred in response and sent out a short scan pulse. Normally, Kaelen kept the sensor feed closed-loop. This time, he let it run. Just for a second.

A flicker.

Something magnetic—low to the ground. South ridge, maybe three hundred meters out. Stationary.

Wiz paused. Scanning again. Then turned his head, ears twitching like he heard something Kaelen couldn't. Something underground or maybe underwater but it's definitely not natural.

Kaelen snapped the interface shut and pressed the seal back into place. "Another time," he said under his breath.

Then he got to work.

He pulled the new gauntlet tighter around his wrist, adjusted the clamps, and started dismantling the cap. Beneath the corroded top, the filter had collapsed in on itself—nothing but rust and sludge.

He dug into his pouch, pulled out a wrapped strip of mesh wire, pressed it into shape, and fitted it inside. Wiz handed him a sealant ring with a mechanical nudge.

One of the nearby children gasped when the valve hissed, then clunked. Water burbled, slow at first, then spilled out into a long-dry basin.

From a distance, adults watched—silent, arms crossed.

Kaelen stood, dusted off his hands, and glanced at the ridge.

Whatever it was—buried or waiting—hadn't moved.

Yet.

Kaelen stood up and dusted off his hands. He glanced back toward the group but didn't call attention to what he'd done.

One of the kids stepped forward. He couldn't have been older than ten. In his outstretched hand was a cracked gear, dulled at the teeth, too worn for use—but cleaned carefully, as if someone had treasured it anyway.

"Might be useful," the boy said, voice flat but sincere.

Kaelen looked at it, then him, and took it without ceremony.

"It might," he said.

A rough voice cut through the silence. "Or maybe he just rigged it to win us over."

A man stepped forward—tall, all ribs and bones, sun-cracked like the others. He jabbed a finger toward Wiz. "That thing scanned the ground. Don't pretend we didn't see it."

Kaelen didn't flinch. "I was checking for structural damage. It's called fixing something before it breaks."

"Or planting something to break it later."

Elara moved beside Kaelen before Dorian could. "We didn't come here to play games with broken water."

The man didn't back off. But he didn't press either.

Tessan's voice rose from the back: "If he wanted to break your well, it'd be broken."

Elara upon seeing the elderly lady from before taking their side, gave a small nod, a sign of gratitude for defending them. Tessan nodded back.

That quieted things. Not resolved. Just… suppressed.

Kaelen didn't speak again. But when he turned away, he made sure Wiz turned with him, no longer scanning.

As dusk stretched across the Godless coastline, the briny wind softened, and the sharp clangs of metal and guarded muttering faded into quieter rhythms. Elara stood at the edge of the clearing, arms folded, watching—not commanding, not leading. Just watching.

She saw Liora near one of the cookfires, crouched beside an old woman peeling roots with a blade that had more rust than edge. Liora offered something from her satchel—a spice blend wrapped in cloth, stolen from some long-forgotten Verdant festival. She didn't announce it. She just unwrapped the cloth, poured a pinch into the bubbling pot, and stirred without asking. When the old woman didn't stop her, Liora gave a small nod and kept going.

Nearby, Arin knelt beside a man with a dislocated shoulder. Her hands worked in silence, movements skillful but soft. She didn't glow with magic—there was no spectacle, no flourish. Just pressure, patience, and a whispered instruction. The man winced. Then sighed. Then nodded his thanks without words.

Further down the slope, where the dust settled into packed soil, Tarian stood with a weathered practice sword. A local teen mirrored his stance, feet too wide, grip too tight. Tarian adjusted the blade gently, tapping the boy's elbow into position with the back of his knuckle. They moved through the form twice, three times. By the fourth, the motion started to resemble something useful. A few others watched from a distance, pretending not to.

Elara didn't speak. She didn't need to.

One man approached Liora's cookfire and dropped a small bundle of dried root vegetables beside her. He said nothing, just tapped the pot once with his knuckle and walked off.

An older woman passed Arin and murmured something about a safer trail—one that cut behind the cliffs and avoided the deeper ravines. Arin nodded, repeating it to Elara when their eyes met.

Even the boy Kaelen had spoken to earlier lingered at the edge of the clearing, watching Tarian's blade lesson as if it were a puzzle he might solve if given enough time.

No one declared them welcome. But the distance between locals and strangers had shrunk.

Not through speeches.

But through choices. Shared spaces. Human need.

Elara finally sat down, her legs folding beneath her. She caught Dorian watching her from across the firelight. He didn't smile, but he didn't look away either.

No one had saved the world.

But for a night, no one had broken it further.

And that counted for something.

Near the far edge of the fire, someone began to sing. A low voice—cracked with age, but steady—carried just loud enough to reach the others. Then a second voice joined. Then a third.

"When fire and soil entwine,
A turning shall unfold in time…"

"Two shall meet, the flames, the green,
The path unseen, the truth between…"

The melody was slow, almost meditative—half lullaby, half prayer. Elara recognized the cadence. The Forgotten Song. But here, sung not in fear or reverence—just rhythm. Something passed down because there was nothing else to pass.

Dorian shifted beside her.

"They're singing it like it's just a song."

Elara murmured, "Maybe that's all it ever was. Until we gave it teeth."

Kaelen's voice came from the edge of the circle.

"Or maybe it had meaning all along. We just listened to the wrong verses."

No one answered. But the song carried on.

And for once, it didn't sound like a warning. It sounded like something that remembered them.

The fire crackled low, casting long shadows that flickered across the worn faces gathered in the clearing. Most had settled into silence, eating or tending to small tasks. But one woman didn't sit.

She stood at the edge of the firelight, arms crossed, one side of her face scarred from what looked like a burn that hadn't been properly treated. Her stance wasn't hostile, but it carried weight—years of surviving without help, years of waiting for promises that never arrived.

"Enough of this," she said, her voice cutting clean through the silence. "You speak softly, you fix things, you patch wounds. But what do you want?"

The group looked up. Dorian rose slowly from his seat near the fire. He didn't reach for a weapon. Didn't square his shoulders like a challenge. He just stood.

"We're not here to lead," he said, steady. "Not to claim, or convert, or beg for loyalty."

The woman narrowed her eyes. "Then what are you? Messengers? Missionaries? Strays with cause?"

Dorian met her gaze. "A risk worth taking."

Silence followed. Not tense, but taut—like something being tested.

She stepped closer, the light revealing more of her features: eyes sharp with suspicion, but not cruelty. "I've seen both sides," she said. "Forgeborne scorched our hills for metal. Verdant let us rot because we wouldn't kneel to their roots. You wear pieces of both."

"I carry what they gave me," Dorian replied. "But I don't serve them."

A few murmurs stirred behind her—some uncertain, some surprised.

The woman looked over at Kaelen, then Elara. Then back to Dorian.

"You're either lying… or you've lost more than I thought."

Dorian didn't flinch. "Both might be true."

That earned a dry, single laugh. Then, slowly, the woman sat down. Not next to them—but not far either. She didn't look at him again. But she didn't leave.

Tarian shook his head like someone who'd just defused a bomb without touching it.

Kaelen tossed another piece of driftwood on the fire. Liora stirred the pot. Arin resumed binding the shoulder of a young girl who'd fallen earlier.

No one clapped. No one praised.

But something old and jagged had been acknowledged. That was enough—for now.

The wind had picked up by evening, dragging with it the scent of salt and charcoal. Liora wandered beyond the edge of the gathering, drawn by the shape of a crumbled structure near the hillside—a squat building with no roof and a bent metal plaque near the door. Whatever it once read had long since rusted into nonsense.

She stepped over broken stone and pushed aside a curtain of dead vines to duck inside.

It was a school. Or had been.

Burned desks were heaped in one corner, and the walls still bore the blackened ghosts of once-painted murals. But what caught her attention were the drawings—smeared but intact—on the far wall. Names scrawled in charcoal. Stick figures in long coats. One child had drawn a hammer. Another, a tree split in half. Beneath one of the drawings was a single word: "Wait."

Liora ran her fingers across the wall.

Behind her, footsteps—light, unsure.

She turned to find three children hovering in the doorway. One held a broken slingshot. Another clutched a ragged toy that had once been a stuffed bird.

"Is this place yours?" she asked.

They shook their heads. "Used to be," said the oldest, a girl maybe eight, maybe nine.

"Well, good," Liora said. "Because I'm awful at following rules."

That got half a smile.

She crouched down, careful not to step on the drawings. "You know stories?" she asked. "The kind that doesn't end yet?"

The girl nodded slowly.

"Good," Liora said. "Because I have one. About a crooked tree, and a sky that forgot how to rain—and what it took to make it remember."

She started to tell the tale. Not from a book. Not polished. Just memory, turned loose. The kids sat. Then others came—drawn by voices, not orders. Soon a dozen small faces filled the ruined space, listening.

Outside, Arin paused near the entrance. She watched for a moment, then stepped inside and sat down. When Liora finished her story, Arin raised a hand.

"Want to know something more?" she asked the room.

A few heads nodded.

She closed her eyes and began to hum—a slow, rhythmic chant that pulsed like breath itself. A Verdant healing cadence, but stripped of its usual formality. No vines, no incantations. Just tone, and repetition.

The children echoed it. Some off-key. Some are too fast. But they followed.

They didn't call it magic.

They just listened. Then joined.

And somewhere between Liora's story and Arin's rhythm, the space that had once held only smoke and silence shifted. Not into hope. Not yet.

But into memory, stirred back to life.

The kind that waits for a reason to begin again.

The sun dipped low behind the craggy cliffs, painting the cloudy sky with streaks of burnt orange and violet. Shadows stretched long over the Godless coastline, softening the jagged edges of broken buildings and rusty towers. In the center of the settlement, a long, splintered table had been cleared of debris. Not built for ceremony. Just repurposed.

There was no feast. No declaration. Just soup—thick with root vegetables and dried herbs—and scavenged bread, dry but warm. Someone had found an old pot. Someone else had kindled a low fire in a half-buried drum. The heat was barely enough to fight the chill in the air, but it was something.

People gathered. Not all. Not close. But some sat beside strangers. Some passed bowls without comment. A few offered seats with curt nods. Silence clung to the corners, but it wasn't as heavy as it had been. It left room for the sound of spoons scraping wood and the occasional crackle of the fire.

Tarian sat between Elara and Dorian, both silent in their own ways. Kaelen leaned against a crate nearby, still fiddling with a valve core he hadn't yet given up on. Liora handed out spoons, one by one, muttering jokes under her breath that only the twins seemed to laugh at.

Tension still threaded the air. Caution, too. But for the first time, no one was armed. No one stood watch. Even the local militia had set their weapons aside—though within reach.

Tarian took a bite, winced at the saltiness of the soup, and cleared his throat.

"So a Verdant priest and a Forgeborne engineer walk into a bar," he said loudly, gaze fixed on no one in particular. "One orders wine, the other orders oil. The barkeep says, 'Which one's for drinking?' They both answer, 'Depends who you're trying to kill.'"

A pause.

Then a snort—from somewhere down the line. Then another. A single chuckle, brittle but real, broke the silence. Even Dorian's lips curved, just barely.

Elara shook her head. "That's terrible."

Tarian grinned. "That's unity."

A woman at the end of the table passed a basket of bread without being asked. A young boy refilled Kaelen's bowl. Two former strangers shared a shrug.

No one toasted. No one led a chant or sang a song.

But in the stillness, in the firelight, in the spaces between suspicion and trust—people shared a meal.

Unity, it seemed, didn't need to be loud.

Just present.

The meal had long gone cold, but the memory of warmth lingered. Smoke curled from the last embers in the drum-fire, curling skyward into a star-scarred night. Most of the settlement had settled into a wary kind of quiet—half rest, half readiness. That balance didn't hold for Sariel.

He returned near midnight, silent as the wind, stepping through the perimeter shadow without stirring a single watcher. Only when he reached the edge of camp did Kaelen notice him. The rest followed his gaze as Sariel emerged from the dark.

Elara stood. "Report?"

Sariel didn't speak right away. His eyes swept the gathered group. Tired, scraped, and bruised—but no longer splintered.

"There's a ridge four clicks northeast," he said at last. "Broken trees, high elevation. Good vantage. I waited until full dark. Then I saw the signal. A glint of glass. Movement."

Dorian stood. "Pirates?"

Sariel shook his head. "Too disciplined. Too quiet. Pirates gawk. They celebrate. These ones watched and withdrew. No fire. No banners. Just observation."

Liora's voice wavered, still holding a sleeping Nyra. "So... scouts?"

"More than that," Sariel said. "Not looking for loot. Looking for us."

Elara frowned. "Verdant forces? Or Aldric's enforcers?"

"Could be either. Or someone new entirely. But they're organized. Trained. And they knew not to be seen until it was too late."

Arin's voice stayed level, but something had changed in her tone. "They know what we're carrying."

Sariel's nod was barely perceptible. "They know enough to track us across oceans."

A long silence followed. Even the wind seemed to hold its breath.

Dorian looked to the horizon, where the ridge sat hidden in the dark. "Then peace was a breath—not a reprieve."

Kaelen closed the casing on his repaired valve core and tucked it into his belt. "We'll be ready."

Sariel's eyes lingered on the children—Sylas sharpening a stick, Nyra curled against Liora, listening even in her sleep. "They're not after a fight. They're after fear. We don't give them that."

Elara stepped closer to the fire. The flames cast long shadows behind her, stretching toward the broken wall behind the square. "Tomorrow, we build. We help. We earn our stay. But we also prepare. If someone's coming for us—let them find us standing together."

She didn't shout. She didn't have to.

One by one, heads nodded. Not in unison. Not dramatic. But enough.

Dawn came slowly, a cautious light edging across the crumbled rooftops and warped steel fences of the outpost. The salty air still clung to every breath, thick with the tang of rust and old seaweed, but something had changed. The town stirred with more than just wariness—it stirred with motion.

Kaelen stood near the well he had repaired, checking the pressure valves and making minor adjustments with Wiz chirping dutifully at his side. A woman came forward and asked if it would last. Kaelen gave a brief nod and said, "Depends on how much faith you put in patchwork and an automaton with bad joints."

She laughed—an actual, surprised laugh—and offered a canteen filled with something sharp and briny. He didn't drink it, but he didn't refuse it either.

Across the settlement, the old forge—silent for years—began to flicker with new heat. Dorian, sleeves rolled up, helped a local blacksmith clear debris from the bellows while Arin whispered healing chants over the man's trembling wrists. Sparks flared. The fire caught. Around them, a few villagers watched quietly—but they didn't turn away.

Liora knew this place. She walked past a cluster of children, her gaze already fixed on the familiar, burned-out structure. She ducked inside, just as she had before. The walls were charred but still standing, and on one of them, drawn in faded dust and chalk, were names. Dozens of them. And sketches—stick-figure families, suns, waves. Fragments of old hope.

She gathered the children, coaxing them gently, much like the last time, and began to tell another story. Not one of kingdoms or battles, but of three animals—clever, scared, and brave—who had to work together to find a safe hill. The children leaned in. They didn't smile at first, but this time, they settled quicker, almost anticipating the familiar rhythm. They listened.

Arin joined them later, settling beside the group and humming a slow, steady rhythm. She taught them a healing chant disguised as a lullaby. No mentions of magic, no show of power—just breath and song. Unlike their initial hesitation, they followed along with less uncertainty now. Their voices, though still quiet, were firmer this time, getting almost used to the comforting routine.

Tarian trained three young militia members on footwork—no titles, no grand speeches, just rhythm and stance. He corrected posture with adept hands, not with commands. Elara watched from nearby, leaning against a post, arms crossed.

An elder approached her then, Tessan. The same one who had doubted them at first. They stood together for a moment, saying nothing.

"You'll leave soon," Tessan finally said. "This place doesn't owe you. But it'll remember you."

Elara nodded. She didn't argue. Didn't promise to return. She just said, "We only came to survive. But if something else grows... then maybe that's worth protecting, too."

From the overlook near the sea wall, Sariel watched the horizon. The water was calm, but he didn't trust it. His hand rested lightly on the hilt of his weapon. His eyes tracked motion that wasn't there yet.

And beneath the ship's hull, Sylas and Nyra sat together, backs pressed to worn wood. They said nothing. Just breathed. Side by side. The air between them no longer filled with fear—but with something new.

The wind picked up.

The town didn't cheer. It didn't rally. But it moved. It continued.

And that was enough.

The Godless Lands had accepted their presence.

But something else had marked it.

And it was still watching.

Chapter 15: Crossfire Waters

The Dawnseeker sliced through the morning mist, its metal hull gliding across an uncharacteristically calm stretch of sea. Spray dusted the deck like powdered salt, and gulls circled in lazy arcs above the masts. It was the kind of stillness that didn't last long in Elyndor—not with the world turning the way it had.

Kaelen crouched near the bow, tightening a filament inside the gauntlet's bracer. The bronze casing clicked into place with a snap. Beside him, Wiz stalked the deck like a restless predator. The automaton had bulked up—no longer lizard-like, but closer to a squat, wide-shouldered drake. New ridge plates ran down his back, and twin stubby wings twitched. Sensors blinked in rhythmic pulses as he scanned the sky and sea, vigilant even at rest.

Kaelen didn't speak, but his focus carried a weight. A rhythm. Every adjustment was deliberate, as if he knew he might need the gauntlet soon.

Elara leaned on the rail midship, her eyes fixed on the endless horizon. The sea was a dull blue, and the wind blew sharp but steady from the east. Her satchel hung by her hip, the relic inside softly glowing through the flap—visible only to those who knew what to look for.

Kaelen did. He watched it for a beat too long before muttering, "That's early."

Dorian stood near the helm, arms crossed, eyes scanning the water with a soldier's tension. His face betrayed little, but he was tracking movement. Waves, clouds, light refractions—anything that didn't belong. He had developed the habit over their last few days of travel, after the last stop in the Godless Lands. Now, every breeze could carry risk. Every shadow could be more than weather.

Sariel sat on the raised quarterdeck, hood up, face turned slightly from the group as he studied the eastern sky. He hadn't said much since they left the settlement. But he watched. Always. His presence wasn't comforting, but it was constant—a silent sentinel who revealed nothing.

Liora climbed the main mast rigging halfway up before calling down, "Clear skies west. No sails in range."

"East?" Dorian asked.

She hesitated, then climbed a rung higher. "Low cloud cover. Could hide a ship, maybe two, if they're tucked under the horizon."

That was enough to bring everyone's attention.

Tarian emerged from below deck, rubbing his shoulder. "Waves feel wrong today," he said to no one in particular. "Like something's pushing from underneath."

Arin appeared behind him, nodding faintly. "I felt it too. Pressure shifting. Something in the water wants to rise."

Kaelen stood, brushing off his hands. "We keep watch in shifts. Nobody will work alone. We've seen too much to believe in coincidence."

Elara adjusted her satchel and nodded. "The relic's never wrong. Something's coming."

The wind shifted again—sharper now, biting at their coats and cloaks. The smell of salt grew thicker. Below deck, something creaked. Not the groan of wood or steel—but a pressure release, like a breath being drawn deep below.

They moved with purpose, their coordination falling into place like a muscle they'd all learned to use. There were no arguments. No hesitation. Just the calm before a storm they hadn't yet seen—only sensed.

And far below the Dawnseeker, beneath the calm veneer of sea, something stirred.

Not Forgeborne. Not Verdant. Something else entirely.

The deck of the Dawnseeker had become something else entirely—a proving ground. Not for dominance or rank, but for rhythm. For balance. For understanding.

Kaelen stood near the forward mast, gauntlet strapped tight to his forearm, copper coils pulsing as energy cycled through. Wiz stood nearby crate, eyes glowing, quietly logging data.

"Mid-range output. Twenty feet." Kaelen flexed his fingers. A small orb of voltage snapped forward from the gauntlet, striking a suspended tin plate with a sharp clang. Not enough to damage, just enough to stagger. Wiz chirped and blinked in confirmation.

"Impact logged. Spread radius at current output: 1.7 meters. No residual shockwave," the automaton reported, voice clipped, efficient.

Kaelen adjusted the dial on the side, then again. "Still too narrow." He muttered, half to himself. "If I'm aiming to disable more than one target, I'll need better arc spread."

Another pulse. Another clang. The plate rattled. Wiz didn't praise—just processed. That was enough.

Across the deck, Elara moved in controlled steps opposite Arin, each of them mirroring the other with a focus that bordered on clinical. Arin feinted low; Elara sidestepped, hand glowing green as vines shot up—not to strike, but to tangle Arin's leg just enough. Arin let herself fall, rolled, came up with a healing glyph already drawn.

They weren't testing strength. They were testing delay—how quickly a spell could reinforce bone, close a shallow cut, restore balance mid-strike.

Again. Arin slashed with a curved staff. Elara caught it mid-motion, not with force but with summoned bark armor timed to the instant before contact.

Again. This time Elara attacked, a controlled burst of thorns grazing Arin's shoulder. Arin hissed, winced, and then cast. The wound closed slower than expected.

"Too much delay," Elara said, stepping back, breathing hard. "I felt that."

"And I saw it coming. You hesitated before casting." Arin pressed fingers to the spot. "Healing has to start before the pain distracts you."

"I'll fix it." Elara glanced toward the others. "We're past guessing."

Near the rail, Liora balanced three water barrels atop each other—impossibly stacked, impossibly still. Her hands moved in careful arcs, wind swirling just tight enough to keep them stable.

A single ripple in the current and the top barrel would tip. She didn't blink.

"Don't think," she muttered to herself. "Feel the weight. Guide it."

She shifted her stance. A gust rose—sharp, fast, corrective. The barrels tilted, then steadied, wind swirling around them like a coiled ribbon.

No spill. No collapse.

She released the wind with a snap of her fingers, caught the falling barrels with a flick of water drawn from the sea, and lowered them to the deck without a splash.

She grinned, then quickly looked around to make sure no one had seen it.

Tarian barked a sharp signal—barely a grunt—and Dorian pivoted behind him, switching stances mid-motion. Sariel ducked under both their arms, leg sweeping to fake a trip. Tarian didn't fall for it. He caught him with a flat strike to the ribs, pulled the hit just before impact.

No orders. No words. Just the rhythm of bodies that had fought side by side for weeks now.

Dorian threw a punch—slow, deliberate. Sariel blocked, turned, and swept. Tarian stepped in, arm low, catching his shoulder before he completed the spin. They held the motion there, tension high but controlled.

They nodded.

"Again," Sariel said.

No one argued.

Evening came. The ship rocked with the steady rhythm of waves, but their footing didn't falter. They had trained through stormy nights and tight quarters, through mistrust and tension and doubt.

But now?

Now they moved like parts of a greater machine. Jokes passed in glances. Commands shortened to gestures. Kaelen didn't have to say "shock incoming"—he just raised the gauntlet, and Wiz beeped twice. Elara turned her staff, Arin adjusted position, and Liora shifted the wind.

They weren't perfect. But they weren't separate anymore.

They were functioning.

Sariel didn't speak at first. He just stared—eyes narrowed against the late sun.

Then he raised a hand. "Sails. Starboard. Three leagues out."

Kaelen stepped beside him. "Pirates?"

"No," Sariel said. "Green and white. That glint on the ridge? I was right. They followed."

Elara was already moving. She shoved past barrels and crew, climbed onto the rail for a better view. The wind whipped her braid behind her, salt sticking to her skin.

Then she saw them.

Two sails. Crisp, structured. No drift in the wind—too disciplined for that. At their center, a gold-inlaid emblem: vines wrapping around a crescent moon.

Her spine went stiff.

"That's House Thalrien's crest," she said quietly. "From Eldoravell."

Arin stepped closer, her voice tight. "Loyalists?"

Elara nodded. "They were always the most vocal. The most… devout." She didn't need to say what that meant. The word "loyalist" did enough. Loyal to the Wardens of Aeldrin. Loyal to the old order. Loyal to the idea that Elara was a traitor.

Wiz chirped beside Kaelen—three rapid beeps in succession. Kaelen pulled the relic from his belt pouch.

It was warm. Hot, even. The runes along its surface pulsed faster now—erratic, like a second heartbeat.

"They're close enough for this thing to know," Kaelen muttered. "I don't think it likes them."

Liora stepped up behind them, face pale. "They'll board, won't they? They'll try."

Tarian answered without looking. "If they wanted a chat, they wouldn't be raising banners."

"Not pirates this time," Dorian said. His voice had dropped low, steady. "They know us."

Sariel didn't flinch. He adjusted the strap around his chest, loosening the twin blades. "Then they know what happens next."

Elara glanced at him. "You've fought Verdant ships before?"

"Yes," Sariel said. Nothing more.

Dorian stepped forward. "Then you know what they'll try first. Disable the rudder. Grapple the rails. Come in staggered."

Kaelen was already at the gauntlet. "How fast can we turn?"

"Not fast enough," Liora murmured.

The ship rocked under a fresh gust, as if the wind itself was bracing.

Dorian's voice cut through it. "Positions. Quickly! No alarm—yet. Let's not show them panic."

Elara moved without thinking, brushing fingers over the relic as she passed. It buzzed again, like it wanted to speak.

Liora caught movement from the corner of her eye—two small figures lingering near the central mast.

Sylas and Nyra.

They had that look again. Eyes wide, not with fear, but with intent. That sharp stillness that came before kids like them did something reckless.

She crossed the deck fast, crouching low beside them. "You two need to hide. Now."

Sylas furrowed his brow. "We can help. I've got my sling—"

"And I can spot from the crow's nest," Nyra added, already half-turned to climb.

"No." Liora cut them off. "This isn't like before. These aren't thugs or sailors. These are trained. Disciplined. And they'll cut through us if we're not sharp."

"But we've—"

"I said no," she snapped, harsher than she meant to. Then softer, "You matter. You don't get to be brave right now. You get to be alive."

The twins exchanged a glance. The kind siblings share when they're weighing whether to disobey. She didn't give them the chance.

A gust rolled through the deck—not wild, but focused. It caught beneath their feet, lifted them just enough to stumble back. Liora moved with it, guiding the air like a shepherd with sheep. The twins skidded down the incline of the deck toward the lower stairwell.

Sylas opened his mouth to shout—Nyra reached for the railing—but Liora flicked her wrist, a sharper burst of wind slamming the door behind them. The latch clicked shut.

She pressed her hand against the wood. "Sorry," she whispered. "But not sorry enough."

Then she turned back toward the prow. The sails on the horizon were closer now.

The banner on the horizon rippled in the wind, vivid even from a distance. Green and white.

Something old.

Something seen.

And something is coming.

The first signal came on a polished silver disc—flashed from the lead ship's bow, quick and deliberate. It bounced off the sun in a specific rhythm. Verdant code.

Elara read it before Liora even asked. She stepped up beside Kaelen. "I know that pattern."

"They're calling for surrender," she said. "Specifically—for me."

Dorian moved closer. "What exactly do they want?"

Elara didn't look at him. "They're invoking a tribunal clause. Old law. Royal edict." Her fingers curled around the wooden rail. "They want me to stand trial… and submit to nullification."

Arin spoke softly from behind. "They're going to strip your magic."

Kaelen winced. "And if you refuse?"

"They'll call it treason," Elara said. "And justify whatever comes next."

No one answered.

The lead ship slowed. Its crew lined the rails in silence—helmets gleaming, weapons not drawn, but ready. A second signal was hoisted—this time, a banner: green and white flanked by a single black stripe.

"They're naming her formally," Sariel muttered. "That's not a warning. That's a verdict."

A voice rang out across the water—amplified by wind, channeled with force. A woman's voice. Controlled. Commanding.

"Elara of House Thorne. Verdant princess. Grovecaller in exile. You will surrender yourself. You will face judgment by the Council. Comply, and your companions will be spared. Resist, and you forfeit all claims of blood or mercy."

No one moved. The waves answered with soft percussion, steady as breath.

Then Dorian stepped into view, framed cleanly against the sun-soaked deck—unmistakable in armor, stature, and presence. The enforcer colors were dulled from salt and time, but the Forgeborne crest still marked his pauldron.

The silence that followed wasn't hesitation.

It was recognition.

New signals flashed.

The voice returned—this time less formal, but more eager.

"Dorian Asher. Of the Titanbreaker. You're far from your barracks, Commander. Forgehelm still pays handsomely for returnees—especially ones who've gone rogue. Surrender to us, and we'll see you delivered to Forgehelm… intact. The rest may walk."

Elara's hand gripped the rail tighter. Beside her, Dorian didn't move.

Another ship emerged slowly from the far mist—no banners, no lights, no declaration. Just presence. The second Loyalist ship, flanking wide and quiet, its position strategic, its angle precise. The net was closing.

Sariel's hand hovered near his blades. Kaelen adjusted the gauntlet, checking the dial. Arin glanced over her shoulder, reading wind patterns.

Elara stared forward—eyes locked on the lead ship. Her breathing was shallow, but steady.

She felt Dorian's hand brush hers. No pressure. No pull.

Just a moment.

Her fingers curled around his briefly—an acknowledgment. Of the risk. Of the choice.

No words passed between them.

But something far heavier did.

The grappling hooks came fast—iron claws clanking against the rail before any final offer was made.

Verdant soldiers vaulted across the gap as the ships locked. Green and white tabards flared behind them like falling leaves—elegant in form, effortless in intent..

Then the first one hit the deck wrong.

Liora stood just behind the mainmast, hands raised. A narrow crosswind spun beneath the boarders' boots, subtle enough to miss until it mattered. Their landings staggered—knees buckled, balance gone.

Kaelen didn't hesitate. "Wiz—wing spike, go."

The automaton launched from his shoulder in a sharp arc, mechanical wings flaring. It slammed into a soldier's side, then released a jolt—not lethal, but enough. The man dropped, twitching as his spear clattered uselessly on the wood.

A second charged—Kaelen fired a pulse from the gauntlet, angled low. The floor beneath the boarder sparked as current snapped through a metal plate, catching him mid-step. Down again.

Another came swinging. Kaelen ducked, rolled. Wiz followed, talons sparking.

On the upper deck, Elara spun her staff—roots surged up through the boards, curling around the stairwell posts. Vines thickened and pulled tight, forming a twisting barricade that blocked the narrow passage without harming anyone.

Two soldiers crashed into it and rebounded hard.

"I'm not killing them," she muttered. "Just stopping them."

"Good," Arin said, crouched behind a crate. "Because I'm not fixing lethal wounds right now."

She popped up just long enough to throw a burst of healing toward Liora, who'd taken a glancing hit to the shoulder. Then ducked as a spear skimmed overhead.

"Field heal two, behind stern rigging!" Arin called out.

Elara angled her hand, directing a growth of moss toward the wound. Liora nodded in thanks, already drawing more wind.

Tarian and Sariel were moving in tandem now—silent, brutal arcs of motion. Sariel cut low, Tarian followed high. Not just reacting. Anticipating.

Near the helm, Dorian stood like a fortress.

Every strike he made was deliberate. One to disarm. One to disable. Always near Elara—always intercepting what she couldn't see.

He didn't speak, didn't shout commands. Just acted. Clean movements. Measured force.

He caught a sword mid-swing with the haft of his hammer, twisted it free, and shoved the attacker backward over the rail.

Another charged Elara's flank. Dorian stepped in, crushed the attack with his shoulder, and knocked the man unconscious with a flat blow to the gut.

"You're not runaways!" a Loyalist soldier shouted, stumbling back with blood in his mouth. "You're trained!"

Elara met his eyes. "No," she said. "We're ready."

The tide shifted.

For the first time, the Loyalists faltered.

The Dawnseeker groaned beneath their boots.

It wasn't from sails straining or the pull of the tide—this was deeper, slower. Like the sea itself had clenched around them.

Kaelen stopped mid-step. "Something's wrong."

The relic flashed once—then again, brighter. Not a pulse. A flare.

Elara flinched as the heat surged through the satchel, and she quickly unhooked it, setting it against the deck.

Kaelen moved first. "That's stronger than Floralis. Stronger than the Godless Lands."

Dorian scanned the deck, eyes narrowing. "So they brought more than we thought."

Tarian scanned the horizon. "Then we hold the line until we can count the rest."

No one questioned it. No one asked if they were wrong.

Because danger was coming. The relic didn't care what it was. Only what it meant.

Then the tremor hit—low and grinding, as if some great beast stirred just beneath the hull. The deck jolted.

"Under the hull—move!" Kaelen shouted.

They scattered moments before the surface broke.

A shape broke the water—not wood, not sails. Steel. Seamless. Moving too fast.

"That's not Verdant," Kaelen said.

The relic pulsed again—deeper now. Like a warning they'd ignored.

Elara whispered, "The relic didn't spike because of them. It was this. It was both."

A metal mass surged out of the sea, displacing tons of water in a roar. Salt spray drenched the deck as it surfaced—jagged plating, streaked with black oil, forced its way into view. Its structure was angular, aggressive, not built for stealth but for intimidation.

And at its head: a black-and-gold crest. The emblem of Aldric's coastal enforcers.

Dorian's face hardened. "Submersible class. Forgeborne naval, special operations."

Kaelen finished the thought. "Aldric's. He doesn't field ships unless he means to erase something."

No warning. No challenge.

The turret turned and fired.

The second Loyalist ship, still circling wide, took the hit straight through its center mast. The explosion ripped clean through the hull. A second shot followed, splitting the deck apart like paper. Fire spilled across the sea. Then came silence—followed by splashing, screams, and sinking timber.

Cheers broke out instinctively.

Tarian let out a shout. "That's one less thing to worry about!"

Liora leaned over the railing. "They saw the Loyalists. They're helping us!"

Sariel stood still. Watching.

Kaelen didn't answer her. He was already pulling the relic free from his belt.

The runes pulsed in a violent rhythm—no longer warm, but white-hot. Too bright to ignore.

Liora looked at him. "Aren't they?"

"No," Kaelen said. Quiet, but final.

She turned, confused. "They just destroyed the—"

"They're not here for them," Dorian said. "They're here because of us."

The submersible adjusted course—closer now, slow, deliberate. The forward hatch began to unwind.

Liora looked from the hatch to Dorian. "But they're Forgeborne. So are you."

"They don't care about that," Dorian replied. "Not when a Council order's involved."

Kaelen held up the relic. "They followed this. We sent it out to mislead them. They must have backtraced the pulse."

Dorian nodded once. "And if Aldric's here in person, they're not here to negotiate. They're here to remove a variable."

Elara moved closer but said nothing. Her eyes were locked on the relic, on the submersible, on the fire dying behind them.

Arin hovered behind her, tense but silent.

Sariel adjusted the grip on his blade.

Kaelen's gaze swept across the group, then back to the emblem on the advancing ship.

"They're not after the Loyalists," he said again.

The relic burned bright in his palm.

"They're here for us."

The submersible's hatch clanked open. Hiss of steam. The ramp extended slowly, like a tongue drawn toward blood.

Then a voice boomed—mechanically amplified, thick with command.

"Surrender the relic. Surrender the rogue Mechcrafter and exiled Titanbreaker. This is not a request."

Kaelen didn't flinch, but his hand closed tighter around the relic. The glow didn't fade.

Dorian's stance widened. One hand rested on his hammer—not drawn, not idle. Just waiting.

Across the water, the remaining Loyalist ship shouted back.

"We give you Dorian Asher. You give us Elara Thorne."

A beat of silence followed—sharper than the cannon's echo.

Dorian didn't move. But his voice cut low, bitter. "They'd trade me like debris."

Elara stepped to his side. "They never valued you. Just your usefulness."

Liora's breath caught. "They're bargaining with us."

"No," Kaelen said. "They're trying to survive. One cost at a time."

Then the Forgeborne enforcer's voice returned, amplified through iron.

"The enemy of my enemy is still my enemy."

"We don't accept broken tools. We scrap them."

The cannons realigned.

Then they fired again.

A survivor—no, more than that. A figure stood atop a floating beam, arms raised. Magic surged around him, the sea bending to his will.

A Sylvanar.

Water rippled and coiled in long, smooth arcs, lifting the injured from the debris. One by one, drowning Loyalists were dragged from the tide and placed on floating wreckage, stabilized by summoned brine and broken mast.

Sariel watched with narrowed eyes. "Some of them still have honor."

"Honor doesn't change the aim of a cannon," Dorian muttered.

The Forgeborne captain stepped forward—his figure now visible on the submersible's upper deck. His armor was darker than regulation, reinforced at the shoulders. No helm. Just a clean-shaved head, a scar down the left jaw, and a voice like freezing steel.

He didn't yell. He didn't posture.

He just spoke—and it carried.

"The enemy of my enemy is still the enemy. I'll not stoop to beg for my kill."

He raised one hand.

Kaelen knew what came next.

The first shell landed just off the starboard bow—close enough to douse the deck in seawater and shrapnel. The second carved into the port railing. A third exploded in midair—Verdant cannon fire—striking a Forgeborne shot before it landed.

Both sides were firing.

Neither was aiming to miss.

The Dawnseeker lurched hard as the deck lit up in flame and splinters. Smoke poured from both flanks.

They were no longer passengers caught in a feud.

They were the target.

Dorian shouted, "Brace for contact!"

Elara jumped for cover behind the wheel. Liora dropped low, summoning air to redirect smoke. Kaelen pulled Wiz behind cover, shielding the relic with both hands.

The Dawnseeker was burning from both sides, pinned between two factions who wanted them gone for different reasons.

They weren't enemies. They weren't allies.

They were bait.

And the sea didn't care.

The Dawnseeker was breaking apart in real time.

The sails hung in torn ribbons, snapped ropes whipping like dust across the deck. The port railing was gone—replaced by open sea and the smoke of a sinking Loyalist ship. Fire danced along the mainmast. The hull screamed with every blast, wood splintering, iron bolts shearing loose. The ship was no longer fighting to win—it was trying to survive.

Kaelen dropped behind a collapsed beam near the stern, shielding Wiz with one arm. The other worked fast, fingers snapping open the automaton's wing module. He dug past the stabilizers and reached the hidden beacon array—a system he'd only half-tested in theory.

"Come on," he muttered, rerouting copper lines into the relay coil. "Power loop through the secondary nodes—filter to wideband—"

Wiz chirped in a rising panic as another explosion hit nearby. The deck tilted hard.

Kaelen didn't look up. "Just hold together. That's all I need from you."

Movement—fast and low—cut across his periphery.

A Loyalist soldier vaulted the debris, blade raised. Kaelen ducked under the first swing, brought his gauntlet up with a snap, and fired point-blank. The pulse wasn't clean—it sent both of them sprawling—but the other man didn't get up.

"Wiz—pulse on my mark. Don't wait for me."

The automaton chirped again and vanished into the smoke, scampering up the rigging.

Sariel appeared beside Kaelen without a sound. He nodded toward the water.

"We need to do something about that submersible."

Kaelen kept his voice low. "You think you can reach it?"

"I'll find a weakness. Or die trying."

Dorian, nearby, looked over. "Don't die."

Sariel gave the faintest smile. "Wouldn't dare. Not with you lot watching."

One splash. No noise. No trail.

He'd leapt from the starboard railing and disappeared into the water. No one saw him dive. No sonar pinged. But Kaelen knew what he was doing.

The submersible's intake vents were vulnerable at range—but only if you could get beneath the armor and past the sonar mesh. It required precision. And speed.

Sariel had both.

On deck, the assault hadn't let up.

Liora staggered as another blast hit, fire curling past her face. She raised one arm against the heat, the other glowing as she summoned. But a spear came from the flank—fast, deadly, clean.

Arin threw herself forward, vines erupting from the deck with raw force. They slammed into place between Liora and the strike, cracking and hissing as steel pierced through the first layer.

The spear lodged in the second.

Arin fell to one knee. "I can't hold that again."

"You won't need to," Liora said, stepping past her shield. Her voice shook—but not from fear.

She raised both arms.

The ocean churned in response.

A whirl began—a spiraling ring of current and pressure, pulling water upward into a tight vortex. The sea twisted around itself, dragging the submersible slightly off axis.

Liora's eyes were wild. "Still think we're prey?"

Liora braced herself on the upper deck, one hand raised to the sky, the other low over the railing. Wind answered first—sharp and biting. Then water. Then heat.

Fog exploded across the surface, dense and blinding.

The others didn't question it. They just moved.

But Arin looked up once. Just once.

"That's not luck," she muttered. "She's not scared of her powers anymore."

Visibility dropped to feet. Shouts blurred. Shapes vanished.

And in the middle of it, Tarian held the deck.

His armor was scorched, one pauldron cracked—but he didn't falter. Two Loyalists pressed him hard, striking from opposite angles. He turned just enough to deflect one blade with his shield, then stepped into the other's swing, took it on the side, and drove forward.

The first attacker went over the railing with a cry.

The second faltered—just long enough.

Tarian dropped his shoulder and slammed into him, hammering the man into the deck.

"You want this ship?" he growled. "You'll have to swim for it."

The hull reverberated. Not from an impact—but something shifting underneath.

Kaelen staggered and looked toward the port side.

"That wasn't them," he muttered. "That's internal."

Wiz emitted a sharp warning tone.

Elara steadied herself, eyes narrowing. "Sariel."

Below deck, Kaelen flipped the final switch on the override array.

"Now!"

A high-pitched frequency burst from Wiz—pure and wide. The submersible's sensors would register it as static, flooding their trackers and throwing off range-lock. It wouldn't last. But it would buy seconds.

That was enough.

Elara moved through the chaos, roots dragging across the deck as she forced back two Loyalists trying to flank Arin. Vines snapped into motion behind her, coiling hard around the boot and blade.

Then she heard it—a shout. Dorian's.

She turned. Across the deck, he was bracing against the rail, hammer raised, shielding Tarian's retreat from a collapsing spar. His cloak was on fire. Blood streaked his forearm.

For a moment, the fight narrowed.

She didn't see the warrior. She saw the man who had stood at her side in Cinderhollow. The man who watched her walk away from a throne, and never once asked her to turn back.

Elara gritted her teeth, forcing her focus back into the present.

Elara saw him stagger as a shard from the last cannon blast tore through his side. He dropped to one knee, hand still gripping his hammer—but barely. Blood poured from under his armor.

She ran.

She dropped beside him, throwing her staff forward. Vines erupted in a crossguard arc, deflecting another projectile aimed for his head.

"Don't you die," she whispered—not a command. A promise. Her voice shook from more than just exertion.

Dorian coughed, red blooming across his teeth. "Was about to say the same."

She pressed her hand to his wound, summoned all the life-magic she could, and poured it in. It wasn't elegant. It was desperation. But it held.

Around them, the battle raged on—a burning ship, an ocean in revolt, and enemies on all sides.

And still, none of them broke.

Kaelen didn't wait for a vote. "Retreat! Now! Get us out of here!"

His voice cut through smoke and cannon-wrought chaos. The moment was narrow—fragile. The Forgeborne submersible had been staggered, its targeting systems scrambled, and its ramp now sealed in molten steel from Kaelen's makeshift charge. The Loyalists were scattered, pulling their wounded from the waves.

It wasn't a victory.

But it was an opening.

Kaelen sprinted toward the stern rigging, digging into his satchel as he moved. Smoke stung his eyes, but he didn't blink. He pulled free a half-fused explosive he'd built days earlier—an industrial welder repurposed for breach lockdown.

He raised it, aimed, and launched it across the gap toward the sub's open hatch.

The device hit, exploded, and sealed the entrance in a violent bloom of heat and blue flame. Welded edges glowed orange. Inside, distant voices shouted, banging against the bulkhead. It wouldn't hold forever—but it would hold long enough.

Kaelen turned. "We're clear for now!"

But the ship wasn't moving.

The Dawnseeker drifted, wounded—its hull splintered, its main mast creaking under the weight of torn sails. There was no wind. No momentum. And nothing else to get them out of range.

Liora staggered to the bow, hands glowing faint, breath shallow.

She didn't speak. Didn't wait.

She dropped to one knee, palms pressed to the deck.

The wind came sharp and fast.

Not a breeze. Not a push.

It slammed into the back of the sail like a hammer from the sky, snapping canvas forward with a deafening crack. The ship lurched as its battered frame caught motion again.

Kaelen held the rail as the Dawnseeker groaned under the sudden force. "Liora—how are you—"

"Just steer!" she shouted, voice raw.

The sails flared with captured wind—controlled, angled. Not random.

Liora stood at the bow, both arms shaking with strain.

"We have to move. Now."

The gust she summoned wasn't chaotic. It was targeted. Controlled down to the thread.

Tarian shouted, "She's giving us the gap!"

The Dawnseeker surged forward—because of her.

Ropes pulled taut. The mast swayed. But the ship moved—fast, cutting through the surf in a line of foam and rising smoke.

Behind them, the Forgeborne submersible remained sealed. The Loyalists' surviving vessel began turning away, prioritizing its wounded over any continued engagement. The ocean held no more orders for them.

Elara reached the side rail and spotted a dark shape in the water. Sariel.

She tossed the rope. Tarian joined her without being asked, bracing his feet against the slick deck. Together, they hauled Sariel up from the sea, armor soaked, eyes alert but drained.

"You all right?" Tarian asked.

Sariel climbed back onto the deck, drenched and coughing seawater, a gash across his shoulder.

"One of their aft stabilizers is toast," he rasped. "They'll have trouble aiming for a while."

Tarian raised a brow. "You swam under a submersible with active turrets."

"Better odds than politics," Sariel said, slumping against the mast.

Kaelen gripped the wheel, keeping them steady. He didn't look back again.

Mid-deck, Arin dropped beside Dorian. He sat slumped against a crate, blood leaking through his side, his face pale.

"Still with me?" she asked.

Dorian coughed. "Until the next volley, yeah."

Arin pressed her hands to his wound. Light bloomed. The gash began to close, but the process was slow. Her magic was nearly spent.

"You did good," she muttered. "Protecting her."

He didn't answer at first. Then: "Would again."

"Let's not need to."

As the Dawnseeker pushed forward under Liora's wind, the crew regrouped.

Kaelen shouted updates from the helm. "Steering's holding. Rudder's cracked but still functional."

Tarian checked the rigging with Sariel, tying off frayed ropes and bracing the mast with makeshift splints from a broken railing.

Arin moved from Dorian to Elara, checking wounds in silence.

Liora remained at the bow, knees planted, arms raised. Her hair snapped in the wind, but she held steady—no panic, no pride. Just control.

The ship was moving again. That was all that mattered.

Minutes passed. The wreckage behind them faded into smoke and floating bodies. Fire smoldered across the waves. The submersible stayed still.

Kaelen scanned the horizon.

No sails followed.

No silhouettes.

Just the trail they left behind—a burning corridor of war no one had asked for.

Finally, Liora collapsed backward onto the deck. Her arms fell limp at her sides.

Kaelen rushed to her.

She was breathing—barely.

He didn't speak, just pulled his coat off and threw it over her.

Tarian sat beside Sariel, armor dented and cracked. He hadn't spoken since hauling Sariel up. Just stared at the deck, sword still in hand.

Dorian didn't move. Elara sat beside him now, silent.

Arin paced once, checked the wheel, then joined the others. No words.

Wiz returned to Kaelen's side, wings still twitching from the earlier overload. It buzzed quietly—tired, almost apologetic.

Kaelen sat beside Wiz, holding him against his chest.

They were alive.

That was the only victory they had.

No one spoke. No one cheered.

The Dawnseeker left fire and blood behind as it drifted into the wide sea.

And no one looked back.

The Dawnseeker creaked as it cut through calmer waters. No longer gliding—just drifting forward, like even the sea was giving them a reprieve.

Smoke trailed behind, thinning with each passing minute. The wreckage of the battle was a horizon away now. But no one felt distance from it.

Kaelen sat with his back against the scorched mast, staring at the gauntlet on his arm. The metal was dented, plating warped from heat, some of the embedded circuitry exposed where a blade had struck during the fray. One of the stabilizer bolts had cracked down the middle. It shouldn't be usable anymore.

But when he flexed his hand, the joints still moved.

"Stubborn piece of junk," he muttered.

Wiz lay curled at his side, eyes dimmed to orange, wings folded tightly. The automaton's frame had hairline fractures up the spine, but it hadn't stopped running diagnostics since they'd escaped.

Kaelen touched the gauntlet's damaged plate again, slower this time. There were burn marks on his wrist underneath. He hadn't felt them until now.

He didn't bandage them.

Behind him, footsteps approached soft on the wood.

Arin lowered herself into a seat beside him. Her braid was fraying, one sleeve torn, and there was dried blood on her collar. She didn't seem to notice—or care.

"We're not the same people that left Smeltport," she said.

Kaelen didn't respond right away.

He didn't need to.

Arin continued anyway. "Back then, we didn't know each other. Not really. Not like this."

He nodded. "Back then, we could walk into a town and pretend we didn't matter."

She looked out across the sea. "We still don't matter. Not to the people making war out of flags. But we matter to each other."

That stuck.

Kaelen glanced down at Wiz, then back at the twisted gauntlet. "We've burned through every plan I had. Every backup. But we're still here."

"That's something," she said.

Across the deck, Sariel sat with his back to the forward rail. His breathing was slow but heavy, like someone who hadn't realized they were exhausted until everything stopped.

His blades were laid beside him—scratched and wet. He hadn't cleaned them yet.

"We shouldn't have made it," he said.

No one asked what he meant. They all knew.

He looked up, catching Kaelen's gaze. "But we did."

Kaelen gave him a nod. Not a smile. Not relief. Just a shared truth.

Up near the bow, Elara stood against the rail. Dorian was beside her, one hand resting on the post for balance. His side was still wrapped, and every gust of wind made him flinch, just slightly.

They didn't speak for a while. Just looked ahead—toward the edge of the sea, where sky met nothing and the world held its breath.

Elara broke the silence.

"You think we can make it to Nocturne's Edge?"

Dorian took a moment. The wind picked up, ruffling his coat and hair.

He didn't look at her when he answered.

"We just crossed the ocean between who we were… and who we need to be."

Elara nodded. "That sounds rehearsed."

"It wasn't."

He didn't smile. Neither did she. But the moment settled between them.

Behind them, Tarian leaned against a broken crate, sharpening one of his smaller blades. Not because he needed to—but because motion helped him think. His armor had been patched hastily with twine and cloth. He hadn't said much since the escape. But every few minutes, his eyes swept the sky like he expected another ambush to crash down from above.

Liora was asleep, finally. Arin had insisted she rest. Her body had shut down the moment they'd cleared the wreckage line. Now she lay curled in a blanket, her brow furrowed even in sleep. She hadn't even had enough magic left to dry her own clothes.

Kaelen watched her breathe.

She'd carried the wind when the ship had no right to move. It wasn't finesse. It wasn't control. It was raw force—and for a few moments, it had made the difference between escape and death.

He didn't know what she'd tapped into. Panic, fear, something deeper. But she hadn't lost control.

She'd bent it to her will.

They all had, in different ways.

For now, the sea was quiet. The Dawnseeker floated toward unknown waters, its sails patched but holding. Smoke drifted lazily behind them, curling into the air like memory.

And no one—no one—asked what came next.

They didn't need to.

They had crossed something. A line they couldn't undo. They were no longer passengers or refugees or tools in someone else's game.

They were the game now.

Kaelen closed his eyes and leaned back against the mast.

He didn't know where Nocturne's Edge was on a map.

But he knew they were heading the right direction.

They weren't fugitives anymore.

They were fighters.

And every faction that wanted them dead was starting to learn that too.

Act V - The Fractured Equinox

Chapter 16: The Edge of Prophecy

The Dawnseeker rode low in the water, sails furled, anchored well outside Irondale's harbor. The city stretched across the horizon—iron towers rising through the haze, smoke trails winding into the dusk. No horns, no flashing signal lights. But they knew better than to trust the silence.

"We stay out of range," Dorian said. "No landfall, no signals. They'll have checkpoints, patrols. Maybe worse."

He stood near the prow, gauntlet tucked behind his back, eyes fixed on the city like it might blink. "If the enforcers are watching, we've already made their list."

Kaelen nodded. "They'll expect survivors. Just not the kind that bites back."

Below deck, the mood was quieter. Restless. Controlled.

Liora sat propped against a stack of canvas bags, the twins flanking her. Her skin still held a faint shimmer—residual magic clinging like dew. She'd spent more power in one battle than most Sylvanars managed in a season. Now, her fingers twitched in her lap, like they weren't done yet.

Kaelen crouched nearby, adjusting a set of makeshift dampeners around the ship's magical array—just in case. He glanced over. "Still breathing?"

"Barely," she murmured. "I think I burned through the last of my sanity somewhere between the lightning strikes and the screaming."

"You're assuming you had any left to start with."

That pulled a weak smile from her. "True."

Nyra shifted closer, resting her chin on Liora's shoulder. "You're going to explode again if someone startles you?"

"I make no promises."

Sylas handed her a dented water flask. "Kaelen says we're safe for the night. Ship's shielded, rigged for silence."

"Shielded," Liora muttered, taking a slow sip. "That's generous. More like 'vaguely disguised by tarp and stubborn hope.'"

Kaelen chuckled. "That tarp cost me three hours of stitching and two fingers nearly blown off."

"Well then," she said, raising the flask like a toast, "I hereby nominate you for patchwork sainthood."

But the joke flattened halfway out of her mouth. Her shoulders sagged, and the laugh didn't reach her eyes. She leaned back again, exhaustion finally pressing past her charm.

Dorian stepped below deck with Tarian close behind. "No signs of pursuit. Not yet. But we can't stay long."

Arin appeared in the stairwell. "Then let them rest now, while they can. Liora's burned out, and the children haven't had a moment's peace since Smeltport."

Liora gave a half-hearted wave. "Still here. Still awake. Technically."

Dorian glanced at her. "You don't look it."

"I'm just conserving beauty."

Nyra tugged on Liora's sleeve. "Are you scared?"

The question didn't hang in the air. It landed. Heavy.

Liora blinked. "Scared of what?"

"Of what's next. Of going to Nocturne's Edge. Of… dying."

Silence. Even the hull creaked softer.

Liora didn't answer at first. Then: "You know, when I first left Floralis, I thought I'd be gone for just two weeks. Rescue mission. Then home."

She paused, turning the bracelet on her wrist—the one Kaelen had given her. The faint glyphwork still glowed, steady and faint.

"This," she said, holding it up, "helped more than you probably meant it to. Kept my focus clean. Let me push harder. It's good work, Kaelen."

He nodded, quietly grateful.

"But magic or not…" Liora looked down at Nyra. "Yeah. I'm scared. Not all the time. But right now?" She gave a brittle laugh. "Right now, I'd give a lot to be in a field somewhere, drinking juice out of a bottle shaped like a fruit."

Nyra didn't laugh. She just nodded, solemn.

Liora leaned down, bumping her forehead against the girl's. "But listen, both of you. After this—after all this mess—I'm taking you on a real adventure. No spies. No gods. Just sky."

Sylas raised an eyebrow. "You're promising something you can't keep?"

"I never said I'd come back in one piece." She shrugged. "Just said I'd come back."

Kaelen looked between them all. "We'll make sure of it."

Dorian's voice cut through the moment. "We're not here to make speeches. We're here to make it count. Nocturne's Edge isn't a place you walk into and expect to walk out again. You've all seen what's coming. The fractured lands, the false peace. The way both sides are rallying behind ghosts and guesses."

Tarian stepped forward. "The people don't want more war, but they're being pushed into it. Prophets, relics, Chosen Ones—it's all firewood for the next burn."

"And we're the match?" Arin asked.

"We're the ones who can douse it," Dorian said. "Or at least shape where it burns."

From Elara's satchel, the relic pulsed once. Not bright. But steady. A slow beat that matched no sound in the room, yet settled into all of them.

Liora rubbed her face. "You're exhausting when you're right."

"You'll live."

"No guarantees."

She glanced out the porthole, toward the city beyond. Lights flickered on the distant shore. Some moving. Some are waiting.

"Still feels like we're being watched," she said.

"We are," Kaelen replied. "Just not by anything that blinks."

That quieted the room again.

Eventually, Arin stood. "Rest while you can. We'll plan at dawn."

Liora shifted, curling slightly around the twins. "Wake me if we're boarded, betrayed, or dead."

Kaelen smiled faintly. "Two out of three, at most."

The air was cooler come morning. Not clear, exactly—but calmer. Smoke still hung thin across the sky, a reminder of what they'd outrun. But the horizon beyond Irondale shimmered with enough light to pretend the world wasn't coming apart.

The Dawnseeker bobbed gently on the water as the group stood gathered at the main deck. None of them were armed to the teeth anymore. Too obvious. Too dangerous. Just cloaks, packs, and the weight of everything left unsaid.

"We'll need parts first," Kaelen said, tightening the strap on his shoulder rig. "Food, replacement wiring, maybe a new manifold if I can find one that isn't corroded to hell."

Dorian nodded. "We go together. In and out. No stalling."

Elara adjusted the collar of her cloak, eyes narrowed toward the city. "We blend. No questions. And we don't stay longer than we need to."

"That a new rule?" Kaelen asked.

"It's the only one that's kept me alive this long."

The twins stood off to the side, quietly observing. Liora remained nearby, still recovering but upright now, arms folded as if posture alone could keep her grounded.

Then Arin stepped forward. "I'm not going with you."

The silence was immediate.

Kaelen turned. "What?"

"I need to go to Hollowgrove," Arin said, voice steady. "My mother is there. And if I don't go now—before everything spirals—I may never get the chance."

Elara blinked. "You think it's safe?"

"No. But it matters."

Tarian nodded once. "It's a long detour."

Sariel spoke, calm as ever. "Not as long as you think. Hollowgrove's only half a day northeast. We're closer than the maps say."

"I can go alone," Arin offered, though even she didn't believe it.

"You won't," Tarian said. "I'll take you."

Kaelen looked between them, clearly calculating risk. "We need your blades in the city."

"And you'll have them after," Tarian said. "Give us two days. If we're not back by then…"

"You'll be back," Kaelen cut in. "That's not up for negotiation."

Elara met Arin's eyes. "Are you sure you're going to be okay?"

Arin didn't answer right away. Then: "I don't know. But I need to find out."

Dorian nodded slowly. "Then we meet here. Two days. No delays."

The group moved in rhythm after that—packs handed off, coordinates confirmed, watches synced. Not rushed, but intentional. A controlled split, not a collapse.

Liora leaned against the mast, still pale but watching closely. "You all realize this is how horror stories start, right? Splitting up before the finale."

Kaelen half-smiled. "We're past stories."

Liora gave him a look. "No one's past stories. They just stop pretending they're not in one."

At the plank, Arin adjusted her satchel. She moved slower than usual, more careful. Not from weakness—just thought.

Kaelen stepped in her path.

"You don't have to say it," he said.

"Say what?"

"Goodbye."

She tilted her head. "That's not what I was going to say."

He raised an eyebrow.

"I was going to say 'don't get yourself arrested,'" she said. Then added, more quietly, "But yeah. I was also going to say goodbye."

Kaelen shook his head. "Don't. Say 'until after.'"

Arin smiled at that, small but real. "Until after."

Sariel passed her a spare blade, slim and plain. "In case words don't work."

"Words rarely do," she replied, sliding it into her belt.

Tarian gave Dorian a brief clasp of the shoulder. "Try not to get into trouble without me."

"No promises."

From the pack slung across Kaelen's back came a faint thud—barely audible, but unmistakable. He shifted, sensing the weight had shifted inside. The relic.

It pulsed once—no flash, just a sudden warmth through the canvas. It's not a warning nor a sign of danger. Just... acknowledgement.

Kaelen didn't say anything. Just adjusted the strap and kept moving.

The city waited on one side. Hollowgrove on the other.

And in the middle, a fragile trust that two days would be enough.

Irondale was louder than it should've been for a city on edge.

The docks clanged with freight, vendors shouted from tarp-strung stalls, and steam hissed from the under road grates in sharp bursts. But underneath the noise was something heavier.

No laughter. No music. The soundscape had all the right shapes—but none of the life.

Kaelen, Elara, and Dorian moved single file down a side road lined with half-shuttered workshops and flickering rune-lamps. They'd entered through a freight gate east of the main square—low security, minimal attention. Still, they walked fast and said little.

Fliers papered the walls around them. Some were torn, some overwritten. Calls for conscription. Propaganda from both the Forgeborne loyalists and a rising faction calling itself "The Balance." No one had taken them down. No one dared.

Dorian scanned the roofs. "Less patrols than I expected."

"They're conserving force," Elara said. "Waiting for something to ignite."

Kaelen ducked into a side alley and came back out with a canvas bag, tossing it over his shoulder. "One circuit board, five charge cores, three bags of powder-sealant. No questions asked, which means we're either welcome or too suspicious to question."

They turned onto a narrow marketplace street, where rows of merchants had set up makeshift stands. Most wore tired expressions. Some avoided eye contact entirely.

Elara walked beside Kaelen, gaze tracking every twitch, every sudden movement. "People here are afraid."

Kaelen nodded. "Not afraid of us. Just… afraid."

A boy ran past them, clutching a satchel too tightly for it to be empty. No one chased him.

A few blocks deeper, Dorian stopped.

The armory was chained shut.

Not just locked—sealed. Steel doors reinforced with crossbars, the emblem of Irondale's military blacked out by smeared paint. A posted sign read "Under Review – Property of the Council."

He stood there a moment longer, then turned away, saying nothing.

"This city's preparing for war," he said. "They just don't know who the enemy is yet."

Kaelen looked up. "Or maybe they do. They just don't want to say it out loud."

Elara's hand moved to her staff, instinctual.

She didn't like this city. Too familiar. Too many corners. It reminded her of Floralis before the riots—when the nobles smiled and the servants vanished.

They pressed on, veering toward a smaller neighborhood tucked behind a guildhall. Kaelen ducked into a shop with no signage—just a pale lantern and dirty windows. Inside, he passed a coin to a woman with missing fingers. She passed him a sack with food, cloth, and something wrapped in wax paper.

"Three hours," she whispered. "Then I shut for good."

Kaelen nodded and left without a word.

The trio regrouped near a blacksmith's shop, long abandoned.

Elara leaned on the wall. "You two feel it too, right?"

Dorian didn't ask what she meant. He just nodded.

Kaelen ran a hand through his hair. "The city's holding its breath. Not sure if it's praying or just waiting for something to break."

In the distance, a bell rang. Not church. Not military. Just a worker's shift bell—but sharp enough to make half the street flinch.

A group of men turned down a side road, speaking in low tones. One wore an armband with a broken scale on it.

"What is that?" Elara asked.

Kaelen squinted. "Symbol of The Balance. They started as a labor movement. Now they're pulling numbers—lots of Verdant and Forgeborne defectors."

"Another faction," Dorian muttered. "As if we didn't have enough lines to cross."

Kaelen's voice was quieter now. "They're not trying to take sides. They're trying to erase them."

They kept moving. The city breathed around them—just loud enough to disguise its own unrest. Just silent enough that if a riot broke out, no one would be surprised.

Dorian led them toward the edge of the industrial quarter. They'd circle back in the evening, make camp in the shell of a broken mill Kaelen had found on his last supply run.

As they passed a mural flaking off brick, Elara touched the wall without thinking.

It was a painting of a tree. Verdant-style. Once bright green, now faded to gray.

Someone had scrawled beneath it in black ink:

WE WERE WHOLE ONCE.

Elara didn't speak. She just traced the roots with her finger, then walked on.

Dorian, Kaelen, and Elara passed by the gallows on their way to the market.

The structure loomed in the center of the square, a grim reminder of the city's laws. Its wood was worn and dark, the rope swaying slightly in the wind. Two nooses hung ready, a sign of what was about to happen.

Dorian had witnessed scenes like this before back in Forgehelm. He walked with steady purpose, gaze unwavering. Kaelen was quieter, his steps measured, while Elara kept her distance, eyes darting anywhere but the platform ahead.

Soldiers lined the square, standing at attention, while civilians watched in silence. There were no cheers, no protests. It wasn't a spectacle—it was a warning. A message that Irondale did not tolerate defiance.

The condemned stood on the platform, wrists bound, heads bowed. A man and a woman. They didn't look dangerous. The woman was older, her face marked by years of hardship. The boy beside her, hardly more than a teenager, trembled despite his attempts to stand still.

Verdant sympathizers. That's what they were called. There was no trial, only the verdict the city had already decided.

Kaelen and Dorian folded their arms.. Elara shifted her weight, glancing toward the edge of the square.

A soldier stepped forward and unrolled a scroll. Their crimes. Their treason. Their betrayal of Irondale and the Forgeborne ideals. The words were spoken, but no one was really listening.

The woman lifted her head. For a moment, her eyes met the man standing next to Dorian.

"They must've known each other." Dorian thought to himself.

There was no plea for help. No anger. Just understanding.

The boy beside her wasn't as composed. He pulled against the ropes, his breath coming fast as the executioner stepped forward.

Dorian had seen it before—the fear, the realization. The moment when defiance gave way to desperation.

Then, the lever was pulled.

Elara turned away, staring at the ground. Kaelen held his breath. Dorian remained still.

The crowd remained silent as the platform dropped. It was over quickly, though the tension lingered in the air.

The bodies were cut down. The next charges were prepared. The city's message would be sent again.

Dorian adjusted his grip on his belt, releasing a slow breath.

Then they walked away.

The alley narrowed as they moved, its stone walls closing in around crates, rusted bins, and the sour scent of vinegar runoff from an abandoned tanner's. Irondale pulsed behind them, but here—no one watched. No one followed.

Dorian's steps slowed.

"Something's off," Kaelen said under his breath, adjusting the strap across his chest. "We shouldn't be this exposed."

"Stay sharp," Elara murmured. Her staff was already half-lowered.

That's when the silhouette stepped from behind the crates.

Slim build. Low stance. Hands visible.

Kaelen reacted first—gauntlet primed, two fingers raised in warning.

But Dorian caught the shape and stopped cold.

"Hold."

Kaelen's hand didn't lower. "You know her?"

The woman stepped into the light.

She looked thinner than Dorian remembered. Pale beneath the collar. Her uniform was downgraded—standard Forgeborne grays stripped of command insignia, sleeves frayed, one shoulder patch removed altogether. Her rifle hung on her back, matte black and shortened—snubbed down for alley work, not long-range flats like she was used to.

Riven.

"Been a while," she said quietly.

Kaelen's brows pulled. "You were there. In the Iron Flats."

She nodded once. "Overwatch tower. Fourth ridge."

"I saw a silhouette," he said. "One shot took out the lead skirmisher. Saved our lives."

Riven shrugged. "Someone had to. I can't just accept that the Forgemasters are giving orders to kill someone who has done nothing wrong."

Kaelen didn't lower the gauntlet. "You're Forgeborne."

"Was," she said. "Technically still am. But these days, I'm mostly furniture they forgot to replace."

Dorian gave no visible reaction. But his next words came easier. A memory confirmed. A trust—fractured, but not broken.

Riven shifted her weight. "I was reassigned after the Flats. Demoted after the prison gate. They didn't trace it directly, but someone knew."

"Why help him?" Kaelen asked.

She looked at Dorian. "Because when the call came to let him rot, I didn't agree."

"And now?"

"Now?" She reached up, removed the rifle from her back, and set it gently against the wall. "Now I'm done playing loyal to people who reward silence over truth."

Elara studied her carefully. "You've got timing."

Kaelen finally lowered the gauntlet halfway. "You saved us before. Doesn't mean we trust you now."

"I don't expect you to," Riven said. "I let too much slide. Let people vanish. You two made it out. I didn't. Not really."

Dorian stepped closer. "You're not here on orders?"

"No. I'm here because the people I trained with are starting to vanish, and the ones who stay are less human each week."

Kaelen looked at Dorian. "Your call." Both men knew they were thinking of the same thing.

Dorian hesitated—but not for long.

He gave a small nod. "Two days. That's all we've got left in this city."

Kaelen shifted his weight—and stopped.

The relic in his pack had grown warm again, pulsing softly. But this time... not alone.

From across the alley, Elara's satchel stirred—its clasp twitching slightly as the second relic responded.

Two pulses. Not bright. Not loud. But synchronized—like breath drawn between sparks.

Neither of them said a word.

Kaelen didn't speak—but he didn't have to. They both felt it. Both understood. And Elara's hand lingered a moment longer on her strap.

Riven nodded. "Two days is plenty."

Kaelen stepped past her but paused.

"You can come with us," he said. "Or leave this city and your post."

Riven didn't flinch. "Understood."

She retrieved her rifle, but didn't re-sling it. She just fell in behind them, silent as shadow.

Hollowgrove revealed itself all at once—like the forest had blinked.

Sariel stepped through the shimmer of woven magic, and the woods parted behind him. Arin followed with Tarian close, blinking as the village emerged from between branches: stone-set homes, moss-threaded walkways, and lanterns strung from root arches.

It was quiet. Hidden. Undisturbed by the world unraveling beyond its veil.

And in the center of it, Arin saw her.

Lysandra stood at the threshold of a rounded stone dwelling, her right arm still in a sling, a thin scar tracing her cheekbone. She looked like she hadn't moved in a month—like she'd been waiting right there.

Arin stopped walking.

She hadn't let herself hope. Not really. After the ambush, after the silence—she'd prepared for the worst. Forced herself to keep moving. But the part of her that had never stopped listening for her mother's voice… that part broke loose.

She stepped forward.

And then she was running.

Lysandra caught her in one arm, the sling slowing nothing. They crashed together, breath hitching, strength vanishing in the embrace.

Arin clung to her—and the sob cracked loose before she could stop it.

"I thought you were gone," she whispered.

Lysandra didn't answer for a long moment. Then: "I thought I might be."

"You didn't write."

"I couldn't. I didn't know if it would be safer for you to think I was dead."

"You were wrong."

"I usually am."

They pulled back just enough to look at each other. Arin reached up, brushing her fingers against the scar. Lysandra caught her hand and held it.

"You look different," she said.

"So do you."

"Don't get sentimental on me."

"You're the one who waited by the door."

Lysandra's eyes flicked away, just for a second. "I told Sariel you'd make it. He didn't argue."

A second figure approached from the edge of the clearing—measured steps, loose posture, young but steady.

Sylva.

She stopped beside Sariel, giving him a nod, then turned to Lysandra.

"You didn't say she'd be that fast," Sylva said. "Nearly bowled you over."

Lysandra gave her a sidelong look. "This is my daughter. Arin."

Sylva studied her without speaking, then offered a short nod. "Welcome to Hollowgrove."

Arin returned it, cautious. "Thank you."

"Lys talks about you when she thinks no one's listening."

"Sylva," Lysandra warned.

"I'm just saying," Sylva replied. "She didn't wait by that door for fun."

Arin turned back to her mother.

They stood there a while, just breathing the same air again.

For the first time in weeks, Arin's hands weren't trembling.

She felt like she was home not because of the walls around her, but because her mother still stood inside them.

Lysandra finally stepped back, looking Arin over once more—this time not as a mother reuniting, but as a soldier measuring a comrade.

"You're not just here to visit," she said.

Arin nodded slowly. "We leave for Nocturne's Edge tomorrow, after we regroup with the rest of the team back in Irondale."

"Then I'm coming."

Arin hesitated. "You don't have to—"

"I know exactly what I don't have to do. I'm coming anyway."

A soft whistle sounded. Sylva leaned against the outer archway, arms crossed. "Looks like I better pack my things."

Arin blinked. "Both of you?"

Sylva grinned. "What, you think she's the only one with a death wish?"

Meanwhile, deeper in Irondale...

The street noise had dulled to background hum—no footsteps close, no shouts overhead. Just the distant hiss of steam vents and the metallic breath of an old city holding tension in its walls.

The trio paused near the edge of a closed square, the kind usually crowded with apprentices and carts. It was nearly empty now.

Kaelen adjusted the strap on his shoulder and stopped.

Not for pain. Not for pressure.

For weight.

He reached back and touched the pack. The relic inside didn't shift—it settled. Like a coin dropped into a perfect slot.

Elara froze beside him. Her satchel gave the faintest twitch—not the flare of alarm they'd felt before, but something deeper. A low, internal click, like a mechanism aligning.

Dorian's brow furrowed. "What is it?"

Kaelen didn't speak at first. Then: "Something just... changed. Not here. Somewhere else."

Elara ran her fingers along the edge of her bag, eyes distant. "Like we were waiting for something to lock into place."

"And it just did," Kaelen said. Quiet. Certain.

None of them knew why.

But back in Hollowgrove, two warriors had just stepped forward. Not as survivors.

As reinforcements.

The market should have been loud—a cacophony of hammer-on-anvil strikes, roaring furnaces, shouting vendors, and the hiss of molten metal cooling in troughs. But the first thing Dorian noticed wasn't the sound. It was the absence of it.

He moved slowly between smith stalls, Kaelen and Riven trailing close. The usual rhythm of the place—metal, motion, noise—was still there, but muted. Caged. Like the whole street had sucked in a breath and was waiting for someone else to exhale.

Ash and dust clung to everything: awnings, boots, brows. Racks of gear sat untouched, polished blades going dull in their scabbards. Half the vendors kept one hand below the counters, likely on hidden blades or panic runes. The others kept their eyes locked on the same corners of the square—like they expected someone to step out and shatter the silence.

Dorian slowed his steps, scanning every line of sight, every exit. Elara was quieter than usual, avoiding the gazes of soldiers stationed at intersections.

The gallows were fresh in their minds—what had happened, what they had watched. The silence of the market carried the same weight, the same warning.

"It doesn't feel right," Dorian said, low.

Riven paused beside him, tracking the rooftop angles with a trained eye. "You're not wrong."

"Feels like a trap," Kaelen muttered. "What are we missing?"

Dorian didn't answer immediately. Instead, he tilted his head toward the eastern edge of the market. Three enforcers cut across the crowd in perfect formation—tight, deliberate, close enough that their shoulders nearly touched.

They weren't watching the vendors. They weren't holding ground.

They were looking for someone.

Dorian kept his voice barely audible. "They're not hunting us. Not yet. But they're hunting someone."

It was in the way they moved—purposeful, not reactive. As if they knew their prey was nearby. The kind of movement that came from orders, not instinct.

Kaelen shifted his pack slightly, adjusting the weight. Elara kept her gaze fixed ahead, determined not to meet any lingering stares.

"Word's out," Riven said, voice just above a whisper. "Not just about you two. About all of it. The Chosen. The Equinox. It's spreading faster than they can contain it."

Dorian's reply came after a pause. His tone was even, but each word struck clean.

"It's bigger than we thought. We didn't just light the match. We started the fire."

For a heartbeat, the air shifted—like the moment before a pressure valve gives.

Across the square, Elara slowed, one hand drifting toward her satchel—not because she meant to, but because something in her reached for it.

The relics didn't glow.

They didn't heat.

But both of them pressed outward—twin pulses, inward and mirrored, like two heartbeats briefly syncing and then pulling apart.

Not loud. Not dramatic. But felt.

Dorian noticed. His glance wasn't long, but it was knowing.

No one said anything.

But the silence after felt different.

They passed a weapons stand. The vendor stared straight ahead, sweat dripping from his brow despite the cold. Behind him, a dozen longswords gleamed, unsold and untouched.

A young boy ran past them with a bag of nails and no shoes. No one stopped him.

Further on, an older woman swept her stoop with more force than needed, casting nervous glances at every armored figure who walked by.

The crowd wasn't dense, but it was tense. Movements were measured. Voices kept low. The noise of industry remained, but it carried a different energy now—a simmer beneath the iron, like something ready to break open.

Kaelen caught fragments of whispered conversations. "Another sermon raided." "They took the woodworker's son." "Said she lit a candle for the wrong name."

Not orders. Not protests.

Fear.

They rounded the corner toward the main junction and saw two more enforcer squads. One stood idle but alert near a smith guild. The other spoke with a shopkeeper, who nodded too quickly at questions he clearly didn't want to answer.

Dorian slowed. "They're pulling in the net."

Kaelen adjusted his pace to match. "Then we stay under it."

They made no purchases, but every step through the market told them more than any intel briefing could. The city was waiting.

Not to be saved.

To erupt.

Irondale wasn't holding steady.

It was bracing.

The sky was heavy with gray clouds as the Irondale team crested the rise beyond the city's eastern edge. The trees that marked the outskirts of their makeshift camp stood still, untouched by wind but dense with the kind of silence that warned them they were no longer alone.

Kaelen stepped through first, followed by Dorian, Elara, and Riven. She walked a half step behind them, rifle slung and posture wary—not deferential, just aware. It was the kind of presence that asked for trust without assuming it.

The camp looked exactly as they left it—tents pitched, embers still faint in the fire pit. But something about the stillness made Kaelen's gut tighten.

"They're not back yet," he said, voice low.

"Or they're watching first," Riven replied.

Dorian scanned the trees, fingers brushing the edge of his hammer's grip.

Then—motion.

Figures emerged from the forest edge.

Sariel came first, cloak slightly damp from the woods. Tarian followed close behind him, then Arin—hood down, eyes sharp, scanning for familiar shapes.

Kaelen took a step forward instinctively.

Arin saw him. And the moment their eyes met, her shoulders dropped with visible relief.

"Kaelen!" she called.

He grinned before he realized it. "You made it."

Elara moved faster than the others, reaching Arin with a short laugh and wrapping her in a tight hug. Tarian and Dorian exchanged a solid clasp at the shoulder—less formal than usual, but real.

Then came Lysandra and Sylva.

Lysandra moved slower, her eyes scanning the camp, her stance deliberate. Sylva trailed close behind, assessing without flinching. Kaelen didn't know who she was, but the way she held herself—measured, unshaken—made it clear she knows how to lead a squad.

For a moment, there was a pause. Everyone stood where they were, looking at the other half of their journey.

Then the dam broke.

Dorian gestured toward the woman beside him. "This is Riven. We used to work together. She helped me and Kaelen escape back in Forgehelm. Without her, I wouldn't be standing here."

Riven gave a sharp nod. "I'm honored to be here—and I'll do what I can to contribute. I know I'm the new one. Just point me where I'm needed."

Sylva raised a brow. "So these are the ones you didn't tell me about."

"I wanted to see your face when you met them," Arin said.

Sylva shrugged. "Fair."

Kaelen clapped Tarian on the back. "Two days, right on time."

"And I see Liora and the twins didn't let the place fall apart," Tarian said, nodding toward the campfire where they were tidying up the last of the gear.

It wasn't a celebration. But it was warmth. The kind that only came after surviving something separately and realizing you'd made it back to the same fire.

Elara looked at all of them—Kaelen, Arin, Sylva, Riven—and stepped into the center.

"If you're here," she said, "you know what this means."

Lysandra met her eyes. "I'm here because I know what it'll cost if we don't."

No one argued. No one backed away.

The group was whole.

And what came next, they'd face together.

Then, from Kaelen's pack, came a sound. Not sharp. Not urgent. Just a shift in pressure—a small mechanical clink as the relic adjusted itself inside the canvas like something settling into its final slot.

Elara's satchel echoed the movement a second later.

This time, they all noticed.

Kaelen blinked, unshouldering the bag slowly. "Again?"

Elara reached for hers too, brow furrowed.

Dorian looked between them. "They've been pulsing since Irondale."

Kaelen opened the flap just slightly, enough to feel the low warmth on the stone's surface. It didn't flare. It just held.

A quiet hum. A steady weight. Like acknowledgement.

He looked at Elara, then back at the others.

"…They were waiting," he said.

"For what?" Riven asked.

Kaelen scanned the circle of faces now standing around the fire.

"For all of us."

The group sat in a loose ring around the campfire, its glow pulsing softly in the dimming twilight. Packs were half-unloaded, boots kicked off, weapons nearby but untouched. It wasn't rest, not exactly. But it was the closest thing to stillness any of them had known in weeks.

The sky had turned to slate, and the wind carried a warning—cool and dry, but full of movement. Somewhere, not far from their fire, a branch cracked beneath the weight of an animal that didn't want to be seen. Liora adjusted the coals with the tip of a stick, keeping the flames low. Elara sat beside her, legs crossed, hands resting in her lap. Arin flanked Lysandra, silent but present. Everyone listened.

Riven stirred the fire with a longer branch before speaking.

"Things are worse than you think," she said. "In Irondale, the Forgeborne are tearing at their own command structure. The Forgemasters' grip is slipping fast. People are talking—openly now—about Dorian and about Kaelen. Rumors say you lit a relic in the scrapyards. That you broke ranks with purpose. Some are calling it treason. Others? Inspiration."

Kaelen's brow furrowed.

"They don't even know the half of it," he muttered.

"They don't need to," Riven replied. "They've made their version of the story. And it's enough to split loyalties. There's already splinter groups forming in some cities. They say the old ways are dead. That the council sold their souls to safety and forgot why we built anything in the first place."

Dorian leaned forward, resting his arms on his knees. "And the enforcers?"

"Some still follow orders. Others are… hesitant. Especially the ones who lost friends in skirmishes with the Verdants. They don't want another war, but they'll join one if the ground gives way. I've heard whispers of whole units going dark. Waiting. Watching who steps forward."

Kaelen glanced at Elara. "This isn't isolated."

"No," she said quietly. "It's a pattern. We're not just being followed. We're being preceded."

Sylva, crouched near the cookpot, glanced up. She stood, brushing her hands clean, and spoke without pause or flare. "Verdant command's no better. The army is fractured. The leadership vanished after the last convoy raids—maybe dead, maybe hiding. No one knows. Their assassin corps splintered. Some stayed loyal, but others? Rogue now. Operating without sanction. They're targeting anyone they think is tied to the Equinox prophecy. Civilians included."

Arin sat up straighter. "They're killing their own?"

Sylva nodded. "They call it purification. But it's fear. Panic dressed up in purpose. The ranks don't agree, either. Some loyalist squads are starting to question the mission. I've even heard rumors of units standing down rather than carrying out kill orders on grovecallers. One Verdant captain reportedly deserted his post and escorted his entire village into exile."

Lysandra frowned. "And the Wardens of Aeldrin?"

She laid it out clean. "Scattered. Some are trying to hold ground. Others are settling scores. No communication. No coordination. And no clear vision of what comes next. They're splintering, and everyone underneath them is starting to see the cracks."

The fire cracked softly, casting long shadows across their faces. The silence that followed wasn't empty—it was dense with implication.

Then Sariel spoke.

His voice was low, but every word landed like iron. "When both sides lose the leash, the wolves run free."

The fire popped again, and no one moved.

The world wasn't just unraveling at the edges. It was tearing straight through the center. And in the gaps where power had failed, something older and more dangerous was beginning to grow.

They weren't just caught between factions anymore.

They were standing in the hollow where something new could begin—or something ancient could return.

Not to stop it.

But to decide what would be rebuilt from the ashes.

The fire had burned down to coals, but no one moved to rekindle it. A chill settled over the camp—thin but constant, like the air itself was bracing. Every member of the group sat within the glow of the dying embers, eyes reflecting not just the flames, but the weight of what they knew waited above the tree line.

Tarian crouched beside the crude map they had scratched into the dirt with a stick of charcoal, a furrow between his brows. "Celestial Heights isn't just high ground. It's convergence," he said, pointing toward the central plateau. "Trade routes. Old war trails. Pilgrim paths. All of them meet here. That's why they chose it. That's why it's sacred—and dangerous."

Lysandra stood nearby, arms crossed, gaze fixed on the drawn lines. "It's not just a symbolic site anymore. Reports say both factions are moving. Armies. Not scouts. Multiple divisions. They're gathering at the foot of Nocturne's Edge."

Kaelen straightened slowly, the weight of the map settling like lead. "They're going to fight on the slope. Turn prophecy into a graveyard."

Elara stared at the map, eyes unreadable. "They think it's destiny. That it ends there, with one side rising and the other burning. That it has to be blood for legacy."

Dorian stood, arms folded tightly over his chest. "And if we don't intervene, they're right. We'll watch both sides tear each other apart just to prove their gods still matter."

A silence followed, longer than usual. Even the fire seemed to dim.

Then Arin said, quietly, "What's the point of fulfilling the prophecy if everyone we know is dead?"

Her words hung there. No one contradicted her.

Kaelen knelt beside the map again, smoothing out a crease in the dirt. "Then we shift it. Control the tempo. Force a stalemate. We've done more with less. We've survived worse odds."

Tarian nodded. "We get ahead of the armies. Offer something neither command expects: reason. Delay. Visibility. A symbol that doesn't draw blood."

Lysandra frowned. "Reason won't hold if the first arrow flies. We'll have one shot to make them listen, and it might not be a long one."

Liora stood, arms wrapped around herself, face unreadable but her voice firm. "Then we use everything we have. Storm, voice, presence. We don't whisper. We roar. Show them we're not part of the cycle. We're here to break it."

Riven leaned against a tree trunk, rifle slung over one shoulder, but her eyes were clear. "I don't care about the prophecy. But if it puts us in the center of that battlefield, then I'm making sure someone walks out alive. Preferably more than one."

Sariel finally spoke, his voice quiet, words even. "When both sides stand on the brink, it only takes one truth to push them back. Or forward."

Sylva, who had been quiet, finally stirred. She moved closer to the fire, kneeling across from Arin. "We go in knowing they won't trust us. That means we speak louder through action. No theatrics. Just clarity. Make them hesitate. Make them question the orders they're dying to follow."

Across the clearing, Liora gently pulled a blanket up over Sylas and Nyra, who had drifted against her shoulders. Sylas had stirred, wide-eyed. "What if they don't stop?"

Nyra, half-asleep but listening, whispered, "Then we make them wish they had."

Kaelen looked up at that, the faintest smile tugging at the corner of his mouth. "Out of the mouths of very small, very dangerous people."

Elara stepped forward. Her voice wasn't raised, but it reached everyone just the same. She touched the edge of the map, fingers tracing the rise toward Nocturne's Edge. "This is prophecy now. But it's ours to shape. Not theirs. Not what's written. What we decide."

Dorian exhaled slowly, glancing toward the north where the outline of the Celestial Heights waited behind low clouds. "Then let's shape it. Together."

The group said nothing more, but no one stood. They sat together in the cold silence, the flames barely flickering now, surrounded by wind and branches and belief.

Nocturne's Edge wasn't just the end.

It was the last chance to change everything.

And they were the only ones left who could.

As the others began to settle down or check their gear in silence, Elara remained near the fading fire, a scroll half-unfurled across her lap. The same one she'd carried since Hollowgrove. Its edges were worn, its ink faded—but the glyphs were still legible under the soft light of the campfire.

She traced the lines with a finger, rereading them slowly—each verse older than any city still standing.

"And so the land called Auravalle was broken,
Where iron met nature and neither bent.
A song was lost. A bond undone.
And light that once stitched god to ground was torn."

She had never fully believed it before. Not really. It always felt like allegory.

But now, with the fire dying and the edge of the world waiting, she wasn't so sure.

"The light returns not through force, but through fracture. Not by fire alone. But by seed and spark."

Nocturne's Edge had been called Auravalle once—when gods still walked beside the people. Before unity cracked and every child was born into one side or the other.

She rolled the scroll tight and pressed it against her chest.

Tomorrow, they will climb.

And maybe—just maybe—the world would listen again.

The morning came gray and cold, the sun a dull smear behind thick haze. Mist drifted low over the ridge, coiling around their boots as they readied their packs. No one spoke much. The fire had long since died, and the silence that followed was neither tense nor calm—it simply was.

They moved like parts of a machine. Straps were tightened. Weapons checked. Canteens secured. The ritual of preparation gave shape to the unspoken weight pressing down on them.

Kaelen secured his gauntlet, adjusting the pressure latch until it clicked into place. He didn't look up as he spoke. "We move light. If we lose speed, we lose initiative."

Dorian adjusted the strap of the two-handed hammer on his back. "We hold formation until the last bend before the ridgeline. After that, expect interference."

Arin offered water to Sariel, who accepted it with a nod. He hadn't slept, but his eyes were clear.

Tarian scanned the tree line one last time. "They'll be watching the skies. If Liora's right about the winds shifting, we might be harder to track until we break elevation."

They all knew what wasn't being said: that every step forward was a step into a storm—political, magical, prophetic. The point where intention meets consequence.

Liora stood apart from the group, her pale face drawn but steady. She remained by the edge of the camp, standing on a wooden platform built near the supply carts, watching them as they ascended the hill toward the ridgeline. The twins stood on either side of her, bundled in cloaks too large for their frames.

She knelt in front of them, adjusting Nyra's hood before brushing a hand against Sylas's shoulder. "You two are staying here," she said gently. "The Dawnseeker needs a first and second mate to keep her safe while we're gone. That's you now."

Nyra's lip quivered. "But we want to help."

"You are helping," Liora said. "By staying. It's too dangerous where we're going. You've both done more than anyone could've asked for already."

Sylas gave a small nod, though his fists stayed clenched. Nyra sniffled. "You'll come back, right? For the adventure you promised?"

Liora smiled faintly, her voice silent but certain. "I will. I don't know how, or what shape I'll be in, but I'll come back."

Nyra looked up at her. "How do you know?"

Liora met her eyes without flinching. "I just do."

Nyra waved silently. Sylas didn't. He just stared, eyes too knowing for his age.

Elara met Liora's gaze and offered a nod. Not farewell. Just understanding.

Sylva was the last to adjust her pack. Her eyes flicked toward the ridge ahead. "We'll make it in time," she said. "But it won't feel like it."

Riven ran a hand along the edge of her rifle and then slung it across her back. "Let's make sure they see us before they decide to stop us."

Lysandra walked past Elara, gave her a light tap on the shoulder. "We've done harder things with worse odds."

"This time it matters more," Elara replied.

Lysandra nodded. "All the more reason to finish it right."

They began the climb.

The eastern ridgeline loomed ahead, draped in mist and myth. The earth grew quieter with every step upward. Trees thinned. The air thinned. No one looked back.

Then Kaelen stopped. Just for a second.

He shifted his pack. Felt it—pressure, not weight.

Inside, the relic had moved. Not on its own—but with purpose. A slow internal pivot, like something had just been aligned.

Across the trail, Elara blinked. Reached for her satchel.

Her relic pulsed once. Not light. Not heat. Just presence.

Kaelen didn't speak.

He didn't need to.

Elara said it for both of them.

"This is it. It's starting."

The ship, the camp, the firelight—everything behind them faded into silence.

They walked not toward fate—but into the storm they'd chosen.

Chapter 17: The Breaking Line

The wind was thin but sharp, scraping up from the valley below. The first ridge sloped upward like a spine, jagged and narrow, each footstep landing with deliberate weight.

Sariel moved ahead without a word, cloak low and eyes cutting through the mist. No one spoke much. Even Liora, usually the first to mutter about weather or incline, said nothing.

A stone shifted underfoot. Kaelen paused, adjusted his stance. When he looked back, Elara was already watching him. She didn't speak—but nodded once. Not reassurance. Recognition.

Somewhere below, a horn sounded—dull, buried in the fog, but there. A signal from one of the camps. Or both.

They kept moving.

When the ridge finally broke open, the view didn't unfold—it *hit*. A steep drop revealed two camps sprawling out like fractured constellations across the valley floor: one Forgeborne, disciplined and lined with black-iron artillery; the other, Verdant—curved, organic formations set in crescent patterns around their banners.

Dorian let out a breath, not quite a curse. "Two gods waiting to be fed."

Kaelen shifted his pack slightly—and felt it. Just the smallest warmth from inside. A relic stir, not a pulse. Like something inside had flinched.

He said nothing. But Elara touched her satchel soon after, as if she'd felt it too.

Verdant banners to the east. Forgeborne standards to the west. Thousands of soldiers. Tents dotted the landscape like pockmarks. The twin encampments glowed with scattered fires, flickering in slow pulses across the darkened field. It looked like a starfield swallowed by the land. Each camp carved into its own stretch of land, separate but converging. And though no horns sounded, and no lines had moved yet, the tension between them was already alive.

Elara squinted at the distant formations. "They're waiting."

"For a sign," Arin said. "For blood. For prophecy."

Kaelen's eyes narrowed. "Or for someone to blame."

Riven stepped up behind them, silent until now. "There's no waiting when they're this close. This is a pause with purpose. Someone's giving orders to stall—until the justification comes."

No one responded.

Sariel knelt near the ridge's edge and traced a line in the dirt with one gloved finger. "There's a route through the shale line. Curves north around the basin. Steep, but shielded. Harder to track. I'd take it if I wanted to stay ahead of a scout line."

"We do," Dorian said, voice low. "We need every second we can steal."

Lysandra adjusted the straps on her chestplate, eyes still locked on the flickering field below. "If it breaks, it breaks fast. The slope will run red before either side pulls back."

Kaelen scanned the mountain range ahead, eyes narrowing at the silhouette of the jagged summit above.

"That's Nocturne's Edge?"

Tarian nodded slowly. "Used to be called Auravalle. Before the First Rift."

Arin glanced up. "The place where gods walked beside men?"

Sariel's voice came low. "And where they stopped."

No one replied right away.

Elara broke the silence. "This is where we stopped being one people."

The wind shifted. No one corrected her.

Liora stood a few steps back, scarf tight around her neck. Her arms were wrapped around herself, eyes fixed not on the path but the sky. She hadn't said much since they crossed the lower passes. Even now, her voice was barely a whisper. "We're not stopping it down there."

"Then we go above it," Sylva said. "Not to watch—but to strike before it begins."

Tarian sat on a rock outcrop nearby, his face unusually still. Tarian held a carved twig in his hands, running his thumb over it. His eyes were on the sky, not the ground. He didn't ask questions. Not anymore.

Kaelen glanced back at the group, then forward toward the shadowed climb ahead. "The relics are quiet."

"They know better than to speak too early," Elara murmured. "Even prophecies know when to wait."

He adjusted the strap of his pack. Something about the weight felt... off.

Not heavier—familiar. Like a presence he hadn't accounted for.

His mind flicked, unbidden, to the tracker from Smeltport. The spider-like device. Forgeborne-make. Thought it was gone. He'd watched it drift away.

But the thing about signals?

They echo.

He didn't mention it. Not yet.

The clouds were starting to roll in behind them now. A slow-moving wall of gray and shadow. Wind swept through the canyon with a low whistle, as if the mountain was warning them.

Lightning danced far in the distance—silent for now. But not for long.

They stood at the edge of everything. Below them, fire and armies. Above, stone and silence. In between, the path they had chosen.

A storm behind them but a greater one ahead.

And the mountain waiting in between.

The trail narrowed as they ascended, the mountain path twisting between sheer ridges and gravel-strewn ledges. Frost slicked the stone in patches, and the mist that curled through the upper branches thickened with every step. Above them, jagged cliffs loomed like teeth. The only sound was the crunch of boots on loose rock and the occasional gust of wind threading through trees too stubborn to fall.

They hadn't spoken much since the overlook. No one wanted to be the one to say aloud what they all felt: the mountain was watching.

Then Sariel stopped without a word.

Just off the main path, half-buried beneath a fallen branch, stood a carved stone. Thin, weatherworn, but unmistakably placed. He brushed the snow from its surface, revealing the faint trace of symbols carved deep into the granite.

Elara stepped forward, eyes narrowing as she crouched beside it. The carving was spiral-shaped—wrapped around a triangle of thorns. She didn't touch it. "This is Verdant," she said. "A warding symbol. Old. Meant to mark sacred ground or warn others away. Not something you just stumble on by accident."

"Looks more like a warning," Sylva said from behind. "That, or a claim."

Kaelen knelt opposite Elara, gloved fingers tracing the edge of the stone. He scanned the terrain around them. "Look at the placement—just off the bend. Good elevation. High visibility to anyone traveling up the trail." He stood, glancing farther ahead. "Tactical. These weren't set for worship. They were placed to control the path."

Sariel moved up a short rise and pointed toward a break in the rocks. Another stone stood embedded in the cliffside—this one marked with a different sigil, still Verdant, but stylized with the same knotwork. "There's another. And another—there."

Lysandra's hand moved toward her sword out of habit. "They're ancient, but that doesn't mean the watchers are gone."

Riven spotted it first—tied to a broken tree limb near the trailhead. A twisted knot of bones, roots, and pale leaves.

Elara froze. "It's a wardbreaker. A warning. Not to us—to the mountain. They've declared us unclean."

Tarian muttered, "Still warm."

Kaelen checked the ground. "They were here. An hour ago. Maybe less."

They pushed farther, and what had started as isolated markers became a pattern. Symbols lined the edges of the trail like silent sentinels. Some were carved into rock, others built from stacked stones and branches, bound together by vine cord and animal sinew. A few were half-collapsed, overgrown with moss, but others were disturbingly fresh.

Riven paused beside one such totem, eyes narrowing. She reached out and pressed her palm against a length of pine twisted with fresh cord. "Wood's still wet. Someone tied this within the week. Maybe even days."

"Someone still is," Dorian said. His voice was flat, but his eyes were scanning the shadows above.

Liora stepped carefully around a rune-marked stone and looked back at the trail. "We're not in a passage. We're in a perimeter."

Arin frowned. "Which means we're not just passing through. We've entered something."

"Sacred," Tarian said quietly. "Or contested."

The wind shifted then. From far ahead, a bird cried—sharp and distant. Not a warning. A signal.

Sylas froze mid-step. "That wasn't an animal."

Kaelen reached into his coat and adjusted the dial on the back of his gauntlet, not activating it, but making sure it was ready.

Elara's hand rested near the relic tucked beneath her cloak. It hadn't stirred. Not yet.

No one spoke after that.

The air grew colder. The slope steeper. They moved in silence, eyes darting from stone to tree to ledge. Every turn in the path felt tighter, every shadow longer. Somewhere, not far, they all knew eyes were watching them—unblinking, patient.

The symbols whispered that they did not belong here. That this path was not meant for them.

And still they walked it.

They were not alone.

And someone had been waiting long before they arrived.

The trail narrowed again, hemmed in by rising stone and mist that thickened with every step. The higher they climbed, the more it felt like the mountain was holding something back—its breath, its memory, its judgment. What had begun as a path now felt more like a threshold.

Each footstep was softer here. The ground had shifted to a dusting of moss and brittle lichen, and the trees grew sparse, crooked, shaped by old winds and older warnings. The silence wasn't peace—it was the kind of silence that watched.

They rounded a switchback, boots scraping against slick shale, when Sariel raised a hand. He didn't speak. He didn't need to.

Everyone stopped.

Figures emerged from the fog.

They came in slow, deliberate patterns. Cloaked in gray-green armor, matte and leaf-textured, they blended into the haze and stone like they belonged to it. Spears tipped with living wood—vines still curling around the haft—reflected no light, only a dull gleam. Their helmets were fashioned with bark-like plating, their faces shadowed but alert.

Twelve at least. Maybe more. They moved without sound, their formation more ceremony than threat.

Kaelen stepped forward, hand near his gauntlet. He didn't activate it—yet. "Hold position," he said, voice even.

Tarian came to his side, one hand lightly resting on his sword hilt. "They're not charging."

"They don't need to," Sariel said. "This is a ritual. You don't rush into sacred ground unless you mean to die on it."

The formation tightened, circling—not trapping. There was space left between them. Not enough to escape, but enough to be heard.

It was not an ambush.

It was a message.

The lead figure stepped forward, his silverleaf bark helm resting over armor tinged with deep green. Faint magic pulsed through the twisting vines etched into his chest plate. He moved with purpose, his presence unwavering.

He stopped ten paces away, raised his chin just slightly, and spoke.

"You trespass on a crownless summit," he said. His voice was low, calm. The kind that didn't need to be loud to carry. "Turn back."

Elara stepped forward before anyone else could. She didn't raise her staff, didn't lift her voice. But the weight in her stance made it clear she wouldn't be moved easily.

"This mountain doesn't belong to war," she said. "And we don't come to claim it. We come to stop what's coming."

The figure didn't move. "The mountain belongs to what it remembers. And it remembers betrayal."

Kaelen's hand hovered near his tools, not out of panic, but preparation. He was already sketching outcomes in his head. Dorian stepped forward to stand beside Elara, his hammer slung high on his back, but his eyes already gauging every enemy angle.

Liora leaned slightly toward Tarian and whispered, "Do we prepare to run or negotiate?"

"Depends on how long they listen," he murmured.

Lysandra shifted, blade half-loosened in its sheath. Her gaze never stopped sweeping the upper ridges. "Too many blind angles. If they wanted to ambush, they would've already. Doesn't mean they won't."

Sylva crouched low beside a frost-covered rock, dragging her fingers through the pale moss. "They're watching posture more than weapons. They're testing how we move, not what we say."

Arin adjusted the straps on her pack but said nothing. Riven remained still behind her, rifle at her back, hands relaxed but ready.

Elara took one step closer, her voice steady. "We are not your enemy. But we know what's coming. If you truly remember betrayal, then you know how it starts—with silence. We speak because we remember too."

There was a pause. A long one.

The leader of the Loyalists didn't answer immediately. He tilted his head, assessing. Behind him, the others didn't move. Not a twitch. Not a breath out of sync.

The fog curled tighter around them, a living wall. The wind pressed in from above, whispering against their cloaks.

Still no strike. Still no retreat.

The line had not broken.

But it had been drawn—and now they stood on the edge of something old.

And something waiting to be decided.

The wind shifted again, carrying with it the brittle taste of frost and something older beneath it—something acrid. The two groups stood in frozen balance, the loyalists unmoving, the companions bracing against a confrontation that had not yet come.

Elara stepped forward again. Not rushed, not bold—just certain. Her staff remained low, but her shoulders squared. She inhaled slowly.

"I am Princess Elara Thorne." she said. "Grovecaller of the Eldoravell. Heir to the House of Thorne. I carry the rites of memory and of peace."

A shift passed through the loyalist ranks—not in their posture, but in the air around them. It was the kind of stillness that follows insults.

"You were," the lead figure said. His voice remained calm, but colder now. "The Wardens have already judged you."

He stepped forward one pace. "You consort with Forgeborne. You travel with weapons designed to poison the land. You carry a cursed relic that pulses even now beneath your robes."

"The relic is not cursed," Kaelen said, his voice low and steady. "It's dormant. And it has saved more lives than you'd believe."

"You fracture your own bloodline's purity," the loyalist continued. "You stand beside oathbreakers and iron-scourged thieves. You would shatter the last roots of Verdant sovereignty for what? Peace?"

Elara didn't flinch. "For survival."

Dorian stepped beside her again. "She's risked everything to keep your war from spreading. You think purity matters more than people?"

Riven scoffed from the back. "Typical. You want someone to blame, and she's the easiest target. Next you'll say you're just following orders."

Another loyalist shifted, spear tip twitching slightly.

The leader held up a hand to silence them. "You misunderstand. We do not blame her. We simply name her for what she is."

"You want to talk about names?" Tarian stepped forward now, chin raised. "Then let's call this what it is: fear dressed up in ritual. You're not defending anything. You're hiding behind a myth."

Arin moved to his side, a warning glance cast between her and the spears. "We don't need more blood on a mountain already soaked in it."

The loyalist leader studied them all—Kaelen with his frown, Dorian like a statue carved for war, Elara with fire in her silence. He turned back to the fog behind him.

"We'll not kill you here," he said at last. "Not yet. You'll carry your corruption higher."

He looked back, and for the first time his voice dipped into something near a sneer.

"That will be enough."

Then he turned, disappearing into the mist with the rest of his patrol.

The group remained still, weapons undrawn. But every heartbeat had become louder than the last.

They were not safe.

Just postponed.

The mist lingered long after the Loyalists disappeared. No one moved for several moments, their breaths still caught in the echoes of what hadn't happened—of what could've. Eventually, Elara lowered her staff.

"We keep going," she said. But her voice didn't carry confidence. Only necessity.

They pulled back to a narrow clearing tucked behind an outcropping of stone. Here, the wind softened, and the trees muffled the lingering tension. No one built a fire. They didn't need warmth—they needed distance, clarity.

Kaelen crouched beside a rough stretch of dirt, drawing a crude map between stones with a stick. "They'll report back," he said. "Probably already have. We'll lose any uncertainty they might have about our presence by tomorrow morning."

"They'll dig in," Riven added, arms folded. "Fortify positions, call for more. Both sides are here, and neither is willing to blink."

"We need a way in," Kaelen said. "Before they close the gates completely."

Dorian, who had been silent since the standoff, finally spoke. "We try diplomacy."

Elara looked at him sharply. "They just called me cursed."

"And they didn't attack," Dorian replied. "That's a thread. We pull it."

Sariel nodded. "Separate approaches. If we show up as a group, we're an army. Split, we might be something smaller. Something they'll listen to."

Tarian crossed his arms. "Assuming anyone's still interested in listening."

"We're not giving them the excuse to strike first," Lysandra said. Her voice was cold steel. "We've walked this far not to start swinging now."

They began to shape a plan.

Two teams. Two missions.

Kaelen tapped the Forgeborne side of the crude map. "I'll go to the Forgemasters. They'll know me by name, even if they don't want to. Riven, you're with me."

Riven smirked. "Good. I've been meaning to return a few favors."

"Lysandra," Kaelen added, "we could use someone who still knows how to talk like a soldier."

Lysandra didn't hesitate. "Done."

Wiz landed behind Kaelen with a soft mechanical thud, wings folding in like armored sails. His frame had changed—taller, broader, the once-smooth panels now layered with ridged plating that glinted dully in the mist. Small, retractable spines ran down his back like a defensive ridge. His optics adjusted in a slow pulse, more complex than before.

Elara glanced at him—then at Kaelen. "When did he become that?"

Kaelen didn't look away from the map. "Somewhere between Forgehelm and now."

Wiz chirped once, low and steady. Not a question. A confirmation.

Elara didn't say anything else and moved on.

Elara pointed to the opposite side of the valley, where the Verdant tents crept up the ridge. "I'll approach the Wardens. Liora, Arin, Sylva—you know their language. Their hesitation."

"I know their rituals too," Sylva said. "Enough to speak to the ones who still remember them."

Arin shifted her cloak. "And enough to know how they'll bend the truth if it suits their fear."

Liora gave a half-smile. "Let's see what they do with someone who can't be pinned down."

Dorian looked between the teams, then at the mountain behind them. "I'll stay with Tarian and Sariel. Between both paths. If anything turns, we'll know first."

Sariel nodded in agreement.

Tarian nodded once. "Two sides. One watch."

Elara stepped back, looking at each of them in turn. "We only get one shot. Speak as one. Even if we walk apart."

Kaelen's eyes narrowed. "Let's find out if anyone up here still wants peace—or if they just want witnesses."

The party moved without further argument, splitting into paths that would define what came next.

The summit was still waiting.

But now, so were its keepers.

The descent into the Forgeborne camp was more like entering a storm than an encampment. Heat shimmered in the air despite the mountain's chill, the hiss of steam and the rhythm of drills echoing through the canyon walls. Smoke and hammer strikes pulsed like breath from a massive, unseen machine.

Kaelen led the way, flanked by Riven and Lysandra. None of them spoke. The clang of metal on metal, the barked orders of overseers, and the roar of smelters gave the camp a weight that didn't welcome words.

Tents here weren't canvas—they were layered plating, iron-ribbed and reinforced with stone. Every Forgeborne soldier they passed wore full armor, their faces hidden behind masks of burnished steel. Some watched them. Others didn't bother. In this place, posture spoke louder than weapons.

They crossed into the perimeter—and immediately drew attention.

A patrol stepped forward. Four soldiers, steam-vented pauldrons and plasma axes slung across their backs. The lead guard raised a hand.

"You're outside the declared boundary. State your designation."

Riven took a step forward to respond, but her voice never landed.

"Riven Locke?" the guard said, tone shifting. "You're listed under internal suspension protocol."

Two soldiers moved toward her, hands not yet raised to weapons—but not far from it either.

Kaelen stepped in, hand up. "She's here under my authority. We're not prisoners—we're diplomats."

"Doesn't change the protocol," one of the guards muttered. "We have orders."

Before tensions could spike, Lysandra stepped between them. Her stance was firm, even as every eye in the patrol clocked her as Verdant. "I'm Lysandra Merrow, former Thornblade of the Verdant army," she said, tone crisp. "We're here under peaceful intent. You want to verify something? Start with that."

That made them stop. The name. The tone. The certainty.

The lead guard tapped a sigil on his vambrace. A low ping sounded. Moments passed. Then he stepped back.

"Confirmed. You're cleared for temporary entry. Weapons will be surrendered. And you'll be watched."

"We came to be seen," Kaelen said. He unlatched his gauntlet and handed it over. "Take it. Doesn't work right without me anyway."

Riven unstrapped her rifle with a roll of her eyes but didn't argue. Lysandra reached over her shoulder and unstrapped the twin-blade from her back, offering it handle-first without hesitation.

They were escorted through a corridor of hammer forges and supply carts, past younger soldiers running drills and older smiths hunched over flame-fed benches. Everyone moved with purpose. No one looked uncertain.

At the far end of the compound stood a reinforced command structure—no banners, just heavy plating and embossed gears framing a sealed door.

A voice crackled from a speaker embedded in the archway: "State your business."

Kaelen stepped forward.

"I'm here to speak with the Forgemasters."

A pause. Then the door clicked.

"Enter."

The metal hissed open.

They stepped through, not as soldiers. Not as enemies.

But as the only ones left who still believed there was something worth saying.

The chamber was sweltering. Not with heat from the forges outside, but with the weight of judgment. The walls were lined with old schematics, fractured relics, and dozens of warforged sigils pinned like medals to thick stone columns. At the far end of the room, the Forgemasters waited—six of them seated behind a long table of blackened steel.

Their armor was ceremonial: riveted plate engraved with oaths, crimson inlays running like veins across the shoulders and chest. Each one bore the rank of centuries.

Kaelen stood at the center of the room, flanked by Riven and Lysandra. Their weapons had been surrendered, their posture deliberate. No one bowed.

"We're not here for alliances," Kaelen began. "We're here to stop a war before it consumes both factions. There's still a path—if we take it now."

One of the Forgemasters leaned forward slightly. "A path of surrender?"

"No," Kaelen said. "A path of reason."

Another scoffed. "You walk with Verdant ghosts and cursed steel, and speak to us of reason?"

Kaelen's voice sharpened. "I speak as a Forgeborne. And as someone who still remembers what the Equinox is supposed to mean."

A pause. Then laughter—not mocking, but cruel in its certainty—rippled through the line of Forgemasters.

"The Equinox," the oldest among them said, "has always served us. It is a furnace. It burns the weakness from the world."

Riven took a half-step forward. "So you'll burn the rest of the continent too?"

A younger Forgemaster replied, "Better to cauterize rot than to let it spread."

Lysandra stepped forward, voice like tempered steel. "You speak of Verdant rot like it's a disease. What you'll create is a graveyard."

"We'll create a future," the eldest said. "Clean. Unified. Undivided."

Kaelen met his gaze. "There's no unity in ashes and ruins."

Another pause. He could feel Riven tense beside him, but she said nothing more.

The Forgemasters didn't rise. They didn't draw weapons. They simply looked down at them like artisans surveying flawed ore.

"Then you've delivered your words," one said. "And we have heard them."

That was the closest thing to dismissal they would get.

The escort returned. No one spoke on the way out.

Only as they reached the compound's outer corridor did someone finally break the silence. A soldier—young, half-armored, face streaked with ash—passed close to Riven.

He didn't stop.

But he spoke just loud enough for her to hear:

"You should've stayed dead."

Riven didn't turn.

Kaelen saw her knuckles go white.

And the door shut behind them.

The shift from stone to soil was subtle but certain. One moment they were on a worn mountain path, the next beneath a green canopy laced with illusions so soft they felt like memory. Light filtered through branches that shouldn't have existed this high on the slope—Verdant magic expanding nature's grasp.

Elara led the group in silence. Beside her, Liora moved with deliberate care, eyes scanning not for danger, but for the unseen rhythms of the forest. She paused to note symbols woven into moss, old totems half-submerged in root. Behind them, Arin adjusted the strap on her satchel while Sylva traced the outline of a bark-carved ward with two fingers. They weren't lost. They were being guided.

The path wound slowly, looping through arches of bark and woven vine. They passed no guards. No watch posts. But they were not unseen.

Figures moved just beyond the edges of vision—Grovecallers and Sylvanars, half-hidden by illusion and enchantment. Their presence wasn't menacing. It was ceremonial. A procession of ghosts watching the living trespass.

Elara stopped at a tree where the canopy opened like a natural gate, a crescent of leaves shifting in rhythm with her breath. "This place remembers," she whispered.

"They've prepared for us," Liora said. "But they won't speak first."

"Then we speak," Arin replied. "Before silence becomes rejection."

A moment later, the trees parted. Not violently—gracefully, as if the forest had simply decided to reveal its heart.

A pavilion stood in the clearing. Grown, not built. Its frame twisted from living branches, its roof a dense thatch of golden leaves. At its center sat a woman cloaked in ivy green and deeproot black. Her presence radiated calm, but not passivity. This was not a priestess who spoke sermons. This was one who had survived them.

Elara stepped forward and bowed—not deeply, but with respect. "High Priestess of Aeldrin," she said. "I am Elara Thorne. I come to speak not of right or ritual, but of survival."

The High Priestess inclined her head, her gaze sharp. "You've crossed sacred ground. You walk beside oathbreakers. You carry a relic no longer sanctioned by Verdant rites. And yet… the trees did not stop you."

"I didn't come to ask for forgiveness," Elara said. "I came because a war waits at the summit of this mountain. And it will not ask for permission before it starts."

Arin stepped beside her. "We seek pause. Not surrender."

Liora folded her arms. "A moment of reason. Or at least one more day."

The priestess said nothing at first. Then: "A day may change nothing."

Elara met her eyes. "Or it may change everything."

The forest thickened around them—not with growth, but with presence. Every root underfoot felt deliberate, every leaf turned in their direction. It was not a place of welcome, nor one of wrath. It was simply waiting.

The High Priestess remained seated in the center of the living pavilion. Her hands rested atop a staff made of elderwood, its thorns shaped into a spiral around the shaft. When she spoke again, her voice carried the weight of centuries, unshaken by Elara's plea.

"The Equinox is no longer what it once was. Whatever purity it held has been blackened. Poisoned by proximity."

She chose her words carefully. "The relic is unchanged."

"No," the priestess said. "It has changed. It hums now with doubt. Its light stammers. It bends toward fire."

"You see only what you expect," Elara said. "The prophecy was never meant to be comfortable."

"Nor was it meant to be rewritten by traitors."

Arin stepped forward. Her voice trembled slightly, but she held her ground. "Please. The path we walk—it's not about conquest. It's about avoiding the slaughter we both know is coming."

"There is always slaughter," the priestess replied. "Some carry it in their hands. Others in their silence."

Sylva moved next, brushing past Elara and Arin to stand squarely in front of the priestess. Her eyes narrowed.

"You're not here to listen," she said. "You brought us here to see how we'd beg. I've read your circles, your casting trees. You let us in because you want the story of our failure to be righteous."

A murmur ran through the grove. Not a voice, but the press of unseen attention.

The High Priestess didn't deny it. "You brought an echo of imbalance into our heartwood. This audience is merciful."

Then a new voice came from beyond the trees. Liora turned, tension immediately curling in her stance.

A Warden stepped forward—older, marked with years of moss and scar. His voice was grave. "Blades have already left for the high paths. Should your companions fail their attempt, or should you lie—there will be no message. No survivors."

Elara's heart sank. "You planned this. You've already decided."

The priestess finally stood. She was not tall, but her presence stretched.

"We did not summon judgment," she said. "You brought it with you. The climb will finish it."

And with that, the grove began to close again. The air thickened with stillness.

The conversation had ended.

And the mountain waited.

Liora lingered near the grove's edge, her face unreadable in the shifting green light. She hadn't spoken once since they entered. Now, as the roots sealed behind them and the threat fully settled into shape, she exhaled slowly.

"I told them I'd come back," she whispered—to no one in particular. "Told them we'd navigate the sea. Just the sky, water and endless stories."

Her voice barely carried. But Arin turned her head slightly at the sound.

"So we'd better survive," she added. "Because I don't break promises."

Sariel returned from his perimeter sweep slower than usual.

"You alright?" Tarian asked.

Sariel didn't answer at first. Just held up a leaf folded into a triangle, a blooded vine pierced through the center.

"What is that?" Dorian asked.

"A Verdant mark," Sariel said. "I found one of their scouts. They let me walk."

"Why?"

Sariel's voice went quieter. "Said my sins weren't mine to atone for. Said the mountain would decide."

The rest of the team returned without triumph. No banners, no terms. Just weary steps and silent glances shared as both squads regrouped at the edge of the mountain's spine.

Kaelen arrived first, gauntlet re-secured. Riven trailed behind him, saying nothing. Lysandra's twinblade remained strapped, untouched, but her stance was coiled. She didn't report failure aloud. She didn't need to.

Moments later, Elara's group emerged through the mist, stepping back into the forest edge like survivors of something half-named. Liora walked at Elara's side, her wind-mussed hair braided again with slow, deliberate hands. Sylva moved behind them, her arms crossed, face sharp with contained fury. Arin's eyes scanned the sky as if still searching for something that might change the outcome.

Dorian was already waiting, Tarian and Sariel at his side.

The two groups reconvened in the clearing below the ridgeline, faces drawn, movements slower than before.

No one spoke at first.

Kaelen dropped his pack with a loud thud. "They won't negotiate."

Elara shook her head. "The Wardens called us corrupted. Said the climb will judge us."

Sylva sat heavily on a flat stone. "So that's it. Two armies. One mountain. One fire."

And then the relic stirred.

Not violently. Not bright.

Just a low resonance from Kaelen's pack—like a held breath becoming audible.

Elara's satchel followed, not a pulse, but a slow warm press—like gravity shifting ever so slightly.

No words.

No message.

But they felt it all the same.

The relics weren't silent.

They were waiting.

For something none of them could name.

"They've made camp mobilizations," Dorian said. "Troop formations shifting, command tents reinforcing their lines. It looks like they're preparing for movement—soon."

Tarian added, "There are prayer rites being held. Funeral robes distributed. Even without confirmation, they're acting like the battle's already decided."

No one spoke immediately. Elara stepped forward slightly. Her voice was quiet, not dulled but distilled.

"Then we climb while they burn."

Riven turned her head, spitting into the dirt. "So that's it, then. One more massacre. Two flags and no memory."

"We were never here to stop them," Kaelen said. "Only to outlast the fire."

Arin shook her head. "We tried. That has to count for something."

Liora's voice came out hoarse. "It will. When it's written down—if it's written down."

Sylva crouched beside the fire, brushing away dirt with the side of her boot. "Then we don't wait to see what the smoke covers. We move before the mountain becomes another name in a war chant."

Dorian's gaze moved toward the ridgeline. "We leave now. Before the first horn sounds."

They began adjusting straps, tightening boots, checking the weight of what they carried—not just gear, but choice.

Elara pulled her cloak tighter. "It doesn't end because we failed to change it. It ends because we walk into what no one else can."

Then Kaelen paused. His head tilted sharply.

A sound.

Faint. Deliberate. A shift in the fog not shaped by wind.

He held up a hand.

The others froze. No one breathed. Every instinct sharpened.

The sound came again—soft metal on stone. Multiple sets of feet. From behind. Above. The fog was moving—not rolling, but driven.

Then Elara's hand twitched. A pulse.

The relic beneath her cloak gave off a faint light—muted, but undeniable.

Across the circle, Kaelen's relic pulsed once beneath his coat, its glow faint but sharp—an echo to Elara's light, as if drawn by the same unseen threat.

Riven unslung her rifle.

"Company," Kaelen said.

And the air began to hum.

The hum grew into vibration.

Wiz chirped once—sharp, fast—and launched into the air just as the first spear tore through the fog.

Too late.

The impact sent Elara stumbling sideways. Sariel turned toward the motion, but a second projectile caught him in the shoulder. He crumpled with a hiss, dropping to one knee as blood soaked the edge of his cloak.

"Formation!" Dorian shouted.

The mountain erupted.

From the ridgeline above and the trees behind, armored figures dropped like thunder. Enforcers—Aldric's, by the way they moved. Precise, brutal, efficient. Their armor glinted silver and black in the half-light, modified for high-altitude warfare, vents steaming as they moved.

Kaelen's gauntlet snapped into full activation. His relic pulsed brighter now, the edges of the relic glowing with searing blue heat. Elara's staff began to vibrate with power, the relic in her satchel pulsing in rhythm with Kaelen's.

Riven took cover behind a broken boulder and fired. One shot, then another—clean, deliberate. She didn't waste breath on a curse.

Tarian stepped forward to shield Sariel, raising his blade to deflect a blow that came down with hammer-like force. The mountain path was too narrow. They were too exposed.

"Push west!" Kaelen shouted. "We hold the higher angle!"

Lysandra spun her twinblade in a tight arc, clearing the path for Elara to drag Sariel back from the worst of it.

A moment of stillness broke the rhythm of chaos.

A tall figure emerged from the smoke.

Armored head to toe, helm blackened but regal. A sunburst insignia half-buried beneath fresh dents. One arm still wrapped in reinforced gauntlets, the other gloved in steel-threaded leather.

Aldric.

Alive.

Focused.

His gaze swept over the field. Then he pointed his weapon—a heavy-bladed polearm—toward Kaelen.

"Target acquired," he said.

And the enforcers surged again.

Elara raised her staff, calling to Liora. "Wind! Scatter their front!"

Liora responded without words, thrusting her hands forward. A current swept down the slope, lifting fog and dust in a wall.

Sylva and Arin flanked Riven, moving in tandem to push the assault line into the trees.

Kaelen stood his ground.

Dorian joined him.

Behind them, the fog turned red.

And the battle began in full.

The slope fractured into chaos.

Steel clashed with stone, fog and fire churned into the air, and the lines between survival and strategy blurred. Enforcers poured down the incline in formation, but the group fought as one—every move calculated, every motion fueled by the knowledge that this wasn't a battle to win, only to survive.

Elara's voice cut through the noise. "We go! Kaelen, Dorian—now!"

Kaelen glanced toward her, his eyes narrowing just for a moment before locking with Dorian's. A shared nod passed between them—no hesitation.

"I'll clear the ridge," Kaelen called.

"I'll hold the break," Dorian replied.

They moved.

Behind them, the rest of the group reacted instantly. Tarian braced himself between two jagged boulders, his blade sweeping low to intercept incoming enforcers. Riven took the right flank, her rifle tight against her shoulder, moving like a specter between stone and shadow.

"Two lines!" Riven shouted. "Anchor and bleed them out!"

"Copy that!" Tarian called back.

Arin crouched low behind Sariel, whose face was pale from blood loss but whose eyes were still sharp. She pressed her hands to his wound, channeling magic in pulsing waves. "Don't move. Don't talk. Just breathe."

"I can still fight," Sariel muttered.

"Not like this," Sylva snapped. She had a short blade in one hand, the other outstretched, flinging pebbles laced with runes to mark terrain behind them.

Lysandra swept in from the rear, her twinblade spinning wide in tight arcs. She caught two incoming enforcers mid-strike and pivoted to cover the left gap Elara had left behind.

The mountain shook beneath the weight of the conflict. Magic cracked the air. Fog twisted under wind pressure. Blood darkened the rock.

Kaelen and Dorian pushed toward the upper pass, feet crunching over uneven stone as more enforcers tried to close around them. Elara followed close, staff raised, her relic burning now like a second heartbeat against her ribs.

Then Aldric came again.

He moved through the smoke with surgical clarity—ignoring defenders, fixated on Kaelen and Dorian. Each step was relentless, his polearm sweeping with terrifying reach.

"He's targeting them," Elara said, spinning to deflect an incoming strike from a lesser enforcer.

"Because he knows what matters," Sylva called out.

Riven fired again, but Aldric deflected the round with a gauntlet. "Go!" she barked at Kaelen. "We'll buy your time with our bones if we have to!"

Kaelen didn't answer. He grabbed Elara's arm and pulled her forward as Dorian turned and parried a blow that would've split the rock behind them.

"We climb," Kaelen said, eyes blazing. "Whatever happens here, we don't stop."

The wind howled.

And prophecy ignited in the clash of steel and breath.

Aldric's path cut clean through the chaos.

He advanced with purpose, polearm slicing air and flesh in wide, brutal arcs. His armor steamed where enchantments burned off impact. Enforcers parted for him without a word—this wasn't his unit's fight anymore. It was his.

Dorian stepped into his path.

He raised his hammer and held the line.

Aldric paused only long enough to acknowledge the choice. "Still hiding behind broken principles?"

Dorian's grip tightened. "Still building legacies out of graves?"

Then they moved.

The clash sent a shockwave through the slope. Hammer met blade, steel singing against steel, sparks flaring with each impact.

Dorian fought without flourish—every swing a lesson in control, weight, and intent. Aldric was faster, more precise, but Dorian was a wall.

They circled each other once, twice. Kaelen, from above, looked back—but Elara caught his arm.

"He has to do this," she said.

Aldric feinted low and drove upward. Dorian blocked, spun, countered with a shoulder check that rocked the old captain off balance. He brought the hammer down—

—and Aldric caught it on the shaft of his polearm. Sparks sprayed like shattered stars. He twisted. The blade edge found Dorian's side.

A hiss of pain. Blood.

Dorian stumbled, arm still locked around his weapon, teeth clenched. He swung again, catching Aldric in the chest and sending him reeling.

Lysandra saw the blood and broke from the defense line. She ran low, cutting past two enforcers before reaching Dorian's side.

"Move!" she shouted.

Kaelen dropped from a ledge and landed beside them, catching Dorian under one arm. "You don't get to die here."

"I wasn't planning to," Dorian grunted.

Then came the explosion.

A blast from the cliff above—a concussive rune charge meant to clear escape routes—detonated. Rock and mist swallowed the slope.

Kaelen shielded Dorian as the shock hit. Lysandra covered them both, back to the wall.

When the dust settled, the line was broken.

Aldric was gone.

Kaelen scanned the rubble. No movement. No body.

Only smoke.

Then—

A new sound. Mechanical, shrill, pulsing like a predator's breath.

Wiz swooped overhead with a low, electric hum—wings flaring wide, twice the size of a dog now. His sensors flashed bright and sharp through the fog.

From the upper ledge, a shadow dropped—a jagged figure in modified Forgeborne armor, leaner and wired with unstable energy cores.

"Clyne," Kaelen whispered.

Clyne stood armored in polished, newly-forged plating and arcane foci, smoke coiling from the tubes at his back. The air buzzed with barely-contained instability, like the man himself was a charged weapon waiting to detonate. He hadn't forgotten their last encounter—his retreat after Floralis, his ruined ambush, the shattered automatons. Now he returned not just to kill, but to prove the failure had never been his. His gaze swept over Kaelen and settled on Wiz, visibly surprised. "Well," he muttered, "you've upgraded. And here I thought I'd already broken your pet."

"Word was you were still climbing," Clyne said. "Fitting that I'm the one waiting at the top—with better gear this time."

Kaelen stepped forward, gauntlet rising.

Wiz screeched and fired a bolt of plasma. Clyne deflected it with a laugh, swinging a wicked glaive charged with unstable kinetic magic.

The slope shuddered again.

"Looks like we finish this," Kaelen said.

Wiz chirped in agreement.

And they charged.

Kaelen didn't charge immediately. He watched Clyne's footing, the twitch of his gauntlet fingers, the simmering crackle of unstable magic pulsing around his weapon. The man hadn't just come to kill—he came to prove he'd evolved beyond failure.

"Why the rune?" Kaelen asked, gesturing toward the shattered cliffside where Aldric had vanished. "You almost killed your own captain."

Clyne shrugged, tapping a control node on his bracer. "Collateral damage."

That was all he said.

A click echoed through the air.

From the upper ledge, something leapt—a humanoid automaton, sleek and plated in reflective bronze, its limbs moving with unnatural speed. Wiz dove forward in response, intercepting it midair.

Clyne smiled. "My finest creation. I've been waiting to test it in the field."

The two constructs collided in a crackle of plasma and metal. Wiz spun with clawed limbs outstretched, grappling with the automaton. The machines roared and sparked as they struck rock, their fight becoming a blur of wings and limbs.

Kaelen didn't wait. He lunged at Clyne, gauntlet sparking as he swung. Clyne caught the blow with a flash of his kinetic shield, the force rippling in a spherical shimmer around his armor.

"Nice try," Clyne said, swinging his glaive low. Kaelen ducked, using the momentum to uppercut into the field. The hit landed. Not fully, but enough to stagger.

Across the battlefield, Elara knelt beside Dorian, her hands glowing green as healing magic flowed through the wound along his ribs.

"Stay with me," she whispered. "You don't get to check out now."

Dorian winced, trying to sit up. "We can't stay still."

A shape emerged through the smoke—Aldric, bruised but alive, armor scorched. He saw the two of them together and raised his weapon, fury in every step.

Dorian surged to his feet. The two clashed again, and this time Dorian was faster. He ducked a sweeping strike and rammed his shoulder into Aldric's chest. The force sent Aldric stumbling.

They reached the cliff edge.

Dorian pressed forward, hammer raised.

Aldric grabbed the edge to keep from falling. Their eyes locked.

Dorian hesitated.

Aldric didn't. "Not by your hand."

He let go.

Aldric vanished into the mist below.

But somewhere, beneath it all, a rune flickered blue.

Back on the slope, the others held the line. Liora hurled spears of wind and fire. Sylva loosed arrow after arrow into the charging enforcers. Riven picked targets with surgical efficiency, dropping two attackers with clean headshots. Lysandra fought beside Tarian, their blades flashing in tight arcs as they held a defensive wedge.

Arin crouched behind a rock, healing Sariel, who now stood again—wounded, but steady.

Wiz bit down on the automaton's arm, tearing it free. The machine staggered, sparks erupting from its severed joint. Wiz twirled midair, using his tail to slam the automaton into the rock wall.

Kaelen dodged another kinetic pulse, rolled under Clyne's sweeping blade, and activated the gauntlet's core with a final twist.

He struck forward.

The punch landed square in the chest.

Clyne's shield flickered. Then collapsed.

The mechcrafter stumbled, eyes wide, breath caught. Sparks sprayed from his armor as circuits overloaded. He fell backward, crumpling into the dirt. His armor sparked once more.

And then went still.

Across the ridge, Lysandra, Arin, and Sariel joined Wiz, who had been caught in a grappling hold. Sariel struck with a focused slash of his sword, Arin summoned a tangle of thick, thorny vines that burst from the rocky ground, wrapping around the automaton's legs and arms, halting its swing long enough for Wiz to recover, and Lysandra cleaved the automaton's knee.

Wiz launched upward, wings catching wind, and with a roar, fired a concentrated beam of plasma.

The automaton melted.

The group breathed, exhausted but alive.

The fog returned with a vengeance, thick and smothering, curling around boots and blades like smoke from a dying fire. The final ridge loomed behind them—jagged, narrow, and steep. Elara, Kaelen, and Dorian were already ascending. But for the others, the battle wasn't done.

Liora stood at the front line, breathing hard, her hair matted to her face with sweat and blood. Her legs shook from exhaustion, but her arms rose again, wind magic swirling in thick gusts that shoved back the front line of enforcers. She gritted her teeth and pressed her palms forward, directing a blast that knocked two attackers into a crumbling ledge.

Beside her, Sariel fought like a dying man who didn't plan on dying yet. He pivoted sharply, slashing his sword into the chest of an approaching enforcer. The impact dropped the soldier flat. Blood seeped through the wrapping at Sariel's side, but he stood tall.

Tarian held the center with brutal clarity. His shield was dented, his sword chipped, but every movement had weight. Precision. Finality. He planted his feet and swung in tight arcs, carving space for the others to breathe.

Sylva moved through the chaos like a wraith. Her bow sang in measured rhythm, each arrow loosed with care. One struck a knee, the next a throat, the third catching a helmet seam with terrifying precision. "Keep moving," she muttered, drawing again.

Riven was last to reposition. She stayed near the trio's path, rifle at her hip. Blood ran into her eyes. Her next shot went wide. She didn't curse—but her silence cracked.

Dorian turned, eyes wide.

Riven moved.

She didn't have time to aim. She just stepped between the blade and its target and fired blind.

The shot missed.

But the shock startled the attacker.

Riven didn't flinch. She rammed the butt of her rifle into the enforcer's face and kicked him backward off the slope.

"Go!" she shouted at Kaelen and Dorian, her voice raw.

The three looked back just once—just long enough to see the line holding.

Tarian shouted orders, rallying Sariel and Liora to shift positions. Arin ran to Sylva's side, checking her for wounds, eyes already glowing with healing magic.

The ridge trembled with the force of so many fighting to stall time itself.

And above them, three figures climbed toward Nocturne's Edge.

The prophecy still burned behind them.

But it hadn't caught them yet.

They didn't look back.

Kaelen, Elara, and Dorian climbed in silence, each step pulling them farther from the ridge, farther from the ones holding the line below. The air was sharp here—thin and cold, biting at exposed skin, clawing at breath. But none of them slowed.

The slope narrowed quickly, rising into knife-edge trails flanked by jagged stone and steep drops. The mountain had no comfort to offer, no signs, no mercy. Only direction.

The relics pulsed again.

Elara felt it in her chest—rhythmic, steady, like a second heartbeat. Her fingers closed around the relic beneath her cloak, and it warmed in her palm. It no longer warned. It called.

Kaelen's relic responded with its own hum, the light beneath his coat flickering in time with Elara's. "They're not trying to stop us anymore," he said, his voice ragged from breath. "They're pulling us forward."

Dorian grunted as he boosted himself over a jagged outcrop. "Then let them. Just means we're close."

The climb steepened. Their boots scraped against gravel, hands gripping cold stone as they ascended through clouds that clung to the mountain like breath. Mist swirled and shifted, sometimes clearing, sometimes thick enough to blind them to each other.

Below, the sounds of battle faded. Steel on steel, shouts, the crack of spells—all of it dulled into something more distant than memory.

Elara looked back only once.

The fog had swallowed the world.

She said nothing.

They pressed onward.

Every breath now was labor. Every heartbeat matched the relics. The climb was not just physical—it pressed on the mind, the soul, demanding not just strength but resolve.

Kaelen stumbled once. Dorian caught him without a word.

Elara reached the next ridge first, hauling herself up with a groan. She turned and helped Kaelen up. Then Dorian.

They stood together for a moment, wind whipping their cloaks.

Ahead, the mountain continued.

Above them, the summit loomed—just beyond sight, just beyond understanding.

They didn't run from the war.

They ran toward the truth waiting above it.

Far below, half-buried in mist and rubble, a gauntleted hand gripped stone—bloodied, shaking, but alive.

Chapter 18: The Fractured Equinox

They didn't look back.

Kaelen, Elara, and Dorian climbed in silence, each step pulling them farther from the ridge, farther from the ones holding the line below. The air was sharp here—thin and cold, biting at exposed skin, clawing at breath. But none of them slowed. There was no room left for fear. Only forward.

The slope narrowed quickly, rising into knife-edge trails flanked by jagged stone and sheer drops. Footing grew treacherous, their steps echoing across silence that seemed to thrum with expectation. The mountain had no comfort to offer, no signs, no mercy. Only direction.

The relics pulsed again.

Elara felt it in her chest—rhythmic, steady, like a second heartbeat. Her fingers closed around the relic beneath her cloak, and it warmed in her palm. It no longer warned. It called.

Kaelen's relic responded with its own hum, the light beneath his coat flickering in time with Elara's. "They're not trying to stop us anymore," he said, his voice ragged from breath. "They're pulling us forward."

Dorian grunted as he boosted himself over a jagged outcrop. "Then let them. Just means we're close."

Their pace slowed, not from caution but exhaustion. Muscles strained. Fingers cracked against cold stone. Mist swirled and shifted, sometimes clearing, sometimes thick enough to blind them to each other. The sound of each footfall grew louder in the silence—echoing off the cliffs like a ticking clock.

Below, the sounds of battle faded. Steel on steel, shouts, the crack of spells—all of it dulled into something more distant than memory. What had once been a roar was now a ghost.

Elara looked back only once.

Through the veil of fog, she couldn't see the others—just the shape of where they had been. Of where they still fought. Her chest tightened. It felt wrong to climb while they bled, to chase light while her friends held darkness at bay. But the relic in her hand pulsed, firm and unyielding. She whispered, barely audible, "I'm sorry." Then turned away.

The fog had swallowed the world. There was no more line of defense. Only the thread they followed upward.

She said nothing else.

They pressed onward.

Every breath now was labored. Every heartbeat matched the relics. The climb was not just physical—it pressed on the mind, the soul, demanding not just strength but resolve. Each meter gained was carved from their will.

Kaelen stumbled once, his leg giving under him. Dorian caught him without a word, gripping his forearm tightly, hauling him up. No thanks were needed.

Elara reached the next ridge first, hauling herself up with a groan. Her arms trembled, legs shaking beneath her. She turned and helped Kaelen up. Then Dorian.

They stood together for a moment, wind whipping their cloaks, sweat cold on their skin.

Above them, the summit loomed—closer now, jagged like a broken crown against the white mist. Just beyond reach. Just beyond understanding.

Their relics pulsed again.

But this time, the hum carried weight. A pressure. A promise.

They didn't run from the war.

They ran toward the truth waiting above it.

The summit inevitably revealed itself. A flat stretch of stone framed by crumbling pillars and windswept silence. The altar stood at its center, weathered by time and elemental fury. Its surface was split clean down the middle—an ancient fracture that mirrored the world below. The air feels heavier here, like the mountain itself does not want what is happening below.

The trio approached slowly, their steps dragging, their eyes fixed on the altar as though the weight of centuries pressed into the space between each stride. None of them spoke. They didn't have to. The silence between them wasn't hollow—it was reverent. Tense. Expectant.

Elara pulled the Verdant half of the relic from beneath her cloak. The relic shimmered faintly in the light, but the warmth she had once felt was gone. Kaelen mirrored the motion, drawing the Forgeborne half from the inner lining of his coat. His hand lingered on the relic for a moment longer.

He looked at Dorian.

Then, with a deep sigh, he stepped forward and extended it.

"It's about time you held your half of the Celestine Convergence," Kaelen said. "You're the one they all saw in the vision. The Chosen one. If it triggers another storm, fine. Doesn't matter now. This is it. One shot."

Dorian didn't move immediately. His brow furrowed as he accepted the relic, as if it weighed far more than it should.

Kaelen's voice dropped lower. "I've carried this since Obsidian Reach. Thought that was my part to play—hold it until you could finish the prophecy."

There was something unspoken in his words. A flicker of bitterness. Not sharp or loud, but settled into the edges of his tone. Weariness, too. The kind that didn't go away with rest.

"I thought I was just the courier," he added. "Turns out even that role nearly killed me."

Dorian looked at him, something unspoken in his gaze. An apology? A recognition? He nodded once, solemnly, and gripped the relic with both hands.

Together, Elara and Dorian approached the altar, stepping toward opposite ends of the broken stone. The wind tugged at their cloaks, dragging their silhouettes apart as if the altar resisted their unity.

They placed the relics gently onto the fractured altar—one glowing with green light, the other pulsing with residual heat. For a moment, the relics seemed to shimmer.

And then—

Nothing.

Elara reached to her belt and drew a small blade, not hesitating as she dragged it across her palm. Blood welled and dripped onto the surface of the Verdant relic.

Dorian followed suit, pressing his bleeding hand to the Forgeborne half.

Still—nothing.

The relics remained inert. Unmoving. Cold.

The pulse that had guided them, sustained them, drawn them together—it was gone. No hum. No light. No transformation.

Elara's breath hitched. She stared at the altar in disbelief, then looked to Dorian, then to Kaelen. Her fists clenched at her sides.

"This is what we bled for?" she whispered, voice shaking. "This is what we sacrificed for?"

She snatched the Verdant relic off the altar and hurled it across the summit.

Kaelen moved before it could vanish down the slope.

He caught it, cradled it in both hands like something still sacred, and stared at the dim, unresponsive stone. Then he looked up, eyes shadowed.

"Maybe it's broken," he said. His voice was low. Hollow. "Or maybe it never worked."

The wind moved through the summit in response.

But it didn't answer.

And the altar offered nothing.

Kaelen stood motionless for a long moment, both halves of the Celestine Convergence held in his hands. Elara and Dorian didn't speak. The wind swirled around them, carrying the taste of stone and storm, lifting the edges of Kaelen's coat like the mountain was trying to turn a page.

The sky above churned with slow-moving clouds—too low, too still. The silence that followed wasn't just quiet—it was expectant. Like the world had taken in its breath and was waiting to see what he would do with it. The summit, jagged and ancient beneath his feet, felt less like a place and more like a threshold—an edge between what was broken and what could be mended.

Kaelen looked down at the relics—one alive with Verdant glyphs, the other lined Forgeborne scripts. They weren't just artifacts. They were declarations. Symbols of power that had torn the world into halves. And he held them like a question no one else had dared to ask. They felt heavier now, not in weight, but in consequence—as if every life lost to the schism pressed down through the metal.

His fingers tensed around them. Not with certainty, but with resistance. Doubt coiled beneath his ribs, a voice whispering: *What if the fracture was never meant to heal?* What if the split was necessary? Safer? Forgeborne and Verdant weren't opposites by accident. They were designed to pull apart. Like two poles of a magnet—purposefully repelling to preserve balance. Was he defying something sacred? Or fulfilling it?

A flash of memory hit him. Forgehelm. The smell of steel. The weight of exile. His uncle Orlan, the last Chosen, standing defiantly before the trial. And then—nothing. Just silence and the echo of what could've been.

Another: In a memory not yet real, a voice that hadn't spoken yet: "You've surpassed me," Kaelen says, placing a hand on the shoulder of someone younger, braver, just as uncertain as he once was. "...it's time for me to go." The words weren't prophecy. But they felt inevitable. Like they were already waiting somewhere down the line, ready to be spoken.

He had walked the center line his entire life.

Was this why?

The relics pulsed—faint, uneven, like breath caught in a dying lung.

He stepped forward.

The air thickened. It pressed around him like unseen hands. The wind no longer moved around him—it responded to him. It swirled inward, as if the mountain itself exhaled for the first time in centuries.

The moment his foot touched the altar's edge, the relics changed.

Not a pulse.

A pull.

Magnetic. Inevitable. The halves didn't wait for permission. They lunged. Snapped together with a force that wasn't violent, but final. Like a wound closing. Like the world saying *enough*.

Light burst between his hands.

A blinding arc carved through the summit—colorless and every color at once. It didn't just shine. It *remembered*. The summit

trembled beneath him—not in fear, but in recognition. As if
something deep within the stone recalled its purpose.

The remembering was loud.

Kaelen staggered, wind shearing past his face. The cyclone at the
summit rose around him, not brutal but reverent. He dropped to
one knee, holding the fused relic against his chest. It wasn't a
weapon. It was a heartbeat. A rhythm that didn't match his own,
but something deeper—older.

The altar stirred.

Cracks split across its surface, glowing with fire and memory.
The mountain didn't shatter. It woke. Veins of light raced down
into the stone, spreading outward like roots seeking connection.
Faint echoes pulsed beneath his knees—each one a heartbeat,
answering his.

Elara stepped back, hand unconsciously reaching for the relic
that was no longer hers. Yet the relic's hum still touched her. It
pulsed through the air, the stone, the marrow of her bones. She
felt it in her scars, in every wound the war had left behind.
Dorian didn't flinch, but something in his stance shifted—as if
gravity had changed. As if the world was no longer beneath
them, but around them.

The light didn't blind.

It revealed.

Symbols long buried emerged beneath Kaelen's feet—Verdant
glyphs and Forgeborne scripts spiraling together, not clashing,
but joining. Unity written in two languages. The floor of the
summit lit up in lines, patterns, circuits of intent. The glow

extended to the outer edge, ringing the entire plateau in incandescent sigils.

The fracture remembered the bridge.

And Kaelen stood at its center.

Not as a courier.

Not as a bystander.

But as something the world hadn't known it needed until now.

Above him, the clouds twisted. Not breaking—opening. A shaft of light pierced the haze, striking the altar. The relic flared in response, casting its glow down the mountain in slow pulses—like a beacon. Or a signal.

And for the first time, he understood:

He wasn't meant to carry the relics.

He was meant to join them.

A line from the song drifted unbidden to the surface of his mind:

"For change to come, a life must part... to mend the world, to heal the heart."

He wasn't sure if it was prophecy, memory, or something deeper.

But he felt its truth like heat rising through stone.

The relic pulsed again.

And the mountain listened.

Kaelen stood in the halo of the altar's light, his breath shallow, the unified relic heavy in his hands. Around him, the summit held its breath. The wind had quieted—not gone, but subdued, like it was holding back in reverence or anticipation. Even the fog seems thinner here, unwilling to cross the lines carved into the stone.

And then, softly, a sound.

A melody.

Faint at first, like a memory surfacing from the depths of some shared ancestral dream. The notes were delicate, as if whispered through time—familiar in the way old lullabies were, or half-remembered verses spoken to a child in the dark. It wasn't from the relic. It wasn't even from the mountain. It was older than both.

Kaelen froze, his fingers tightening around the relic.

Then, without realizing, Elara began to hum it. Her voice was soft, hesitant, but perfectly matched to the rising tune.

The melody wrapped around them, drifting through the summit like smoke through branches, neither wholly seen nor ignored. It stirred something deep—something before memory.

Dorian blinked as though waking from a trance. "That song…" he whispered. "I've heard it before. My mother used to hum it when I couldn't sleep. She said it was older than the war. Older than the bloodlines."

Kaelen turned to them, eyes wide with understanding.

"It's the Forgotten Song," he said aloud. "I thought it was just a myth. A footnote in the scrolls."

He stepped back from the altar, the light casting his shadow in two directions. His eyes dropped to the swirling symbols etched around his boots—Verdant glyphs and Forgeborne scripts, once conflicting, now pulsing together in rhythm.

He looked between Elara and Dorian. "It was never about the relics," he said slowly, as if the words were building themselves through his breath. "It was about us. Verdant and Forgeborne. Together."

His voice steadied, deepened.

"That's why it never made sense apart. Why every generation failed. We kept trying to force power into objects, into symbols, but the truth… the truth was in us."

The relic glowed brighter, responding to his words with a shimmer that lit the carved edges of the altar.

"But…" he trailed off. A furrow crossed his brow. "The song says something about sacrifice."

The words left him like a breath he didn't want to name. "You mean one of us?"

Kaelen shook his head, visibly rattled. "No. No, that's not it. That's not right." He glanced at the altar, then back at the relic. "It doesn't say someone must die. Sacrifice doesn't mean giving life away—it means giving something that matters."

"Given?" Elara asked, stepping closer. "What does that mean?"

Kaelen didn't answer right away. His eyes were locked on the relic, now glowing with a golden hue that seemed to pulse in time with the song.

"I don't know," he admitted, "but I think we've been asking the wrong question. It's not about power. It's about what we're willing to lose to become whole."

Elara nodded, not in agreement—but in understanding. "Unity has a cost."

Dorian nodded. "And it's never paid in blood alone."

The song rose again, clearer than before. The summit seemed to hum with it, as if the mountain remembered the melody too. The lines carved into the altar flared gently, casting shapes across the trio's faces. Their shadows no longer split in three directions—they merged into one.

The altar continued to glow.

And the summit watched in silence, waiting for the final choice to be made.

The silence didn't last.

A shift in the mist—a ripple, not of wind, but of movement. Heavy. Deliberate. The echo of boots against stone echoed through the summit like a heartbeat from something dark still pulsing beneath the surface.

From the fog at the edge of the summit, a figure emerged.

Aldric.

His armor was battered, scorched along one shoulder, a smear of dried blood streaking from his temple to his jaw. One arm hung slightly heavier than the other, but his steps were firm. His eyes locked onto the trio with the intensity of someone who had followed them through fire and refused to be denied his final act.

"You think you're chosen?" he spat, voice low and cracked. "Chosen by what?"

The words echoed. Not theatrical—genuine. Bitter. He stepped closer, dragging the glaive through the dust. His glare didn't falter. Kaelen took a step forward, relic pulsing in his grip, but Aldric's eyes snapped to Elara.

"That's the problem," Aldric said, voice rising. "Everyone wants to believe they're special. That their suffering means something. But it doesn't. It's just pain."

He lifted the glaive slowly, leveling it at her. His voice dropped.

"Killing Dorian would be too easy. He'd endure it. He'd turn it into meaning. But her?"

His lips twisted into something between a grin and a grimace.

"That's where it'll break him. And the prophecy."

He lunged.

Elara flinched, unable to react in time.

But Dorian did.

He threw himself between them, just as the blade swung down. The glaive cut across his ribs and shoulder, opening a fresh wound over the one barely sealed. Blood sprayed in a wide arc as the blow drove him back into Elara.

She caught him with both arms, her knees buckling under the weight. "Dorian!" she cried, lowering him to the ground. Her hands glowed with the beginning of a spell, but the blood was coming too fast.

He gritted his teeth through the pain, one hand still gripping the haft of his hammer. "Don't let him touch her," he hissed, forcing the words out like they were heavier than his wound.

Kaelen moved. Not rushed. Not reckless. But with resolve. He stepped in front of them, between Aldric and the others. The relic in his hands pulsed harder now, as though responding to the presence of something wrong.

Aldric squared his stance, raising the glaive again.

"I should've ended this back in the flats," he muttered. "You were nothing then. Just another broken apprentice clinging to scraps in a hollowed-out forge. Scrapforger."

"And now?" Kaelen asked, his voice calm, clear. "Still afraid of what a failure might become?"

The wind stirred.

Not gentle.

It howled—wild, furious. The sky above began to churn, and the relic's glow deepened into something that wasn't just light—it was memory. Purpose.

Aldric didn't pause.

But this time, neither would Kaelen.

Elara dropped to her knees beside Dorian.

His blood soaked the stone beneath him, seeping into the fractures of the summit as if the mountain demanded its toll. Crimson pooled around him, hot and vivid against the cold gray of the altar. His face had lost all its color. His breaths came shallow and sharp, every one of them a protest. But his eyes—his eyes were still open. Still locked on hers.

She pressed her hands over the wound, feeling the wetness, the heat, the way the muscles spasmed beneath her fingers. Her magic stirred at her fingertips, sluggish and strained. She had drawn on too much already, burned through more energy than her body had to spare.

Still, she pushed.

Verdant light spilled from her palms, silver threaded through its glow. The energy seeped into Dorian's torn skin, crawling slowly across the torn flesh like ivy over cracked stone. But the wound resisted. The magic buckled against the damage, like it was fighting something deeper than the cut itself—fighting the violence behind it.

"You're not dying," Elara whispered. Her voice trembled with fear and fury. "Not like this. Not now."

Dorian reached up, his hand shaking as he brushed the edge of her sleeve. "This isn't the end of us," he said, voice barely above a breath.

Tears rimmed her eyes, but she didn't let them fall. Her lips pressed together. The tears held. The magic didn't.

"No," she whispered back. "Just the beginning."

She poured more into him. More magic. More of herself. Every drop of energy drained from her limbs into her hands. Her shoulders quaked from the effort. Her head swam. Still she gave. Still she refused to stop.

The light grew stronger—pulsed—then began to flicker.

Her breathing turned ragged. Sweat dripped down her spine, soaking into her tunic. Her fingers started to tremble from the strain. The spell was holding, but just barely. Like trying to plug a wound with silk.

The wound slowly closed. The angry red began to pale. The bleeding stopped. Flesh knit together.

Dorian's breath evened. His hand dropped limply to the ground.

Elara's hands slipped away from the wound. Her arms hung at her sides.

Then she slumped forward.

Wiz roared as he intercepted Aldric's next strike, the automaton's metal frame colliding with the glaive in a burst of sparks. Kaelen didn't look back—he trusted Wiz with his life.

He was already running.

He slid to his knees beside Elara, catching her just before she collapsed. She sagged into his arms, her breath shallow, her strength all but gone. Her eyes fluttered open, lips parting to speak, but no sound came out.

"You shouldn't have done that," Kaelen said, voice barely audible.

"I had to," Elara whispered. Her voice was dry, nearly gone. "I won't lose him. Not here. Not after everything."

His nod was slow. Weighted. He didn't look away from her—not even for a second.

The glow from her spell faded completely. And with it, something deeper—some reservoir of strength she might never reclaim.

But Dorian lived.

And Elara, in that moment, needed no other answer.

The mountain wind howled above them, but here, in this narrow circle of light and blood and breath, it was quiet.

The cost had been paid.

Now came whatever came after.

Aldric rose from the edge of the altar, battered but unbroken. His glaive scraped a jagged arc in the stone as he turned, the blade trailing sparks. His armor was fractured in half a dozen places, one shoulder pauldron barely clinging to its straps, but he still moved like a predator. His face twisted with fury, and through blood and grime, his eyes locked onto his quarry.

He moved toward them—toward Elara, slumped against the altar, too weak to raise her head. Toward Dorian, breathing shallowly beside her. The relic in Kaelen's hands pulsed once, sensing the threat before Kaelen's own instincts could respond.

Aldric raised his weapon.

Kaelen stepped between them.

"Not this time," he said.

Before Aldric could strike, a roar split the air.

Wiz barreled into him from the side, claws extended, engine scream echoing off the summit walls. Sparks flew as the massive automaton collided with Aldric, slamming him into a stone pillar with enough force to crack the base.

Aldric grunted, twisting, his glaive arcing in a tight circle that caught Wiz's shoulder. Sparks and plating flew in a spray, but Wiz didn't stop. He pressed forward, larger than he had ever been, wings spread in full as his metallic tail snapped around to parry Aldric's counter.

Kaelen didn't flinch.

He watched, measured the space, then shouted, "Take him up."

Wiz surged forward again. This time, he locked his talons around Aldric's chest and waist, claws embedding deep into Aldric's cracked armor. Aldric snarled, thrashing, trying to wrench free—but Wiz's wings snapped downward in a powerful burst, generating a gale-force updraft that launched them into the sky with sudden, breathtaking speed.

Stone shattered beneath their launch. Wind exploded outward from the force, knocking Kaelen back a step as the two figures—one steel and magic, the other bone and wrath—rocketed skyward into the clouds.

The sky above the storm clouds opened—vast, sunlit, and deadly still. Thunderclouds loomed below, swirling with the chaos of the armies fighting beneath them. The summit vanished in mist.

High above it all, Wiz released his grip.

Aldric dropped like a stone.

He plummeted through the clouds, his armor flashing once in the sun before disappearing into the thunderclouds below. He didn't scream. He didn't cry out. He just fell, arms wide, swallowed by the storm and the ruin he had helped create.

For a long moment, there was only silence.

Then, the clouds parted.

Wiz reappeared, wings flaring, stabilizers hissing as he descended back toward the summit. Scorch marks laced his armor. One of his wing joints sparked erratically, but he flew steady.

He landed beside Kaelen, crouched and breathing in heavy metallic huffs, tail sweeping behind him for balance.

Kaelen stepped forward and placed a hand on Wiz's neck plating.

"Good work," he said.

Wiz chuffed a low mechanical whine—part acknowledgment, part exhaustion.

Kaelen turned. Behind him, Elara stirred. Dorian sat up slowly, still pale, still alive.

And before them, just beyond the altar's light, the final stretch of the prophecy waited.

Clear.

Silent.

And ready.

Kaelen approached the altar, each step heavy with the weight of every moment that had led him here. The summit pulsed with tension, the wind circling in reverence. He could feel the relic vibrating in his hand—warm, steady. Not demanding. Not threatening. Simply ready.

Behind him, Dorian stood with one hand still pressed to his ribs, his armor bloodstained but standing firmly. Elara leaned against the altar stone, her breath shallow from the toll of her healing, but her eyes never wavered from Kaelen. There was pain there, yes, but also belief.

Kaelen reached the altar and let his hand trace the etched surface. His fingers brushed against ancient stone worn smooth by wind and time—then found the groove. A narrow slot, carved long ago, concealed by centuries of moss and forgetting, now illuminated by the light flowing from the unified relic.

He looked at the relic one final time. It glowed not with dominance, but with promise. With unity.

Then he placed it in.

It clicked into place with a resonance that echoed deep into the mountain.

The ground trembled—not violently, but with purpose. As if something dormant had taken its first breath in an age. The altar shuddered beneath Kaelen's hand, and then—

Light exploded outward.

Concentric rings of brilliance raced from the center, spreading in all directions. They illuminated the summit's carvings, the ridges, the veins of stone and root that had been split for centuries. The lines glowed like stars etched across the ground, golden-white and humming with energy.

The mountain groaned as if exhaling. The tension in the wind shifted—what had once been hostile became something reverent, almost sacred. Thunder cracked above them, a sharp crescendo that shattered the sky's silence.

From the altar's central spire, a flare of energy surged upward, cutting through the storm clouds in a single, radiant beam. The clouds parted in its wake, revealing a break in the storm clouds, sunlight cascading down in fractured beams.

Elara lifted her hand to shield her eyes, stunned by the intensity. Dorian turned his face into the wind, squinting into the golden halo that now surrounded the summit. Kaelen didn't move. His gaze stayed locked on the light as it gathered, focused—then twisted inward.

And from that light, a figure began to form.

Rindun Veladra.

But not as they had seen him before.

His shape coalesced in waves of energy, His features emerging like a sculpture being carved from starlight. His robes, once ragged and simple, now shimmered with threads of light and gold that danced like embers. His once-withered frame was tall, regal, radiating a presence too vast for the space he occupied.

His eyes opened—twin stars set in a human face, burning not with rage, but with clarity. Every movement radiated stillness, like a sea that had finally stopped storming. He was no longer cloaked in shadow. He was presence made whole.

He stepped forward.

And with care, He placed a hand over His chest, as if acknowledging a wound that no longer remained, a break once felt not in bone, but in being.

"The fracture is mended," He said, His voice neither booming nor soft, but impossibly clear. It echoed through stone, wind, sky—and something deeper.

"I am whole again."

The light around Him pulsed once more, not to blind, but to affirm.

And the mountain, long divided, stood silent in recognition.

The light did not fade.

It shifted—became something deeper. More intimate.

A glow that wrapped the summit in stillness, not silence.

It was as if the mountain, having exhaled, now waited—not in anticipation, but in reverence.

Time felt suspended, stretched thin like the space between one breath and the next.

He stood at the center of it all—radiant, steady, and known.

To Kaelen and Dorian, He was Rindun Veladra—the mysterious watcher in the scrapyard, the guide who lingered in Obsidian Reach. The same face, the same stillness. Always near when the path bent.

But to Elara, He was Revand Durlain—the custodian of the Great Canopy, who offered no counsel, only questions wrapped in old pages.

None of them spoke, but all of them knew.

There was no divinity in His expression. Only recognition.

As though He had waited lifetimes for this moment—not as God above, but as a broken truth, finally made whole.

He spoke, and the sound of His voice was not a declaration, but a chord—ancient, harmonic, inevitable.

"I am the name you split to survive.
 The chord you sang in halves.
 The people of Auravalle called Me Druvalandrine."

The name filled the summit, echoing through stone and wind. The sky quieted. The relic, still embedded in the altar, pulsed once—its glow flickering in confirmation.

"Once, I was the center.
 Flame and root. Invention and soil.
 The breath between opposites.
 But the rift did not break Elyndor.
 It broke Me."

He began to walk, slowly. Not pacing, but weaving presence into space, threading silence with memory. His eyes moved between Elara and Dorian, then settled on Kaelen.

"The rift took no sides.
It took syllables.
Voice became echo.
Purpose, a rumor."

He raised a hand, and behind Him, the air shimmered. Mist peeled back, revealing fragments of the past, stitched together by memory rather than time.

"You wondered why the relic slept beneath rust and ruin."

An image sparked: Kaelen, crouched in a scrapyard, fingers brushing the artifact.

"I placed it where only wonder could reach.
Not to be hidden.
But to be chosen by the hands of someone who deserves it."

Another scene: Kaelen slipping past guards.

"Eyes turned blind. Gates turned loose.
I whispered where your feet should fall."

Then Elara in the Great Canopy.

"I wore ink upon My fingers and silence in My robes.
The words she sought were not given—they were guarded."

Obsidian Reach flickered next.

"I walked that forgotten place.
Spoke in fragments.
Wove riddles into alleys.
The lost do not need directions. They need belief."

The forest—Liora under green light.

"She called herself lesser. I called her wind.
 Told her the elements are not rivals, only songs awaiting breath.
 And that you three would come—not to lead, but to lift."

Now the ocean—gray, vast. A storm. A ship.

"I captained the Dawnseeker when time still bent for Me.
 But fragments cannot steer fate.
 So I stepped aside when the tide called for another."

He paused. Then stepped forward. The summit glowed brighter, the wind circling but never touching.

"Rindun Veladra. Alden Varidnur. Revand Durlain.
 Names I wore like cloaks.
 Vardun and Aeldrin. Names that people know like blades.
 You were never meant to war—only to wander.
 To forget me, so you could remember each other."

He placed His hand over His chest, where a soft light pulsed like the heartbeat of the mountain.

"And you—Kaelen, Elara, Dorian—
 You are not echoes.
 You are the silence made whole again."

His voice dropped, silent as a falling ash, steady as the dawn.

"To heal a world, you do not need to conquer it.
 You need only choose it—over and over.
 Choose each other."

The relic in the altar answered—its glow deepening, then spreading.

The mountain pulsed with light once more.

And when the light dimmed, He was gone.

No trace. No farewell.

Only warmth where He had stood, and the faint scent of smoke and wildflowers.

The light from the summit stretched far beyond the altar—beyond the trio, beyond the stone, beyond the battle.

It reached the valleys below.

Across the battlefield—where Forgeborne and Verdant clashed in a chaos of steel, flame, and fractured oaths—soldiers slowed. The scream of blades dulled. The fire of spells flickered out midair. All eyes lifted toward the mountain.

They saw it. A column of radiance cutting through the storm. A golden pulse from the peak, too bright to be flames of battle, too calm to be a weapon. The storm that had shadowed the skies for generations split apart, light pouring down through the break like sunlight through old stained glass.

And the fighting paused.

No order was given. No horn was sounded. But still, they stopped. Verdant and Forgeborne alike stood still, weapons lowered, breath held. Something ancient had moved. And they felt it.

Kaelen glanced down from the summit, eyes tracking the battlefield far below.

The lines were no longer holding. Command banners fell, not to fire—but to confusion.
 Soldiers dropped their blades. Others turned from the fight and simply stood, staring up toward the light breaking through the storm.

Elara stepped beside him. "They believed in blood," she said. "But now they're watching something that doesn't ask for it."

"Not a victory," Kaelen said. "A reckoning."

At the summit, the wind ceased.

The mountain was still.

The altar, once split and crumbling, now shone with a soft and steady glow. The relic, embedded within its center, pulsed with purpose—no longer demanding, no longer fractured, only present. Like a heartbeat.

Kaelen stood near the edge, his silhouette outlined against the rising light. His coat fluttered gently in the new calm, a whisper in the breeze that had finally softened.

Elara leaned against Dorian, her legs weak beneath her. Her hand still glowed faintly, a last ember of the magic she had poured into him. Dorian, pale but alive, held her steady, his own wounds forgotten in the gravity of what they had just survived.

They had come up the mountain broken—scarred, divided, uncertain.

Now, they stood together.

Kaelen turned, facing them both.

"The Equinox wasn't just about peace," he said. "It was about clarity."

Neither Dorian nor Elara answered. They didn't need to. It was in the air. In the way their shoulders no longer sagged. In the light that no longer demanded anything from them.

The glow from the summit extended across the world.

And for the first time, they weren't afraid of what came next.

Footsteps echoed against the stone.

From the broken trails winding below, the rest of their companions emerged one by one—tired, bloodied, but alive.

Liora arrived first, one hand wrapped in a makeshift bandage, wind swirling lightly around her boots, reacting to her presence. Her eyes were red from smoke or tears—no one asked which.

Tarian and Lysandra followed, armor cracked, shields nicked, but heads held high. They scanned the summit like old soldiers checking a final perimeter.

Arin came with Sariel at her side, his arm over her shoulder for balance. Though still holding on to his ribs, Sariel walked unaided for the last stretch.

Sylva trailed close behind, her bow across her back, her face still taut with caution. But when she looked up and saw the trio—saw the light—something in her eased.

And finally, Riven, her rifle hung low, her limp heavier than before. But her pace never broke. She nodded once at Kaelen, then moved to stand watch.

They gathered in a circle around the altar.

No one spoke.

Not because there was nothing to say.

But because silence felt right. Felt earned.

They had all made it.

They had seen the prophecy to its end—not with triumph, not with spectacle, but with understanding. With unity.

And together, they would begin again.

Not to restore what was lost.

But to build something new.

Act VI - The End

Chapter 19: The New Dawn

The smoke was gone. Two years had passed since the Equinox, and the banners—once stained in faction colors—were now faded, re-stitched into awnings above forges and greenhouses alike. Vines coiled up scaffoldings, and luminous leaves filtered the morning sun into prism-like hues that danced across cobbled streets.

The city—still unnamed—stood at the border of what was once Verdant and Forgeborne territory. Not by accident. Not by convenience. But by choice. A new start had to begin somewhere neutral, somewhere claimed not by war, but by wearied hands willing to rebuild.

The hum of steam conduits drifted alongside the rustle of treetop canopies. Street vendors called out prices in two languages. Children darted through alleyways lined with moss and metal, their laughter a small miracle in a place where screams once echoed.

A patchwork canopy stretched over the central square, where a mural was still in progress. Half Verdant glyphs. Half Forgeborne scripts. In the center—unfinished—was a figure holding a divided relic.

Elara watched from a stone bench nearby, a soft cloak draped over her shoulders. Her eyes tracked the brushstrokes of a young artist working in silence. No grand symbols. No glowing magic. Just color and patience.

Dorian stood beside her, one hand resting lightly on his healed ribs. He was quiet, but not distant. Not anymore.

"It's not perfect," he said.

Elara nodded. "No. But it's growing."

Across the plaza, Kaelen leaned against a railing, watching gears turn in the framework of a new tram system. Wiz hovered nearby, wings tucked, scanning the calibrations.

Kaelen adjusted something on a control panel, then stepped back. The carriage groaned, then glided forward a few feet with a soft hiss.

Wiz chirped in approval. Kaelen smirked, just a little.

This was peace—not the kind forged by treaties or sealed in blood, but the kind that emerged slowly. Earned. Built from splinters.

A new dawn didn't erase the scars. But it lit the path forward.

The city lived, and so did they.

Kaelen stood beside an open scaffolding, sleeves rolled past his elbows, a new generation of apprentices gathered around a makeshift table strewn with blueprints and salvaged parts. He spoke plainly, pointing to a schematic for a pressureless conduit, while Wiz projected a glowing schematic from his core. The students took notes with stained fingers and furrowed brows.

He didn't lead them with grand speeches. He asked questions. Made them think. Gave them tools, then walked away so they'd learn how to hold them on their own.

Across the city's healing quarter, Elara knelt in a garden overrun with vibrant moss. Her hands worked not with spells, but with poultices and root-thread. Grovecallers gathered in circles, following her lead—not just in how to heal, but how to listen. She rarely used the word leader.

But they followed her anyway.

In the university annex, Dorian stood beneath the frame of an old bell tower turned forum, chalk in hand, the board behind him filled with phrases in both Forgeborne script and Verdant glyphs. He taught tactics, yes, but also history—how stories shaped nations, how choices shaped myths.

When he spoke, his voice was steady. But those who knew him best could still hear the weight of battles beneath the syllables.

The three had not drifted apart.

If anything, the world had pulled them tighter.

In the evenings, they would meet again—no longer out of need, but out of choice. On a rooftop. Around a workshop. In the peaceful bloom of Elara's garden.

Elara and Dorian often walked side by side, hands touching but rarely clasped. No rings bound them. No ceremonies defined them. But the way she tilted toward him when he spoke, and the way his eyes tracked her without effort—those were truths.

They didn't wear rings. Not yet.

And somehow, that said everything they needed to.

Liora stood at the helm of the Dawnseeker, a seafaring vessel strung with sails and glyph-woven canvas, its hull patched in places with mismatched wood and metal—proof of adventures no port had fully documented. The sea stretched wide before them, each wave another road unmarked. Beside her, the twins—Sylas and Nyra—argued over navigation, trading quips and corrections as they adjusted charts and recalibrated the compass. They weren't just older now. They were capable. Confident. They had learned to read tides as easily as faces, and steer through both with equal finesse.

They didn't sail for fame. They didn't sail for fortune. Their legend didn't grow because they chased it.

It grew because they never stopped moving.

In the western borderlands—once scarred by barricades and bloodlines—Arin now stood across from a delegation of minor leaders, her tone steady, deliberate. Behind her, Tarian stood like stone—arms crossed, his silence sharp. Arin didn't negotiate with promises. She offered pathways. Rebuilding terms. Justice rooted in compassion, not conquest. Tarian kept the edges clean. The few who tried to intimidate her didn't make the mistake twice.

Together, they turned no-man's-land into a place where trade routes thrived, schools reopened, and people no longer whispered when they said the word future.

In the cities, the neutral guard had become more than a symbol—it had become structure. No longer bound to Verdant vines or Forgeborne banners, their uniform bore silver threadwork over deep slate gray. At their helm, Lysandra walked the line like it was a blade. Fair. Precise. Unyielding when it counted. Sylva, ever at her flank, saw what others missed. Her bow wasn't raised often, but when it was, no second arrow was needed.

The two of them weren't just enforcing peace. They were enforcing accountability.

Riven oversaw the outer defenses—never stationed, always moving. She had no sigil, no office, no subordinates to bark orders at. But every wall she passed, every tower she leaned against, became steadier. Her name alone was enough to freeze most disputes. Those who tested the perimeter never tested it twice.

And Sariel?

He was gone.

No grave. No final word. Just a space in the circle that hadn't been filled.

Some whispered sightings—on the cliffs beyond Varn's Teeth, or in the ruins of Hollowgrove. Always alone. Always leaving before anyone could speak. But those who'd walked with him didn't need proof to remember.

They kept his name alive not out of obligation, but out of love.

Because the world they fought for still stood.

Not perfect. Not whole.

But standing.

And those who shaped it now carried it—each in their own way.

In the wake of the Equinox, neither the Forgemasters nor the Wardens of Aeldrin remained.

Some stepped down in silence. Others vanished without formal word, their followers drifting into the wind or folding into new communities. A few issued farewell decrees, written more like apologies than declarations. Most simply stopped answering when the old summons rang.

The institutions didn't fall to fire. They fell to choice.

The world no longer answered to the councils that tried to bind it.

In their place rose the Circle of Accord—a provisional council made up of scholars, mediators, tradespeople, and former soldiers. No crowns. No emblems. No factional seats. Its chamber was round, its walls lined with murals of both Verdant and Forgeborne craft. Anyone could speak. Everyone had to listen.

Public forums replaced private halls. Arguments were loud. Slow. Messy. But they were heard.

It wasn't unity through power. It was compromise through voice.

The Circle didn't claim to be the answer. It only promised to ask the right questions. And after millenia of silence from above, that was enough.

No thrones remained.

Just voices.

And that was the beginning of something else entirely.

The workshop smelled of copper and lavender root—equal parts Verdant and Forgeborne, fused now in more than just material. A low hum filled the space, rhythmic and patient.

At the front of the hall, Kaelen spoke to a circle of young inventors, blueprints and scrap spread across their tables. But the real lesson wasn't coming from him.

Wiz paced the perimeter of the workshop—not scuttling, not hovering, but walking on stable clawed limbs, tail curling in the dust, wings tucked and alert. He pinged corrections to student tablets, projected schematics midair, and emitted short instructional tones when someone's weld burned too hot.

The students didn't treat him like a tool. They thanked him when he nudged a design or offered a fix.

He wasn't machinery anymore.

He was a symbol.

A companion.

An emblem of what could come from broken pieces, refined.

Kaelen watched him quietly from across the room, arms folded, a rare smile tugging at the corner of his mouth.

Wiz had started as a device. A prototype. An escape plan.

Now he was something more—adaptive, unexpected, and necessary.

Just like the world they were building.

Just like Kaelen himself.

The garden hadn't changed.

The same lavender rows curved in gentle lines beneath the wooden trellis. The same low hum of bees drifted lazily through the air, pollinating flowers with diligence. The same warmth radiated from the sun-drenched soil as Elara pressed her palms into it, grounding herself with each breath.

But something felt different.

Not in the garden. In her.

There was a tension she couldn't name—restless and still all at once. It didn't interfere with her work. It lingered, subtle and quiet, just beneath her skin, like the prickle before a storm that hadn't yet broken the horizon.

The dreams had returned.

Not nightmares. Not visions. Just fragments—disjointed glimpses of places unfamiliar, yet saturated with meaning. Valleys blanketed in frost where no birds sang. Skies gray and endless, not with weather, but with absence. The dreams never showed her danger. She always woke in the same way: still, breath slow, the sense of something unfinished coiled behind her ribs.

She hadn't spoken of them.

Not yet.

She had buried them under routine. Let herself get swept up in the rhythms of healing, teaching, replanting. In the rebuilding of something soft, something grounded.

But this morning, as she trimmed back the ironroot blossoms the way she always did, she found herself humming. A tune. Low and instinctual.

Familiar.

The moment her ears caught it, her hands froze. It wasn't just any tune—it was a fragment of the Forgotten Song.

Only a few notes, but unmistakable. She hadn't meant to hum it. She hadn't even realized it had left her lips.

The air shifted.

The breeze through the garden moved gently past her shoulders, but it carried a chill she hadn't felt since the early months after the Equinox. She paused, turned slightly, and looked to the forest edge that bordered the outer paths—where sunlight filtered through tall grasses and mist often clung to the roots.

There was no movement. No shadow.

But she felt it.

Not fear. Not even warning. Just awareness. The sense of something drawing breath far away, and in doing so, brushing against her own.

She wiped the soil from her hands slowly, not because she was finished, but because she wasn't sure what to do with them. Her eyes didn't leave the trees.

Sariel used to say the wind always knew first. She hadn't believed it then. But now...

Now, she wasn't so certain.

Something was coming.

She didn't know when. She didn't know what form it would take.

But she would speak of it soon.

Not yet.

Today, the world was still whole. The garden still bloomed. The peace still held.

And she wanted to remember what that felt like—for just a little longer.

The summit was quieter now than it had ever been. No relic pulsed. No prophecy echoed. Just wind and stone—and Kaelen.

He knelt near what remained of the altar, sleeves rolled up to his elbows, forearms dusted with grit and pale earth. The fractured stone ring that had once marked the convergence site had crumbled with time. Some of it collapsed under the weather. Some, he had dismantled himself.

Not out of bitterness.

Out of purpose.

He rebuilt it slowly, deliberately—stone by stone—not as a monument, but as a space for learning. A place where ideas could grow instead of fracture. The new circle didn't rise above the ground; it settled into it, low and wide, ringed with carved markers that bore no names of heroes or gods. Instead, they bore questions.

How do you hold power without breaking?

What must be remembered when peace feels easy?

How do you know when the fracture is truly healed?

Small tiles ringed the site, etched with diagrams, timelines, half-solved problems, and alternate approaches to power and connection—unfinished, imperfect, challenging. Kaelen didn't offer conclusions. He offered tension. Apprentices came here in small clusters, sometimes silent, sometimes eager to argue. They brought ideas. Left with better questions.

And sometimes they stayed behind just to watch the wind move over the stones.

Wiz sat nearby, wings folded tight, posture upright. He didn't monitor—he listened. The whir of his internal systems had softened over time. He no longer projected schematics unless prompted. He existed like a presence now, more mentor than machine. Occasionally, he adjusted a student's grip, repositioned a tool, or replayed a memory of Kaelen's early missteps so others could laugh and learn.

Kaelen reached out and brushed his fingers along the edge of a freshly set stone.

He whispered to it—not loudly, not urgently. A habit, maybe. A reflex. Or something else.

"It wasn't the relic that needed reforging," he murmured. "It was us."

The wind stirred against his back, wrapping around the circle like a slow breath.

The summit didn't hum anymore.

But somehow, it never felt more alive.

Kaelen stood and looked out over the valley below—green, silver, scorched, and seeded. The world had changed. The scars remained.

But like the stones beneath his feet, they had been placed with care.

And every piece still fits.

Even the broken ones.

The sunlight that warmed Elara's garden bent—not as if interrupted, but as if remembering something. No wind moved. No shadow passed. But Kaelen felt the pulse echo from the old stone sundial nearby, a low vibration that hummed against the soles of his boots. Something—somewhere—was stirring.

Kaelen paused. He felt it even before he saw the glow.

In the silence that followed, the space beside the ancient oak shimmered—not in brilliance, but in focus. As if something stepped into a moment rather than a place.

And Druvalandrine appeared.

No thunder. No divine proclamation. Just presence.

He was taller than they remembered, not in height but in bearing. The robes were simpler now, woven in gray and gold threads, edges faded. His skin no longer glowed, but something beneath it did—like a fire banked for warmth, not war. His face was lined. Familiar. Human, almost.

Not godlike.

Guiding.

Kaelen straightened. Elara turned. Dorian stood without speaking.

Druvalandrine looked at each of them. Not with reverence. Not with judgment. Just the truth.

He didn't offer praise. He didn't ask questions. He only said one thing.

"The fracture is healing."

A pause.

His gaze shifted—not upward, not inward, but outward.

"But the Veil still bleeds."

His voice fell lower now, the sound of old stone cracking beneath ancient roots.

"Beyond lies what the old gods feared to name.
 Not a god. Not a man.
 A hunger that waits where balance falters—
 Not to strike, but to inherit."

He looked at Kaelen—and in his eyes, not command, but burden shared.

"You sealed the wound. But not all wounds close.
 Some remain open, not from failure…
 …but because they are not done bleeding."

The moment stretched, held in silence.

Druvalandrine stepped forward, robes drifting in the forge-wind. His form shimmered not with fire, but with memory—like the mountain remembered Him.

Then, He spoke—not with warmth, but with weight.

"When joined at last, the halves shall shine,
 Yet fractured lies the ancient line..."

He paused.

Elara's breath caught. Her lips moved on instinct, words emerging unbidden:

"Evil shall rise as light divides,
 Lest hearts converge and hope survives."

The verse hung in the air—half dream, half awakening.

She blinked. "I don't... I don't know how I knew that. It's the last verse of the Forgotten Song."

Kaelen and Dorian turned to her, the silence between them newly charged.

"You have forged what many feared: not peace, but potential.
 Elyndor breathes beneath your bond, but peace alone is not enough.
The wound is closed... yet something stirs beyond the scar."

Elara stepped forward. "We united the factions. Isn't that what the prophecy wanted?"

Druvalandrine inclined His head, voice distant and low.

"The prophecy spoke of union, yes.
But it was not faction alone that fractured the world.
There is a third silence... one left to fester.
A force born not of fire or soil, but of severance."

Kaelen frowned. "The Great Discord."

"Yes.
Born not in spite of My will,
But from it.
For I gave My creations choice.
And they chose... division."

Elara whispered, "The people of the Godless Lands…"

"They abandoned Me, as I allowed.
They rejected unity, as was their right.
But that freedom bred more than silence.
It birthed the Discord—
A hunger that feeds not on conquest,
But on collapse."

Kaelen looked down at Wiz, then back to God.

"I gave life to a machine. I understand the fear of what comes next."

Druvalandrine turned His gaze on Kaelen.

"And thus you understand Me.
I, too, was a maker.
And I, too, must bear what My creations become."

Dorian's voice was hard. "Then why not stop it?"

"Would you cage your child to keep them safe?
Force them into silence for peace?"

He paused.

"Unity cannot be forged by force.
 Only revealed—when all else has failed."

Elara's hands clenched. "You want us to go back into the fire?"

"You are not chosen for comfort.
 You are chosen for consequence.
 The Great Discord rises beyond the Veil.
 And only those forged in fracture can face what waits."

The three looked at each other—scorched, worn, but standing.

Kaelen nodded slowly. "Then we go."

Druvalandrine's form began to fade, light stretching upward like the dawn.

"Go not as bearers of peace,
 But as reminders that peace is possible.
 Not as weapons,
 But as witnesses."

The morning after the unexpected visit was calm.

A courier arrived at the edge of the garden where Kaelen had been tinkering. Dust on his boots. A sealed message in his hand. He bowed once and left as quickly as he'd come.

Liora's name was on the wax.

She hadn't sent a dispatch in weeks. Now her message simply read: "Delayed. The sea's not right. The winds have changed."

Kaelen read it twice. Then handed it to Elara, who had just joined him on the rooftop where the trio often met. Dorian arrived a moment later, carrying fresh bread and three mugs of warm tea.

They sat in silence for a while, the letter between them, the weight of it heavy despite the few words. A shift had come—not loud, not clear, but undeniable.

In the distance, beyond the far mountain range, storm clouds and lightning flickered at the edge of the sky.

Kaelen didn't smile. Just stared at the horizon. "We saved the world once."

Elara tucked a strand of hair behind her ear, eyes on the horizon. "Now we protect what we've built."

Dorian raised his cup.

"Together."

The wind stirred the leaves. Below, the city still lived—still healed. But above it all, something old had begun to move again.

The world was no longer broken.

But the Veil—was beginning to bleed.